LOOKING FOR MR NOBODY

LOOKING FOR MR NOBODY

A Novel

SUE RANN

NO EXIT PRESS

Published in 2003 by No Exit Press
18 Coleswood Road, Harpenden, Herts, AL5 1EQ
http://www.noexit.co.uk

A CIP catalogue record for this book is available from the
British Library.

ISBN 1 84243 066 1 (Trade Paperback)

2 4 6 8 10 9 7 5 3 1

Typography by Able Solutions (UK) Ltd, Birmingham.
Printed and bound by CPD, Ebbw Vale, Wales.

To my husband Dave
and daughters Rosanna, Joanna and Hanna
with love

Acknowledgements

Thanks to the Royal NL Embassy, London;
Maud Goudberg and B.V.
of the Royal NL Navy Office of Public Affairs;
Kathleen Canham Ross
of the Office of the Chief of Public Affairs,
US Army, Los Angeles Branch;
John Heffernan for chemistry above and beyond;
Pien Schepel
of the SBA Schepen Binnenstad, Amsterdam;
Helen, for airmiles and encouragement;
Garry Sutton of the Stafford Tattoo Studio;
Michael Thomas, for believing when nobody else did;
Ion and the No Exit Press gang, for taking the risk,
and to Lorraine who saw it first.

LOOKING FOR MR NOBODY

1

CHRISTMAS. Time of good cheer, generosity, love and peace to all men, etcetera, etcetera, etcetera.

Alternatively: Christmas—time of stress, isolation, mad debt and huge aching disappointments.

No prizes for guessing which scenario I was currently playing out. My wonderful plan of running away to Europe to become a penniless artist had mutated under the harsh light of day into a luxury I couldn't afford, except for the penniless bit. I managed that with no effort at all.

Any money I made went out faster than it came in, and social life was a roller-coaster on the never-never. That's what cities are like; Amsterdam more so than most.

So when I got home from work a week or so before St Nikolaas, in a light-headed state somewhere beyond tired, to find that my apartment had been broken into, it was just the latest in a long-running series of indignities.

I plodded up the last flight of stairs to the third floor, yawning and fumbling in the debris at the bottom of my shoulder-tote, trying to locate my keys by touch.

My fingers hunted through familiar terrain. Lip-salve, tissues, palmtop, the half chocolate bar I'd been saving that had gone sort of fluffy in its wrapper, cellphone, pen with no top, billfold, lime green fur-fabric notebook, rape alarm, loose coins, Mace spray . . . all the stuff a girl ought never to be without. Oh, and the gun, of course, zipped into the cosmetic compartment at the side. My baby, my secret vice.

I glanced over my shoulder at the dark hallway before starting the game of find-the-keyhole. The frazzled light-bulb that dangled in the narrow stairwell still hadn't been replaced.

I kept meaning to bug old Schama about it but so far I hadn't raised the necessary energy. Like his building, my landlord was old, grimy and clapped-out. It took an immense effort to get him to do anything besides collect the rent. It was funny—in a strictly non-humorous way—how he always managed the stairs when there was money owing.

Today had sneakily turned into tomorrow while I wasn't looking. The luminous green readout on my wrist-watch said 04:25. My stomach had been grumbling in a rebellious fashion since about midnight, and I knew without having to look that the fridge was just about empty, as usual. The club manager at EyeKon had doled out a little cash-in-hand overtime tonight, and the thought of shopping in the Albert Cuyp market for real food—fresh bread, and crusty smoked bacon, and beefsteak tomatoes and cookies—was a pleasurable diversion from my feet, which hadn't gone quite numb enough not to hurt.

The key stuck in the lock and I jiggled it. Come *on*. The mechanism gave with a scraping noise. I shouldered the door open and dumped my bag on the floor. The heavy panel clicked shut behind me, and I pressed the deadbolt down and sagged thankfully against the wood for a second. *No snow, no wind, no music, no people.* I tossed my wet jacket at the coat-rack, and yawned, rubbing at the nape of my neck with numb fingers. Home safe.

A line of light showed under the kitchen door. I froze in the act of kicking off the hateful court shoes. I never leave lights on. Over the sudden thunder of my own heartbeat, I heard the shuffle of feet.

A tidal surge of flight hormones paralysed me for a second. I had to fight for control of my legs, which were attempting to scurry out of the door.

Primeval fury came a close second to terror. *In my apartment?* A nasty gritting noise turned out to be my teeth grinding together. I relaxed my jaw with an effort. Get a grip, Carlson. What's that dumb thing Marik's always telling the students? *The power is in the ability to take action.* You've got the ability, dummy. So take some action.

It took a second to control my breathing. I moistened my lips and muttered, 'OK. OK. Come on, Robin, you can do this.' Well, I mean. You don't expect to have to take your work home, do you?

My knees wobbled. I crouched, fumbling to remove the second shoe. I wiped my palms on my dress, then reached for my bag and slid out the Glock-17.

Even in the dark my hands knew the gun. It was cool in my grasp, solid but not heavy. A birthday present from Daddy, back when I was still his golden girl, still a chip off the old Carlson block.

Light, precision-machined ceramic. The mechanism was state of the art, smooth, almost impossible to jam. Daddy had made certain that I bought one of the original models, with no safety catch to forget. The man in the shop had approved his choice. A nice little ladies' gun, he'd said. The creep.

It had been tricky, bringing the Glock into Holland. When they first appeared, journalists were quick to grasp on to the fact that, being made of ceramic, they did not show up on airport X-ray scanners. Neglecting, in their enthusiasm for a good headline, the fact that several parts of the mechanism were manufactured from steel, including the firing pin. Bullets would be a whole separate world of trouble.

Any putative terrorist with one of these babies would have to lock themselves into the aeroplane toilet for half an hour to unpack and reassemble all the bits—provided, of course, that they hadn't been accidentally loaded on to another plane en route to Heathrow or Bogota, along with the terrorist's roll-on deodorant and clean underpants.

Mom had always maintained (usually after her cases had gone soaring off to Atlanta again instead of following her to Dulles) that baggage handlers thwarted more hijack attempts than the airport police ever did.

So, it had been a challenge, and for once I was glad to be the daughter of a five-star General in the US Army. It was a sure thing that Daddy knew I'd used his name to pull strings. The thought left a nasty taste in my mouth. *There Ain't No Such Thing As A Free Lunch* should be carved in stone on the Carlson family crest: TANSTAAFL. But there was no way I'd have left the Glock behind. It was my security blanket.

Inside the kitchen, small sounds indicated that someone was busy. I moved up to the door in two silent paces. There was a click, followed by the clatter of metal on metal. I twisted the handle, and flung the door open.

'FREEZE!' Legs straddled (as far as they would go in a satin sheath dress). Gun gripped in both hands, levelled like an accusatory finger. The burglar was bent over the sink. A man.

A very familiar man. My jack-in-the-box entrance made him start so violently that he dropped whatever he had been holding with a clatter and spun round, white-faced. 'C-Carlson! Bloody hell, woman, put the gun down!'

'*Bowman!*' I slammed the gun on to the worktop so hard, it was a wonder it didn't go off anyway. Too late to explain to my body that it had been a false alarm. My legs were jelly-shapes. I pushed past Bowman to right the coffee machine, upside-down under the mixer tap. 'Did you put some coffee in the filter bit?'

'Y-yes,' Bowman said, and watched while I filled the jug and plugged it in. Sucking and bubbling noises started up, followed a few seconds later by a trickle of brown liquid.

'Cary,' I said, in a level voice that fooled neither of us, 'how did you get in here? I don't recall giving you a key.' I folded my arms and leaned against the worktop, next to the gun.

'You didn't,' Bowman admitted. 'I called the Fight Club. That Neanderthal character you work for told me you were moonlighting over at EyeKon till about four. I thought I'd drop in for coffee and surprise you. I need to ask you something, Robin.'

'You broke into my apartment to ask me something at four-thirty in the morning?' My voice cracked.

'It's urgent.' He refused to look at me, hands stuffed into his coat pockets. He had turned the frayed corduroy collar up, as a concession to the cold. The coat fitted: country-house English, the ancestral gilt imperceptibly worn off.

'Cary, what's happened?'

'I'm sorry,' Bowman muttered, and glanced at me. There were dark shadows under his eyes. 'I shouldn't have . . . I—I haven't been thinking very clearly. Sorry,' he repeated, and rubbed at his forehead as if trying to erase something. 'Perhaps I'd b-better go . . .'

'Perhaps you'd better sit down,' I interrupted. 'You look as if you need a drink.' I pulled a chair out, and after a moment's hesitation, he sat.

'Sorry about the melodrama.' He sounded tired.

'Will you stop apologising already?' The coffee hadn't finished perking, but there was enough for two cups. I brought the jug with me to the table. Bowman met my gaze with an attempt at his usual humorous, half-shy flicker.

'Do you want to be mother, or shall I?'

'Be my guest.' I slid into the seat opposite him.

Bowman righted the thick white cups in their saucers and poured a thin stream of dark liquid. A frown dug a line between his brows as he concentrated. I took advantage of the fact that he wasn't looking at me to study him.

Bowman had a lean, freckled face with a nose that had been broken once and badly set. His teeth were crooked too but very white when he smiled, which was often. He had curious tilted eyes the colour of weathered copper. His lashes were thick but so fair they hardly showed. The reddish fair hair needed cutting. He looked like a battered thirtysomething, but I had a feeling he was older. I'd never felt the need to ask.

It was a good, uncomplicated friendship. Bowman had made a pass at me the first time we met, and scored high points for smarts in accepting that it just wasn't going to happen. So far, he hadn't repeated the endeavour, but the thought that this might be the reason for his presence made my insides curdle suddenly.

Don't be stupid, I told myself. *This is Cary, remember?* All the same, the fact that he'd forced his way into my home like this disturbed me more than I was willing to admit. The whole point of paying for my own place was so I could keep people at arm's length.

Crazy, really, because in the ordinary way of things, I could really have let myself fall for Bowman.

I had found myself wondering, lately—with increasing irritation—if there would ever be an ordinary way of things again.

Hell, I thought, with a small stab of alarm, *I sure hope so.*

It occurred to me suddenly that in the eighteen months or so that we had been friends, I had never visited Bowman's apartment. Oh, sure, I knew where he lived—a bachelor one-bed pad in a classy 1920s building in the New South—but I had never done more than drive past in a taxi. I remember thinking that it looked too expensive for a lowly university lecturer.

All our contact was on neutral ground. Email, of course, and cafés, parties, movie theatres, parks . . . the fact that I had never noticed it before unsettled me now, for no reason that I could name.

Belatedly, I wondered how long Bowman had been here before I arrived. Vivid recollections of the mess in my bedroom and the heap of dirty laundry filling the shower stall made me close my eyes. *He must think I'm a complete slob.*

'Here you are.' Bowman slid a cup and saucer across the table. He pulled a packet of cookies out of his coat pocket and placed them on the table. 'Peace offering?'

'No need,' I said, and scraped back my chair to reach inside a drawer. The bulbous bottle I placed beside the cookies was more than half empty.

'Apricot brandy?' Bowman unstoppered it and sniffed, grinned. 'Strong stuff.'

'I said you looked as if you needed a drink,' I pointed out. 'It's great in coffee. Here.' I took the bottle and tipped a generous measure into his cup, then my own. '*Sláinte.*'

'I shall be,' Bowman muttered, and swallowed. His eyebrows shot up, and he coughed. 'Gordon Bennett, Robin, are you trying to g-get me drunk?'

'You gotta love it.' I inhaled deeply and sipped the scalding coffee with eyes shut, savouring the tendrils of warmth that spread out from my belly. I was furious with myself for not being able to hold his gaze, but sitting here alone with a man, even Bowman—no, who was I kidding? *Especially* Bowman—was bringing back all the old symptoms of incipient panic. I drank, and forced myself to breathe. *It's time you were over this, Robin. He's a nice guy.*

'So.' I crossed my arms on the table in front of me. 'Are you going to tell me what's wrong?'

'Oh—er, y-yes. Yes, of course.' He put his own cup down a little too hard, and coffee slopped on to the table-top. 'Damn! Sorry . . . '

'It's OK, leave it.'

'All right.' He glanced at me, glanced away. 'Robin, I, er—I think I might be in a spot of bother.'

A spot of bother. I would remind him of that phrase, later. Now, all I said was, '*Bother?*' with LockStock images jumbling in my head of police and court appearances, or (worse) some broken-faced heavy with a tyre iron, waiting in the shadows of the classy apartment building.

'It's a long story,' Bowman said. He was playing with the heavy gold signet ring on his left hand, turning and turning it so that the greenish stone winked in the light. It had belonged to his father, and he referred to it caustically as 'The Family Curse', but I noticed he never took the thing off.

'Go ahead,' I said eventually. 'It's my day off, I've got plenty of time.'

'*Robin.*'

'What?' I unwrapped the first cookie, popped it into my mouth, crunched and swallowed, trying not to look at the packet too obviously. I glanced up to find Bowman looking at me. '*What?*' The word came out in a shower of crumbs.

'D'you trust me, Robin?'

'In what way?' The pause had been too long. He looked down, fiddling with the ring again.

'Never mind.'

I hurried to cover the gaffe, cursing inwardly.

'Look, you're my friend, Cary. What—' I realised I didn't have a question to fit after the 'what', and trailed off. I reached over to touch his hand. 'Are you OK? You don't look so good.'

'I slept rough last night,' Bowman said. He twitched at a sudden noise from the coffee maker, and ran a hand over his hair. 'Sorry. Bit jumpy.' His smile was unconvincing.

'I can see that.' I frowned at him. 'What the hell's going on, Cary? What's this spot of bother?'

'I can't tell you.' Bowman shrugged and avoided my gaze, twisting his cup in its saucer. 'Sorry, but I—well, it's just not a g-good idea, that's all. It's not that I don't trust you—'

'The hell it isn't,' I said. My stomach growled audibly. I reached for another cookie, and ate it in two bites.

'Hell,' Bowman said plaintively. 'This is going to be more difficult than I thought. Robin, I—*can't*—*tell you*. I wish I could.'

'And that's it? I have to trust you, but you won't trust me? That's hardly fair, Cary.'

'Don't be so childish,' Bowman said, sharply. 'I just don't want you to end up in the same mess I'm in. Honestly, Robin. It's b-better if you don't know.'

'If you'd just tell me,' I said, after a moment, 'then maybe I could help.'

'All right,' Bowman said eventually, and rubbed both hands slowly over his face, as if just waking up. His voice came out muffled. 'I have to find someone, an acquaintance. A Dutch guy, he was looking into something for me—'

'The bother?'

'Yes, the bother. He's a PI, does that sort of thing for a living. I asked him to find out about . . . the bother, dig around a bit and see if I was just being p-paranoid. He said he'd look into it, and . . . well, the long and short of it is, he's disappeared. G-gone.'

'Maybe he moved house,' I offered, then, at Bowman's impatient shake of the head, '—well, did you call the cops? Fill out a Missing Persons or something?'

'It's not that simple.' Bowman shrugged and looked embarrassed. 'He's been missing for almost five months, Robin.'

'*What?*'

'You have to understand,' Bowman said in a rush, 'it seemed all above b-board to start with. Him vanishing like that, I m-m-mean.' He reined the stutter in with an effort. 'Anyway. When I hadn't heard from him for a few w-weeks, I went to the place where he worked. PI agency called FIXX, over on Kerkstraat. Just a little outfit, three or four people. B-boss called Jerry something. They said he'd left, just cleared out his desk over the weekend and done a bunk. He faxed his letter of resignation from

Germany. They showed me. Gone off climbing or hiking or something, said it was time for a change, urgent personal reasons, apologised for lack of notice, etcetera. They were a bit p-pissed off about it, to tell you the truth.'

'And you didn't think this was a little odd, him just leaving like that? *Cary.*'

'It all seemed kosher,' Bowman protested. 'He had all kinds of hobbies like that, from what I can gather. Sailing, rock-climbing, that sort of thing. Real m-man's man, Grizzly Adams type. I assumed he hadn't found anything, that's all, or he would have left me a note or something. End of story.' He shrugged. 'Well, till now.'

'So what suddenly changed your mind?' I poured more coffee from the jug and made a face at the taste. I topped it up with brandy.

Bowman pulled a piece of paper from his coat pocket, folded small. He spread it out on the table between us, and I leaned forward with a little jump of excitement. 'An email? Is it from him? What's it say?'

'Well, that's the problem. It came last night. And yes, I think it is from him.' Bowman handed it to me. After a second I dropped it back on to the table, puzzled.

'This is garbage. A whole page of 'o's and 's's? Someone's spamming you, that's all. It's just junk.'

'I don't think so.' Bowman retrieved the sheet, and smoothed it out. 'If you look carefully, there's a pattern. See?' He pointed. 'SOS, then again, SOS, and again, all down the page. There's no spacing, that's what makes it look like garbage.'

'I don't know, Cary.' I pushed the paper back across the table. 'It isn't even a personal address, it was sent from a cybercafé. What makes you so sure it's from your guy?'

'It was sent to a private email address,' Bowman said. 'I set it up specifically so he could contact me. It couldn't *be* anybody else.'

'You know email addresses aren't that secure.' I sighed and shook my head at his intense expression. 'OK, tell me the rest. Did you go to the cybercafé?'

'He'd already gone.'

'Well, did you ask the waitresses? Maybe someone saw him.' Against my will, I found that I was curious. Bowman shrugged the question off.

'Of c-course I asked. He was in there about ten-thirty, sent the message, paid cash and left.' He hesitated. 'The girl I spoke to remembered him because he had blood on his face.'

'Maybe he'd been in a fight. Did she say anything else? I mean, is he a regular?'

'She hadn't seen him before. She said he looked stoned, and a bit rough.'

'What, rough meaning sick, or—'

'Street rough.' Bowman got up and rinsed out his coffee cup in the sink, then sat down again and half-filled it with brandy. 'That's better. You?'

'Sure.' I pushed my own cup across and watched him pour half an inch of neat spirit. 'So,' I said after a moment's silence. 'You're going somewhere with this, where?'

'I—I don't know. Maybe nowhere,' Bowman muttered, and put down his cup. 'It was just something I remembered that he said he was going to do, back when I first asked him to look into the . . . um, b-bother.'

'What?' I prodded.

'We discussed the possibility of him going under cover,' Bowman said. He did not look at me. 'He was g-going to pose as a tramp, a vagrant.'

'For five months?'

'No.' Bowman frowned at me. 'Just a few days, but—well, we discussed it, and he agreed it was too risky. He went off on another tack, and I didn't hear from him—'

'And then he disappeared.'

'Mm.' Bowman tossed off the last of his brandy. 'I wish I knew what to make of all this. So bloody tired I can't think.' He rubbed his hands over his face. The gesture made him seem suddenly vulnerable. I leaned forward in my seat.

'Look, say I take your word for it, the mail's from this guy. Why all the cute Morse code stuff? This is weird, Cary.'

'You don't know how weird,' Bowman murmured. 'But if I can just find him, talk to him . . . '

'What,' I said, lightly, '—we'll all live happily ever after?'

'Something like that,' Bowman said. 'Something.'

'And you can't tell me anything else?'

'No.' Bowman looked sheepish. 'Look . . . I'm afraid this has rather p-put the wind up me. I want to lie low for a day or two, make a few calls to some people I know . . . I don't want to go back to my place.'

The question hung there for a few seconds, delicately unspoken. I glanced up at him over the rim of my coffee cup.

'You're welcome to sleep on the couch. I, uh, I don't have too many guests just now, you know . . . '

'Robin, you're an angel.' Bowman stood up, smiling. He looked relieved. 'I'll pitch in, honestly. I'm a m-mean hand at washing dishes.'

'Oh, uh . . . thanks.' Probably the wrong moment to reveal that I lived off junk food and only owned one dish. I smiled back, getting to my feet as well because in his coat he was towering over me like a highwayman. I folded my arms firmly over my misgivings. 'So, uh . . . want the grand tour?'

Bowman nodded towards the clock, hanging lop-sided above the door. 'If it's all right with you, I'd like to get a wash, then catch up on some sleep. I never really appreciated what a filthy place a street is until last night.'

'Oh. Sure.' I gathered up the coffee cups and carried them to the sink to rinse them. My voice came out in an adolescent mumble. 'Look, I don't know if I can get any time off work just now, but I'll try to help you find your friend.'

'Thanks.'

'Yeah, well, don't thank me yet.' I banged the cups into the drainer and turned to find him still standing there, studying me with a faint, infuriating smile on his face.

'I'm not making a move on you, you know.'

'I know.' I never had been any good at lying. His smile turned wry.

'You did make it pretty clear, that time.'

'Yeah.' I turned back to the sink. 'I guess I did.'

His voice was very soft. 'You can't carry on being frightened for ever, Robin.'

'Oh, that's good, coming from a guy who's too scared to go home.' I folded the tea-towel over the rim of the sink, and smoothed it with unneccessary precision.

'That's different,' he said, and I could tell he was smiling even though I didn't look up. '—and you're changing the subject.'

'The bathroom's through the living room on the left,' I said.

He was silent for a few seconds, then I heard him turn and walk towards the door. I closed my eyes. *Damn.*

'Robin?' He had stopped in the doorway. I turned my head a fraction.

'Yeah?'

'I'd like to pay you a bit of . . . well, rent, I suppose. Seems only fair.'

'Oh!' I hesitated, embarrassed. 'Oh, no no, really, it's nothing . . . '

'Well, we'll talk about it tomorrow,' Bowman said, comfortably. 'Perhaps there's something else I can do.'

I lay awake for a long time after I had closed the bedroom door between us. The first half hour—after a blitz raid on the bathroom to scoop up the laundry and wipe down the chinaware—I spent not-reading a book, and listening to the small movements and noises which meant that he, too, was having trouble getting to sleep. After that it went quiet. I was relieved that he did not snore.

I put the book down, and rolled over to pull my sketch pad out of the bedside cabinet. The last page was one I'd abandoned yesterday over breakfast with the vague intention of working at it a little harder when I got the time. It was supposed to be a montage of oceanic imagery. I shoved it out to arms' length and squinted at it critically: *looks like an explosion in a whaling station.* Unfinished cetacean body-parts everywhere. I scrubbed at the mess with my eraser, but it just smeared. I pursed my lips and picked up the pencil, scribed in a few lines more heavily, then groaned and snatched the page off the pad, crumpling it in my fist. It's always the same, I told myself tiredly: you try too hard to do something you care about and you screw up, Carlson. Everything's always got to be *right.* I tossed the ruined sketch at the wastepaper basket, and wriggled down so that the pad rested on my knees, but found myself just tapping the point of the pencil on the paper. Stalled again.

Outside, a police siren emitted a single abortive *whup* that made me jump. Amsterdam was as quiet as it ever gets at night, only an intermittent rumble of traffic and a faint thump-thump of music from a night-club a couple of streets away, a muffled, jittery heartbeat.

I thrust the pad and pencil guiltily back into the bedside cabinet, and padded over shivering to peek round the drapes.

It was still snowing. There could not have been any wind, because the flakes fell straight down, thousands of tiny white dots hurrying to the ground. I peered upward and tried to fix one flake in my gaze and follow it to the place where it landed, but my eyes were tired and refused to co-operate in the game.

I blinked down at the street: everything was blank and empty, tall crooked houses shoulder-to-shoulder above smooth white sidewalks, the jigsaw of gables and chimneys looking like some kind of mad Christmas cake. The dotted line of car roofs at the kerb were mushroomed with snow.

The stillness made me feel for a second as if the city was waiting for something—something huge and a bit scary, which would bound on from the wings with a *Ta-dahhh!*, shatter the silence with its vitality and start the clocks ticking again.

I shivered, suddenly irritated by my own whimsy. *Carlson, don't be ridiculous.*

I checked my watch, and powered-up the little palmtop computer. Might as well see if anyone I knew was online. The chirping and whirring as the modem connected seemed antisocially loud all of a sudden.

The V-zone was crowded. I used the last of my Zone credits and bought a pair of shades for my rather basic athletic-female avatar, then wasted almost half an hour click-navigating around the topiary garden and the water park exchanging greetings with total strangers who almost all tried to hit on me.

A few months back, I'd met someone in the Zone who I was best buddies with in Base high school: Zia Roccaro. Yeah, *that* Zia Roccaro. Knowing her is my one claim to fame. Finding out that she was right here in Amsterdam was like all my Christmases came at once. At least till I found out exactly how rarefied the atmosphere was up there where she lived. Still, we were both e-savvy; no reason to lose touch completely.

Tonight, Zia's expensively-equipped persona was nowhere to be seen: pity. I chatted to enough passers-by to ensure that nobody else had seen the distinctive silver android, then exited, bored, and logged into my email account instead. V-zones could be alarmingly like the waking world sometimes, even down to the aimless banality of the small talk.

I typed quickly, tucking a wayward strand of hair behind my ear.

Hi Chili!
Missed you in the Zone tonight. You'll never guess who's sleeping over here

tonight—remember Cary Bowman? English guy, tall, devastatingly handsome?
Only sleeping on my couch as I type, girlfriend . . . ;-)
Don't kill yourself from jealousy, will ya?
See you soon.
Red
xx

I hesitated, biting my lip, then shrugged and pressed SEND. If Zia wanted witty, she'd have to wait till morning. The guys at EyeKon kept trying to get me to use the same crappy stimulants they did, but I wouldn't. If that meant I lost the sharp edge at this time in the morning, well, tough. Minding the doors and washrooms in a night-club is hardly life-and-death stuff. If I got a little slow, I just got one of the bar girls to slip me a little shot of cola-concentrate. Just enough caffeine to keep my head up. I could sleep when I got home, which was more than you could say for the idiots who'd been popping pills all night.

I hopped back beneath the covers and curled tight, like a hibernating animal, until my own body heat created a nest of warmth and the touch of my own hands on my skin didn't make me want to shriek.

I lay still and breathed deeply, evenly, waited for sleep to come. I found I was thinking about Bowman and the way he'd said *you can't carry on being frightened for ever*. Like a challenge.

I sat up crossly, and drank a glass of water that I didn't need, just to break the rat-run of my thoughts.

My heartbeat was a little fast, my skin warm when I felt for my pulse, as if I was coming down with a virus.

Hell.

This had better not turn out to be anything serious.

2

THE BLOND MAN lay on his back in a tangle of bedding and watched cold light grow in the basement windows a few feet above his head. Pale straw hung down in wisps among the cobwebs, ghosts of old weeds that had taken root in the rotted wooden frames.

It was a comforting sight to wake up to. It meant that he was in the guest-bed—a grandiose title for an old mattress and cast-off bedding—in the basement of the squat on Geldersekade. Eddy and Cara and their ever-changing roll-call of residents were the closest thing he had to friends. It was good to wake up now and then among friends.

How he came to be here was less clear. Accustomed to not knowing, he waited placidly for enlightenment and let his gaze wander.

Frost had inscribed the dirty glass cobbles of the skylight with an ephemeral icy forest of ferns and flowers. Big peeling flakes of pale blue paint sagged off the damp brick walls, beaded with tiny glittering gems of frozen condensation.

He ran a tongue over furry teeth. His mouth held a flat metallic taste, like blood. His nose felt stuffy, as if he was coming down with a cold.

He twisted his head to look at the pillow beside him. It was flattened, but cold and a bit damp when he put out a hand—dream-fashion—to feel it. Had there really been somebody here?

The man ran one hand through his pale hair, a preoccupied gesture. He was called Jan Wolf. It was not his real name but he used it when he needed to—usually when trying to get work. The menial jobs that came his way were always strictly cash-in-hand. Nobody ever asked for identity papers—which was a good thing—but experience had taught him that they did like you to have a name.

About his real name he was fatalistic. It would come back to him when it was ready. Curiosity had taught him some painful lessons over the last few months, which had left him—among other things—with a twitch in his left eye. Under provocation, it erupted in a flustered spasm of blinking, a silent stammer. People on the street read it as the dubiously-earned stigma of a drunkard or a madman, and gave him a wide berth.

He had thought long and hard about this. To the people who lived in the city, and to the tourists who flocked and peered and waddled like fat pigeons, he was just another *clochard*. Derelict by virtue of alcohol or other abuses, human refuse to be pushed out on the streets with the rest of the sweepings. A receptacle for the embarrassed charity of strangers.

It was an estate in which pride became a handicap rather than a virtue. Wolf felt sometimes that the enforced humility of his existence might be good for him; it didn't make him like it any better.

He had spent a lot of time over the summer months on his knees in Dam Square or Leidseplein, head down, concentrating doggedly on whatever Rijksmuseum postcard he was reproducing that day on the flagstones. He'd copied the idea from art students, and was surprised but gratified to find that he was good at it. He blended the chalk with his fingers. The silky feel of the pigments on his skin was soothing.

The arrangement suited Wolf. He did not have to talk to people, or even look at them if he didn't want to, they still gave him money and somehow it didn't feel like begging.

It had been a short, almost contented interlude that ended with the first real rains in September. He sold the chalks to buy food. The colours that stained the tips of his fingers faded in a week. He drew the line at panhandling, so he had to find work. Cleaning, carrying. Not many people wanted to employ a madman.

In black moments, he reminded himself a bit grimly of the eleventh commandment: Thou Shalt Survive.

He jammed knuckles into his bleary eyes and rolled up on to one elbow, pushing back the covers. Hunger was a familiar pinch in his belly. He realised suddenly that he was stark naked, and looked sharply round for his clothes. They were just beside him, piled in an untidy heap.

Wolf subsided on to the bed, relieved. *Sleeping in the nude, now there's a novelty.* His skin from the waist down was pale. Torso and arms and face were tanned, from long summer days spent dozing in the parks or crouched over a chalk drawing, but the tan was fading; the sun had darkened and blurred his tattoos and they re-emerged now like developing photographs, sharp in the half light.

Wolf ran experimental fingers over the still-taut muscles of his chest, where the tattoo altered the texture of the skin. He liked the star tattoo, with its bright, bold colours and the two dolphins swimming their never-ending circle, inscrutably-smiling nose to tail.

The tattoos were one of the only things he had left from before the hospital. He felt it, sometimes, like half-recognising a face in somebody else's photograph album. When he stripped to wash he always looked the designs over, one by one, as if by some miracle they would suddenly yield and tell him what he most wanted to know. Even now, he found he was holding his breath, willing the stab of memory.

Foolishness. Wolf sighed and slid his hand down to caress the small round scar under his ribs. It was ticklish and tender, a baby's fingerprint. Its counterpart on his back was larger and less neat. It ached in the damp.

Wolf lay back down again with a little grunt of resignation. No job to go to, and nobody was hassling him to get up, so why not enjoy the boon of privacy and a real, clean (well, almost clean) bed while he could?

There'd been something nagging to gain his full attention ever since he awoke. Pete. Yes, that's right, he'd been worried . . . He gazed into the growing light through half-closed eyes, and pulled memory about him along with the blankets.

He'd been leaning on the iron railings down by Oude Schans, watching a coot duck and dive around the houseboats. It seemed much longer ago than just yesterday.

He'd been eating rye bread out of a paper bag, savouring the chewy, dark-smelling morsels, and dropping crumbs into the water to tempt the coot closer.

A woman in fluffy slippers came out on to the deck of the houseboat below and started pulling washing in off a line stretched between two steel hawsers. Wolf stared off into the middle distance and felt she must be looking at him, but he was too hungry to care—the bread was the first thing he had eaten in two days.

He preferred to eat in the privacy of a room, if he had one, or a café. At times, as now, the street had to suffice. Wolf disliked it enough to have his own rules, points of order in his otherwise chaotic life. One, what he ate in public he ate casually, a man enjoying a snack; and two, he never admitted how hungry he was, even if that meant leaving food uneaten. Or sharing it with an ungrateful bird, he amended. The coot was steadfastly ignoring his little flotillas of crumbs and pecked industriously at some submerged weed.

The afternoon had been dry and still—unusual for late November. The water was the flat polished grey of sheet lead, edged with a bubbly scum of dead leaves and sickly rainbows of diesel, bits of floating trash. Better than it was even fifteen years ago, since the big clean-up in the Eighties, but still, not the sort of stuff you'd want to drink, or even drown in.

The air was hazy with exhaust fumes. Buses and trams and cars and a resigned-looking traffic-cop waving big white gloves, attempting to bring order out of the chaos. Some hope. Four-thirty on a Friday meant everyone cramming on to the roads in a vain attempt to begin their weekend early. Most would spend the next hour just clearing the central canal ring.

Flocks of cyclists swooped and sped like brightly-coloured birds among the slower-moving vehicles.

Wolf rolled and half-smoked a cigarette while he finished the black-brown crust of the bread, then pinched out the glowing end and pocketed it. He'd smoke the crumpled butt later, right down to the last tarry ember. It had become a ritual, one last lungful of wholesomely-unwholesome normality before his nightly drowning.

At the hospital, months ago, they had given him pills to send the nightmares away. The tablets slowed the world to a crawl and affected his speech. The bad dreams merely receded so that he walked a grey maze in his head every night, searching for them.

There are worse things than nightmares, Wolf discovered. The maze almost sent him crazy before he unofficially discharged himself.

Wolf rubbed the side of his nose and half-smiled at the memory: those last few days in the stuffy disinfectant air of the ward, the fluttery excitement and the sick feeling when he thought the nurses might stop him and bring him back. It was like looking back through an open doorway at a child's memory, solitary games played in the sunlit safety of a family home. He had walked out of that door almost five months ago.

Street lights were winking on, Wolf's internal signal to start moving. The sleight-of-hand onset of twilight took him by surprise. Only a few days ago, it had still been light at this time. He chewed slowly on the last of the bread to trick his stomach into believing it was getting more than it was, and pushed himself upright. The stiff breeze from the harbour had little icy teeth in it.

He'd better start looking for shelter. There were sleeping-places that he favoured, but you could never guarantee that some other body or bodies would not get there first. He took care to find privacy at night and that, with a population of transients as large as Amsterdam's, was not always simple.

Instead of pinching them up and stuffing them in his mouth, he scattered the last few breadcrumbs for the pigeons and dusted his palms together with a small sandpaper sound.

White specks whisked in the quickening breeze, grains of snow. His breath clouded up around his head as he turned towards the bridge. The traffic had turned into a string of yellow fairy lights, all moving. It made him slightly dizzy. The bread really had not been enough. Perhaps he should stroll up to the back of the station later, get some free grub in his belly.

He tried to consider such necessities dispassionately, but if he was truthful with himself it rarely came off. He felt like a fraud standing in line with the beggars and bag ladies. Something in him did not fit, and he knew it even if nobody else seemed to notice.

He set off towards the bridge. There was always the squat in that ratty warehouse on Geldersekade. If things didn't pan out elsewhere, maybe Eddy would let him crash in the basement.

He had crossed the wide bridge and dodged through the crawling traffic to the opposite kerb, when the sound of frantic barking made him turn and look back the way he had come. A shaggy grey mat of a dog was racing across the bridge, short legs pistoning. Dragging some way behind was a man on the end of a long nylon lead, waving a carrier bag and mouthing curses at the dog. The dog wove through the cars to Wolf's feet, and sat as if trained, grinning.

'Hello Pete.' Wolf bent to smooth the dog's silky white eyebrows, which seemed to have been filched from a much larger, cleaner animal. Pete huffed and lolled a black-mottled tongue at him, then wandered off to lift a leg against a nearby lamp-post.

Rustling and out of breath, the dog's companion emerged from the stream of traffic and balanced on the kerb edge to execute a deep bow.

'Jan, my man!' American-accented English today, though Wolf knew for a fact that Pete Susskind could speak Dutch. He was tall and thin; the archaic obeisance made Wolf's mind flash to the mating dance of a crane. He smiled.

'Hello Pete. Been anywhere?'

'Waterlooplein,' the human Pete answered, pleased. 'Want to see? Got some beauties.' As always, he had an air of barely-suppressed excitement. His hair was an electric halo. Sparks snapped from watery blue bug-eyes. He looped Pete-the-dog's lead round his arm and shook the bag open, tilting it so that Wolf could see inside.

Wolf peered dutifully at a jumble of cheap bric-a-brac. Pete inserted a dirty hand and lifted something out for him to see: a glass eye, the iris deep brown feathered with gold. It winked at Wolf from between the grimy finger and thumb. 'Isn't it great? Gotta keep an *eye* on things, huhu!' A bony elbow nudged his arm. The eyeball vanished back into the bag, and a picture in a cheap plastic frame came out in its place. Wolf recognised a gaudy depiction of the Eye on the Pyramid, and took a guess at the current direction of Pete's obsessions.

'They're very nice.' He bent down again to rub Pete-the-dog between the ears, not really listening to the non-stop talk going on above his head.

Pete talked all the time. It was mostly recycled, little speeches that Wolf had heard ten times before, laughter, snatches of song in an off-key baritone, phrases shouted out of the blue. It was difficult to guess at any context. There probably wasn't one. Wolf had to put up with people thinking he was a madman: Pete was the genuine article.

From a handful of disjointed conversations, Wolf had the bare bones of the man's story. Pete had used drugs, once upon a time, a decade ago when he had been a teenager fresh from the Kansas cornfields, anxious to kick over the traces into Amsterdam's exciting urban-Bohemian lifestyle.

Whatever brightly-coloured landscape Pete inhabited now, inside that curly-topped cranium, it most certainly was not Kansas.

Wolf straightened and said firmly over the flood of verbiage, 'Got to go now, 'bye Pete.' He walked off towards the turning for Geldersekade, shouldering his way through a contrary current of Metro-bound commuters. After a few yards he heard Pete clomping after him, the dog's untrimmed claws scrabbling on the sidewalk.

'Jan, wait! Anni said—said . . .' The effort of lucid communication contorted his face like a toddler's. His long fingers plucked at the tangled beard. 'Anni, uh . . .'

'What did Anni say?' Wolf was just curious enough to wait for the answer. Pete seemed more agitated than usual, a gawky puppet jittering head and shoulders over him in the twilight.

'Anni said that a . . . a guy was asking questions. 'Bout me.' He was practically plaiting the straggly ends of his moustache, and the blue eyes had a feverish quality. 'Why'd anyone ask questions 'bout me, Jan?'

'What sort of questions?'

'Don't know, just questions. Are they goin' to take me away?' Pete grasped Wolf's sleeve and looked so pathetic that Wolf took pity and clumped him reassuringly on the shoulder.

'Pete, nobody's going to take you away. Nobody, you understand? Anni's crazy, she was thinking of someone else. Not you.'

'Not me? You sure?' Pete's eyes lit up, and he gave a jerk on the dog's lead that hauled the mutt right out of the gutter where it had been foraging. 'Oh, thanks Jan! 'Cos that sorta had me worried, you know. Kind of freaky, huh. Look, I've gotta get along now, get Pietje his bones. Sally Chin, she works at the Chinese on Kloveniers, she saves them for him. Thinks he's cute. She's nice to me,' he added, grinning, already walking away backwards. His long arms semaphored at the corner of an alley. 'She's always nice to me! *Tot ziens!*'

'*Tot ziens,*' Wolf shouted after him. He tucked in to the side of the nearest building and turned his coat collar right up, fastening the highest button. It was still spitting hard little flecks of snow and the temperature was dropping. He'd got chilled standing talking.

He set off again. There was still time to hike round a few likely places, but he might just stick his head in at the squat first, see how things stood. They might even give him some food. Saliva sprang in his mouth and he quickened his pace, pushing Pete out of his mind.

Funny, though, that business with Anni: he knew her by sight, a wide-arsed mare of a woman with colourless eyes and a droopy little goldfish mouth. She was always to be seen around Waterlooplein and the other markets, stumping along on bulging conical legs that ended in surprisingly small feet. She had a sweet, high little-girl's voice that unnerved people into staring at her, as if they thought she might be a minor in disguise.

Wolf curled his lip and shrugged deeper into his coat: the woman was a bit touched in the head, sure, but why should she go telling Pete that some man had been asking questions? Ach, why anything with these crazy people? He was one himself, and he didn't know.

His first port of call, a herring stall whose owner sometimes gave him bags of scraps, was not in its usual place. Wolf detoured around the neighbouring streets for almost fifteen minutes before giving up in disgust. It was late. He was just getting cold and hungry mucking around like this. He set off for Geldersekade and Eddy with renewed determination, visions of soup and soft white bread swimming enticingly in his head.

Outside the Chinese supermarket, the traffic was snarled by an accident: a bad-tempered cacophony of car horns and shouting voices spread out from the mess of crumpled panels and smashed glass. Wolf took advantage of the gridlock to cross the square leisurely towards the Waag, which looked even more like a picture-postcard than usual with its twin pointy towers crusted with snow.

The electronic howl of an ambulance started up, almost behind him coming down Geldersekade. Wolf jumped and looked that way automatically as it nosed through the junction.

Just that reflex turn of the head, or he would never have seen what happened next.

A black car pulled to the far side of the square, as if to avoid the ambulance. Its windows were tinted black. The detail made him look—rich people and police go for the expensive black glass, no reason for anyone else to bother. He caught a glimpse of the driver's hands through the front screen.

The rear door on the far side opened and a second later three men hustled out of a dark alley mouth towards the car. The two either side were bulky, efficient, muffled in dark coats. The third man bobbed out of stride between them. His face was a pale blob under the street-lamps. The mouth was a black hole that opened and shut as he talked. He was tall but thin, scarecrow clothes flapping in the breeze. Straggly corkscrew hair waved to the world. It was Pete.

The lanky American seemed to be arguing, resisting the men who flanked him. As they reached the car one of the heavies grasped him brutally by a handful of hair and thrust him into the opening. The two piled in and the door slammed. The car pulled out with a squeak of tyres, nosing north up the Zeedijk.

'Pete? *PETE!*' Wolf's surprised bellow turned heads. He shoved past people, threading through the stationary traffic towards the black car.

He'd thought for a blank second that it was the cops, but why in hell would they be whisking a filthy bum like Pete off in an unmarked car when they knew they could just pick him up off the pavement any time? It didn't add up. And where was the dog? Pete said he was taking the mutt to the Chinese restaurant on Kloveniersburgwal to get his bones. What was he doing here, alone? Wolf had never seen the two friends separated by more than the length of that silly red leash. For some reason that scared him more than the sudden casual violence.

The car was picking up speed. Wolf ran across the middle of the busy junction in its wake. Cyclists whirred past. Wolf gasped for air. There was a coach, a big EuroCruiser, coming the other way. Its airhorns blared a warning. Wolf put on a last desperate spurt, yelled again, 'PETE!'

The driver's window scrolled half way down on a hard, heavy-jawed face. Insect eyes of dark glasses regarded Wolf coldly. A second, no more, then the window slid shut. The car accelerated away. Winded, Wolf stared after it, chest heaving.

The horns blasted again, appallingly close. Wolf jumped aside cringing as the coach roared past. A rack of blank faces stared down at him behind the green-tinted glass. A soot-black maw belched diesel fumes over him. The noise made his innards shake.

Wolf made it to the sidewalk on legs that trembled. He felt as if something heavy had hit him on the skull. His bad eye refused to stop blinking. He wiped a hand over his face. It came away slick with perspiration. *The driver . . .* Like a damaged disc, repeating senselessly, *the driver, something about the driver . . .*

'Hey, you!' A traffic cop had witnessed Wolf's antics. He gestured peremptorily from behind a gaggle of hurrying people.

Wolf backed away round the nearest car, tripped and sat down in the gutter. Commuters started aside, a jink in their steady stream.

The white-helmeted cop was closer now, looking sour. He was fat, and walked with a sort of unstoppable roll, a glacier grinding down a valley. The black night-stick attached to his belt waggled with every step.

Wolf struggled to his feet and ran, pushing people out of his way. Behind, he heard the cop give a startled shout.

Three, four steps clear, running down the side of Geldersekade. In the cycle track, damn it. A man in a shiny purple helmet shouted at him and grabbed his sleeve. Wolf twisted free and heard the cyclist go down with a crash and a yell of outrage. He did not stop.

Bicycles chained three deep by brainless anarchists protruded into his path. Wolf tripped, dodged. Why couldn't the man just give up and let him go? He felt like a sideshow. People were pointing, stopping to look. He slogged on, pressing a hand against the pain in his ribs. That crazy dash after the car had knocked all the breath out of him.

A tic of pain started behind his left eye. He rubbed it, unnerved. *Pete, that's right. What happened to Pete? Can't think straight running like this.* He dropped to a limping jog.

Ahead, he caught sight of the yellow-painted door of the squat. Refuge. He veered towards it.

A shriek of brakes and the blare of horns jerked him back. A man's red face popped out of the window of a white van. 'Oi!'

Wolf returned the man's obscene gesture automatically and banged on the side panel of the van with the flat of his hand, heart hammering. The road lifted and dropped under his feet like the deck of a ship.

'All right, you!' A heavy gloved hand grabbed his lapel and yanked him back out of the way of the traffic. It was the cop. Wolf winced at the manhandling. He babbled wildly, 'No, please, I haven't done anything wrong, please—'

The cars were moving again now, crawling past in a solid line down the side of the canal. The policeman was big as well as wide. Fists like pink hams almost lifted Wolf off the floor.

'Shut up!'

'I'm sorry, OK, I'm sorry—' Wolf begged off with upraised hands, breathing fast. He ducked his head aside in an embarrassed attempt to avoid the cop's eyes. The man was frowning blackly.

'Okay, *Menheer*, let's see about this, shall we? No need for any trouble. Would you just step over here away from the road, please?'

Cop talk, polite but with that menacing sub-text. Wolf nodded, numb, and allowed himself to be shepherded over to the railings. His eyelid convulsed.

The policeman let go of Wolf and extracted a notebook and pen from his uniform jacket with forbidding, ponderous movements.

'What did you think you were doing, hey? Running out into the traffic like that? Bloody fool.'

The needle of pain behind Wolf's left eye-socket pulsed, white-hot.

'Now, *Menheer*, how about some identification?' The cop looked up, pencil poised.

'Jan?' The soft voice jerked Wolf back to early-morning sunshine and the cold, musty smell of the cellar. He blinked, dazzled. A semi-naked girl was picking her way down the brick steps. Wolf clasped the blankets to his chest like a startled old maid, struggling to sit up. The girl noticed this and chuckled. 'No need, really.'

'Really?' A blank splat of real panic; how could he have slept with someone and not remembered? Had he got drunk? He felt sure he had seen her before, but he could not even recall a name.

She must have seen it in his face because she laughed and sat down on the end of the bed. *She's a child*, he thought, no bosom to speak of and a boy's slim hips and flat belly. Her face was pretty, even scarred at the jaw with a red mottling of acne. Her short black hair was shaved at the sides to show off a gleaming row of gold earrings.

She was clutching a red-stitched army blanket round her shoulders but he could see white panties and the pale pink point of one small breast. The sight started a warm ache in the pit of his belly. Some internal clock told him it had been a long time.

'Yes, really, and no, we didn't. Oh, I *slept* with you,' she added at his twitch of a frown towards the rumpled sheets at his side. She pulled a face, mock-outraged. 'But that was it. You were in a seriously wasted state last night.'

'So I didn't . . . uh, we didn't . . . ?' He gestured helplessly. The girl chuckled again, an infectious sound, and pressed his toes where they poked the blankets up. He noticed that she had rings on every finger. One in her navel, too, with a tiny gold ball on it. Her Dutch had a southern burr.

'No. You walked in the door all messed up and bloody, had a couple of beers and passed out. Eddy and Willem cleaned you up and brought you down here to sleep it off but . . . ' She stopped and looked thoughtful. 'Well, I came down after a bit to see if you were OK.'

Wolf hunched his shoulders and rubbed a hand through his hair, scratched round his adam's apple where the beard ran out. 'Scare you?'

'Nooo . . . well, a bit yes,' she admitted. 'You were shouting stuff in your sleep, thrashing about, you know.' A one-shouldered shrug. 'Eddy'd said something about . . . well, he thinks you're a bit crazy if you really want to know.' Diffident, as if she thought he might bite.

Wolf shrugged and grunted—he was Eddy's pet eccentric. So what if the guy thought he was one sandwich short of a picnic, when he got fed and watered and allowed to sleep here sometimes? He realised the girl was looking at him still, worried that she'd offended him. 'I get nightmares,' he volunteered shortly. 'That's all.'

'You don't need to tell me,' the girl said. 'I got the full *son et lumière* last night. Someone screwed you up well and truly. Was it drugs?'

'I don't know,' Wolf muttered. 'That's the problem. I can't remember.' He felt himself colour at her look, grabbed his t-shirt and started to jam his arms in. 'It's true.'

'Well and truly shafted.' The girl shook her head and made a face. 'Hell, we have to look out for each other. I mean, someone's got to give a damn, right? Nobody else is going to.' The cynical expression was replaced by sly good humour. 'Hm. Anyway, you're lucky I was still here, Jan. If you'd've left it till next week you really would have been on your own.'

'You're leaving?'

'Sure. London, Paris . . . ' An insouciant shrug, not quite pulled off. 'Wherever. I've got a friend mails me sometimes from Berlin, says the club scene's really hot. I might go there for a bit, see if I like it.' Her grin widened. 'You don't remember my name, do you?'

'No,' Wolf admitted. He knew he was blushing again. 'I know I've seen you before, here I guess, but that's all. Sorry, uh . . . '

'Maartje,' she said, 'Maartje Rijk,' and stood up as he began to struggle with his socks. 'You going already?'

'I shouldn't outstay my welcome.' Wolf cocked an eyebrow at the upper levels, and she wrapped the blanket more firmly around herself, heading for the steps. He could not tell if she was disappointed or not—he did not know whether to be disappointed or relieved, himself. She turned at the top of the steps.

'It's snowing again, a bit. I'll make coffee before you go, OK? Take your time, it's early.'

Early could mean any time before noon, Wolf supposed. There was no sound of movement in the squat apart from Maartje's quiet footsteps in the kitchen overhead, but a steady grumble of traffic in the street made him think it must be mid-morning at least. Time he was moving. That thing with the men in their dark coats and the black car . . . it had rattled him. He wouldn't be easy in his mind until he'd seen Pete and made sure he was all right.

When he had tidied the bed and made himself as presentable as he could without the aid of water and a mirror, Wolf climbed the steps into the dim high-roofed kitchen. Pots and crockery, caked with the remains of old meals, were piled in the sink and on the worktops, interspersed with towers of beer glasses and empty bottles. The room smelt of baked beans and burnt toast.

Maartje seemed to have appointed herself his guardian angel. She stuffed a wad of cash into his pocket as soon as he appeared, like a mother sending a child off to school with its lunch money. Wolf half expected her to whip out a comb and tidy his hair.

The two didn't exchange many words while they drank their coffee. Maartje let him out of the yellow front door in silence, just a grin and slap between the shoulder-blades as he stepped out into the new covering of snow, as if they were old friends. When Wolf turned back to say something, she was already hidden behind the closing door. Only her hand was visible with its solid row of rings, delicate baroque knuckle-dusters.

She'd packed a carrier bag with food. When he opened it standing on the doorstep, there were even cakes—two chocolate croissants, a bit squashed, and a piece of Mika's space cake, marbled in a swirl of violent colours.

He kept the croissants with tomorrow's breakfast in mind, and donated the space cake to a beggar squatted shivering in a shop doorway with 'STARVING' pencilled on a piece of cardboard strung round his neck. Life was weird enough lately without resorting to hallucinogens.

There was bread folded round thick ham and smeared with mustard, and almost a whole packet of stale Lebkuchen. Wolf chewed and gulped as he strolled along Geldersekade. OK, think. Where's Pete going to be?

He'd try over on Waterlooplein first. Pete was there all the time. Even if Wolf couldn't track him down, there would be people who had seen Pete last night, or maybe even this morning.

I just want to be sure he's OK.

Colder today, definitely. Snow squeaked under his boots. Gusts of frozen drizzle clawed Wolf's cheeks above the line of his beard. He cocked an eye to inspect the clouds but there was nothing to suggest that they were contemplating anything worse— nothing better, either. His forehead ached with cold.

There was a grey rime of ice at the edge of the canal, sleek hard bubbles like glass jewels tangled in the hair of old reeds. Cars crawled past. There was the usual number of crazed all-weather cyclists, swooping and swerving in the *fietspad*, tyres whirring and hissing in the slush.

Memory was playing unkind tricks on Wolf this morning: rows of numbers marched and somersaulted in the back of his mind. He ignored them as best he could. After all this time incommunicado it seemed irritatingly useless to suddenly be remembering phone numbers.

It was like having someone else's private phone book in your hands, but with all the names torn out. One could call them up, but what to say? 'Who's calling? Well, I was rather hoping you could tell *me*.' No. If they were going to resolve into something, they would have to do it by themselves. Curiosity, he had learned, did not just kill the cat, it skinned it alive and nailed its hide to the door. He had no particular wish to court its displeasure.

The mess he had been in, yesterday . . . He flinched inwardly. As if things weren't bad enough. Twice now, it had happened: crushing pains in his head then blackout and waking up hours later with a raw bloodied gap where memory ought to be. He had had similar episodes in hospital, before they started doping him up, but the summer had passed without incident and he'd naïvely thought himself recovered.

Fugue, the doctors called it. 'An interval of flight from reality' was how Henrik, the counsellor, had described it. He showed Wolf a video tape of himself standing, sitting, talking quite naturally to nursing staff and counsellors and this frightened Wolf badly because he had no memory of any of it. Now it had started again and he had no recourse to stop it.

The first time, it had been sparked off by the antics of a rowdy bunch of German football fans spilling out of a bar on Singel. The image glittered in his head: they'd picked up one of their number, struggling, swung him by the arms and legs and tossed him into the canal.

The man seemed to hang for an instant at apogee, sprawled in the air with his mouth agape, before he plunged beneath the surface. He bobbed up a second later spouting water and dog-paddled round yelling insults and trying to splash his mates, prostrate with laughter on the quayside above.

Wolf—who chanced to be walking across a nearby bridge—shivered in the breeze and wondered nervously at the sparks of pain that arced between the bones of his skull. His hands and legs trembled as he walked away.

Hours later, while nursing his worsening headache, he had fallen backwards off a bar stool in the smoke-filled basement of a jazz club. He landed spreadeagled on the floor, which knocked all the breath out of his lungs. The circle of faces that closed in around him stretched and distorted and span away like a cheap television special effect. He drowned that night in thick black water that tasted of his own blood.

It's like being burgled, Wolf thought morosely. Or raped. Whatever I did, wherever I went last night, it might just as well have been someone else doing it—someone else looking through my eyes, walking with my legs, touching with my hands. The notion was oddly repellent.

Don't I have enough enemies without ganging up on *myself*?

A sudden memory-flicker of the stranger's face, the driver of the black car, made his eyelid wince. He rubbed it tenderly with his fingertips, but the stabbing pains that had signalled the start of the seizure yesterday did not come. Still, he didn't feel much like eating any more. He dropped the last of the Lebkuchen back into his pocket.

Wolf filled his lungs with the rumbling cold city air. It was undeniably invigorating to be setting out with a definite purpose in mind, however odd or futile that purpose might turn out to be. If he was going to tilt at windmills he was in the right place for it.

Ever since he woke, he'd had a feeling—somewhere between fear and anticipation. Things were changing. Perhaps there were answers after all. Perhaps there was a way back.

It didn't seem likely, but living on the city streets had taught Wolf that all kinds of unlikely things happen every day.

3

WHEN CARY BOWMAN banged on my bedroom door at eleven o'clock in the morning, I knew last night's forebodings had been right. I struggled upright and stared blearily at the clock. Five hours' sleep? He had to be joking.

'Wakey-wakey!' Bowman shouted sadistically outside the door, and banged again. I groaned and rolled away from the noise.

'Go 'way, 's too early . . . ' I jammed the pillow over my head and burrowed deeper under the covers, groping after the cushiony darkness.

'Rise and shine, we've got work to do.'

I surfaced, glaring. The effect was spoiled somewhat by my inability to keep my eyes open. 'C-coffee, Madam,' Bowman said, mock-suave, bending to indicate the bedside table—as if this was a Bond movie and he was the eccentric butler serving breakfast in bed to the exotic bit of fluff—and walked out.

The exotic bit of fluff shot upright in the bed and threw a pillow, but the door was already shut.

'Breakfast's ready,' Bowman added, from the safety of the living-room.

'OK, OK, I'm up, I'm up!' I croaked, and threw back the covers before I could change my mind.

Ugh. Cold. I could see my breath. I grabbed my robe. Coffee, right. I took a searing sip, and pulled a face. Filter coffee was too much on a hung-over stomach. That'd teach me to drink brandy at five in the morning.

Forget it. Drink coffee. Hmm. Better get dressed. Definite psychological disadvantage to being seen slobbing around the apartment in grubby old t-shirt and shorts with a moth-eaten pink robe on top. Especially as I'd lost the belt for the robe. Some Bond girl I'd make.

I stuck a chair in front of the door before I stripped, and spent ten minutes staring into the half-empty wardrobe and panicking. What had I been *thinking*?

Bowman was in the living-room crunching toast when I shuffled in en route to the bathroom. Veiled amusement in his eyes as he took in my distressed-refugee look. His tone was perfectly courteous.

'Good morning.'

'Not really.' I sipped my coffee and poked at my hair: it felt like a Halloween wig. I tried to comb my fingers casually through it and got them stuck.

'Hungry?' Bowman proffered the plate of toast.

'No. No, thanks.' He had opened the drapes and the winter sunlight stabbed at my aching eyes. 'Ow. I, uh . . . think I'll just go wash up.'

'Don't take all morning.' Bowman was rooting in his big black sports bag. I made a face at the top of his head, and banged the bathroom door a little more vigorously than I'd intended: *who exactly is the interloper here, Mister Bowman?*

Half an hour was longer than I liked to spend on anything apart from taking a bath, but stubbornness made me stretch my toilet out. As a result, I emerged feeling a good seventy-five per cent more human—hair brushed to a shine, teeth flossed and polished, breath fresh, face glowing. I had even taken the trouble to trim my nails and paint them a vivid metallic blue. Doing my nails always made me feel good. Shame the inside of my head still felt as if it was stuffed with kapok.

Bowman was still sitting on the couch, frowning at a mess of papers he'd spread on the coffee table. The toast was gone. He glanced up at me as if I had only been absent for a few moments.

'Bit more awake now?' No detectable irony in his voice. I perched cautiously on the arm of the couch, unsure of my next move now that my flagrant tardiness had been ignored. I peered at the papers. There seemed to be a lot of charts and diagrams and scientific symbols. 'So, uh . . . what is all that stuff?'

'Oh, just stuff,' Bowman said quickly, pulling the nearest stack towards him. 'I came out in a bit of a hurry and it's all mixed up. I was trying to find the background notes I kept on our missing PI. Look—' He gestured distractedly, 'why don't you go and get a fresh coffee, then we can go through it together. The perc's on.'

I hesitated, then scooted into the kitchen. Was he really acting strange, or was I just being hyper-sensitive? *Probably both*, I told myself, pouring coffee from the jug.

I'd hoped that the mundane aspects of having Bowman using my bathroom and sleeping on my couch would defuse some of the sexual tension I'd experienced last night. If anything, it seemed to be having the opposite effect.

I snapped the lid on to the pot and slotted it back into the bubbling percolator. Well, I'd just have to make the best of it. I could hardly ask him to leave because he was giving me hot flashes, could I? *Besides*, I braced myself, *however much I don't want to admit it, he's right. I can't stay frightened for ever. I'm just not sure any more if I'd recognise the right time and place and person.*

Back in the living-room, I slid down to sit on the floor and tucked my hair out of the way. 'OK, shoot.'

'Right.' The papers had been stacked into a rough pile at the far end of the table. Bowman pushed one sheet towards me. 'Try this for starters. Service record.'

I studied the official-looking form. 'Cary, this is in Dutch.'

'Oh—oh, sorry, I assumed . . . ' Bowman leaned over to run his finger down the lines. His arm brushed mine, distracting me. 'Er . . . well, it's a c-copy of his service

record with the RNLN—the Royal Dutch Navy. Er, let's see, name, Kristian de Haan
. . . he was in for six years, seventy-eight to eighty-four, rank Sergeant—seems he was
offered promotion twice and declined—deep-water specialist—'

'A what?' I interrupted. There was a passport-sized blob at the top left that must
have been a photo. The copier had rendered it as a greyish-black morass, like a toddler's
crayon drawing.

'A diver,' Bowman said, still frowning at the densely-written form. 'Marine salvage
or mine clearance, that sort of thing, I suppose. He served on HNLMS *Tacticus* and *Wolf*
. . . A f-few disciplinary blips, but nothing serious . . . Um. That's about it, really. It's only
a summary. Oh, sorry about the photo, there's a b-better one somewhere about . . . '
He started rifling through the mess at his end of the table. I drank coffee in an attempt
to jump-start my brain cells.

'What did he do after he quit the Navy?'

'Oh, this and that. Arty stuff m-mostly, he was in the archive service at the Boymans-
van Beuningen Museum in Rotterdam for a while, cleaning and restoring old paintings,
sticking b-broken vases back together, that kind of thing.'

'Patient guy,' I murmured, thinking of a woman I'd watched once, in the New York
Metropolitan Museum, manoeuvring tiny broken fragments of an ancient pot into
place on a clay model using tweezers. A painstaking jigsaw with a thousand pieces and
no picture to help you. 'What did you say he looked like?'

'Big bloke,' Bowman said, '. . . er, blond, six foot . . . ' He trailed off, gazing at the
piece of paper in his hand. It was another scientific-looking jumble. I wiggled my
fingers to get his attention.

'Hello? Planet Earth calling Cary?' His startled blink made me smile.

'What—? Oh, sorry . . . ' He stuffed the paper back into the pile, and retrieved a strip
of four small colour photographs, which he tossed my way. 'Here, this is him.'

'What *is* it about passport photos?' I studied the tiny images mock-critically.
'Everyone comes out looking like a complete psychopath. I mean, *look* at this.' I held up
the photographs for Bowman's inspection. 'He's all weird and starey-eyed, see? And
his mouth's hanging open in that one. Yuck. I wouldn't let him on *my* plane. No way.'

'Yes, well,' Bowman drawled, and dropped the photo-strip on to the table. 'We all
know how p-picky you are when it comes to men, don't we? A shifty-looking private
eye wouldn't stand a chance.'

'I didn't say that.' I snatched the photos back for a second look while I took another
swallow of coffee. 'He's not so bad. Kind of Nordic. Blue eyes, hmm. Say, is he married?'
I slid a teasing look sideways at Bowman. He uttered a short chuffing noise and looked
martyred.

'Bloody hell, I don't know. D-divorced, I think. Anyway, he's too old for you. C-can
we get on now?'

'Sure, what's next?'

'Hang on a sec . . . ' Bowman sorted through the top strata of the stack, and pulled out a shabby manila folder. 'Oh, here we are, you'll like these. Got 'em from his old place. Seems you're not the only one that m-mucks about with art in your spare time.'

'You're kidding.' I put down my cup to pull off the perished old rubber band holding the folder shut. A heap of sketches spilled out, along with a stub of soft pencil and a putty eraser. I fanned the drawings across the table, and puffed my cheeks out in disbelief. 'Whoa, these are really *good*, I was expecting—you know—'

'Watercolours of windmills?' Bowman grinned at me. 'Told you you'd like them.'

'You were right,' I murmured. I traced the fluid pencil lines with one fingernail. Whales, dolphins, sea-stars . . . It was as if someone had rifled through my brain for all my best ideas and then drawn them better than I could ever hope to. Several sketches had been worked up into striking, detailed designs, executed in black ink and signed in a round, incisive hand *KdH*.

I went through the heap again, examining each piece, front and back. Bowman leaned over my shoulder, disconcertingly close. His breath tickled the small hairs by my ear.

'This isn't *Murder, She Wrote*, you know.'

'What do you mean?' I twisted to look at him. Bowman nodded at the sketches.

'Looking for phone numbers or secret formulas or whatever. In m-my experience, people aren't usually that accommodating.'

'Oh, your experience, riiight,' I drawled. 'Cary, someone who gives lectures on Hollywood movies every day of their working life could be considered just a tad out of touch with reality.'

'Oh, v-very funny.' Bowman lit up a cigarette, and waved the smoke away from me. 'Sorry. D'you mind?'

'No, it's OK.' I got up to fetch a foil takeaway carton from the kitchen. 'Sorry, I don't have a real ashtray.'

'This'll be fine.' Bowman balanced his cigarette on the edge of the carton, and tilted his head to look at me. A flicker of amusement. 'Kris de Haan has an eidetic memory.'

'Sorry?'

'A photographic memory. Never any need for him to write things down.' Smoke trickled from Cary's mouth and nostrils as he spoke, like a magic trick. 'You know, you've never asked what I did before I came to Amsterdam. I wasn't born a Film Studies lecturer, you know.'

'Well, OK.' I hugged my knees and recited mock-obediently. 'What did you do before you came to Amsterdam?'

'I was a p-private investigator,' Bowman said, and smiled wryly behind the thin veil of smoke. 'Surprised?'

'Yes,' I said, and sipped coffee. He raised one brow.

'What's wrong, have I g-grown horns and a tail?'

'Of course not, but . . . well, why didn't you tell me before?'

'You didn't ask.' He shrugged and smoothed at the nape of his neck. 'It's one reason why I left England.'

'To hide?' I frowned at him. He smiled again, and shook his head.

'To lay the ghosts of the past.' He spoke lightly, but avoided my gaze. Bowman's reserve was iron shutters behind those deceptive eyes; this tenuous strand of revelation was fragile as a soap bubble. I nodded, not wanting to break the mood.

'I know the feeling. I thought I could lay a few ghosts myself by coming here.'

'And did you?' Bowman tilted his head again to look at me, his eyes hooded.

'I don't know. I think . . . I think you carry the ghosts inside you,' I said, and shrugged. 'Hell, you know what my life's been like. It's kind of hard to run away from your own memories.'

'Perhaps you need some new ones,' Bowman said. He slid down to sit on the floor at my side, leaning back against the couch and drawing on his cigarette. I stayed still, but moth wings fluttered in the pit of my belly. I moistened my lips.

'What do you mean?'

'I mean perhaps you're just approaching your ghost problem in the wrong way.' Bowman turned his head to look at me. The smoke and the pale sunlight-shapes from the window slid over his face like a disguise. 'Sometimes the only way to exorcise a bad memory is to crowd it out with good ones.'

'You mean, like new . . . uh, new memories?' I could not quite bring myself to meet his gaze, and stared instead at the scattered pile of sketches. The topmost drawing was one of the inked-in designs. It depicted a pair of dolphins coupling merrily, sinuous bodies entwined in a trail of bubbles. The eroticism jolted me like a static charge. I hugged my knees tight.

'Question.' The light from outside gleamed in Bowman's pale eyes. He let the word hang in the air for so long that I grew uncomfortable.

'What?'

'D'you trust me?' It was the same question he had asked me last night, I realised— and he knew it, he'd said it like that deliberately. I had flunked the question last night, and we both knew that, too. I stuck my chin out.

'Yes.' My voice came out in a whisper, and I cleared my throat, irritated, and repeated, in a firmer tone, 'Yes, of course I do.' *I think. Oh, help . . .*

'Then come here.' He put his hand out slowly, palm up, and added, on a small plume of tobacco smoke, '—please.'

'I thought you gave up smoking,' I said after a moment. I did not move yet. Bowman half-laughed, and shrugged.

'It's the stress.'

'Stress . . . ?' My heart was battering at my ribs.

'Of being rejected,' he explained. 'It gets to a man after a while.'

'Oh.' I reached out my hand until our fingers brushed; his skin was warm and dry. 'I would hate to be the cause of you starting smoking again.'

'Really.' Bowman's fingers curled around mine, and I allowed him to draw me closer. I baulked at the last moment.

'Cary—'

'It's all right,' he said, and let go of my hand. I gulped back a nervous laugh, and fumbled for his fingers again, pressed them hard.

'No, I—look, is it OK if we just take this very . . . *very* slowly?'

'That depends.' The lines at the corners of his eyes were laughing. I made a face at him.

'Changing your mind already?'

'Definitely not.' He ran his hand up my arm.

'I don't know if this is going to work, Cary.' I didn't seem to have the breath to speak properly.

'You don't know anything until you try.' Bowman said. His hand drifted up to stroke my hair. 'Look. Like this . . . ' He held my gaze quite deliberately as he leaned down to kiss me.

I felt I knew now exactly how a rabbit feels, frozen in the headlights of an oncoming truck: my body seemed to have turned to frozen jelly, if that was possible. He pinned me against the couch, curled against me hip to hip. My arms were trapped between us in a ridiculous gesture of defence, hands flat against his chest. His fingers slipped beneath my hair to caress the nape of my neck, and I shivered.

'Cary—'

He drew back a fraction, but his heartbeat was rapid under my fingers. The translucent irises of his eyes refracted the pale glimmer of sunlight.

I kissed him. His mouth was warm, and softer than I'd imagined. His skin smelt of cinnamon and salt. A couple of millimetres of sharp gingery stubble scratched my chin, but you can't have everything. It was so good to be held like that. It had been so long. I still couldn't get my breath but it didn't matter. I wriggled my arms free and wound my fingers in his hair.

Bowman groaned deep in his chest. His kisses strayed over my jaw and throat. His hands traced the shapes of my body, his movements becoming rough.

Panic, like a bullet in my belly.

'Don't.' I caught his hand and pushed it away, breathing rapidly. 'Cary, stop. Please.' The acrid bite of bile in my throat. I gulped convulsively.

The pale lashes flickered, and I saw his nostrils pinch slightly. 'What's wrong?'

'I'm sorry.' I wriggled out of his grasp, getting to my feet. Hot and cold in equal parts. 'I—I just can't . . . go there. Not yet. I'm—I'm so sorry. We shouldn't have started this.'

'No, it's OK, I understand.' Bowman slumped against the couch, running his hands through his hair and breathing deeply through his nose. It didn't look OK, not one bit, but he was trying to be all British and gentlemanly about it. Half of me wished he would yell and get unreasonable. The other half navigated a wobbly course between guilt and relief.

I snatched a glance at the clock: twelve forty-two. My one o'clock self-defence class would be lining up in the hallway at the Club. I groaned and clutched my head. 'Dammit, I'm going to be late for work!' I scrambled for my coat and boots, aware that work was just a good excuse to leave.

Bowman appeared in the doorway while I was struggling with my bootlaces. He looked tired. 'Can we talk about this?'

'What's to talk about?' I kept my head down over my boot. 'Maybe the whole thing was just a lousy idea.'

'You don't really believe that,' Bowman countered. He grasped my sleeve as I straightened up. The green eyes were clouded. He gave me a little shake. 'Robin, come on—'

'We'll talk later,' I mumbled, 'I'm late already.' I twisted out of his grip to open the door.

Bowman did not say anything else, or make any move to stop me. I wasn't sure if that made me happy or sad. I helter-skeltered down the stairs, stamping along the landings as if I could pound my feelings back into shape.

I paused in the silent hall, and sighed gustily. Love *sucks*.

❖

Four different classes made for an arduous afternoon. I worked myself into the sort of manic good humour that comes from using physical activity as an emotional pressure-valve.

Living in the moment. It was what had drawn me back towards the martial arts. The submerging of the whole self—mind, body and spirit—into something that seemed on the surface wholly physical. It scratched an almost-subliminal itch.

The last class was a practice session for some of the younger kids in the Kung Fu club. The Spawn of Satan, I privately termed them: springing around the floor in sparring practice like a boxful of hyperactive crickets and driving *sensei* Robin nuts by not listening. Marik gave them to me as a joke. I had to work twice as hard as the other teachers to avoid becoming the punchline.

After the last stragglers had been herded away by harrassed parents and au pairs, I turned the lights off and ran through *kata* one more time, alone, as a final, private wind-down.

The neon sign of the kebab house across the street threw fantastical colours over my reflection in the big wall mirrors. The afternoon light was gone, leached away into a sullen twilight. Sweat drying on my neck made me shiver. Step, punch, block, sweep . . . I mirror-gazed shamelessly. It was reassuring to know that here, at least, I was in complete control.

Ten minutes later, skipping down the last flight of stairs past the weights room, I smelt a gas heater going and heard the tack-tack of a manual typewriter. Over the grumble of traffic outside, a violin sang.

I leaned in at the office door, still towelling at my sweaty neck. 'Hey, Sunny. Koos said there was a call for me?' A plastic Santa dangling from the door-frame tickled my shoulder with its fuzz-trimmed boots. I batted it to one side and entered.

The stink of the heater was strong in here. The wave of moist warmth was like walking into a sauna.

Wall-to-wall, Marik's treasured collection of Bruce Lee posters glared down, peeling at the edges from damp. Since last week, they had been augmented with twirly Christmas garlands and foil lanterns with tassels, in an assortment of shocking colours. Chinese restaurant crossed with Santa's grotto. Vital clues to the identity of its owner.

Marik's girlfriend scooted her swivel chair backwards from her desk and grinned smugly at my dishevelled state. As always, her own starling-black hair was sleek, lipstick in place, not a nail extension chipped. I had been intensely envious of Sunny's nails, until I discovered that they were thirty-five per cent nylon.

'Jeff Bloem. He's on line one, over there. Have the babies been giving you a hard time today, darlin'?'

'It's the other way round *entirely*, believe me.' I wrinkled my nose, reaching for the handset. 'I don't know how you can stand that stench, Sun-yi. I can hardly breathe in here.'

'I'd ra'ver have the stink and be warm,' Sunny pointed out. Even at that, she was wearing a fancy fur-trimmed Afghan coat that made her look like a Tibetan princess.

'Good point.' I pinned the receiver between shoulder and ear. 'Hello, Jeff?'

'Hey, Robin, how you doing?' Not a real question. I started shaping the 'f' of 'fine, thanks', and as usual got cut off as Jeff barged on in his ripely-accented English, 'I need you for a gig tomorrow, it's urgent, how are you fixed?'

'Uh . . . ' I extemporised, pulling horror-movie faces. I switched the handset to my other ear. 'What's the gig?'

'Media junket, sweetie. Someone out there likes you. Big Tree are launching this huge TV campaign for some medical research charity, and they specifically asked for you—'

'Wait a minute.' I switched ears again, hoping it would sound different. 'Is it the one for NERVE?'

'Oh, you've heard of—'

'Find someone else.' A queasy feeling, as if I had inadvertantly swallowed a slug. 'I can't do that gig, Jeff.'

Jeff sounded startled. 'What do you mean, you can't? It's good money, it's not even a whole day's work—'

'It's not the money,' I said. 'It's . . . it's just something personal, OK? Get somebody else to cover it.'

'No way.' The business edge in Jeff's voice. 'Robin, you owe me so many favours I lost count. The launch is going to be at the charity's HQ, it's one of those new places down on the Ringweg. Europa Victor Business Park, number 4. I want you there, tomorrow, twelve sharp, smart dress. OK?'

Another non-question. 'OK,' I muttered, defeated, 'OK.'

'That's better. Beggars can't be choosers, huh?' Miffed at my lack of proper gratitude. A sound of papers being shuffled. 'I'm putting you on Jean-Paul's team.'

'*Jeff*—' I recognised petty vengeance, closed my eyes and took a deep breath. 'Thanks.'

'You're welcome,' Jeff said, deadpan. 'Bye.'

'Bye now.' *Sonofabitch.* I banged the handset down with a growl of annoyance, and rolled my eyes at Sunny's inquiring look. 'He's only gone and put me on the same team as Jean-Paul Didier.'

'Ooh. Be'er brush up on your self-defence, duck.' Sunny waved a languid hand at the plastic clock on the far wall. It hung slightly lopsided on a torn cinema poster of *Enter the Dragon* and said 17:35. 'Last lot all gone?'

'Yup. Nobody seemed to want a shower today for some reason.' We shuddered and giggled in unison: the showers in this place were a running joke. Since last week, all they had been running was ice-cold water. Word got around.

I hugged the towel tighter round my neck and rotated my head, wincing at a creak of tendons. I rubbed at the sore spot with cold fingers. 'Sunny, could I have a few minutes alone in here? I want to make a call before Marik gets in.'

'Personal, is it?' Sunny, who, I thought, must have developed some pretty advanced survival techniques to live with Marik Washington for eleven years, unfolded her compact Asian-Barbie form from the swivel chair and indicated the empty seat. 'Go on, love. I'll run down to Dvaar's and get us somefin' nice, shall I? Danish and coffee? Got half an hour before the next class, we might as well push the boat out.'

'You go, girl.' I stood aside to let Sunny out of the door—there really wasn't enough room for two people in the cubby-office—and wiggled my fingers at her as she pushed through the glass doors into the street. A burst of traffic noise boomed in the lobby, then faded again as the doors closed.

I blew out both cheeks in relief and lugged my shoulder-bag up on to the desk to search out my palmtop and the little cellphone.

I yanked Sunny's phone jack out of the wall box, and plugged in.

As soon as the tiny computer connected, a warning pinged, and I saw the familiar *You've Got Mail!* banner. I tapped the trackpad to open the message.

Can-can music blared from the speakers, and a line of minuscule frou-frou'd dancers high-stepped across the screen with a small chorus of squeals and whoops. As they lifted their skirts to display bold pink lettering where their byte-sized knickers ought to be, I read GOT YOU A JOB HONEY—YOU CAN THANK ME TOMORROW—CHILI XXX

The dancers cartwheeled off the edge of the screen one by one. I slumped in Sunny's swivel chair and groaned out loud: the junket for Big Tree Media. Jeff said they'd asked for me. Zia must have done it. As the screen 'face' of NERVE, she had the clout just now to get most anything she wanted. She knew I was strapped for cash, so she had got me a job at her next press launch. She was obviously expecting me to be delighted.

'Oh, no . . . ' I clutched my hands over my face, then sighed and tapped the trackpad again to make the message go away. It wasn't Zia's fault if I had a love-life like a Croatian minefield.

I disconnected the palmtop and dropped it into my bag, then picked up the cellphone and dialled the number of my own apartment. The ringing tone chirped in my ear. *Come on, Bowman, pick it up.*

'Yes?' A flat businesslike snap. I injected hurt into my response.

'Oh, and hello to you, too, Cary.'

'Robin! Sorry, I was expecting a call.' He had the grace to sound sheepish. 'Look, about this morning . . . '

'Forget it,' I mumbled. 'Bad timing, that's all. Listen, Cary, Jeff Bloem just called.'

'Oh?'

'And, you know you said that if there was something you could do for me, I should just ask . . . '

'I don't think I like the sound of this,' Bowman groaned, then sighed. 'Go on.'

'I want you to come with me on a job tomorrow.'

'Robin.'

'Come on, Bowman, you promised.'

'I lied,' Bowman said. 'Robin, I'm in hiding, remember?'

'Oh, come on, Cary, what can happen to you in the middle of a security team?' I sighed. 'Look, I'm sorry, I didn't mean to just drop this on you. We'll talk about it later, OK?'

'All right,' Bowman said after a pause. 'Want me to wait up?'

'I can look after myself.'

'That's n-not what I meant.' Exasperation in his tone. 'We didn't really get very far this morning before . . . um. Anyway, I'd like to finish going over some of the stuff about our missing man.'

'Well, it'll wait till tomorrow, won't it?' Being jogged at the elbow brings out the mule in me. 'I mean, he's been missing for five months, another day here or there isn't going to make any difference. Anyway, I'll be here at least till nine, maybe later, and I promised Sunny I'd go back for coffee. We'll do it in the morning. I'm a quick learner, we'll get through it in no time, I swear.'

'I don't know . . . ' Bowman sounded tired. I rode over his objection.

'Well I do know, Cary. Go to bed with a nice book and a cup of hot chocolate, or whatever you pussy English do to get to sleep. OK?'

'All right.' He was definitely smiling this time, I heard it in his voice. 'Bossy cow.'

'Goodnight, sweet prince.' I folded the handset up with a snap that I hoped would ring his ears for him, and smiled at Bruce Lee for a totally superfluous length of time before Sunny came back with apricot Danish and polystyrene cups of creamy-hot *koffie verkerde*.

❖

I did not know whether to be indignant or relieved when I let myself into the apartment, late and cold, head buzzing from Marik's treacle-black Turkish coffee, and found Bowman asleep.

He was curled in the nest of blankets on the couch, a paperback book splayed on his chest. His hand lay just touching the spine of the book, as if he had fallen asleep reading.

I picked the book up, carefully so as not to wake him, and put it on the coffee table, then draped a fold of the blankets over him. He stirred, and muttered something, but did not wake.

I tiptoed into the bathroom to brush my teeth, feeling curiously disappointed. I'd told him that I could look after myself.

I just hadn't expected him to take me at my word.

4

NIEUWMARKT was the usual lunchtime free-for-all. Wolf stepped off the pavement, meaning to quicken his pace on the salted road and get past the mess of would-be commuters outside the Metro station. A couple of taxis were waiting, motors idling, and Wolf skipped round the offside of them. A slab-sided white van was stopped too, right on the no-parking strip, and Wolf's gaze swivelled at the sight of a cop leaning into the open cab window.

It was the same traffic cop who had chased him yesterday. The moment stretched as he took in the man's size, the bristly cuff of flesh that bulged at the back of his neck. He was less than a metre away. If Wolf had wanted, he could have beaten a quick tattoo on the man's expansive backside as he passed.

Wolf changed direction on the instant. There was a tram humming towards him and he skipped across its path with a metre to spare, heart hammering. Traffic was moving slowly. He jaywalked, slow-quick-slow, and gained the north side of the square. His mouth was dry, lips gummed together. He risked a look back: the cop was still standing at the side of the van. He hadn't even turned round.

Fool, Wolf thought—relieved all the same—and walked straight on down Kloveniersburgval.

When he had put a decent distance between himself and the square, he stopped and leaned on the canal railings. Across the way, poking up over the gable-ends, the clock on the Zuiderkerk tower, gold on red, winked at him VI past XI. His left eye winked back and he rubbed his lids crossly, feeling stupid. *Damn, but I need a cigarette.*

Wolf put down his bag and fumbled a paper from one coat pocket. His other hand nipped up a pinch of dark tobacco to sow along the waiting curl. His fingers still shook a bit.

He passed his tongue along the edge of the cupped rectangle and rolled the tiny tube without looking. That reaction when he saw the cop . . . it scared him, he had to admit. He had set out to find Pete, make certain that he'd been mistaken over what he'd seen last night. But if his memory of the traffic cop was correct—and it seemed it was—then finding Pete might not be a certainty at all. He gazed thoughtfully back towards Nieuwmarkt.

Across the water, a woman stood beneath a sycamore tree, throwing fistfuls of seed into the snow. Pigeons crowded thick around her feet. The constant crawling ripple of their iridescent grey bodies put Wolf in mind of lice. His scalp itched reflexively and he ran a hand through his hair with a grimace. Lice were one reason why he avoided the shelters. The woman smiled the blissful smile of one visited by angels, and strewed more seed into the seething mass.

Wolf stuck the slender paper cylinder in the corner of his mouth. The fuel in his lighter was almost gone but it sprouted a tiny round bud of yellow on the fourth try and he sheltered the frail thing inside his coat collar while he lit the end of the cigarette and puffed gently.

There's nothing like really bad weather, he reflected, to take all the residual fun out of being homeless and destitute. In summer it's possible to kid yourself that you actually like sleeping out under the stars and strolling the streets and parks all day. Not so now. The past few weeks, Wolf had woken with a homesick ache in his belly.

Tiny ice-pellets skirled about his face and spat cold water down his neck. Wolf picked up his bag and walked on, hunched into his turned-up collar.

He had bought the coat from a thrift store down by the Albert Cuypmarkt, a week or so ago. It had taken most of his last pay packet but it was worth it: thick black worsted with double-stitched seams. You could see the marks where there had been rank patches—Navy most likely, the man in the shop had said. That pleased Wolf, though he could not have said why. More prosaically, it had a high collar that he could turn up against the cold, big deep pockets, and was long enough to keep his backside warm when he sat down.

Thanks to the forbidding presence of the traffic cop barring his way down Nieuwmarkt, Wolf had to take a dog-leg route, down Kloveniers and backtrack across two more bridges, before the ugly white bulk of the Stopera hove into view. The stinging whip of the wind off the river welcomed him to Waterlooplein.

He ducked in among the jostling makeshift stalls, glad to shelter from the spasmodic slap of sleet that could not quite make its mind up to be proper snow.

Almost the first person he caught sight of was Anni, rummaging through a pile of second-hand clothes like a truffle-hound hot on the scent. The stallholder looked resigned.

Wolf realised that he had half expected Anni to have vanished, bundled away at midnight in a big black car by sinister men in dark coats and sunglasses. Relief made him feel foolish: of course she was here, where else? Pete was probably just round the corner of the next stall. He must have been mistaken after all, there was a perfectly reasonable explanation, and Anni was just the person to expound it to him.

He ate the last iced biscuit, tiny and shaped like a snowman, in optimistic celebration.

❖

Later, standing in line with a stained wooden tray, Wolf wondered if he had been right to come into the Mensa.

It wasn't that he felt people were staring—the University quarter wasn't like that. You could hold loud imaginary conversations with a rubber chicken in here and the worst that would happen would be some wispy-bearded type inviting you to the next meeting of the debating society. Or, possibly, inviting the chicken; you never could tell.

And it wasn't as if this was a private dining hall. People wandered in off the streets all the time. There was hot, cheap food here: word got around among the sorts of people who might not care about décor or *haute cuisine*, but for whom the next Euro was an uncertain proposition.

Wolf had been here himself more than a few times but today, he could not shake off the feeling of being exposed. Perhaps that was exactly the trouble—the place was too public, when what he really wanted was to find a nice quiet place out of the wind and have a smoke.

He felt dirty and rumpled, ill-prepared for what the day had thrown at him. When he stopped over at the squat he almost always used their bathroom to get a hot shower and wash his hair. The fact that he could smell his own sweat disgusted him faintly. It was a marker on a path he had hoped never to travel.

Well, there was nothing to be done about it. He'd come rushing out after Pete, and where had that got him? He should have stayed put and used the bathroom, then at least he wouldn't stink. He pushed the line of thought away irritably. He felt like some kind of fugitive.

But from what, or whom? The police, if they were still looking for him. The men who had taken Pete, perhaps. Maybe the unknown person who'd shot him. The list seemed to be growing.

'Sausage or herring?' The uninterested drawl from the opposite side of the steel counter brought him back to the greasy lunchtime miasma of cooking smells.

The woman was all but invisible—a pair of hands clutching plate and tongs, an expanse of green-striped apron.

Wolf stared at the patchwork of pitted metal trays in front of him. One contained what looked like a sub-species of hot dog, slender and slick, swimming in some briny yellow stuff. A school of limp fish appeared to have drowned nearby. He shook his head.

'C-can I have an *uitsmijter*?'

'Next counter,' the voice said wearily. Wolf muttered an apology and shuffled up a couple of places in the line. *Not much they can do to a sandwich, is there?*

Chewing the thing a few minutes later, he reflected that perhaps he had been over-optimistic. The ham was sliced meanly thin and the limp supermarket bread was a joke.

At least the egg wasn't fried solid. Wolf licked a dribble of orange yolk off his fingers and felt the warm food filling up the void inside him: truly, it was hard to think of much else when your belly was empty.

Maartje Rijk appreciated that. He thought of her pretty, child's face and felt warmed by her unlooked-for kindness. It was the cash she'd shoved into his pocket that was paying for him to eat like this today, else it'd be scraps from the herring stall again, or yesterday's bread from a bakery, or maybe nothing at all. He should drop in at the squat later and thank her properly.

Wolf took a huge bite of the hot bread and butter. Never mind that once upon a time he'd have turned his nose up at greasy grub like this: today was today and he was . . . well, he was as he was.

I yam what I yam. What was that, Popeye? He grunted with laughter at the image and felt better.

The place was filling up, the general clatter of trays and plates loud counterpoint to the muted blatter of voices.

Wolf lingered over his coffee cup, making it last out of habit. In the interest of calming the flutterings of worry in his belly, he forced his mind back over the events of the last twenty-four hours or so. Map it out, *dom*, get it all lined up on the formica in plain daylight and you'll see there's nothing to get worked up about.

So. He took a considering sip of coffee. Pete going off with those hard types in the black car—that's what had started it all off. He, Wolf, had recognised the driver of the car. No—*recognised* was too strong a word. No point in getting worked up over what might just be a coincidence.

Then there'd been the business with that fat cop, hauling him out of the traffic . . . he'd run for it when the man asked to see his ID papers, he remembered that much— got a bit of distance between them and dodged through a couple of alleyways. They'd brought him up on Nieuwezijd with its strings of tacky red fairy lights and boudoirish windows, bored-looking girls in their neon-lit cubicles. Pink neon, he remembered, and glittery bodystockings that glowed electric blue under the UV lights—they put him in mind of those things you see on the meat counters. Fly wobbles past enticed by the sweet putrescence of meat, sees light, gets the urge for intimacy—poof.

That's where it all got hazy, because the headache had been really pounding by then. He'd been sick, dizzy, pulses of pain like grenades going off in slow-motion inside his skull. He remembered the panicked fumbling for privacy, and a dark place reeking of garbage . . . nothing more. He'd woken in the flop bed, seventeen hours later.

That did knock him back on his heels. *Seventeen hours* missing! Wait, calm down. Maartje'd said Willem helped Eddy carry him down into the basement, so he must have got there after midnight. Willem tended bar at an *eetcafe* on Kloveniers, and barely ever got back to the squat before twelve. Wolf did the maths in his head and was less than reassured: ten hours sleeping it off in Eddy's basement still left seven when he was out there in the city doing … . well, exactly. Doing what?

Skip it, he told himself firmly. You could go crazy trying to figure out that sort of thing.

So. More coffee. It was lukewarm dregs by now, but he wrinkled his nose and drank it anyway. Pete. It all came back to Pete, again: scared because Anni had told him some men were asking questions about him.

Wolf leaned back in his chair, dissatisfied. Anni had remembered the men, sure enough. When he bought her a bag of *frites* and a Coke, she'd been eager to remember anything she could for him. There just hadn't been much to remember.

Two men, she'd said. Black overcoats, suits under. Not police, no, wrong type and anyway, they weren't Dutch. German maybe, or American? Asking stupid questions about Pietje. What questions, Wolf had prompted. Oh, just you-know, where does he hang out, anybody close to him, all that. Kids, wife. I told 'em, just the dog. They both laughed at that. Everybody knew about Pete's dog.

It turned out Anni had seen the men before—a couple of weeks ago perhaps—talking to other people, but she hadn't bothered herself to find out why.

Wolf left her to finish her Coke and asked around a few people he recognised, but nobody had seen Pete after about four o'clock yesterday. Wolf had spoken to Pete himself around four-thirty. Nobody at all after him.

Wolf sat in a small puddle of cold and silence in the warm bustle of the Mensa, and wanted—with a sudden stab of need that took him by surprise—to be among friends.

❖

The yellow street door from Geldersekade was unlocked. Wolf stepped tentatively over the high metal sill.

The warehouse was as gloomy as a chapel. Greyish light filtered down from the lofty windows on the second floor, subdued by grime.

Wolf hesitated, listening. A radio played somewhere, muffled by intervening walls and doors.

Above his head, water gurgled through pipes and the blowtorch roar of the boiler started up. Across the passageway, one of the gigantic cast-iron radiators whistled and ticked quietly. Wolf pressed his hands against its metal ribs, and felt some of the cold-ache melt away. He had no gloves and the morning's aimless wandering had stiffened his joints in a way that made him feel suddenly old.

Upstairs, a door slammed, and footsteps reverberated on ancient boards. Another door opened with a squeak of hinges.

'Eddy?' No answer. Echoes clattered upward.

Wolf mounted the iron stairway and pushed open the kitchen door. A dog yipped from under the table.

'Jan! Hi, missed you this morning!' That was Cara, brisk Midwestern gal as always. Eight years in Amsterdam hadn't diminished her Iowa accent at all. She was applying Egyptian-queen eye make-up in Eddy's shaving mirror, which she had propped against the ashtray on the kitchen table, mouth in an 'o' of concentration. A flowery satin bag gaped open at her elbow, and a bewildering array of brightly-coloured cosmetics spilt across the table. Beside it, the battered radio was tuned to a pop channel, some unidentifiable band churning out a heavy rock beat.

Cara's black-dyed hair was already back-combed and stood out around her face like exotic plumage. Sweet smoke spiralled from the roll-up in her free hand. 'Siddown,' she added, raising her voice over the noise of the radio. 'Party later, ex-pat Christmas thing, I sent Eddy to git a wash.' She returned her attention to the mirror.

Wolf glanced around the room. Cara bought her grass from a licensed stall in Albert Cuyp. It was mild and too sweet for Wolf's taste. The atmosphere in the kitchen put his stomach on edge. The underlying smell of baked beans and burnt toast hadn't changed from this morning. If anything, there seemed to be more dishes piled on the sides than before. Nobody ever seemed to wash up in this place.

Not for the first time, he wondered where all the crockery came from, and what would happen when the last plate or cup was finally used up. The really puzzling thing was that, in all the months since summer, *this had never happened*. It was mystifying.

At least it was warm. He stretched his legs out under the table and reached into his coat pocket for cigarette papers and tobacco. The sudden movement of his legs produced a growl from the dog hidden beneath the table, and he drew them back, peering into the shadows.

Startled white eyebrows grafted on to a grey doormat. Pete-the-dog skinned his lips back off discoloured teeth in an apologetic canine grin and shuffled forward to dab a cold wet snout at Wolf's hand. He smoothed the silky brow tufts in wonder.

'How the hell did you get here, *jongen*? Where's Pete, uh?' He tried to take hold of the dog's collar, but Pete ducked aside and retreated under the table again. Wolf looked at the little dog more closely: he was filthy—nothing unusual there—but there were dark patches of blood matted into the grey coat. Wolf lifted startled eyes to meet Cara's gaze. 'Is Pete here?'

'Nope. Poor little thing came home with Willem this morning. You know he works at that bar on Kloveniers? Well, he found the mutt hanging around the garbage cans and brought him back here. Won't let anyone else touch him, so we've gotta wait till Willi gets off shift tonight.'

Apparently satisfied with her eyes, Cara was drawing a sharp-pointed cupid's-bow on to her lips. Wolf watched in silence while he rolled his cigarette. His feet were regaining a little sensation. His socks squelched as he wiggled his toes.

'Want a light for that thing?' Cara paused with a vivid purple lipstick half way to her mouth, and tossed her zippo across the table. Wolf caught it. It too was purple.

'Thanks,' he murmured, and nursed the little roll-up into life with a noxious whiff of dark smoke. Cara took her lighter back and waved his fumes away with ostentatious disdain.

'Don't know how you can smoke that stuff, whaddayacallit again?'

'*Drum*,' Wolf supplied, and shrugged, smiling. 'Just like it, I guess.'

'Huh, can't imagine why. Make it out of camel-shit from the colonies, don't they? I mean, I know you can't afford much, Jan, but *puh-leeze!*' Cara inhaled with exaggerated pleasure on her spliff. Wolf shrugged again and laughed.

He didn't know why he liked the stuff either, but he wasn't going to tell Cara that. When he first got up courage to go into a tobacconist's, the red-and-blue packet had stood out to him like a lighthouse, familiar as his own face. The stuff inside was dark as treacle, and harsh as a raven's croak, but it was the *right* one, and that was comforting.

Wolf puffed lightly, savouring the dark bite of the smoke, and jerked his chin towards the ceiling.

'Maartje around?'

'Say again?' Cara peered up from the mirror. The sudden regard of her violet eyes, masked in their alien sweep of black and silver eyeliner, made Wolf stutter.

'J—just wanted to know if Maartje was around, I—I, I'd like to talk to her,' he finished lamely. Cara stubbed out her cigarette with a flamboyant sigh.

'Wouldn't we all, honey. Eddy let her go without paying into the food for this week, and now I'm a couple hundred Euros short. Girl eats like a horse. This isn't the goddamn Sally Army.' She sighed again, sharply, and shook her head. Wolf frowned.

'Let her go? Go where?'

'Hell should I know? These guys come knocking at the door, say Klaas sent them. Got a job for her, good money. She was out the door so damn fast she almost left skid marks.'

'What guys?' The smoke made Wolf feel suddenly sick and he crushed the roll-up into the pile of greyish debris in the ashtray. His fingers trembled. 'Cara, what guys?'

The look on his face made her stare. She reached out a silver-painted talon to turn off the radio. 'You OK, Jan? You've gone white as a sheet. You're not gonna get sick again, are you?'

'Did you check her room, I mean,' Wolf gestured. '—did she take all her stuff? Everything?'

'Every last thing,' said Cara, then added as an afterthought, '—oh, except for some tapes she borrowed off Mika? They were on the bed. Hell, I got nothin' against her, she was good fun, ya know? And nice, too, sorta quiet but a real deep girl, if you know what I mean. I just wish she'd given us a bit more warning.'

Wolf blinked at her, distracted into imagining Maartje's reaction to such a description. Her throaty chuckle was one of his newest and most-visited memories. *A real deep girl.*

'Jan! Hi!' Eddy Boersma slammed through the kitchen door, putting a comb through his slicked-back hair. His grin faltered at the sight of Wolf's white face. 'Whoa there, mate, you'd better sit down. You sure you're all right?'

'I was just telling him about those guys that came round for Maartje, and he went and got all weird on me.' Cara laid a hand on Wolf's sleeve with a discordant clash of silver bangles. 'Jan, you really look terrible. Eddy's right, come on, siddown.'

'I'm fine,' Wolf mumbled, but allowed himself to be steered to a seat while Eddy fetched him a medicinal shot of Wild Turkey from the cupboard under the sink.

His fingers trembled and the alcohol didn't make him feel better, just made his mouth numb and muddled his thoughts. He pushed the glass aside. Cara placed a cool palm on his forehead, peering into his eyes.

'Jan, what's wrong?'

'Who sent them?' The abruptness of Wolf's question threw her.

'What? Who?'

'The guys, you said somebody sent them. Told 'em about Maartje . . . '

'Oh! It was that dirty old guy that begs on Stationsplein, the skinny one—now what's his name, ohh, I said it just a minute ago . . . it was Klaas.' She patted his shoulder and nodded decisively, pleased at having remembered correctly. 'That's right. *You* know Klaas.'

Wolf nodded to show that he was listening. Under the table, Pete-the-dog whined unhappily.

Wolf felt like whining himself. Perhaps he would finish that glass of whisky after all.

Five hours later, huddled with his coat collar turned up in the open porch of a café-bar, Wolf switched from one numb foot to the other and tried to rid himself of the feeling that he was making a complete fool of himself. As if to taunt him, the doors shivered in the stiffening wind and belched a bubble of warm air over him, fragrant with cigarette smoke and beer.

Wolf sniffed and pressed his face closer to the glass: the man he was watching had turned a little towards him. A filling in the side of his mouth glinted as he laughed. His companion hunched opposite, clasping a half-empty glass of *jenever* between his hands as if afraid that it would be forcibly removed. Wolf recognised Klaas' ancient, shrunken face. The man with him wore a long black coat.

Wolf berated himself for not thinking of this place sooner. It would have saved him a lot of trouble, getting jostled and trodden on in the dozen or so other bars he'd already been in tonight after leaving the squat. He was frozen and exhausted. His feet felt distant, as if they belonged to someone else.

Street people were tolerated in this down-at-heel brown café, and street people seemed to be what the Black Coats (as Wolf had privately christened them) wanted. For what reason, he had no idea, but somehow he could not bring himself to believe them benevolent.

Inside the café-bar, hours worth of cigarette smoke drew lazy thermals in the air above the heads of the drinkers. The stranger was suddenly animated, brisk: he swallowed the last third of his beer in one long gulp.

Across the table, Klaas took a slow, savouring sip from his spirits. The brown-tinted glass of the swing doors gave the scene a sepia cast like an ancient movie. The stranger was on his feet now, his face visible as he bent over the old man, still talking.

Wolf cupped a hand close to his eyes, his breath misting the glass, but the man's face was the wrong shape and fiercely furrowed round a falcon's beak of a nose, the hair dark. It was not the driver of the black car.

Wolf's shaky exhalation obscured his view for a few seconds. He wiped at the moisture: in the hazy vignette revealed by his hand, the dark-haired man was leaning over Klaas. Something—money, perhaps? Paper, at any rate—changed hands, and then the man was coming for the door, shrugging his coat into place and buttoning it as he walked.

Wolf stood completely exposed in his ridiculous peeping-tom posture. His heart knocked like a broken engine.

Someone shouldered past to push through into the bar and Wolf ducked his head and followed.

For a charged second he was shoulder to shoulder with the stranger. The doors whuffed to and he was gone.

Wolf passed both hands over his face and felt his fingers tremble. He blew out a sigh of relief and headed for the door at the rear of the café marked *HERREN*. The muscles of his thighs quivered with the release of tension.

When he emerged a few minutes later into the warm fug of beer and cigarette smoke, Klaas was gone.

Wolf had walked almost to the door before he spotted the beggar: he had moved over into a booth and sat blinking into the cloudy depths of a fresh glass of *jenever*. An open bottle stood at his elbow. It seemed he was going to drink his way through his fee—if fee it was—in one sitting. Wolf wondered how much he had got for putting the men on to Maartje.

The Black Coats, the professional gentlemen with their expensive car and their terrifying casual violence—somehow, he didn't know why, they held a key that might open his past. And they wanted people—vagrants, homeless nameless street scum that nobody would miss.

People like Jan Wolf. The thought insinuated itself into his mind almost casually.

The short hairs on the back of his neck bristled. If that freeze-frame image of the driver's face was not some pattern thrown up by a cracked brain, then it was an image, a person from his past—and no pleasant memory, either. But he had to know.

When Wolf sat down on the other side of his table, the old man looked up, then back to his drink. His face was grey, dirt in a million tiny particles grained into the pores and lines of his skin. His voice was a bronchial rattle. 'Table's taken.'

'Not this seat, Klaas.' Wolf shrugged and spread his palms at the old man's black look. 'Look, I saw you talking with that bloke. He gave you money.'

'So?' The black-mittened hand crept protectively around the earthenware bottle, and the *clochard* knocked back the rest of his drink in one absent-minded gulp. All the while, his coal-seamed eyes glittered into Wolf's as if daring him to take the stuff away.

The glass clopped on to the formica table-top, and was refilled, brimming. This time Klaas shoved it across at Wolf. 'Here. You look as if you could do with it.' The awkward magnanimity of the suddenly-rich.

'Damn cold out there tonight,' Wolf agreed, and savoured the hot-chilly bite of the alcohol. It thawed the tip of his nose and made his ribs ache exquisitely. He made appreciative noises and pushed the glass back to its owner. 'Thanks, Klaas. I needed that. That bloke in the overcoat . . . '

'*Ja?*' A cautious growl. Wolf groped for inspiration.

'Just . . . I'm short of cash—' A snort—who among them wasn't? He hunched over the table, confiding. 'Anni told me there were men coming round, asking questions, leaving money . . . They gave her a hundred Euro.'

'Huh?' —disgruntled. He must have settled for less.

'Are they still around? I mean . . . what do they want, what are they paying for?' Wolf's frustration was only half acted. He shrugged, ducking his head closer to the old man's face. 'Klaas, give me a break, OK?'

'Listen, *jongen*,' with a judicious air, spinning out the sudden attention. 'This man. He buys me a drink, tells me he wants to find some girls. I'm not a pimp, see? Not into that sort of business at all. I tell him to take a walk down the *Wallatjes*, easy get a girl there if he wants to pay. He says no, not that sort of girl. He says there must be girls who live on the streets, beggars and that, runaways and all, and could I give him any names or anything. You know, where he could find them. He said he had a proposition to put to 'em.'

Wolf frowned. 'Sounds like a porn merchant casting a movie.'

'No, no, it's nothing like that,' Klaas sucked another measure of gin down, wiped his lips with the back of his mittened hand. 'Research, he said. They'd be paid, afterwards. Bit up front to show good faith. He said they had to be single, no ties sort of thing. Nobody to miss 'em being away for a bit. He said it was medical research.' He nodded again and scratched at his bristly jaw, pleased at recalling the turn of phrase. 'That's it. A medical research programme. Anyway, I remembered that skinny little cow that's been hanging around the squat with Eddy and Cara these last two-three months . . . You get round there, don't you? Seen you, mm. Just a kid, fifteen or sixteen, wears all these pretty things, rings and such. Run away from her family, she did—farmers down near Maastricht—well, I was in there the other day with a message for Eddy and he said something about this girl was looking for work, needed a bit of cash, so I put 'em on to her. Done her a favour, like.' He took another swig of spirits, blearily complacent.

'How much did they pay?' Wolf had to fight to keep his voice soft. Klaas must have seen some of the tension in his face and hands. The old man finished his drink in one gulp, and scooted sideways out of the booth.

'Now that's my business, I'd say—'

'Sit down.' Wolf's hand flashed out to grip the old man's shoulder. Klaas yelped and dropped back into his seat. It was hard to tell which of them was the more surprised.

Klaas rubbed his shoulder. 'Hurt my bloody arm, you have! There was no call to go grabbin' me like that—'

'Shut up.' Wolf put on a scowl to cover his own startlement. He had no idea where that move had come from. He felt ashamed of using physical force on an old man. Still, it seemed to have had the desired effect. He pressed his advantage by reaching across the table and grasping a gentle fistful of Klaas' collar.

'Now. Tell me about these men.'

5

'NOW DON'T YOU WORRY about anything, my friend. Not a thing.' The white, confident grin flashed at Wolf out of a lean, tanned face and worried him immensely.

He grinned back at the man as best he could while the hairs on the back of his neck were standing up stiff as a wire brush, and nodded his head up and down. Nervous, eager to please, not too bright. *Don't overdo it, you idiot.*

Wolf tried to moisten his lips but his tongue was dry as an autumn leaf. He rubbed the back of his hand across his mouth instead. Look at that—his hands were trembling, and he hadn't even told them to. Just a sign of how swimmingly things were going. If you wanted to look at it that way.

He reminded himself, a bit sourly, that he *did* want to look at it that way. When you were a hero, you did things like tricking the enemy into transporting you to their secret hideout so that you can discover all their dastardly plans.

Rather to his surprise, that bit had gone off without a hitch. The case of advanced orthodontics sitting across from him had been amused to be approached by a volunteer. You heard what—? Yes, and you need the money, of course we understand completely. But you do understand as well, Menheer Wolf, that you will be in isolation during the programme? There isn't a Mevrouwe Wolf—? No little wolves, hahaha. Nobody? Relatives, friends? Excellent, then if you could just sign this right here, we can do business . . . That's it, OK. Excellent.

It seemed to be a favourite word of his. He had quite a lot to say, unlike his partner who sat at Wolf's side in a Cro-Magnon silence. They both wore the coats, long black wool FBI-style overcoats, just like something out of *The X-Files*.

Wolf seemed to recall liking *The X-Files*, some time before life turned into a murder mystery with him playing the corpse. A distracted corner of his mind noted that this must mean that he had once had a television, and presumably a room to put it in. Cheering thought, in any other circumstances.

Orthodontic Man leaned forward in the dim cosy cave that travelled in the back of the black limousine. Wolf had to stop himself from leaning backward in response. Breath-mints wafted about him, and for the second time in as many minutes, the guy was clapping him on the shoulder.

'Really, now, I'd just like you to sit back, take a load off. I know you're probably worrying about all the medical stuff—' Dismissed with an airy wave of the hand as if it was an incidental. '—but you won't be inducted into the programme until tomorrow at the earliest. Really. The doctor will want to see you, get all your details, allergies, that kind of thing. She'll fill you in. She's very thorough, insists on the most stringent precautions. And in the meantime we'll give you a nice warm bed for the night.' A hammy glance at the expensive-looking wrist-watch. '—what's left of it! Almost five a.m. No, but you just relax, you hear. I wouldn't like you to think this was some two-bit outfit. We're not cowboys, my friend. No indeed.'

If he claps me on the shoulder even one more time, Wolf thought with regret, I am going to screw this up completely by punching his lights out. His stomach was empty and ticklish, a fit of nervous giggles straining to get out.

He sat up a little straighter and stared out of the window: it was snowing again, a fog of fat flakes blatting down out of the yellow-grey night. The driver had the wipers going double speed, and the road had taken on the drumming sound of ice.

They'd come off the motorway on to one of the industrial park roads up northwest of the harbour. Signs passed too quickly in the snow to read, but Wolf was aware of shapes in the grey, storage tanks like a giant's game of boules left out to rust. He recognised them but couldn't think of the name of the road. His momentary blip of optimism faded.

When someone calls you *my friend* every other sentence when you've only just met, and pours out twenty excellent and unsolicited reasons why you shouldn't worry about something they're going to do to you . . . well, frankly, it was worrying. Very worrying indeed.

The future threatened to be both eventful and brief.

Wolf was not gratified in the least to discover that he was right on all counts. It could only have been an hour since he arrived at what the Black Coats called the Hole, and things were going decisively to the dogs.

Wolf rubbed cold palms up and down his goose-pimpled thighs and sighed: it was being buck-naked in the middle of winter among people who were fully clothed. It put one at an immediate social disadvantage. Not that there was much social give-and-take going on.

When you live on the streets, people who inhabit the parallel universe of work and time and money look at you in a certain way, if they look at you at all: it is an embarrassed look, full of bile. It resents and pities and condemns you as a shiftless layabout all in one sideways flicker.

Wolf would have preferred any number of such looks rather than the way they looked at you down here, as if you were a piece of meat.

He glanced up at the inscrutable black lens of the security camera high up in the corner of the room, then away again. Too much curiosity about his surroundings might prompt suspicions about his true purpose here.

True purpose. The thought made Wolf snort: *purpose* was a grandiose name for what had brought him to this pass. *Gross stupidity* would be closer to the mark.

Getting here had been a cinch: he'd felt so damn clever, offering himself up like a lamb to the slaughter. The only trouble with tricking villains into taking you to their secret hideout, he thought, is that in the movies, there's always another good guy—an assistant hero—following you, or using an ingenious tracking device to pinpoint your whereabouts. In short, backup.

Oh, Wolf added drily, the bit I haven't got. Didn't it occur to me that the reason they let me come here was because it didn't matter? They seemed to leave an awful lot of doors unlocked down here, and it occurred to him suddenly that this might be because they weren't worried about anybody being able to get out. No exit. Except feet first, maybe.

When he came to think about it, perhaps he ought to have planned this in a little more detail. Including, say—just for the sake of argument—some means of escape.

Idiot.

When they hustled him from the car, it had been snowing hard, but even the gusts of white could not obscure the fact that the building they entered was derelict. A broken plastic hoarding outside clapped against the brickwork in the wind. Through a wooden door into an echoing corridor, then into a cheaply-outfitted office lit by a single flickering fluorescent strip. Another corridor ended in a set of wide lift doors.

Orthodontic Man punched a seven-digit number into the electronic key-pad, trusting in sleight-of-hand as safeguard. Wolf caught the first four digits, and repeated them to himself a couple of times as the men ushered him inside the opening lift doors. Seven, five, nine, eight . . . then what? Chagrin at missing the vital digits segued into the sweaty onset of panic.

From the outside, this looked like a goods lift, battered and basic. The interior was much different: carpeting that came half way up the walls and tinted mirrors all round. There were some imperfectly-removed rusty stains on the otherwise-immaculate beige of the carpet. Wolf tried not to seem as if he was looking at them.

The doors hushed shut again, and there was an imperceptible jolt as they started moving, downwards. That startled him, and kicked off unpleasant speculations about what might be going on in a locked cellar. He gazed as his boots dripped slush on to the nice beige twist, and tried to look suitably cowed. It wasn't difficult.

It was when the lift doors opened that Wolf realised just how much trouble he was in. This was much, much more than just a cellar.

God knows what it had been originally—a nuclear bunker, maybe, back in the bomb-paranoid Sixties. It showed signs of having been hacked about and adapted many times. The little metal room Wolf was currently sitting in looked as if it might have started life as one of those walk-in meat lockers you find in freezer packing plants. There were still steel slider rails bolted to the ceiling. Wolf could imagine frozen sides of lamb or whatever hanging in rows.

He could just as easily imagine himself hooked up there, dangling, and he pushed the image away with a shiver. *Nothing really bad has happened yet*, he reminded himself. As a calming mantra, it left a lot to be desired.

Orthodontic Man and his monosyllabic companion had disappeared in the first few minutes, leaving Wolf to the tender mercies of the most muscular set of orderlies he had ever seen.

Wolf knew a bit about orderlies—they'd been a daily feature of his life in hospital—and he thought he knew the type: chatty, matey, some brisk, some laid-back. These men barely spoke except to snap orders at you, and they had that Look, which said that what they were seeing was not worth noticing. They didn't look like hospital workers, they looked like mercenaries playing at dress-up.

The doctor, whose head barely topped their 48DD chest measurements, and who also rapped out orders—though with a delectable French accent rather than Middle-Eastern—was a woman.

Wolf contemplated the little circular Band-Aids that decorated his arms. One shouldn't complain when a doctor was as pretty as this one—blonde, with an elfin face, lissome even in the all-enveloping scrubs everyone wore down here—but she was bloody careless with needles. She'd tweaked the final one as she slid it out of his flesh, and his bellow of surprised agony had earned him a cool, pitying look from her beautiful grey eyes.

She turned away and sealed the vial of blood, laying it on the steel trolley at her side before she spoke, with a quick sigh as if addressing a recalcitrant child. 'Don't be such a baby. Here,' peeling the backing off another Band-Aid, '—press this on and hold it.' She pushed the trolley out of the door and left Wolf sitting there clutching his wounded arm and feeling acutely foolish.

It occurred to Wolf at that moment that all his time on the street had failed to imprint an important lesson. He'd relaxed when she walked in the door, as if her full lips and sleek cheekbones and long-lashed almond eyes were some sort of guarantee of good character. He'd believed it, right up to the moment when she fixed him with that cold gaze.

All doctors everywhere speak over your head to their cohorts in a sort of verbal shorthand, and doctors all over the world tell little white lies like 'This won't hurt much.' These things are a given in the doctor/patient equation.

But this French girl was not your average doctor. Wolf found himself wondering, if she didn't care about hurting him, what sort of things she might tell little white lies about—or great whopping big ones, at that. It didn't make for restful speculation.

He felt like a side of beef, and when she looked at him with that Look, he knew in his heart that she was just sizing him up, preparatory to cutting him into the proper joints for roasting.

They left him alone for a while after that, sitting on his plastic chair. The air down here smelt of ammonia and some sickly deodorant perfume that made Wolf think with longing of the freezing air up above. This would not have been his first choice of ways to spend a Sunday morning.

When the doctor came back in and ordered him to take his clothes off, Wolf only hesitated a moment. He had the feeling that the so-called orderlies would enjoy making him do it. He stripped without a word.

The lady doctor was giving him that look again that said he could have made it a strip-tease and she still wouldn't have raised an eyebrow. Pieces of meat aren't sexy, or embarrassing, or pathetic. They're just pieces of meat.

More verbal shorthand, and they'd led Wolf out of the room clutching his clothes, and down a harshly-lit concrete tunnel to a row of green-painted doors. One was open, revealing a grey metal box of a room equipped with a prison-style hole-in-the-floor toilet, a hinged plastic flap seat where he piled his clothes, and a dingy hospital bed with one threadbare blanket.

'Wait here.' Wolf heard the latch drop on the outside: evidently there was some point in the procedure past which doors *were* locked. Also evidently, he had just passed that point.

That had been ten minutes or so ago, and Wolf was getting chilly waiting. He let his gaze wander, curious as a cat. He had just slid to the floor with the intention of testing the door, when he heard the doctor's voice outside. He made it back on to the bed just in time as she entered with a clipboard in her hand and two of the biggest orderlies pushing another trolley behind her. Metal clattered beneath coyly-draped linen, and Wolf's mouth went suddenly dry. The Frenchwoman tapped her biro on the clipboard.

'OK. Just to confirm before we get started, please: you do not suffer from hypertension, or have any diagnosed heart condition, or diabetes . . . '

'No—no, nothing like that.' Wolf watched her brisk movements anxiously, as if they might tell him something he didn't already know. She tucked a strand of blonde hair behind one ear and wrote with the bunched fingers and earnest concentration of a toddler. Wolf swallowed, or tried to. The sides of his throat stuck together. He coughed. 'Can I have a drink of water?'

She shook her head while she finished scribbling on the sheaf of papers clipped to the board.

'Not yet. Afterwards.'

'But—'

'If you drink now it will make you vomit,' she said. 'Lie down, please.'

'But—' Her expression shifted into displeasure, and the orderlies were there, one each side of the bed like really large guardian angels—if angels wore surgical scrubs and expressions of surly violence; Hell's Angels, possibly.

'Listen to me.' The doctor placed the clipboard on the trolley and snapped on a pair of whitish latex gloves as she spoke. Wolf had the impression of a speech performed many times. 'In a moment I am going to give you an injection. Before I do that, these gentlemen are going to put you under restraint. This is for your own protection and ours. Your body will react very quickly to the introduction of the test substance, and the symptoms can be violent. I can't pretend that the next few hours will be pleasant ones—' A slight shrug—*it isn't happening to me,* 'but the induction will go much better for you if you do exactly as I say.'

'Violent? Is it . . . ' Wolf had to pause and clear his throat again. 'Is it dangerous?'

'That's the reason for the medical,' the woman reassured him. 'For someone with high blood pressure, or diabetes, or a bad heart . . . well, the result could be very bad.' The corners of her supple mouth turned down a little to show him how bad. Another shrug, very Gallic. 'But you are healthy, so I don't see any problems here.' End of speech. A jerk of her head to the guardian angels. They grasped Wolf's arms, one each, and looped jellybean-orange plastic cable round his wrists. A metal ratchet clip turned the stuff into a sort of instant handcuff, with a shortish length dangling from each wrist and terminating in a heavy-duty snap ring. The plastic was warm where it touched his skin. Wolf looked at it in disbelief.

'Look, is this really—' He was smiling, a little desperately to be sure, but the doctor cut him off.

'Lie down. I assure you that you won't like it if they make you.'

Wolf flung himself off the bed, lashed the cable in the nearest angelic face.

They swatted him like a fly.

Crushed under several hundred kilos of muscle, Wolf felt his arms stretch. Snap rings went clink. Someone was twisting cable round his ankles: it tickled as it slid under his feet, then ceased to be funny as the someone drew it taut. Another clink, and he realised they were tying him down to the ring bolts in the floor. Wondering why made his guts go watery with terror: no going back now, *dom.*

Dizzy with the lack of oxygen that comes from having your face squeezed in another man's armpit, Wolf tried to indicate that he was co-operating—look, guys, not struggling any more—but they held him tight. He couldn't breathe, let alone yell.

The stab of the needle in his unprotected flank would have made him yelp if he hadn't already been suffocating in an atmosphere composed of five parts garlic, five parts stale testosterone.

He heard the doctor's voice say something testy. His assailants pried themselves off him and lumbered back. Wolf lay panting, eyes closed. Even the foetid recycled air smelt good after that.

'That was very stupid.' The doctor was shucking the translucent gloves, a pinched expression on her face. 'If you refuse to co-operate, this will be much more difficult. For you,' she added sharply.

Wolf bared his teeth at her: he was held fast, arms tugged straight down on either side, as if he were pointing at the floor, feet tethered by a cable that ran through a steel ring in the end of the bed. His muscles felt like overdone noodles. He had never imagined he could be this frightened. He shuddered suddenly, cold in his chest and belly, as if he'd swallowed ice.

Over by the wall, one of the orderlies made a small noise in his throat—a giggle or a sigh, quickly muffled. Wolf looked across. It was the man he had hit in the face with the cable: a red weal struck across his cheek and chin as if someone had attacked him with a lipstick. He looked as if he was enjoying Wolf's discomfort more than would be quite appropriate in a medical professional.

Waves of cold rolled in. Wolf could not stop shivering. His skin seemed to be trying to shuck itself off his bones. The ceiling spiralled down to meet him in a whorl of nausea.

His last memory for some time was of puking helplessly over the edge of the bed.

6

A STEEL DOOR SLAMMED. When Wolf's ears stopped ringing, he was alone again. It was a relief, of sorts. They'd taken the bed away. He picked himself up from where they'd dropped him and limped as far from the door as he could go.

The cell was small, the walls as well as the door constructed from steel. They had turned off the lights but Wolf could see quite well. Everything was bathed in a clear pearly grey light that jiggled at the edges with smeary rainbow colours, like a pigeon's wing. The observation porthole in the door blazed like a miniature sun, and more yellow light forced its way under the threshold, thin as a knife-blade but bright enough to hurt his eyes.

Wolf sank into a huddle in the corner, wrapped his arms tight and pressed his face into his knees, overwhelmed.

Everything was magnified: sound, sight, touch, taste—even his nose was sharper. He could smell his own sweat and the harsh soap they'd just used to wash him down, and a faint chemical-and-shit stink from the toilet in the far corner.

Wolf's heart boomed against his breastbone so loud it was making his ears hurt. He'd never noticed before that his ribs moved when he breathed; now he felt each individual bone as it slid and flexed in its cage of tendons. It didn't hurt exactly, but it was excruciating. As if his nerve-endings had been hot-wired and re-tuned at a higher pitch.

His mouth was dry. He remembered asking the doctor for a drink of water. He hadn't got it.

It felt like hours ago. How many, he didn't know. Hours in which he had puked and sweated and frozen by turns, stretched on his slab like a human sacrifice with the green-clad angels performing strange rituals on his helpless body. Needles and tubes featured prominently in that bit of the nightmare. He'd blacked out and come to three times that his spinning head could recall—once to the nasty sensation of his own limbs twitching.

He'd grunted and strained against his bonds, and heard the Frenchwoman's voice close by, too loud in his stinging ears.

'Don't fight, you'll just make the transition worse.'

Transition. It sounded frighteningly permanent and he did fight then—swore and jerked and heaved against the infuriating plastic string, until light fell on him in a shower of painful sparks and a sliver of pain in his thigh spread a grey blanket over his agitation: he subsided, hearing his own breath whistle in short jerky spasms. Heart jumping in his chest.

The Frenchwoman was still there and he looked at her, muzzy, trying to focus. Blonde. Big grey eyes like a kitten's. She was scribing on a sort of clipboard, and glanced up at him only once. Her voice had a dry edge. 'I keep warning you not to fight.'

'You would.' He'd jerked the words out without thinking. 'If someone was doing this to you, you'd fight.' There was a short pause.

'You're getting paid, aren't you? Nobody said it was going to be a day at the beach.' She punched buttons on the IV stand near his head, and scribbled some more, not meeting Wolf's gaze. The busy-busy, in-control scientist, the big-shot doctor. Whatever had been in that shot she'd given him was making it difficult to concentrate, but he summoned the energy to sneer at her.

'You must think . . . I'm really stupid.' This time she stopped and looked into his eyes, thoughtful for a second. Then she smiled.

'You came here, didn't you?'

She has a point, Wolf thought, and rocked in his huddle. Even that tiny movement set infinitesimal echoes whispering and racketing off the steel walls. He cringed and held still, shuddering. His own breath sounded like a storm wind in his ears.

What was going on? Those orderlies were military of some sort, he'd bet his boots on it. *Military* brought a whole raft of associations with it—of torture and hostages, secret chemical weapons, biological warfare. But really, it couldn't be that, he reassured himself. There weren't enough contamination precautions. They didn't even wear masks, let alone those space-suit things with their own oxygen supply. Anybody mucking about with contagious diseases in a working environment as sloppy as this one would soon be as dead as their own lab rats.

In any case, if he'd been infected with something, shouldn't he be feeling ill by now? How long had it been? His skin prickled but he hadn't noticed a rash at all. Wolf looked at his legs and arms but there were no marks except the shallow pink weals where the plastic cuffs had cut into his flesh. The terrible roiling nausea was gone, and aside from the over-sensitive twingeing of his senses, he felt better than he had for a long time. So he wasn't going to die screaming in his cell from some hideous disease.

It was only a relief until you started thinking of the alternatives. Because they'd put *something* into his body. Wolf shivered at the memory. *What are they doing to me?*

To *us*, he corrected himself. There were others down here. He stared at the thread-thin line of brightness at the base of the door. Six green doors in all. Maartje, and Pete . . . He groaned aloud at the thought of how badly he'd let them both down, charging in as if bravery was all that was required. What an idiot.

Wolf was surprised to find that they'd left him his clothes. He got up and went to paw through his pockets. He was less surprised when he turned up tobacco and papers but no lighter. His pen was gone, too, and the last of Maartje's money, all except one cent. All he had left beside that was a half-used tram ticket and a grubby paper tissue. He rolled the tobacco pouch up and stuffed it back into his coat pocket.

Well, they hadn't told him he couldn't get dressed. He pulled his clothing on, gritting his teeth: garments that had seemed perfectly soft before chafed his newly-sensitised skin as if he was wearing a suit woven of horse-hair. He grimaced and paced about until the sensation wore off to a bearable level.

He peered out of the spy hole in the door, but the light made his eyes water, and there was nothing to see beyond a slice of corridor and the door of the little office room.

His body seemed not to be tired, but he slid down to sit against the wall anyway, and closed his eyes.

❖

'Got to get out of here. *Now*. Got to. Get. Out. Now—'

Wolf jerked awake mumbling like a madman. He bit off the singsong muttering and coughed, grumbling to himself as he sat up.

His throat was dust dry and his tongue stuck to the roof of his mouth. That drink of water's a long time coming, he reflected bitterly. What now, are they seeing how long it takes for me to die of thirst?

He massaged his deprived belly, but it didn't feel noticeably different from usual—less hollow, if anything. How was that possible? He could swear he hadn't eaten since they brought him down here. Before that . . . a plastic ham and egg sandwich, he thought. If I'd known it was going to be my last meal, I'd have had something better.

That must be yesterday now—or was it longer than that?—it was impossible to tell. But he wasn't the least bit hungry. Even thinking about food made him nauseous.

Wolf squatted over the noisome toilet hole to relieve himself, then took himself back to the opposite corner. The camera up above the door whined, mosquito-fashion, and he scowled into the lens. It felt good to be fully clothed, though if he was honest it was making him hot. Hell with it: he wasn't stripping off again for their benefit. He'd roast first.

Wolf leant his head back against the dimpled metal wall, closed his eyes and listened. In the cell next to his, someone was moaning, a quiet ululation that made his spine prickle. He thought it was a woman, though he couldn't have said why exactly.

Whoever it was in there, they were in a bad way. Wolf was almost glad to be distracted by noises from the other direction.

Doors whoofed and creaked, and let out a boom of noise that sounded like heavy-duty extractor fans going. Steps whispered and padded on the plastic flooring—maddeningly difficult to tell one person from another when they all wore those silly paper bootees over their shoes. Wolf heard a man's voice say, in aggrieved Dutch, '—told you, the revised sequences just aren't showing the same percentage as yet.'

'And I told *you*,' the doctor's voice replied, testy as usual, 'that they'll accept anything in the mid nineties. How many times do I have to remind you, Alex, we're not aiming at perfection down here. The client will take care of development after the deal is closed. All you need to worry about is getting the socket right in the modified protein because without that we don't—' Another door clappered to and cut off whatever else Wolf might have overheard, for all the good it would have done him.

The person in the next cell was still moaning, up and down like the edge of a saw. Further away—in tissue-thin layers of sound so vivid he felt as if he was sitting next to them—Wolf heard a man cough painfully, and another voice—another male voice—whispering nonsense to nobody. He had barely formed the question in his mind of whether this last one might be Pete, when he dismissed it. The instinctive certainty gave him pause.

In the pause, the noise from the woman in the next cell—and now that he came to really think about it, he knew that it *was* a woman—grew in volume. The mindless distress in the sound dragged across Wolf's already-quivering nerve endings. He banged on the wall and yelled, '*Shut up!*'

The noise stopped, and he heard a shuffling, close to the wall. There was a tiny slithering noise. Wolf held his breath.

'Jan? Jaa-an!' Her voice was dreamy, a little hoarse, but otherwise just as he recalled. She giggled, as if she was drunk. 'You there, Jan Wolf? Or're you 'nother dream? Huh?'

'Maartje?' Wolf pressed his palms against the wall, as if by some miracle of empathy he could touch her through a foot of concrete. 'Maartje!'

'Jan, is that really you? What're you—what're you doing down here?' The dreaminess rippled into panic. She beat at the metal with her fists. Wolf jerked back with his own hands clenched. The drumming stopped as suddenly as it had started. Maartje caught her breath in a huge sob. 'I can't stand it, they keep coming back, they hurt me Jan—' Her voice cracked into tears. Wolf heard her teeth chatter. He kept his own voice level with an effort.

'Maartje, listen to me, is Pete down here? Did they bring Pete—?'

'Jan, oh don't, don't! Pete . . . Pete's gone, they took him away, they didn't want him . . . ' Muffled, as if she had her hands over her face. A cold dart shot through Wolf's heart. *Gone* could only mean one thing down here. He'd made his one-man cavalry charge too late. A lifetime too late.

'Maartje . . . Maartje, it's OK, I'm here, i-it's going to be OK, just hold on, we'll get out of here, I promise . . . ' He was gabbling nonsense in the dark, and they both knew it.

The thought of Maartje there, just inches away, filled Wolf with anguish. She'd been good to him, treated him like a real person when even Eddy and Cara had left him howling in the basement like a sick dog. She shouldn't be down here.

No one should, he reminded himself grimly, and slid down to sit with his back against the metal panelling. On the far side of the wall, Maartje sobbed quietly. Two cells away, the crazy man was declaiming fragments of poetry and weeping at the happy bits. Wolf rested his head on his knees and groaned out loud.

God help us all, none of us should be down here.

❖

'This wasn't exactly what I had in m-mind,' Bowman muttered, 'when you said there was something I could do.' He tugged at his collar and shot a jaded look at the jostle of white vans that filled the car park, satellite dishes and aerials aloft. 'Spending the afternoon with a couple of hundred TV journalists isn't what I call keeping a low profile, Robin.' His vehemence left a white cloud hanging in the air, as if for emphasis.

'Cary, we're going in the back door, nobody'll even know you're here. If you're worried, all you have to do is stick around the guys on the team. Just relax.' I glanced down at myself and brushed non-existent lint off the lapel of my suit jacket. 'Are you sure this is smart enough?'

'You look fine,' Bowman said. He flattened himself against the wall as a techie in a black Motorhead t-shirt scurried past backwards, laying cable. 'What did you say this gig was again?'

'Big Tree Media,' I said. I reached past his shoulder to press the buzzer beside the steel security doors. 'It's a press junket, some big charity thing.' Not the whole truth, but I was feeling cowardly.

'You should take your own advice and relax, Carlson. Your back's like a piece of concrete.' Cary inclined his head at a clank from behind the doors. 'Here we go.'

'Hi, Taz, it's me.' I waved at the hairy face just visible as the door opened a few inches. 'Let us in, it's cold out here!'

Taz—who looked as Humpty Dumpty might have, given a tux and a really heavy weights programme—hauled the door wide open. He scowled blackly. 'He can't come in here.'

'Sure he can,' I soothed, laying my hand on Taz's bulging sleeve. 'I know someone who's on the PR side of this circus, I got him a pass, I just didn't pick it up yet. Hmm.' I peered up and down the pristine corridor. 'Bit of a change of pace. Is there a crew room?'

'Yeah.' Taz let the fire door thunk shut, and gestured. 'Up here. It's got a fridge and a water cooler and toilets and everything.'

70

'Well, anything would be better than the rat-hole Riddermark gave us,' I reminded him. It had become legendary in the firm, a sort of benchmark of dross. 'That one smelt like it *was* the toilet. Look, would it be OK if my friend sticks around down here while I go get his pass?'

'Sure, Robin.' Taz held open another door, then led us through one end of an empty, over-decorated conference room. His arms hung out at the sides, gorilla-style, and ruined the cut of his cheap jacket because they were so heavily muscled. He did not quite propel himself along by swinging on his knuckles, but probably only because nobody would employ him if he did it in public.

His redeeming feature was a stolid lack of curiosity about anything that didn't directly affect his own paycheck.

'Here.' Taz stopped by an open doorway and waved us inside. He pointed to a jumble of equipment on a table nearby. 'You might as well pick up your earpiece now.'

'—And you might want to explain to *me*,' a nasal voice added, 'why you've brought a member of the public into the crew room?' Jean-Paul Didier came through the far door, zipping his flies.

I summoned the warmest smile I could manage while my skin was crinkling into gooseflesh. 'Hi, Jean-Paul. This is Mr. Bowman. He's on the guest list, but he hasn't got his pass yet, I was going to leave him down here and pick it up on my way round.'

'Jeff better have OK'd this,' Jean-Paul threatened, and tossed me a head-set. 'Here. Put this on and get out there.'

'OK, OK.' I shucked my jacket, and pushed it at Bowman, who was standing looking glum. As an afterthought, I handed my bag over too. 'I'll be back with the pass as soon as I can, I promise.'

'No hurry,' Bowman said, resigned.

This wasn't the biggest conference centre in Europe, but it won points for sheer glitz. I gazed around me as I hurried towards the hive-noise of the junket, tucking the headset into my hair. The whole building was based on some geometric shape—I forgot which, a hexagon or an octagon or something. No time to count walls. The floors were all expensive stone inlays like a mall, and there were lots of glasshousey bits where corridors met. I adjusted the tiny mike in front of my lips. 'Testing,' I muttered. 'C'n you hear me Jean-Paul?'

'Turn the volume up, you silly cow,' Jean-Paul snapped in my ear. I grimaced.

'Sorry, sorry . . .' I twiddled at the controls. 'Is that better?'

'Yes. Now hurry up, you're supposed to be on doors at the main office suite with Karl. They'll be letting the press people in four at a time, ten minutes only. Got that?'

'Main suite, press in four at a time, ten minutes only,' I recited in waitress monotone. A thought struck me. 'Jean-Paul, who's going to be in the main suite?'

'The sainted doctor, of course,' Jean-Paul growled. 'Who did you think, Genghis Khan? The Spice Girls?'

'Nothing,' I mumbled, feeling foolish. 'I'll be right there.' Dumb question. This whole thing was Domi's show, naturally she'd want to be the one to open its secrets to the press. I just wished I could be someplace safely invisible, like the washrooms.

The last set of glass doors whisked open. A wave of noise crashed over me. I winced.

The central concourse was a huge, many-sided space. The walls were a solid crust of mosaic in rich, vivid colours. The only blank spot was a huge video wall. Currently all it showed was the NERVE logo, in garish green.

I could not resist looking up as I walked forward. The room was the hole in the Polo mint. The ceiling was the roof of the building, which—of course—was the biggest and most dramatic glass dome yet. It was like standing in the bottom of a gasometer decorated by Gaudi.

From a sort of artificial coppice of greenery near the doors, sprightly classical music played, the sort of thing you hear on phone systems when they put you on hold. I caught a glimpse of penguin-suited musicians sawing and tooting behind the disguising fronds.

The concourse was already a melee of bodies, and I had to squelch a sudden panic attack. Sweat sprang under my arms. Hospitality was in full swing. Elbows everywhere, and braying voices, the stink of beer and spirits, clashing perfumes. Hostility, I remembered with a desperate stab at humour. That's what Dad calls it. Boy is he right.

I caught sight of the main office suite—handily labelled 'Press Interviews'—and began to wind my way through the drinking, chattering mass towards it. A few faces looked familiar—politicians, maybe, or minor celebs. I jumped when a big man in a light grey suit waved at me.

'Robin!'

'Hey, Tom, good to see you!' I smiled broadly at the friendly face, and allowed myself to be whirled round in a bear-hug and kissed on the ear. 'What're you doing here?'

'Loafing,' Tom Barnabas said, putting me down. He popped a sausage roll into his mouth. 'A good soldier never passes up free food, Private Carlson,' he added indistinctly. I pulled a face, and brushed crumbs off his shirt front.

'Yeah, right. A good soldier never consorts with the enemy either, and I'm, get this, *working* for the enemy today. One of life's little ironies, I guess.'

'Michel?' Tom always had been quick on the uptake. I nodded, and screwed up my nose.

'Stinks, doesn't it? I just hope to hell he isn't going to be here, that's all.'

Barnabas considered, then shook his head. 'Bad bet, kid. What I hear, Rancoul's payrolling this whole thing, wants to up DCI's business ethics profile. He'll be here.'

'Hell, I can hope, can't I?' I shrugged it off with a queasy smile, and changed the subject. 'Did you see Zia yet?'

'Al Roccaro's little girl? Sure,' Tom nodded, and gestured with a canapé, grinning. 'She is some piece of work, that friend of yours. Got TV cameras following her round this place like they was little lambs.'

'It's not exactly surprising.' I shrugged, and grinned too. 'Zia's a pretty arresting spectacle.'

'Tell ya . . . ' Barnabas engulfed the canapé and chased it down with a glass of champagne, leering ludicrously. 'She c'n arrest me any time. *A-ny* time.'

'I'll be sure and tell her that when I see her.' I pressed his hands. 'I have to go strut my stuff now, Tom. Dinner Tuesday night?'

'Sure, sure. My turn to cook this week.' Barnabas grinned and lifted his glass in a mock toast. 'Later, baby bird.'

I waved and headed for the 'Press Interviews' sign at a fast clip, ignoring the mutterings from Jean-Paul in my headset.

A waiter eeled past, a tray of glasses balanced on one hand like a conjuring trick. I reached for a glass, against regs, and drained the champagne in a couple of nervous gulps. My neck and shoulders were taut like piano wires. I'd end up with a headache if I didn't calm down.

My attention was suddenly snatched by a blond-haired man standing in a tight cluster of faces to my left, over near the musicians' dais. He was laughing at some comment, head thrown back and tilted to one side. The mannerism jolted me back nine years in a single second: it was Michel Rancoul.

His presence hit me like a fist in the face.

Our eyes met. I knew I was doing a terrific impersonation of a goldfish. For a moment, I couldn't even breathe. Michel's brows elevated. There was a spark of malicious humour in the brown eyes.

With exquisite timing, Jean-Paul's voice bleated in my earpiece. 'Robin, where are you? I need you at the back door *now*.'

I was trembling. Even my earrings vibrated, tickling my neck. For quite a few years now, I had been kidding myself that I really didn't remember much of what Michel had done to me any more. When I cared to look—which wasn't often—all that remained was a nasty, compressed moment of revulsion and pain.

I had been wrong. The memory unfolded at a touch, like an unpleasant origami trick. That had been at a party, too. And he'd laughed at me afterwards exactly as he was laughing now: boyish, charming, so sure of himself.

It just goes to show, I found myself thinking a little hysterically, *that all it takes is the right trigger.*

I turned and thrust my way through the crush, sick to my stomach, muttering automatic apologies. In my earpiece, John-Paul squawked, *'What are you playing at?'*

'Nothing.' I grabbed another glass of champagne from a passing tray, and gulped it down. 'On my way.' The wine left a sour taint in my mouth.

I shouldn't be here, I thought dully. My mouth felt hot from the alcohol that I'd swallowed.

I had been naïve to think that Michel would have changed. I swallowed a hot lump that had lodged in my throat. For years, the teenaged boy I remembered had haunted me like a malignant ghost, and now here he was—prosperous, a twenty-eight-year-old man with all the polished assurance that privilege and position and lots and lots of money could bestow on him. Only the malice in his eyes hadn't changed.

It didn't seem fair somehow. The man was CEO of one of the biggest conglomerates in Europe, but it all seemed so effortless, at least on his part. Perhaps he had a portrait tucked away in a loft somewhere, like Dorian Grey, growing gross and dissipated while he prospered.

But he did have a portrait: Domi was a true likeness as only a twin can be, even if she was sister not brother. And she certainly took up a lot of slack on Michel's behalf. I found my gaze swivelling to look for the bright waterfall of blonde hair. Dominique was easy to spot in a crowd. Sure enough, she was over by the drinks tables, frowning as she talked at some scientist types.

If Dominique was acting as moral surrogate for her twin, it didn't seem to have affected her looks at all. Not a wart or a freckle. I had to squelch unworthy disappointment, and wondered—for the hundredth time—just what it was about the other woman that brought out such an intense desire to see her fall flat on her pretty face.

Perhaps it was that for one excruciating week last summer, she had *been* the other woman, with capital letters.

Cary's one-week fling with Domi was barely a blip on the horizon any more. He had developed an ironic take on his 'seven-night stand', as he referred to it.

Ambivalence and Domi had always gone hand in hand. It might have something to do with the way she always seemed to talk down to you. She was older than Michel by a full ten minutes and to hear him talk, she'd always taken her responsibilities as eldest too seriously. Michel used to tell amusing stories about how they had covered for one another as children. Domi listened to them with a severe, big-sisterly tolerance. I never said so, but it seemed to me that Domi was always the one doing the covering, hastening behind her lazy, charismatic sibling like an anxious pet-owner with a poop scoop.

It was entirely like Michel to come and hog the photo-opportunities at what should have been Domi's glory day. And entirely like his big sister to let him.

Once I got back into the web of white corridors, and left the stifling crowds and noise behind, I breathed more easily. So Michel was here. Worst-case scenario. Big deal, Carlson, you can handle one spoilt-brat ex-boyfriend. Even as I braced myself up with the words I knew they were a lie. Michel was a seismic event in my life. Referring to him as my ex was simply an attempt to trivialise what he'd done.

I just hoped I could get through the afternoon without disgracing myself. I'd promised myself that I'd be professional. I picked fiercely at a hangnail, and pursed my lips. *Pardon me, but who are you kidding, exactly?*

'Robin, step on it if you want to keep your job!' Jean-Paul again, throwing a hissy fit.

'Almost there, almost there,' I chanted, and broke into a trot for the last stretch of corridor. No harm in appearing to be on the ball. I stopped myself in the doorway of the crew room. 'What's wrong? I thought you wanted me on doors with Karl?'

'I do,' Jean-Paul said, looking up from his control board. The prissy little wet-lipped mouth was pursed. 'It's your friend. You might tell him I'm not your secretary.'

I scanned the room, anxious. 'Is he all right?'

'I wouldn't know,' Jean-Paul said primly. 'He asked me to give you a message to meet him at the back door. He took your stuff!' he shouted after me as I ran down the white corridor towards the fire doors.

I banged through the swing doors into the empty conference room, heart thudding in my ears. I disconnected my headset and stuffed it into my pocket with trembling fingers. What the hell had gone wrong?

I burst into the last corridor, and wilted, panting, at the sight of Bowman standing by the fire door. He was holding my coat and bag. I rested my hands on my knees till I got my breath back, then managed, 'What's . . . going on? Jean-Paul said you had to leave?'

'We b-both have to leave,' Bowman corrected me. He shoved the metal bar and let in a slice of bright white daylight. 'Come on, I'll explain on the way.'

'Cary, I'm working.' I straightened. 'I can't just *go.*'

'Why not?' Bowman was peering out the half-open door like a spy. I made an impatient noise.

'You know why not. This is my job—you know, the thing that pays my rent?'

'I'll pay your rent,' Bowman offered, still looking outside. I rolled my eyes.

'No you won't.' I grabbed at my coat. He resisted.

'Robin, please. We can't stay here.'

'What are you *talking* about?'

'DCI,' Bowman snapped, grabbing my arms and giving me a little shake. 'You didn't tell me this was anything to do with b-bloody Dominique! I've got to leave before she sees me.'

'*What*?' I broke his hold on my arms with a practised movement, angry. I wrenched my bag and coat out of his grasp. 'I can't believe you're still bothered what that bitch thinks, Cary!'

'It's n-not that.' Bowman coloured. 'Don't be stupid, Robin, just come *on*.'

That's all the explanation you're going to give me for doing something that's going to lose me my job?'

Bowman stepped back, eyes dark. 'Are you coming?'

'No, I'm not coming.' I folded my arms over my possessions, and stuck my chin out at him. 'You know I can't just walk out like this, you're being ridiculous. I'll see you later,' I added, and walked away. Bowman did not answer. I had only gone six paces when the fire-door slammed shut.

Damn. I carried on walking, but I could not stop a big bubble of misery from welling up in my throat. *And I thought the day couldn't get any worse.*

7

THE HOUR THAT FOLLOWED was too busy for me to do anything but concentrate on the job in hand. Domi had taken up residence in the main suite, and I was caught up in the sheep-driving routines of a junket.

Six relays of four reporters to be branded, herded and corralled—and presumably fleeced too while they were in the big office with one of the Rancoul twins. Everyone understood these occasions, I thought, as I chased down the last group of four getting lubricated at the drinks tables. The press were fed, watered and given loads of freebies, were handed a batch of great photo-opportunities and sound-bites, and went away to create positive publicity for a charitable foundation that wanted the world and his dog to know who they were. Simple.

The door closed behind my wayward sheep, and I arranged myself in front of it, feet apart to spread my weight evenly and give the useful illusion of my being an immovable object, arms folded. I'd do the head-sweep—Taz and some of the other guys did it habitually, skulls swivelling in a sinister manner as if on ball-bearings—but I already had a stiff neck and anyway, it made me dizzy. It wouldn't look very professional to fall over sideways.

'Red! *Sweetheart*, where've you been? I've been looking for you all over!' Zia was on me like a pouncing lioness, all flashing eyes and perfect white teeth. I found myself enveloped in a light, warm hug, then she pushed me out to arms' length, flaring her eyelids as she drank my appearance in more slowly. 'So,' she drawled eventually. 'These are your work clothes. I like the ear thing, very *Star Trek*.'

She definitely looked more like the Zia that gazed out from a hundred magazine covers than the girl with goofy teeth and braids I had known at high school. DCI had paid big money to get her in the NERVE TV campaign—a celebrity with the looks of a supermodel and a social conscience into the bargain—and they were pumping the link for all its worth.

And Zia Roccaro was worth a lot. Her black hair was caught back in a complicated knot, secured with two murderous-looking silver pins. Her make-up was minimal, ingenuous, *which probably means*, I mused with a touch of envy, *that it took longer to put on than mine*. A midnight-blue satin sheath clung to her like a desperate lover. Only her eyes were a little off-putting—they were iridescent blue. I blinked. She must be wearing coloured contacts.

The famous smile burst again. Heads turned, cameras flashed. I flinched despite myself. Zia linked her arm through mine, oblivious to the attention. 'I got your mail. Sooo, what gives with Cary Bowman? C'mon, tell me—I want to know everything.'

'We're just friends.' I knew I coloured at Zia's disbelieving look. I wished I'd thought to turn off the headset. For once, I was glad to be wearing shades. 'It's true, I swear to God.'

In my ear, Jean-Paul said, 'Robin, stop gabbing with your girlfriend and keep your mind on the job.'

'Hmm . . .' Zia narrowed the sparkling blue eyes and feathered her long, manicured fingers in the air in front of her, as if testing invisible currents. The corners of the glossy, mobile lips turned down. 'Hmmm. I do believe it's true.' She shuddered theatrically. 'I bet you haven't even kissed the sucker, have you?'

'Uh . . .' I grabbed the tiny boom mike with my hand and mouthed, *'Can we talk about this later?'*

'Oh. Ohhh, sure, sorry, honey.' Zia pulled conspiratorial faces, and made a zipping gesture across her generous lips. 'Sorreee, me and my big mouth! You going to be in the Zone later?'

I nodded. 'How about eight-thirty?'

'Oh, sweetheart, that's a little early,' Zia whispered, crestfallen. 'We're having a launch party over at Big Tree for the cast and crew. I've got to be there or Marcus will, like, *crucify* me.' It was like Zia to give the impression that you were a part of her huge circle of acquaintances and knew who she meant without her having to elaborate. I rolled my eyes.

'Midnight?'

'Cool.' Zia perked up, nodding. 'Catch you later, honey. I don't envy you having to guard Dominique's door. Bitch queen from hell. I think she thinks I'm after her precious little brother, as if.' She gave me a quick hug, and her smooth cheek rested against mine for a second. 'Mwah. Be good, Red. Take care of yourself.' She sketched the famous smile again, and twinkled her fingers over her shoulder as she walked off.

I had no illusions about her keeping the midnight rendezvous: having Zia for a friend was like having a fairy godmother with a nanosecond attention-span. The rest of the world was competing for that nanosecond.

I heaved a sigh, and turned the volume back up. Jean-Paul was in mid-rant: '—think you can just waltz in and out as if you were a guest—'

'Jean-Paul—' I cut across his tirade crisply. He paused, wrong-footed by my tone. 'Ms Roccaro is an old friend,' I said. Innocent, helpful little ol' me, only stretching the truth a tiny bit. 'She would think me very rude if I didn't speak to her, and as you keep on telling me, we *are* here to keep the clients happy.'

A heartbeat's pause. 'Well, in future, keep me informed about your esoteric society contacts!' Typical. As if I had kept the information from him out of spite.

'Sure.' I moved to the side as the door behind my back opened. 'That's the last batch out of here, Jean-Paul. I'm going on my break now.' I turned the headset off before he could disagree, and walked towards the food tables. Tom was right. A free feed was a chance I couldn't afford to pass up, even if that meant my diet consisted of salmon-and-spinach quiche and rubbery dim sum.

I filled a plate with food and took it off to a quiet spot behind a fig tree in a huge ceramic pot. I started working my way methodically through the canapés, but my gaze skipped across the crowds. No sign of Michel. Zia was moving from group to group with artless ease. Surprisingly, Dominique was nowhere to be seen. The video wall showed some nervous-looking geek being interviewed by a TV reporter. From the reporter's glazed expression, I guessed he was getting one word in five of the man's technobabble, and that was one more word than I was getting.

'You haven't got a drink.' The soft voice at my elbow almost made me choke on a vol-au-vent.

A young, bearded man stood at my side, holding out a glass of wine. 'Better than choking,' he said with a smile. I shook my head and pushed the glass aside.

'I'm on my break, I can't drink. Thanks anyway,' I added awkwardly. The man looked familiar, but I could not recall where I might have met him. He had very long, henna'd hair and a pointy nose, and was dressed in a green satin shirt and a high-collared black velvet waistcoat. He didn't look like a reporter. He shrugged and sipped at the wine himself.

'No trouble. I saw you drinking earlier, so I thought you must have some kind of policy about it.' An Irish accent.

'Ah . . . ' Damn. I grimaced. 'We do, but it's anti, not pro. I'd better not drink any more, my boss is pretty much mad at me already. Thanks, though.'

'That's cool.' He sipped again, studying me with a sideways flick of hazel eyes. 'You don't recognise me, do you?'

'Uh . . . not exactly,' I admitted. I was sure I was going red. 'I know we've met, but I can't—'

'EyeKon,' the man said. 'I run the new smart bar on the top floor.'

'Oh!' I hit myself between the eyes with a clenched fist, mortified. 'Oh, what a klutz! You're the herbal smoothie guy.'

'That's right. Gabriel.' He introduced himself with a slight, mocking bow of the head. 'And you're Robin Carlson.'

'I am.' I shook my head. 'Sorry, Gabriel, I'm a little distracted today . . . '

'I can see that,' said Gabriel, and grinned. 'Look, could you do me a big favour? Only it's pretty urgent. Tell Cary to call me?'

'What?' I stared at him.

'Cary Bowman,' Gabriel said. 'Tell him TG are ready to rock an' roll.' He produced a

79

business card from his waistcoat pocket and proffered it. 'Here. Think he might have lost my number.'

The card read simply 'Tekno-G', with a phone number printed below it, and an email address. Gabriel slotted a pair of shades on to his face, and inclined his head at me with a grin. 'See youse.'

He sauntered off. I hesitated, then sighed and stuck his card in my pocket. The reminder of Bowman had taken my appetite away. I left the plate where it was and made my way back towards the offices, turning my headset back on.

'Jean-Paul? Robin, I'm going back on over to the main suite now.'

'Where have you been?' Jean-Paul crackled. 'I've been trying to bleep you. They're doing the TV thing early, grab Taz if you can see him.'

'OK.' I blew out a disgusted breath. Michel was up there on the big video screen now, blond hair shining in the television lights, smiling.

He's so good at this. I paused to watch, glancing around for Taz. Michel was in full flow, smiling at an over-lipsticked reporter who was nodding like her head was on gimbals. '. . . but people must understand that biochemistry is the new industrial revolution, and as with any revolution there will be detractors, nay-sayers . . . '

'And these detractors seem to have picked on your laboratory in a very personal way, Monsieur Rancoul,' the reporter said unguardedly, forgetting where she was. The smile vanished from Michel's face.

'Shoot-from-the-hip Luddites,' he snapped. The smile crept back, pained by a short-sighted world. 'These are fools, who fear the future and what it might bring. I—we at NERVE—invite you to embrace that future, a future that holds out the promise of freedom. Freedom from disease, from premature death and ageing . . . '

I scowled and looked down. His voice was unbearably familiar—so smooth and pleasing to the ears that it almost escaped your notice that you were being bullied and coerced. Slimy sonofabitch.

Taz was standing over near the offices, drinking out of a styrofoam cup. I fiddled with the volume control on my headset and speeded up, threading my way between people nimbly. ''Scuse me, comin' through . . . Taz, Jean-Paul wants us to police the TV crews, finish your drink quick—'scuse me sir . . . thankyooo . . . '

A blond man, right in my path. I cannoned into him with an *oof!* that made heads turn all over the hall, and landed hard on my ass.

I sat up. There were people all round, and things standing on tripods, and lights. And Michel Rancoul stood over me with a malicious smile of recognition on his face. He had my headset in his hand. The reporter who had been interviewing him was hovering, microphone in hand.

'Give that back.' I scrambled shakily to my feet, and held out my hand. Michel held the headset up coyly. His voice was pitched rather loud.

'Aren't you going to apologise?' The challenge was plain. A ripple of laughter from the onlookers, and speculative looks.

'Give me that, you asshole!' I snatched the headset out of his hand and put it back on with trembling fingers. 'Jean-Paul?'

'Apologise to Monsieur Rancoul immediately!' Jean-Paul sounded as if he was frothing at the mouth. I narrowed my eyes. Michel was looking at me with that mocking smile again, head on one side, waiting. A circle of eyes glinted behind the bright lights.

The hot ball of humiliation in my belly shrank to something tiny and dense and singular. I turned the volume up on my earpiece, and moistened my lips. 'Jean-Paul? I think you might want to listen in on this.'

'Good, good, get on with it,' snapped the voice in my ear.

'OK,' I murmured, and turned to a passing waiter. 'Excuse me, may I—?' I appropriated his tray, which was almost full, wheeled and flung it full-force at Michel. The tray of glasses burst on him in an explosion of bubbles. He crashed to the floor in a ringing mess of broken glass.

'I *quit!*' I shouted into my microphone, and tossed the redundant headset on top of Michel's struggling form. The TV crews were filming imperturbably, but several other people tried to grab at me as I stalked away. I shrugged them off and slid into the milling crowd. My head pounded. I didn't know whether the sensation in my chest meant I was going to laugh or cry. Both, maybe.

'Hey, my baby bird! Was that you I just saw trashing the joint?' A heavy hand on my shoulder. I turned, with an effort.

'Tom! Yeah, that was me. I, uh, have a headache, I was just going to get my stuff.' Even to me it sounded like running away.

'Hey, you got my vote,' Barnabas confided with a wry grin. 'He was way outta line there, kid.'

Over Barnabas' shoulder, I saw Taz emerge from a doorway, eyes scanning the crowd. I stepped sideways so that Barnabas' bearish bulk blocked me from his sight. The effort of not crying made my voice sound tight and funny. 'Tom, I'm really not feeling too hot. I—uh, my friend Cary, he was supposed to wait for me, but he, uh, he just left. Can I hitch a lift home?'

Barnabas' brows shot up, then he grinned. 'You got it.'

'You're sure?' My heart jumped as Taz appeared in my line of sight. He was walking my way. Barnabas grunted in amusement.

'You'll be doing me a favour. All this *yak-yak, chit-chat* stuff, I swear, it makes me want to gip.'

'You sound like Dad.' I grinned foolishly at him. 'When can we go?'

'Just give me a second to call my boss, let him know I'll be AWOL for an hour, then we can get moving.'

My head thudded with a wave of pain, and I pressed my fingers over my eyes. 'Ow.'

Barnabas took a firm hold of my elbow. 'Let's go get you some headache pills, kid. You're looking a little peaky. Come on, now.'

I hung back. 'I don't use drugs.' There was a short, mulish pause. 'You know I don't, Tom. Not since Mom. I won't.'

'Today,' Barnabas said, 'you'll take what I say you'll take, and no questions asked. Is that understood, soldier?'

I freed my arm. 'Get real, Uncle Tom. You retired, remember?'

'And you flunked boot camp, remember? Ask me, you've been beating yourself up over what happened to your Mom for long enough. Ruth wanted you to be happy, Robin. Do her a favour and stop punishing yourself.'

'Don't go there, Tom.' I could not put my usual conviction into the warning. Do *Mom* a favour? Barnabas renewed his come-along grip on my elbow.

'Kid, you look like shit. Just let me take care of you, OK? Now march.'

❖

'OK, baby bird?' Over the snarl of the Cherokee's engine, Barnabas' question was almost inaudible. I took advantage of this fact to avoid responding.

Fog had come down during the afternoon. Amsterdam had turned into a ghost city of out-of-focus stick figures that scurried between yellow-lighted doorways on unfamiliar white sidewalks. The untidy patchwork of neon signs overhead floated eerily in the mist. Fairy lights in the trees on Rembrandtsplein were clouds of cold fireflies zipping past.

I let out a shaky breath, and shivered. I stuffed my fists up my sleeves, and Barnabas looked at me sideways in the spooky half-dark.

'There's a blanket in that box behind your seat.'

'Oh. Oh, thanks.' I rummaged it out and wrapped it round me like a big shawl. It was soft and smelt slightly of diesel oil. I cuddled it around me and leaned back in my seat. My voice sounded a little hoarse.

'Well, that's that.'

Barnabas chuckled drily. 'Was it worth it?'

'I don't know,' I muttered. My head felt heavy and I rested it on his shoulder. 'I knew I should have stayed away and I let Jeff bully me into doing the gig. If that's not dumb, I don't know what is.'

'Go to sleep,' suggested Barnabas. 'You did what you had to, that's all. Don't beat yourself up over a scumbag like Michel Rancoul.' His deep voice purred through the bone under my cheek.

'I think I had a little too much to drink.' I licked my lips, and sniffed, yawned. 'Ohh, um. Sorry.' I wondered fuzzily if it was a good idea taking painkillers on top of alcohol, then dismissed the notion: *anything* would be a good idea if it made me feel better about this afternoon. My mouth tasted funny, and I wondered if it was the drug. It had been so long since I'd taken any sort of pill, I couldn't remember.

Tom had stood over me, earlier, and made sure I swallowed the little white torpedoes he'd given me. Then he sat with me in his shiny blue Jeep, listening to football scores on the radio, until the pills started to take effect. He hadn't even asked any questions.

It was Tom who had taught me how to fire my first gun, back when Dad was stationed at Fort Polk near New Orleans and I had knobbly knees and braces on my teeth. Barnabas would come over to the house when he got off duty on a Saturday, with a big bag of cookies and an old range pistol. That was when he'd started calling me 'baby bird', because he said I never stopped eating or squawking.

Ruth Carlson hadn't much liked him giving her daughter shooting lessons. I could see her now, leaning in the doorway of our quarters house one evening, arms folded. Her voice always got quiet when she was angry. I was gnawing the tip of my pencil in lieu of doing homework in my room, and I recognised the tone.

'Tom, I appreciate your spending your day off with Robin, but I can't have you giving her firearms training. I'm sorry.'

'Well, hell, Mrs. Carlson, so am I.' Barnabas' deep voice carried through my open window, and I held my breath lying there on my bed, books forgotten, willing him to think of some excuse. I vividly recalled the dawning horror as he went on, 'you see, I caught your daughter playing with her Daddy's spare pistol twice in the last month. Bawled the kid out, a'course, but what can you do? Kids are kids, Ruth. They always want to play with things that go flash and bang,'specially if their Mom says no. Fact of human nature. Now, Robin's twelve already, she's plenty old enough to take in basic firearms training. I'm not talking about anything formal here, just safety stuff, a little target practice on a weekend. She needs to learn a little respect for guns. Come on, what do you say—?' A snort, and an imagined shrug and grin. 'At least this way, nobody's gonna get shot by *accident*.'

Tom always had been good at talking his way round people. Mom had laughed, and—miracle of miracles—hadn't said a word to me about my father's pistol. The lessons went on all summer. It must be almost fifteen years ago now.

He hasn't changed a whole lot, I thought, glancing sideways at him in the ghost light of the dashboard dials. Those big bear shoulders, the buzz-cut fair hair turning fairer on its way to being white, the bulky frame—spreading a touch there, I fancied—but overall the same big, comfortable man.

Tom had been there for me after Mom died, when even the sound of my Dad's voice was enough to make me break out in a rash of teenaged turmoil; he was still there for me, a homely constant, and that's all that mattered.

His shoulder was warm under my cheek, and I curled against him, sighing. My eyes hurt, so I closed them, just for a second.

❖

I woke with a cold feeling and wondered for a second, crossly, who had stolen my pillow.

'Robin.' It was Tom's voice. I pushed myself upright, mumbling. He was a big dark silhouette, leaning in the open car door from the street. Sodium light cast a heartless illumination behind him. 'Robin, we're here.'

'Here. Right.' I rubbed at my eyes, embarrassed. 'OK.'

I scrambled over the seat and down into the snow. My natty little Gucci loafers went ankle deep into the grey drift at the kerbside. The shock of ice up my pants leg finished the job of wakening me. We were double-parked, right outside my building. I tugged my bag after me, out of the footwell, and hooked it over my shoulder.

'Thanks, Tom. I'm sorry I had to drag you away too.'

'Hell, you did me a favour, I hate those things, remember?' He slammed the car door and moved to my side. 'Now, I'll just see you to your door, and I'll be on my way.'

'Oh, no! No,' I gabbled, mortified at a sudden vision of explaining my boyfriend troubles in the hallway. 'Really, I'll, I'll be fine.' I stood on tip-toes to peck him on the cheek. His stubble scratched my lips. Out of the fog of tiredness, I summoned a grin. 'I'm a big girl now, remember?'

'Tell that to the Marines,' muttered Barnabas, but he shrugged and didn't follow me to the street door. 'You take care now, baby bird.'

'I'll be OK,' I called, and waved as he settled behind the wheel, then let the heavy door swing to. The squeal of hinges, and the *clunk* as it shut itself, seemed very loud.

I stood in the cold, dark hallway for a few seconds. Canned applause burst against Schama's closed front door, and I smelt cabbage. Probably his TV supper. Yum.

A grey residue of the afternoon's headache made me sluggish; I took my time on the darkened stairs. It was a relief to slam my front door behind me.

The lobby was in darkness, but a line of light showed under the living-room door. My innards did a quick Mexican wave, and I placed one hand flat on my midriff. Damn. Hadn't I suspected that romance would ruin a perfectly good friendship? Down, girl.

'Cary?' I shucked off coat and bag on to the floor. The ruined Guccis joined them, and I raised my voice, walking into the kitchen. 'Hey, Bowman! I'm back!'

The light from Zbiggy's tank on top of the microwave cast a peaceful, golden glow into the room. I tapped on the glass as I passed, and the little black Fighting Fish inside darted to the movement, mouth working belligerently. It looked very much as if he was scolding me.

'Sorry,' I whispered. 'Sorry, baby.' A piece of pizza crust was still sitting in its box on the drainer, and I floated it carefully on the surface of the water. Zbiggy butted it and did a quick circuit of the tank, looking even more depressed.

I bobbled the stale bread encouragingly with my finger—*Look! It's alive!*—but the little fish had already recommenced his endless, neurotic round-and-round swimming. Despite guilty over-feeding, meant to compensate for neglect, he never seemed to grow. Maybe he doesn't like pepperoni pizza, I thought. Or maybe he just doesn't like being alone all the time. Yeah, well, that makes two of us.

I flicked on the kitchen strip-light. It binged a couple of times, then settled with a buzzing noise. The harsh light hurt my eyes.

A glance at the plastic wall clock reoriented me at six p.m., give or take. It felt like the early hours. I'd a vague idea that Tom and I had left the junket about four-thirty. Surely an hour and a half couldn't be right? Even allowing for the usual manic city traffic, it should only be half an hour's drive from the Ringweg to here. No, I must have got the time wrong. Or maybe the clock's battery was running down. I couldn't think. My headache was coming back.

I put the kettle on, and walked into the living-room with two mugs dangling from my hand.

'Want a coffee? —Oh.' I'm not the world's most conscientious housekeeper, so I habitually focus past a certain level of mess. It took a couple of puzzled seconds for it to sink in. I stared, the mugs clenched in my fist.

The table-lamp lay on its side on the floor, blinking fitfully. The blankets Bowman had slept in were flung on the couch, the cushions scattered on the floor with a mess of CD cases and crumpled papers. The doors of the bureau hung crookedly open.

A light shone in the bathroom. I placed the mugs on the coffee table and strode across, my heart hammering, to fling open the door. Nobody.

Make-up was scattered on the windowsill near the mirror, and my bath-towels were a damp-smelling heap on the floor. Bowman's toothbrush and shaving stuff were missing from the shelf over the sink.

I straightened the eye-pencils and lipsticks automatically. My fingers trembled. Why had he done this to me?

Everything smelt of lemon and lime. A bottle of expensive bubble-bath had fallen into the tub and made a glutinous, greeny-yellow river into the plug-hole. I yanked the light cord and slammed the door shut. Talk about money down the drain. Terrific.

In the living-room, I noticed the untidy stack of papers was gone from the coffee table. The mess on the floor was my stuff, not his. I checked behind the couch: Bowman's big black holdall was missing.

'Hell, Cary,' I muttered, and walked back into the kitchen. A dull ache in my stomach, as if he had punched me in the midriff. The deliberate mess seemed so petty, a childish tantrum.

I sat down at the kitchen table and rested my hot forehead on my arms, too miserable even to cry.

❖

Grey walls, locked doors. Wolf lay on his side and gazed through half-closed eyelids at the shiny scuffed metal of the floor.

He pretended to himself that he was dreaming, that he was back in the maze. That pretty Frenchwoman had been here, shining sharp light into his eyes. Mademoiselle la Docteur. She'd taken more of his blood. He did not speak to her this time. A dream, that's all, or a ghost. *Only a crazy man speaks to ghosts, and I'm not crazy yet. Not quite yet.*

Maartje's voice kept breaking into the dream. Wolf wished that he couldn't hear her. She whispered his name on the other side of the grey walls, and wept and wept. It took all his strength to push her away.

And he was strong. The irony of it made him want to lift up his voice and weep as well.

They'd come back twice now. The first time, two of the orderlies held him while a third used some kind of hypo-gun to administer more of the drug. Wolf had surprised himself at the ease with which he shook them off.

The second time there had been no attempt to restrain him. One had distracted his attention, and another jumped forward and stuck a taser gun in his side.

Wolf shuddered at the memory: an electric charge doesn't produce the kind of pain that you can resist with manly silence and gritted teeth. It swaddled him like sheet lightning and nailed him to the floor.

The orderlies hobbled him with the ubiquitous orange cable. Their paper-muffled boots clumped through his line of sight, big brutal cartoon shapes. Cold cobbled metal pressed into his face. The hypo-gun stung his neck.

When he could breathe again, Wolf had thrown himself at the locked door in fury. Hammered, kicked, screamed his defiance. He could see the marks he'd made in the steel, a smear of blood on the little glass porthole where he'd slit his thumb open on a metal burr.

None of it made him tired in the least. He wasn't hungry or thirsty. His body hummed like a well-tuned machine.

He'd stopped eventually, not out of exhaustion but because it was humiliating. He could scream himself hoarse, batter at the door until he was bloody, and nobody would give a damn. Faces peered in at intervals, and the video camera whined on its wall mount—unfortunately out of reach. Wolf lay still.

He did not know how many hours had passed since the men left him alone. It didn't matter. They would do whatever it was they wanted with him, then they would kill him.

He should have been dead—what—four, five months ago? In the hospital, he'd heard the nurses whisper between themselves that it was a miracle he had survived.

But it wasn't a miracle. It had just been an oversight. A mistake. Now the error was going to be rectified. Wolf gazed at the ripple of muddy colours in the grid-pattern of the floor, and hoped that it would be soon.

Solitary confinement is a rarefied torture. It isn't, as most people think, just the pain of being alone: nobody to talk to, nobody to see, touch, smell. All this is part of it, but not all. The worst is the sheer drab sameness.

Down here, there wasn't even the comfort of sunlight through the prison bars, peaceful darkness, a waft of sweet outside air—just the never-changing artificial light, the ammonia stink, the dim whum-whum of the air-conditioning. Always the same, as if time stood still.

And just as he thought he was getting used to it, had achieved some sort of equilibrium between fear and boredom, the bolt would bang back and they'd be there again: his harsh paper-wrapped cartoon guardians with their electrical persuasion. Barking orders, taking their samples of blood and flesh and spittle and urine. Then gone, like jacks-in-a-box.

Up the corridor, there was a sudden squabble of raised voices. Wolf blinked and climbed to his feet. The lift had just come down—he'd heard the thump as it hit bottom a few seconds ago.

Wolf craned at the reinforced-glass peephole in the door, heart bumping. Black Coats. He recognised Orthodontic Man's cave-man buddy, struggling to keep control of his portion of a tall, fair-haired man that they were trying to manhandle from the lift doors into the office. The man was fighting extremely dirty. Cro-Magnon Man squirmed on the floor suddenly, clutching himself; another yelled and stumbled back pawing at his eyes.

More Coats crowded into the limited corridor space, and Wolf saw the man go down. Muffled noises of agony came to his ears. The door to the little bare office room closed on the hubbub.

Another derelict, snatched off the street? Wolf lingered, staring at the closed door.

The man had been dressed in a shirt and suit—they had jammed the jacket down over his elbows to hobble his arms. Good leather shoes. He looked as if he'd been snatched from a dinner party, not out of the gutter. And he'd been shouting in English, Wolf was sure—though not all the words had been familiar. What was he doing down here?

Wolf waited for a few minutes, but things seemed to have gone quiet again. A mumble of men's voices from the office.

Wolf hunkered down in the corner and pressed his ear to the door-jamb, curious despite himself. If he shut his eyes and concentrated, he could make out words.

'—expect me to *believe* that?' A whiny tenor voice, an American. Wolf pressed his ear closer to the tiny gap. The man kept lowering his voice, which made it difficult to follow the sense of what he said. Another question. Then the fair-haired man, sounding bewildered.

'I told you, you're m-making a mistake. I work for the Free University—' He broke off with an exclamation of pain. Wolf flinched. The American again. His tone was reasonable, almost friendly.

'We can keep this up a lot longer than you, my friend. You're a professional, you know what we can do to you. What's it matter if you tell us? Nobody's gonna blame you. We'll get the information we need, sooner or later. You could save both of us a lot of time and trouble. Come on, buddy, how much does the girl know? You're not gonna make me go after her for the answers, are you?'

'. . . don't know what you mean.' Monotone, obstinate.

'Are you screwing her, huh? Is that it?' Confiding, man-to-man.

'What girl—I, I don't know what you m-mean. Please—' The sound of a blow. The man grunted in agony, and Wolf grimaced. He felt like some kind of pervert, eavesdropping like this, but it might gain him some nugget of information—*something*. He screwed his eyes shut and listened.

More questions from the American. What was the man's real name, and who had sent him, and the girl, what about the girl, how much did she know? Over and over, into tedium. All interspersed with the odd, dull sounds of flesh punishing flesh. Wolf could hear the fair man's breathing after a while, ragged gasps between the animal noises they forced from him.

Wolf found he was trembling, fists clenched. He half wished that the man would capitulate. *Nothing's worth that much*, he pleaded silently, *just tell them what they want to know*—then felt like a stinking coward because the truth was that he simply didn't want to have to listen to it any longer.

Wolf got to his feet and paced the length of his cell and back again, in the soft-shoe shuffle the hobble forced him into. He ran hands through his hair, and wished that they'd left him his lighter because he dearly needed a cigarette.

The *whoof* of the swing doors dragged Wolf's attention back to the porthole. There was the familiar rattle of a trolley. He was just in time to see the doctor enter the office, followed by two green-clad orderlies. She didn't bother to close the door after her, and he heard her voice quite clearly.

'That will be enough.'

'I got my orders.' The American sounded sulky; a little boy getting in trouble for pulling the wings off flies. The doctor's tone was cutting, as always.

'I give the orders down here, Mulder. Out.'

'But Mam'selle, the Major—'

'Out, out! If you wish to play at tough guys, you can find somewhere else to do it. And you can tell the Major so from me,' she added, pointedly. Wolf saw three Black Coats file sheepishly out into the corridor. The door banged shut.

One of the Black Coats was the dark-haired man Wolf had seen in the bar that night with Klaas. He was carrying his coat, shirt-sleeves rolled up, and Wolf guessed that he must be the owner of the whiny voice. Mulder. He looked rumpled and peevish. Sadists are no good at deferred gratification.

Wolf dropped to his knees and pressed his ear to the crack again. The doctor's voice was a muted mumble, too low for him to catch more than a few words.

'—came down here straight away . . . didn't credit you with being so stupid.' A wealth of spite in her tone. The fair man's voice was hoarse with exhaustion.

'Oh, shut up, you stupid cow. Think. If I don't report back, my people are going to be very *very* angry. Angry enough to act on the information they already have.'

A nasty satisfaction in the doctor's voice. ' . . . not stopping you from reporting . . . fact, I'm going to give you a *personal* perspective. Prep him.'

'*Nooo!*' The man yelled. There was a crash. Shouts of alarm from the orderlies, scufflings and grunts of effort. Harsh, desperate sounds.

Wolf sank into a huddle, hugging his legs. Above the door, the little video camera rustled and turned on its mount. Wolf buried his face in his knees, fuming at his own helplessness.

They were—what was it the doctor had called it?—*inducting* him. The yells had subsided into a dry, terrified sobbing. Wolf jammed his hands over his ears until he could hear nothing for the rushing of his own blood.

Poor sod. If I'd known what was going to happen when she stuck that needle in me, I'd have gone berserk too.

8

TIME WAS RUNNING OUT. Wolf had tried to ignore what went on around him, but with senses sharper than a tray of knives, it was impossible. Besides Maartje, there had been two others, both men. One—the poet, as Wolf thought of him—had been taken away yesterday, weeping and struggling. Shortly afterwards, Wolf had suddenly ceased to hear his voice. He had not come back.

The last voice stopped just as abruptly. A cell door had banged open, there was the usual welter of busyness. Wolf braced himself for the snap and sting of the taser. He didn't know why he felt it when the others were hurt. Maybe he was going crazy and it was his own mind doing this to him, suffering by proxy or something. It seemed as plausible as any other explanation.

Except that this time, the taser wasn't just a finger-click of discomfort. It shot a lightning-rod of pain straight through Wolf's body. He fell to the floor, unable to move. In his head, he heard Maartje scream. His heart jerked and fluttered. Then it stopped.

A blank second of disbelief. He was still alive. Maartje was still alive.

After a few minutes, they brought the gurney and wheeled the old man's corpse away.

The orderly pushing the gurney whistled a perky little tune as he went down the corridor. Business as usual.

Wolf sat up, and passed trembling fingers over his face. Bile in his throat.

Is that the way Pete had gone, after they realised he was too crazy or too sick to be useful to them? How long before he had to listen to Maartje's death throes, hear them wheel her body away?

How long after that until they came for Jan Wolf?

Common sense told him that he should lie back down, spin the grey labyrinth about him again, and wait for the inevitable. It might even be a kind of release.

No. No, screw common sense. Wolf rubbed his cheek where the metal floor had left its imprint, and drew a deep breath. He had to get out. He had to *try*. What can they do, he realised with a wintry smile, except kill me? Perhaps I can take a stab at being the hero after all. Anything to disoblige Mademoiselle.

He hunkered down against the door jamb and rubbed thoughtfully at the warm plastic strands that hobbled his ankles. They were monofilament, practically unbreakable—he had the friction burns and bruises to testify to his attempts at snapping them.

Wolf rolled the clip between finger and thumb. Steel, a kind of double ratchet affair, so that the whole arrangement could be pulled tight but not easily loosened.

He peered at it more closely: where it joined on to the plastic, it was crimped on, the edges hooking into the filament itself with three sturdy little claws. The metal was thick and shiny.

Wolf flicked a glance up at the tiny camcorder on its mount above the doorway. He must be right in the periphery of its picture down here. He hunched over and dropped his head forward in a despondent pose. Now the hobble clip and his hands were masked from the camera's prying eye. He grasped the clip and twisted as hard as he could.

Nothing. He examined the tiny, infuriating thing. His efforts had done nothing more than flatten it slightly and drive the little barbs deeper into the orange plastic. He was as securely hobbled as before.

Wolf gave the hobble a last disgusted tug and let it drop into a limp figure eight. At least they hadn't pulled it too tight. It tickled his bare ankles above the padded cuff of his boots. He scratched absently, mind idling.

Idiot!

Wolf sat down in the corner and fumbled at his bootlaces with trembling fingers, cursing at his bitten-down fingernails. He wrenched off first one boot, then the other, slipped the loose hobble cord off over his bare feet, and stamped back into the boots. Done.

Wolf squatted down again, stuffing the hobble into his coat pocket. His heart banged in his throat. His bad eye twitched. Wolf pressed fingertips into the spasming lid and tried to keep his breathing level. Damn. If only they'd all been distracted. If only they hadn't seen . . .

Too many *if onlys*, he scolded himself. He scratched nervously at his beard, and imagined them, grouped around a monitor screen, watching him. Then he imagined them going about their business, unaware of his duplicity.

The black iris of the camera stared enigmatically and gave no hint which scenario was correct. Wolf was acutely aware of his unfastened bootlaces, but he did not dare draw attention by tying them. He had to force himself to relax—to appear relaxed, at any rate—and wait for an opportunity to present itself.

Wolf leaned his head back against the cool metal. Not long now. He could hang on just a little while more. Just a little while . . .

Noises distracted him.

The lift was coming down. The venetian blinds in the office room crinkled as someone leant against them. There was the usual *clonk* as the lift cage hit bottom, then the doors rasped open and people traipsed out coughing and muttering. Four sets of unmuffled shoes. Wolf guessed Black Coats.

He got to his feet and craned up at his spy-hole again, curious. The office door stood open. As Wolf watched, a couple of Black Coats came out into the corridor, supporting the fair-haired man with one arm round each of their shoulders—like a couple of good old mates taking their friend home after an all-night drinking session.

The fair-haired man looked the worse for wear all right, but not from alcohol. His face was swollen and discoloured with bruises. Wolf saw dry blood caked on his chest inside the roughly-buttoned shirt.

Wolf squinted critically at the man: he looked as if he'd been tranquillised. His eyes were sleepy, half closed. A muscle relaxant? He could barely keep his feet. His head lolled with each step as his gaolers guided him gingerly towards the lift doors. Spittle drooled from one corner of his mouth, to the obvious disgust of the Black Coat whose shoulder it landed on.

Wolf grinned. It wasn't much in the way of payback after what they'd done, but it was a satisfying moment all the same. A burst of kinship warmed him for a second. The lift doors closed.

Wolf sank back down on to the floor. The fair-haired man had people who would be very, very angry if he died. Well, bully for him. So far as he knew, nobody would feel any strong emotion if the same fate befell Jan Wolf. If he really meant to get out of here alive, he would have to make his own luck. He wasn't sure he knew the recipe.

Wolf worried at his thumbnail, and waited.

❖

In the event, the opportunity came so unexpectedly that he almost missed it.

Hours had dragged past. Wolf was listening to Maartje's faint movements in the next cell, and wishing he could tell her what he planned, when there was a clatter at the door, and the doctor walked in.

Wolf froze. His heart was going for broke.

'You are an awkward customer,' the doctor muttered. The light dimmed as she bent over him. She was wearing high-heeled shoes and a smartly-tailored suit under her white coat instead of the usual scrubs. The arrival of the fair-haired man had obviously brought her out here in a hurry.

Wolf flickered a glance at the door and saw a single orderly standing in the corridor, staring off into space, submachine-gun dangling. Wolf let his eyelids droop.

The doctor took hold of his wrist and lifted it, feeling for the pulse. 'Fast,' she stated after an interval, 'but well within tolerance levels. You're hurt?' Wolf had winced as her fingers pressed a bruise. She turned his hand in her grasp, manipulating it without much care. Wolf gave a small gasp, and she bent towards him, frowning. 'What—?'

Wolf straightened his arm with a violent suddenness that took her by surprise. She fell hard against the wall. He scrambled after her, grappling desperately. She shrieked and flailed, but he barely noticed the rain of blows. He choked one arm up tight under her jawbone and forced her to her feet in front of him. The orderly in the corridor gaped. The gun swung up, late.

'Drop it!' Wolf's voice was somewhere between a yelp and a snarl. The man hesitated. Wolf stretched the doctor's chin an inch higher. She gave a croak of alarm. 'I'll break her neck before you can pull the trigger. Now drop it!'

The gun thudded on to the carpet tiles. The orderly sprinted away up the corridor, yelling.

'Keys,' Wolf demanded. 'Quickly.'

The doctor fumbled at the pocket of her white lab coat. Her perfume filled his nostrils: he recognised *Tendre Poison*. Appropriate, Wolf thought. His nose tickled. Her body twisted against his. The intimacy of the sensation was distracting, to say the least.

She almost pulled it off. Only the tiny mosquito-whine of the charge warned him, a split second before she snatched a taser out of her pocket and drove it backwards at his face.

Wolf twisted it out of her fingers. She gasped some very naughty French words at him, and went for him with her nails. Wolf shoved her out to arms' length.

'I don't need you awake for this, Mademoiselle.'

She must have set the taser at max. When he pressed it to her neck and thumbed the button, she dropped instantly.

'Bitch,' Wolf added, and sneezed. He limped to the doorway to peer into the corridor. Nobody was in sight yet. He picked up the dropped gun and dragged the doctor into the corridor by her feet.

Wolf pulled open the next cell door. 'Maartje?' The lights were off, but he could see her, hunched against the far wall. She did not respond. Wolf shot a nervous glance up the corridor. 'Maartje! Come on!'

'Jan . . . ?' A whisper. She lifted her head and squinted at him. Her face was grubby and streaked with tears. She did not move.

'Come *on*.' Wolf strode into the cell and yanked her to her feet. She was naked, and he got a stab of the same slightly disturbing emotion she'd first roused in him: *she's just a child. But.* He squashed the feeling grimly, like a bug. 'Quickly. We're getting out.'

He left Maartje leaning against the door-frame while he dragged the doctor into the cell. Maartje's eyes got very round. Wolf felt her disbelief dissolve into vengeful pleasure. 'What did you *do* to her?'

'Zapped her with her own stun-gun.' Wolf held it up between finger and thumb. A flicker of a grin on Maartje's face. She took a startled, whooping breath and started to cough. It was a full minute before she stopped, and sagged against the doorpost, panting.

'Sorry. It's the damn drug.'

'Are you OK now?' Wolf studied her pale face. His own chest seemed a little tight. Perhaps it was just the anxiety. Maartje nodded, though she didn't open her eyes.

'Be fine. Give me a second.' She wasn't fine, but Wolf didn't see the point in arguing.

'OK.' He craned to peer through the glass porthole in the door. Still nobody in sight. A certain amount of muttering and shuffling around the far corner. Wolf ducked back inside the cell and stripped the doctor of her white coat. The orange plastic hobble went round her wrists. He tossed the coat to Maartje. 'Here.'

'Bit short,' she complained, but stuck her arms in and pulled the material together across her bare breasts. 'Thanks.'

'Keep an eye on her.' Wolf jerked his head at the doctor. He went to look up the corridor again, holding the gun in one hand. It had gone quiet. He stretched his ears and heard several men trying to breathe silently. Wolf allowed himself a small, grim smile. They'd provided him with the edge—now see how they liked to have it used against them. He retreated into the cell.

Maartje was fastening the last button on the lab coat. She prodded at the doctor's supine figure. 'Bitch is awake.' Her voice was hoarse.

'Good, I don't want to have to carry her. Can you walk?' Wolf waited for Maartje's nod, then held up the gun. It resembled a good-quality children's toy. 'Ever use one of these?'

'Of course not.' Maartje took it with obvious reluctance. 'I don't think I can shoot this thing straight.'

'Just point it and pull the trigger.'

'You take it.' She held it out. Wolf shook his head.

'I have to go first, with her, or we don't stand a chance in hell of getting out of here.'

'But—' Maartje broke off into another coughing fit. This time when she straightened, her face was greyish and sweaty, and she was wheezing audibly. She said nothing, but wiped her palms on the white coat before taking a businesslike grip on the gun. Her hands were bony and long-fingered, nails trimmed short. They looked vulnerable without the profusion of rings.

'Stay close,' Wolf said. 'There's a pair of swing doors half way up the corridor. Laboratory, I think. If anyone sticks their head out, shoot it. You don't have to hit them, just scare them. All right?'

'I think.' She was trembling, hands white-knuckled gripping the gun. Wolf pressed her shoulder gently.

'You'll be fine.' He bent to jerk the doctor to her feet. 'Come on, up. Time to go.'

'Get your hands off me, *emmerdement!*' The doctor attacked him in an unladylike flurry of elbows and knees. Wolf had to pin her against the cell wall with his body before she subsided, gasping. Up close, her eyes glittered almost silver. Her mouth twisted. 'You should leave the girl behind. You can't help her.' A flicker of the long lashes, as if she were trying to evaluate his reaction. Wolf stared into the grey eyes and blinked, once.

'What do you mean?' He placed one hand gently round her neck. 'Tell me.'

'None of the females in the test programme has survived. The drug reacts badly to female body chemistry. She's having breathing problems already. That's damage to the central nervous system. She has a short time left, then—' A shrug. '*Kaput*.'

'You're lying,' Wolf said, and hoped the dread did not show in his voice. 'You're just lying to save your own skin.'

'I'm not lying.'

Wolf hesitated. 'How long?'

'Till what?'

'Till *kaput*.'

She laughed in his face. A sly flicker of the beautiful eyes at Maartje.

'Get moving.' Wolf gripped her by the shoulders and spun her around. She submitted to the rough handling, but he could still see that infuriating smile. Maartje was expressionless.

He was just pushing the doctor ahead of him into the doorway when a man's voice boomed down the corridor.

'Hello down there!'

Wolf yanked the Frenchwoman backwards against him, and clapped a hand over her mouth. She wriggled and tried to bite him, and he whispered fiercely in her ear, 'I told you I don't need you conscious for this! I'll carry you if I have to, you bitch. Understand?' He relaxed his grip long enough for her to give a grudging nod. 'Good. Now you tell your friends up there to call the lift down, then back off. Tell them!' He uncovered her mouth, and she moistened her lips with the tip of her tongue before she shouted.

'Mulder!'

There was a short pause before the man's voice called back. 'Are you safe?' It was the Black Coat with the whiny voice and the sadistic tendencies. The hairs on the back of Wolf's neck prickled.

'Of course I'm not safe, you idiot!' The doctor's voice rose half an octave. 'If you don't let them go, he's going to break my neck. They have a gun. Now get back!'

'Falling back now,' the man responded. An urgent murmur of voices.

'Don't forget the lift,' Wolf said, close to her ear.

The doctor hesitated, then shouted, 'Call the lift down!' Her chagrin was plain.

'Better,' Wolf breathed, and relaxed his grip enough so that her feet could just touch the floor. 'Now. Let's go for a little walk, nice and slow. We wouldn't want you to get damaged.' He grasped her jaw in one hand, and folded his other arm across in a parody of a tender embrace, gripping her shoulder. 'After you.'

The corridor seemed both too short and impossibly long. Wolf shuffled slowly forward. The Frenchwoman's hair tickled his neck. Her bound hands dug into his midriff. *Tendre Poison* got up his nose and made him want to sneeze. He held his breath and kept shuffling.

Ahead, there was a whine as the lift descended the shaft. Apart from the scuff of their own feet on the floor, Wolf could hear no other movement. A bit of heavy mouth-breathing round the far corner. He fretted over what the Black Coats were doing. He should have got them all down in the cells and locked them in. No time to think.

An awful lot rode on how badly they needed the Frenchwoman alive. He'd gambled that she was as important as she acted. If either of them was wrong, then all three of them were going to die.

'You'd better be right,' Wolf muttered. He could not have said to whom he was speaking.

❖

The mail-man was late. I heard the squeak of his brakes as he stopped outside, then the slop-slop of boots in slush. I heard it because I was lying in bed wide awake, only the tips of my ears and nose poking from beneath the covers while I tried to decide whether it was worth getting up now I was unemployed.

Only partially unemployed, I reminded myself. Marik would be expecting me to turn up for my classes as usual if I wanted to get paid.

I snuck a peek at the clock over the heaped-up bedding: it was just gone eleven. My first class today was a sparring session at three. Four hours' downtime and I couldn't even sleep.

My back ached, and I wriggled about for several minutes trying to get comfortable before giving up and getting out of bed. That mattress ought to have a health warning on it: *The Surgeon General Has Determined That Sleeping In This Bed Will Turn Your Spine Into A Pretzel.*

I stretched, groaning, and crawled into the nearest clothes that looked clean, then padded into the kitchen to put the coffee machine on. My mouth tasted sort of furry. The kitchen floor was cold.

While the coffee was perking, I put the front door on the latch and trotted downstairs to the freezing lobby, jingling the keys on their ring, to check my mailbox.

There was a large Jiffy bag in the box. My name was scrawled on it in marker pen. I glanced uncertainly from the slim mail slot to the bag. There was no way it could have fitted through the slot. Maybe Schama had unlocked my box and put it there, he had a set of keys. I carried the bag down the hallway to check.

'I don't provide a mail service,' were the landlord's first words on opening his door to me and the package. I held it up, frowning.

'You mean you didn't put this in my box?'

'I don't provide a mail service,' repeated Mr. Schama firmly, and closed the door in my face.

'No, or any other service either,' I muttered, and jogged back up the stairs with my prize.

I slit the parcel open on the kitchen table, a flutter of nervy excitement in my stomach. The contents slid out on to the table.

I recognised the tattered manila folder straight away. It was the sketches, the ones Bowman had shown me. My heart gave a leaden thump. I slipped the worn-out rubber band off and opened the flap.

As well as the sketches, there was an official-looking brown envelope, already opened. I glanced at the contents: all in Dutch, some kind of municipal rent demand or something like that. It was addressed to K. De Haan. I dropped it into my bag to look at some other time, and returned my attention to the folder.

The little strip of passport photographs was in there, and the photocopied service record Cary had translated for me, along with a few odd sheets of paper, some typewritten, some just scrawled notes. They all seemed to be about De Haan—a photocopy of a decree absolute, dated several years ago, terse little scribbles like 'no surviving relatives', and 'respect, yes—liking??☹' with an arrow pointing to the name 'FIXX'. Wasn't that the place where De Haan used to work?

More to the point, when had Cary put the package in my mailbox? The thought of him lifting the key from its nail in the kitchen when my back was turned made me feel ill.

Something hard slid among the papers, and I fished after it: a little brass key with a card label attached. On one side of the label the word 'QUESTOR' had been printed in faded red felt tip; on the other, in biro, was written 'Just in case. Love, Cary. xx'

'What the hell—?' I stared at the little innocuous thing, then dropped the key into my pocket. What was Bowman playing at? Storming off like that, leaving my apartment in a mess and my self-esteem in tatters, and now love and kisses? Aloud, I said, softly, 'You and your dumb-ass spy games.'

I sat down with coffee in an attempt to wake up, and ended up leafing idly through the heap of sketches. After a while I reached for my cellphone, and dialled.

'Sunny? Is Marik awake? Listen, I need a really, really big favour . . . '

❖

By the time it got to two o'clock, I'd copied all the stuff about De Haan into my notebook using my best handwriting. I even paper-clipped one of the photos to the first page. I wasn't sure why I bothered, except that I thought it'd fill up the time and stop me from brooding over Cary. It didn't work.

I left my bag at the flat, hidden under the dirty washing, and stuck a rape alarm in one coat pocket and a very small taser in the other.

Down these mean streets a girl must walk . . . *and heaven help anyone who tries to lay a finger on her*, I appended with a last lingering look in the bathroom mirror. I tucked the ink drawings into an inside pocket, and tugged a bit self-consciously at the plait on my left shoulder. *Hey, go get 'em, Lady Croft.*

I hopped a couple of trams, and got off on Rembrandtsplein, into the fume-hung busyness of shoppers and crawling traffic. I had put on my best black cowboy boots, fancy tooled-leather work bought in Mexico on my last holiday with Daddy, two years ago. The left boot leaked where the silver filigree toe-cap had peeled away from the leather, and my sock was getting wet. The tips of my ears stung with cold.

The slush had frozen into a treacherous sheet of marbled ice, and I was glad of the trampled trough down the middle of the sidewalk. Sand and salt had eaten scabrous, dingy holes in the ice.

I queued outside a hole-in-the-wall *broodje* bar, trying not to let unladylike loops of drool run down my jowls at the aroma of bread-rolls and roasting meat, while a huge man dictated his order in slow and portentous Dutch. He seemed to be ordering one of everything.

I was hungry enough to consider using the taser to gee him up a bit, but restrained the impulse and paid for a warmed-over chicken roll and a cone of hot *frites*. As a concession to healthy eating, there was salad in the roll. I picked out the warm lettuce leaf and bits of cress with finger and thumb, and dropped them in a trash can.

I ate while I walked.

❖

The Fight Club smelt of chlorine and the gentle decay of rubber crash-mats. I leaned into the office on my way past. 'Hey Sunny. Is Marik upstairs?'

'You bet.' Sunny waved an upraised fingernail under my nose. 'Just don' get any funny ideas about me covering for you whenever you fancy a day off, all right? This is stric'ly a one-off. If it was anyone else, I wouldn' be doing it at all.' Tigerish words from someone as soft-hearted as Sun-yi Choong. She wrinkled her nose. 'You smell of fas' food.'

'Hon, you know I appreciate you.' I winked at her and made a sharp exit before Sunny could think up a penalty clause. Also before she noticed the mess of melting snow I had trampled in from the street.

Marik was in the attic, going through wind-down with a couple of dozen serious-faced acolytes, all of them barefoot and dressed in the proper black pyjamas.

I slipped in and stood at the back of the class. It felt oddly improper to be here and not working. I waited, feeling self-conscious, until the students were trailing out the door before I strolled to the front.

'Robin! Yo stranger!' It's natural, I guess, that ex-pats hang together, even if there's a little detail of continents between our points of origin. Geographically, Marik's place of birth was a heck of a lot closer to Amsterdam than to the USA, but half his friends and clients were ex-pat Yanks like me. I tell him it's because we're easily charmed by weird English accents, and they don't come much weirder than the British Midlands. Marik had been raised on some awful housing project, an inner-city 'hood in Birmingham—*Bermingum*, he called it. The way I said it always made him laugh.

He loomed over me, gawky and muscular, wiping sweat from his face with a threadbare yellow towel. 'In a hurry, aren't you? Wish you were this early all the time.' His grin sweetened the tartness of his words.

'Here.' A hoarse whisper. I pulled the squashed cone of frites out of my jacket pocket, and waggled my eyebrows conspiratorially. 'I brought you these.'

'You trying to get me in trouble with Sunny or something? You know what she's like.' Marik bugged his eyes, but there was a hungry gleam in them. I shrugged and started eating the frites myself.

'Well, don't say I didn't offer. We walking?'

'You must be joking, I've got the Harley round at the lock-up. This weather gets on me tits.' Marik sniffed and rubbed his nose, accepting the frites. 'Ta. Just don't tell the Diet Gestapo you've been feeding me this greasy rubbish, eh?'

'If you say so.' I licked salt off my fingers. 'You're such a pussy, Washington. No willpower. I can't believe you got your eighth dan.'

The look I got in response to this little witticism was all raised brows and flared nostrils. Marik spoiled the effect by stuffing the last handful of frites in all at once, like a greedy child. He saw me looking at the tattoo on his shoulder and leaned down to give me a better look, posing self-consciously. 'Nice, eh?'

'Mmm. You know, I never knew they could work in white like this. Looks like chalk or pastel or something.' I traced the coiling spine of the Chinese dragon down his biceps. 'Cost you a lot?'

'More than the other one,' he admitted, sheepishly, 'but Sunny likes it.' He dabbed the towel tenderly over the glistening creature. 'I've only had it two weeks, the sweat makes it itch something chronic.'

'I never knew anyone could work up a sweat doing *kata*,' I teased. 'Hmm, say, you're not getting out of condition, are you, Washington? Maybe you should retire.'

'Cheeky cow.' He thrust the towel into the bag. 'Girl, you got a nerve. I could fill your job like *that*, but you just don't care, do you?'

'You know, you are *so* right,' I shot back. Marik rolled his eyes at me.

'Not going to throw something at me, are you? Saw you on the TV news this morning. You should get that PMS seen to, love.' He dropped the black silk belt into the bag, pulled out a red and grey fleece blazoned with FIGHT CLUB AMSTERDAM, and wriggled into it. The short crop of dreadlocks sprouted from its neck like a sudden bunch of exotic black flowers. His voice was muffled. 'Did you bring the pictures?'

'Got 'em right here.'

'Great. Let's go, then.'

Marik shot this over his shoulder at me as he walked off towards the stairs. I hated this as much as the rest of his little autocratic habits. I felt like his dog, panting to keep up and listen to instructions at the same time.

'Something to do with Mister snotty-film-critic, is it?' Bowman and Marik had met once or twice. The dislike had been instant and mutual.

'Something.' I jogged down the narrow treads after him. Two earlybirds for the next class had to squeeze aside on the stairs. I sketched a polite smile for them as we barrelled past. 'So, where are we going?'

'Rob says Kurt Heller's the man for black and white tats. I've seen his stuff, he's good. He's German, but he's lived here so long he's practic'ly an Amsterdammer. He's a doctor, does like charity clinics, goes out with the paramedics as a volunteer and stuff like that. The blokes in the fight scene call him the Horse Whisperer.'

'Oh, that's reassuring.' I shook my head in disbelief. The Horse Whisperer?

Marik's route to the lock-up where he kept his Harley-Davidson included a short-cut through an unpaved back alley. Stacks of boxes tottered under a roof of snow. Mounds of garbage-bags, rats that scrabbled and rustled. Half-frozen puddles of unidentifiable crud. I muttered fervent curses under my breath as water oozed through the hole in my boot. I hoped it was water.

'Hurry it up, girly.' Marik glanced back as we emerged on to a blank, ugly residential street, and set off at a smart clip. He grinned down at me as I caught him up, breathing through my nostrils. 'What's wrong, I thought you liked a bit of exercise?'

'I like lots of things,' I shot back. 'And look where it gets me. Six different kinds of crap on my shoes. Thanks a lot.'

'Come on, we're nearly there,' he said—unruffled as if I hadn't spoken—and strode ahead again. I had to scurry to keep up with him, cursing inwardly at my runaway mouth. Marik didn't have to be here. I was damn lucky to have been able to schmooze him into coming along on this wild goose chase and letting me off work into the bargain. And you're going to bitch at him? Right on as usual, Carlson.

❖

Suikerbakkerstraat was barely long enough to get the name-plates on the walls—the kind of nowhere side street that would look grimy and uncared-for even in summer. A clutter of neon signs overhead advertised everything from live sex shows to express pizza—or maybe it should be the other way around—posters peeled from vacant shop windows and rubbish blew underfoot. A cosmetic coating of snow and ice frankly didn't do enough for it.

The house Marik pulled up outside fitted right in. The stained brickwork was crumbling, and all the ground-floor windows were blanked with peeling black paint.

I waited for Marik to heave the Harley on to its stand, running fingers through my hair where it had been squashed by the helmet. 'Is this it?'

'Yeah,' Marik said, '—bit scruffy, isn't it? Hang on a sec.' He straightened from the bike, and pressed something on his key-ring. 'Fitted a proximity alarm,' he explained.

A stilted artificial voice said, *'Please stand clear of the vehicle. This is a warning.'* A heavy sizzling sound followed, suggestive of damaging voltage.

'You're joking,' I said after a second.

'Rocks, doesn't it?' Marik beamed fondly at the big bike, then swivelled in the snow, the glossy black helmet still dangling from one hand. 'Bought it yesterday, I mean seriously, it was worth every penny. Come on, let's get inside.' He shepherded me over to the door, and pressed a buzzer that I hadn't noticed. The typed label behind the yellowy Perspex panel read *KK TATTOO STUDIO.*

'This guy doesn't seem to go much on PR,' I muttered.

'Doesn't need to, love. Most of his business is word-of-mouth. Here we go.' The buzzer gave a loud click, and Marik pushed the door open with the flat of his hand. 'Open sesame.'

9

AT FIRST SIGHT, the tattoo studio wasn't the treasure-house that Marik's introduction suggested. There was a wall of cheap boarding just inside, a jerry-built lobby. A thumb-tacked gallery of polaroids—no faces, I noticed, but arms and legs and pecs, an impressive expanse of somebody's buttocks—all tattooed. I stepped further in, stamping snow off my boots, and saw a pinboard with *This Week's Specials, €10* written above it.

'What is this,' I whispered, 'a menu?' Marik peered over my shoulder at the three brightly-coloured designs thumbtacked to the board, and made a noncommittal face.

'Mm, nah, don't think I'll bother.'

Past the thin boarding, I could hear a machine whining over the high-energy chatter of a radio programme, and the murmur of a woman's voice.

'All right,' Marik said, and squeezed past me to go through the rough doorway first. 'Hiya, Kiki.'

I trailed him into the studio, feeling out-of-place. A ferociously-maned woman with a bold but unhandsome face that appeared to have been pierced in every place possible was bent hard at work over the rear end of her client, a sleek gamine entity with cropped fair hair and an unfortunate smattering of acne. It was the tattoo gun in the pierced woman's hand that made the dentist's-drill sound. She glanced up at Marik with a grin.

'Hi, Marik. Rob said you'd be coming by, how are you? Keeping that dragon clean?' Her hands, clad in white surgical gloves, continued to stroke the steel pen over the smooth skin of her client's hip with short, precise movements, colouring in the scales of what looked like a lizard. She wiped away the blood that beaded on the surface with industrial paper roll that she held wadded in her lap.

I realised I was staring, and gazed round the walls instead. There were hundreds of designs, a bizarre mosaic of daggers and skulls and roses and gothic lettering. I saw a unicorn, and a howling wolf's-head outlined against a full moon. There was a rash of small, delicate designs obviously targeted at women with somewhat less than two brain cells to rub together: hearts, flowers, bluebirds, butterflies, dolphins—even a little apple with a bite taken out. Yuck.

I stepped closer to the wall. The sheer compression of imagery into such a small space was trippy. Bugs Bunny winked rogueishly at me from the midst of a clutch of crucifixes. Snakes and bat-winged dragons shared space with bosomy mermaids and portraits of Arnold Schwarznegger. I swivelled on my heel: fighter planes, Taz blowing his trade mark raspberry, sea-horses. Crude death's heads and dribbly, sinister candles. Knives and guns, Betty Boop, yellow smiley faces and marijuana leaves. Some of the drawings were breathtakingly bad.

'Found anything you like?' Marik's voice at my side made me jump, and I shook my head with a quick grin, embarrassed by my absorption.

'Isn't he here?'

'Upstairs,' Marik explained. 'They live over the studio. Kiki just gave him a call, he'll be down in a minute.'

'He's down now.' Kiki slapped her customer on the undecorated buttock and thumbed her machine off. The noise dwindled. 'Greet, we'll finish this tomorrow, OK? Hold still—' She fixed a surgical dressing over the area with micropore tape. 'OK. Keep it clean, no tight clothing, you know the drill—' It certainly looked as if Greet would remember what to do: her arms were tattooed solidly from wrist to shoulder. The glimpse I got of her breasts as she hopped off the padded medical-style couch was of psychedelic fractal spirals curling round the flesh.

Kiki propped her gun in a tank of blue fluid and swivelled towards us again, stripping off her gloves, which she dropped into a yellow plastic bin marked *BIOHAZARD*. In contrast to her client, she didn't appear to have any tattoos at all, but the array of silver rings, chains and studs that decorated her face and ears were enough to make your average needle-phobic faint dead away. 'Go on through,' she said, and gestured with her chin towards a doorway at the rear, screened with a bead curtain. 'He's expecting you.'

The Horse Whisperer was waiting for us, seated at a small wooden kitchen table which was covered with a lacy white cloth. I'd been fantasising about Robert Redford in a cowboy hat, but Kurt Heller did not fit the fantasy.

He was smoking placidly, and smiled as we sat down opposite him. He was squat and powerful, with a shaved head and heavy drooping moustache dyed indigo blue. The voice growled, like a big cat.

'I see Rob's sending me pretty ones at last.' He gave me a piratical grin. He had odd, silvery-grey eyes that darted and danced and refused to take you seriously. His face was a mask of black, Maori-style tattoos. The ends of the blue moustache were braided. 'You must be the American girl he was telling me about, yes?'

'Yes,' I managed. 'Hi.'

'Kurt Heller,' the man said. 'Kiki's better half, uh. You have some drawings for me to look at?' His physical presence would have been intimidating. The stylised grimace of rage made his face enigmatic. I fumbled the wad of sketches from my inside pocket and handed them to him.

Heller's hands were hairy, the knuckles a line of clumsily-drawn blue stars. He saw me look at them, and grinned again, stubbing out his cigarette in a glass ashtray. 'My first try at tattooing. I was eighteen, in jail and bored to death. Did it with a pin and a bottle of ink.'

'Ah.' I nodded, feeling foolish, and indicated the papers. 'I, um, need to know if these are your tattoo designs. Marik's guy said you specialise in black and white tattooing.'

'Uh. Let's see, then.' Heller pulled off the rubber band and placed it on the table. He fumbled a pair of steel-rimmed pince-nez from his shirt pocket and placed them on the bridge of his nose, peering closely as he leafed through the papers. I watched him, trying to guess at his expression and failing.

Finally Heller sat back, one broad hand caressing the edges of the paper. With the other, he removed the pince-nez with a delicate, sleight-of-hand motion.

'Where did you get these?' His tone was light enough, but I heard the warning in it, and abandoned any ideas of lying.

'I was given them.' I gestured at the drawings. 'Are they yours?'

'Yes and no.' The grey eyes studied me without blinking, and I returned the stare with as much brass as I could muster.

'Sorry?'

'I am trying to figure you out, uh. You don't want me to tattoo these designs on you.' It was a statement. I shrugged.

'No.'

'Then I think to myself, why these designs? I have a very good memory, and I remember these. You get people come in all the time, they'll want the flash—the designs on the walls out there. I have quite a few bring a photo in, or a picture, and they want my take on it. You know, most people are content to allow me to be the judge. That's what they pay me for. But this guy wanted it exact, he was an artist and he knew what he wanted—this—' and the blunt fingers flicked through the papers, stabbed down on a brightly-coloured compass star ringed with swimming dolphins. '*This* I remember because it was the only coloured one I ever did for him. Right here,' indicating his barrel chest. 'He had me mix the colours specially, pig of a job. All the rest were mono—arms, shoulders, back—'

'Mono? Black and white?'

Heller inclined his head. 'Black and white, yes. I am wondering what you wanted with him.'

'I don't want anything with him.' I held out my hand for the drawings. Heller handed them over with a doubtful look. I snapped the rubber band round the sketches and stuffed them back into my coat, trying to sound businesslike. 'His name's Kris de Haan. He's in some kind of trouble. A mutual friend asked me to find him. That's all. The drawings were given to me by the friend. I thought they looked sort of like tattoo designs . . . ' I shrugged, '—so here we are. Have you seen him recently?'

'Yes and no.' Heller's grey eyes sparked at my look. 'I haven't done any work for him for maybe a year, bit less. That colour job was the last. He dressed well, seemed as if he could afford decent stuff. He had an ear stud done, I remember. Twenty-four carat sleeper, pricey. Always clean, always on time, not your average artist. Hard sort of guy, high expectations, uh.' He spread thick blue-patterned fingers, and the mask of his face wrinkled in an expression I belatedly read as astonishment. 'Then I don't see him, maybe for eleven month, twelve month.'

'And?' He was getting to something, but I was all out of patience. Under the table, Marik kicked the side of my foot. Heller dropped the theatrical face.

'Well,' he said, 'then last week I was out fixing the buzzer on the front door, and I saw him walking past, right out there.' My eyes swivelled fatuously to follow his gesture. 'But now he's dressed rough, his hair's longer, got a beard . . . looked like he'd been living on the street for a while. I'd say he has bad times, uh? Maybe you're right when you say he's in trouble.' He scratched behind the braided moustaches, thoughtful.

'Did you speak to him?' I had a dozen more questions waiting to spill out if that one came up trumps, but Heller was already shaking his head.

'No. I was busy, it was raining . . . No. He wasn't a friend, understand, just a client. Tell the truth, I was surprised to recognise him when he was so changed. Sorry I don't have any more help for you.' A shrug. 'If I see him again, I'll tell him you were asking. What's your name?'

'Robin Carlson—but he doesn't know me. Uh, tell him Bowman is worried about him. That's B, O, W, M, A, N.'

'Bowman is worried,' Heller repeated, and reached over to scribble the message on a scratch-pad beside the phone. 'OK. I'll look out for him, but I can't promise anything.'

'Thanks, anyway, it's a lot more than I'd hoped for. We'd better get out of your way,' I added as a hint for Marik, getting to my feet. 'And thanks again.'

'No problem, Robin. Any time, OK. You just shout.' Heller exchanged some kind of complicated buddy-buddy handshake with Marik, and showed us out.

It was snowing again, tiny powdery flakes wandering down out of an innocent dove-grey sky. I fastened the snap-buckle on my helmet, and clambered on to the Harley behind Marik.

What was De Haan playing at? Living on the street, Heller had said. Why didn't he just get in touch? Why the weirdo email? *Why do I keep asking so many dumb questions?* I grumbled, then had to grab round Marik's waist as he gunned the big bike away from the kerb.

I didn't take Bowman's fears seriously, even then, but how was I supposed to know?

A trembling against my ribs distracted me. I tugged at Marik's sleeve and yelled through my helmet, 'Hey, wait up! Phone!'

Marik pulled the bike up at the side of the street and waited, engine idling, while I rootled in my coat pockets, struggling to take off my helmet one-handed.

'Hello?'

'Robin?' It was Tom Barnabas.

'Tom, hi.'

'Kid, listen, I'm over at the University Hospital.'

'Hospital—?' Blank. Tom in hospital? 'Tom, are you OK? What's happened?—'

'Robin . . . ' Barnabas' tone was gentle. 'Cary Bowman was brought into the Emergency Room a couple of hours ago. He's in a pretty bad way.'

'Oh my God.' In my ear, Barnabas was saying, 'Robin, are you all right?' I swallowed an empty feeling.

'I'm OK. I . . . Tom, what—what happened? Is he sick?'

'Seems he was attacked,' Barnabas said. 'A car dumped him in the road outside the local police precinct. Listen, Birdy, where are you?'

'Uh . . . ' Marik was scowling a question at me. I flapped a hand at him *shut up!* and he threw up his arms and killed the bike's engine. I rubbed a hand over my eyes. 'I'm . . . um, somewhere off Nieuwendijk, I think . . . '

'OK. Can you meet me at the hospital? Get here OK?'

'Yeah, of course. But—' I was talking to a dialling tone. I lowered the handset from my ear. My skull buzzed. The snowy street around me seemed to have changed in some subtle way while I wasn't looking.

'What the hell was all that about? Hey,' Marik angled in front of me, arms folded, a dreadlocked genie. 'Robin? You all right? You look a bit funny.'

'It's, uh . . . I'm OK. Fine. I'm fine. It's Cary. He's been mugged or something . . . I have to go to the hospital.'

'Come here a minute.' Marik grasped me by the shoulders and steered me over to the side of the street. He stooped over me as if I had suddenly become infirm and a touch deaf. 'D'you want to go straight there? It's no sweat.'

'Yeah.' I nodded. My eyes filled with tears, and I smeared them away. 'I, I thought he'd just disappeared because we had a row, and all the time . . . '

'You weren't to know,' Marik stated. 'Come on, let's get you there.' He fastened the buckle on my helmet, and rapped his knuckles on the top. 'It'll be all right.'

I held on to him more tightly than usual during the ride to the University Hospital, and for once it wasn't just because he was driving too fast.

❖

There were fairy lights strung round the entrance to the Emergency Room. Barnabas met us just inside the door. He looked tired. 'You OK, Birdy?'

'I'm fine.' I tried to smile. There was a kid screaming blue murder just a few seats away, bright red blood soaking through the towel someone had wrapped round its arm. The mother was rocking it, making senseless shushing noises. Her eyes were blank with shock. I looked away sharply. 'Can we get out of here—I, uh, I mean . . . '

'Sure thing, kid. Come on.' Barnabas hooked one arm round my shoulders.

I hesitated, twisting my head to look back at Marik. 'Marik, thanks for bringing me . . . '

'Look, no sweat, all right? I'd better get back, let Sunny know what's going on.' Marik took the helmet out of my hand, and nodded at Barnabas. 'Look after her, eh.'

'Sure,' Barnabas said. 'Don't worry about it, I'll make sure she gets home later.'

Marik stared hard at him for a moment, then grinned and tugged my hair. 'Take care, all right?' He jammed his own helmet back on and strode off.

'Geez, you sure attract the protective types, don't you?' Barnabas tucked me closer against his side, apparently unaware of any irony, and led me away from the harsh lights and noises of the ER towards a quiet corridor. 'Down here.'

'Tom—' I pulled away from him. I hadn't been inside a hospital since—well, for as many years as I could arrange, let's say. The disinfectant taint in the air makes me nauseous. Too many memories mixed up in that smell. I licked dry lips. 'Tom, what happened?'

'They're not sure.' Barnabas shook his head. 'Like I said, he was dumped outside the police station down the road. I went over to check on his place, but there's no sign of a break-in. Guess he just got unlucky.'

'How bad is it?' I wondered how my lips and tongue could work when I couldn't feel them. Barnabas looked uncomfortable.

'It's not good, Birdy. The doctors had to sedate him. He's taken some kinda drug and it made him violent. He broke a nurse's arm.'

I stared at him for a second. '*Drugs?* But Cary doesn't do drugs, he despises that whole scene. I—I don't understand. Tom, he just *doesn't*—'

'Let's go see him.' Barnabas' face told me he thought I was being obtuse, but did not want to upset me further. I bit on my tongue, nodded and pushed my hands into my pockets. I shivered as I followed Barnabas' broad back down the corridor.

Barnabas waited outside the glass partition beside the nurses' station. All but one of the venetian blinds were shut, and the cubicle was dimly lit. The nurse who shepherded me inside kept a light grip on my sleeve. Her voice was hushed.

'Just to warn you. He's taken quite a bad beating, I'm afraid, and he's a little confused. That could be due to the drug he took. We can't tell what it is yet and it's having some unusual effects. We've had to restrain him to prevent him from injuring himself, and he's under sedation.'

My voice sounded too loud in my own ears. 'Why is it so dark in here?'

'Too much light distresses him,' the nurse said. 'Also loud noise, so please keep your voice low. The sedative should be wearing off now.'

We had reached the bedside, and the nurse moved out of the way to allow me to see.

'Oh no . . . ' I was barely aware that I had spoken out loud. My voice sounded quivery and small. In my coat pockets, my fingernails dug into the palms of my hands. The nurse's grasp on my sleeve tightened.

'Shh. It's all right.'

It was far from all right. I took in the sight of him in little vignettes of shock.

Bowman's face was distorted, one eye puffed shut. Purple and black bruises disfigured his jaw and cheekbones. His uninjured eye was half-open but there was no spark of intelligence in it. He did not seem to be aware of his surroundings. Clear tubes were taped across his cheek and vanished up his nose. Wires trailed from patches on his chest and ribs and throat to a bank of daunting machinery on the far side of the glassed-in cubicle. I stared at the screens and dials and tubes. For a second, memory had me in a choke-hold. I moved on with an effort of will.

The rails on the bed were up, and Bowman's wrists were secured to the steel tubing at his sides with Velcro, wrapped tight. More tubes ran from plastic cannulae in his hand and arm to an IV stand nearby. He was very pale.

'Cary . . . ?' I pressed the back of my hand to my mouth. Tears in my eyes again. The nurse squeezed my arm.

'It's not as bad as it looks. Go on, talk to him. He needs to hear your voice.'

'OK.' My voice seemed to have gone into hiding. I cleared my throat, and nodded. 'I—I can do that.'

'Good girl.' The nurse patted my shoulder and moved round to the opposite side of the bed to peer at the readings on the machinery there. I stepped up to the bedside, feeling foolish.

'Hi there.' Whispering again. I blew out my cheeks and sniffed. 'Uhm, I came as soon as Tom called me. It's Robin,' I added. No response. I shot a worried look at the nurse. The woman nodded at me.

'Just keep talking. He can hear you, I got a blip on the monitors when you spoke, see?' She pointed her biro at a spiky graph that spooled out of the front of one machine. 'You can hold his hand if you like,' she added, scribbling on a chart. 'You won't hurt him.'

'OK.' I waited until the woman had walked away, then slid my fingers round his, squeezed gently. 'Hey Bowman. Can you hear me?'

No change in the lax idiocy of his expression, but the fingers that touched mine moved, just a little. I pressed them harder, and leaned over him. 'Cary, come on, wake up. You have to tell me who did this to you.' There was a smear of blood at the corner of his mouth. His face was slack, sallow as if from long illness.

My heart squeezed painfully. 'Can't leave you alone for a second, can I? Some 'spot of bother'.' I wiped at the blood with a corner of tissue, and hesitated. 'I got the package,' I added in a whisper. 'Cary, you were right, De Haan's living on the street. He must have gone undercover after all. I talked to a guy who saw him less than a week ago. I, I don't know what to do—'

The bruised eyelid flickered. Bowman's mouth opened and shut, then he swallowed and said faintly, 'How did . . . ?'

He moved his head restlessly, as if plagued by invisible flies. I gripped his hand tighter. Relief swelled in my chest like a shot of pure oxygen. 'Cary . . . come on, wake up, talk to me, *please.*'

'Robin . . . ?' The tremor in his voice did it: I was on the edge of the bed, hugging him, choking on tears.

'How are you?'

He was trembling, but I heard the smile in his voice as he said, into my hair, 'That's . . . very English question. You do realise . . . I'm supposed to say . . . 'Fine, thanks'?'

'Yeah, right.' I pulled back to study his swollen, sweaty face. His one good eye was a dark hole. 'You look . . . awful. Really awful.'

'Thanks.' He looked too tired to even smile, but his gaze never left my face. His fingers gripped mine as if he was afraid to let go.

Up close, I realised that the darkness of his eye was an illusion: the green iris was still there, a fragile ring round a gaping black pit of pupil. His pale lashes flickered at my scrutiny.

'What?'

'Your eyes,' I whispered. 'You look stoned or something.'

'Wish I felt that good,' Bowman muttered fervently. He swallowed again with an effort. 'Tell . . . tell Kris he was right about Nemesis . . . can't imagine anybody off their chump enough . . . to want to feel like this . . . for fun.' He stopped, panting. I frowned.

'You mean De Haan? But—' Abruptly, I realised that I was speaking too loud, and lowered my voice. 'Cary, we didn't even find him yet. I—I don't understand . . . '

'They made it.' Bowman moistened his lips. 'Tell Artemis they . . . did it. Everything— everything . . . '

Is he even talking to me? I touched his cheek, appalled. 'You're in the hospital now, Cary. You got beaten up, the doctors are trying to help you.'

Bowman gave a humourless bark of laughter. 'Was . . . doctor . . . did this to me.'

'A doctor?' I leaned in close, ducked my head to intersect his wandering line of sight. 'Cary? Who did this to you? Who was it?'

'You know,' Bowman whispered. His good eye flickered white. 'Doctor . . . Do—'

'OK, OK. A doctor. I got it. You really are out of it, aren't you?' I shook my head in exasperation, and tucked a dangling strand of hair behind my ear. Behind the glass wall, Tom Barnabas was drinking coffee from a styrofoam cup and looking grim. I leaned close to Bowman's ear. 'Cary, listen, I got the stuff you left me. The papers and the key and everything. Tell me how I can help. You want me to find Kris de Haan, right?'

Bowman shut his eyes and leaned his cheek against my hand. His skin was hot to the touch. 'I'm sorry . . . sorry I couldn't tell you,' he said, fretfully. 'Just . . . not possible.' His tone sharpened. The one clear eye opened again, sought mine with a feverish intensity. 'Robin—Robin, they followed me—'

'What do you mean?' I stared at Bowman, perplexed. He was hyperventilating, a sheen of sweat on his face. A vein pulsed in his temple.

'They—they took me . . . yesterday, after I left . . . bloody stupid . . . Caught me on the hop.'

'What do you mean, they took you?' I tried to catch his eye, but he was too agitated. *Yesterday?* A nasty empty feeling crept into my belly. 'Cary—'

'. . .danger, Robin . . . ' Bowman craned up off the pillow, panting. 'They know. Understand? *Danger,*' he repeated earnestly.

'Sure, I understand. It's OK,' I soothed. Bowman stared past me, chest heaving. White showed right round the iris of his good eye.

'You can't . . . go back . . . *they* sent him—' His eyelid flickered. 'Mustn't . . . '

'Shhhhh. Shhh.' I pressed him back down with my hands on his shoulders. He was surprisingly strong.

'Not safe,' Bowman said listlessly, and moved his head on the pillow. His lashes drooped. 'Not—safe . . . '

'Cary!' I wanted to shake him back into lucidity. I groped for his hand and squeezed, hard. 'Cary, don't fade out on me.'

'Oh God . . . ' A quiver in his voice. The line of his mouth trembled. '—'m scared, Robin . . . going to die . . . '

'Shhh, don't be scared. You're not going to die. I'm here now.' I stroked his hair. It was damp with sweat. 'They're going to help you, Cary.'

'They don't have . . . what I need . . . ' Another pause. Bowman passed his tongue over his lips and swallowed, panting. 'Got to find Kris . . . Kris has it . . . '

'Has what? Cary, what are you talking about?'

'Look after the . . . Family Curse for me, Robin.' A random lucid spark. I shook my head. The signet ring was a part of him.

'No way, Bowman. You're going to be fine—'

'No.' He shut his eyes. 'Not.'

'I won't take it.' Tears threatened to choke me again. Bowman's fingers flexed against mine.

'Want you to have it—just in case,' he added as I started to shake my head. 'Please.'

I scowled at him. 'All right. But I'm only babysitting it, OK? I'll give it back to you when you're better.'

'Yes,' Bowman agreed. He sagged against the pillows, as if he had come to the end of something after great effort. 'Nurses . . . have it. Tell them I said it was OK.' Another, deeper flicker of the pale lashes. Bowman's voice dropped to a drowsy murmur. 'Be . . . careful, Rob'n . . . ' His hand in mine relaxed.

'I promise I'll be—' I stopped. He had drifted back into unconsciousness.

'I'll find the sons of bitches who did this to you,' I said softly. I rubbed my thumb across the lines on his palm and wondered which one was the lifeline. A bad train of thought to get on to. I clasped his hand in both of mine instead. 'I swear I'll find them, Cary. Swear.' Not very eloquent, as declarations of war go, but soldiers generally leave that side of things to politicians.

I leaned over and kissed Bowman on the forehead. The numbing antiseptic stink made it impossible to smell the cinnamon-and-salt aroma of his skin. Just one more thing they took away from me.

I unlaced my fingers from his and straightened up. The quiet imperturbable noises of the machinery across the room went on.

I drew a deep breath, and walked out to where Barnabas waited for me.

❖

I closed my apartment door and sagged, blowing out what felt like a week of pent-up breath and blessing whatever emergency had prompted Tom's employers to call him away so suddenly. His clumsy solicitousness made me want to reach for my gun. But he'd gone when the phone-call came, threatening grievous bodily harm if I wasn't ready and waiting when he came to pick me up for our weekly dinner-date tomorrow.

'Family,' I muttered through lips numb from smiling, and pushed myself upright. I was going to take a long, hot bath.

❖

Forty-five minutes later, I put down the cellphone and stretched out my left foot to twirl the hot tap. Steam plumed up, and I drew my feet back from the sudden influx of boiling water.

It had been all I could do to stop Sunny coming over on the spot. Marik had gone straight home from the hospital and she'd had time to work up a fine head of steam by the time I called. I managed to persuade her that a quiet evening in would do the most good. If I ever got one.

I stared at the moisture-spotted ceiling and practised deep breathing while the tide of scalding heat crept and eddied around my body. So many things to think about. Bowman, and the key, the whole damn weird thing with Kris de Haan . . . it was like trying to do logic puzzles in your head, I couldn't hold on to all the slippery threads at once. However I shuffled the information, nothing made sense. I needed something new, something from outside the loop of data I already had.

Something from outside the loop. I sat up with a jerk. Water slopped over the side of the bath. One of those Archimedes moments, I guess.

I climbed out, grabbed a towel to wind around myself, rubbing perfunctorily at my wet hair. The air seemed colder than ever after the hot water. My feet left dark prints to the door.

Wet hand into jacket pocket. Tissues clung to my fingers. Cookie crumbs. The cold little brass key with its enigmatic label.

The card. I pulled it out and turned it over, brushing off tendrils of wet tissue. *Tekno-G. Gabriel.*

I sat on the wooden toilet seat and dialled the number quickly, before I could chicken out.

'Yes?' A man's voice.

My heart jumped: he'd picked up right on the first ring. My tongue suddenly felt like a strip of Velcro. I swallowed with difficulty.

'I, um, need to speak to Gabriel.'

'What do you want?' The voice flat, cautious. I clawed the hand with the card through my dripping hair. Cold droplets spattered on to my back and made me shiver.

'I don't know, I—look, I need to talk to Gabriel. He asked me to tell a friend of mine to call him.'

'Robin?' Gabriel's voice, startled out of hiding. 'What the hell's going on? Didn't you pass the message on to Cary? I told you it was urgent.'

'Cary's in hospital,' I said. 'He's been hurt.'

'*What?*' Gabriel recollected himself. 'What happened?'

'He was beaten up and dumped outside a police station,' I said. 'The hospital say he's been doing drugs, some stuff they don't recognise. He's really sick.' I took a shaky breath. 'Look, Gabriel, Cary didn't do drugs. I told them that at the hospital but I could see they didn't believe me. He turned up at my place Friday night and he was scared, he wouldn't say what of. He didn't want to go back to his place. And he said he had to find someone, a Dutch guy—'

'I know,' Gabriel cut in. 'He called me from your flat. Look, Robin, how much did he tell you about the project?'

'I—what?' I floundered. 'He never mentioned any project, he just asked me to help him find this guy De Haan.'

'I think we'd better meet.' Gabriel said.

It was only after I put the phone down that I realised what I'd done. I wanted to bite my tongue off. I'd said that Cary *didn't* do drugs. As if he was already dead.

10

AS I LET the café door swing to behind me, I noticed a snowflake melting on my glove.

If there was such a thing as a scale of brown-café-ness, *De Stuiver* would be towards the beige end. This meant that the floor was parquet instead of lino scattered with sand, and the tables were draped with small faded Turkish rugs instead of a scattering of beermats. After the crisp night air outside, the thick auburn mist of beer and tobacco smoke was like walking into a wall of warm water. I breathed deeply of it and felt myself begin to thaw from the inside.

Most of the tables were taken and there was a constant muted hullabaloo of voices. A radio behind the bar played tinny jazz. It was comforting and ordinary.

Gabriel was waiting for me in a wooden booth near the kitchens. His mane of carroty hair was held back with a twist of copper wire, and he was dressed in an Army surplus greatcoat instead of satin and velvet, but he still wore shades indoors, and the goatee beard and the smile were the same. 'Robin, hi. I got you a beer, is that all right?'

'Sure.' I sat, and blinked at the round goblet of frothy brew. I clasped my bag on my lap. 'Look . . . uh, would you mind telling me why we're here?' I twined the bag strap through my fingers and it snagged on the Family Curse. I twisted the signet ring between finger and thumb, rubbing the smooth metal as if I could conjure a wish-granting genie. The unfamiliar weight of it clunked on my hand like an iron manacle. I remembered that Cary worried at it all the time when it was on his finger, like a child picking at a half-healed scab. The habit seemed to have transferred to its new owner.

'You want to help Cary,' Gabriel said. He had bony spatulate fingers with bulbous ends, like a tree-frog, and he fiddled incessantly with his immediate environment while he talked. 'Maybe I'd better explain our involvement for a start. Tekno-G . . . well, we're kind of a group now. Started off just as friends, we're all hackers of one sort or another, come from all over the place, mostly the US and Europe—' (Tidy crumbs into a zigzag, scatter and reform them into a spiral.) 'There was one of us in London, Cassandra.' Not fiddling at all suddenly, and I registered the past tense with a jab of understanding, just as he was saying, 'She was a club queen, Cassy. Used some stuff—we all do, E mostly—but there were people with her who'd swear it wasn't E she took the night she died.'

'I'm sorry . . . ' It was clumsy, and I wished I hadn't said anything. Gabriel shrugged it off, while arranging the salt and pepper shakers in a more pleasing pattern.

'Cass died almost two years ago. There was a big scare on the club scene around then, don't know if you'd remember it. Big public outcry, police warnings on the telly, all that crap.' Difficult to tell if he was looking at me; I couldn't see his eyes behind the ultra-dark sunglasses, and as he was sitting half turned away, he appeared to be talking to my left shoulder. I don't think I'd realised before how annoying shades could be.

'It was on CNN,' I said. 'The cops in the States were all geared up to nip any dealing in the bud, but it never happened. Wasn't it called Mach2 or something?'

'Mach5,' corrected Gabriel. 'Pretty nasty synthetic compound. Pretty bloody ingenious too, not your average street drug at all. Way too sophisticated. There was another one you might remember. OmegaBomb, it was called. Went the rounds in Glasgow a few months previously. Same basic story. New drug appears, free samples. Take one of these, you could dance non-stop for a week, but that was just scratching the surface. These substances were way too complex to be recreational drugs. We think they were released on to the streets as a test measure.'

'Test—?'

'White mice, guinea pigs,' Gabriel nodded at me rapidly, and balanced a sugar cube on top of the salt cellar. 'You know. As in *laboratory test*. When OmegaBomb appeared, the hospitals in Glasgow post-mortemed all the victims for the local fuzz, but when Mach5 turned up and the London police called Glasgow up to compare notes, the path reports were gone.' Another cube on top of the first. I raised my eyebrows.

'They lost the autopsy reports?'

'Well, it looked that way, but when the Met finished its own reports for the Mach5 victims, they disappeared too. By the time it came to light, it was too late to redo the tests, so the whole thing was written off. There were no further deaths, the stuff had vanished off the street. The case was dead as the proverbial Dodo.'

'I don't understand what this has to do with Cary,' I said, after a short pause in which Gabriel added two more lumps to the sugar tower. It was leaning a fraction to the right.

'We—Tekno-G, I mean—employed him to find out some stuff for us,' the Irishman said. 'We can handle the electronic side of things, but we needed someone who could be our eyes and ears in the real world. One of us had met Bowman a few times socially, heard a few things about him.'

I sipped at my beer. 'How did you find out he was a PI? Cary isn't exactly forthcoming about his personal life.'

'Police records,' Gabriel said, and grinned. I lowered the glass from my lips.

'*Criminal* records?'

'Sure. We ran a background check. Mister Bowman spent two years in Wormwood Scrubs detained at Her Majesty's pleasure. Soon as he got parole he shipped out here and I don't think he's ever been back.'

'Prison?' My mouth was hanging open. I shut it.

'Yeah.' Gabriel straightened the sugar tower. 'He was a good PI, from what I could find out, but he was a lousy judge of women. He fell for this girl he was supposed to be investigating—fraud, I think—anyway, it was pretty damn messy. Two cops got killed before the end of it.'

'You don't think—'

'Nah, he didn't kill 'em,' Gabriel said. 'He was charged as an accessory, got off pretty light. But his computer records let us track him. Devilish little bloodhounds that we are. We got an old acquaintance of his from London to call in some pretty heavy favours. He took the job.' He dismantled his sugar-lump tower, and popped one cube into his mouth. He sucked it for a few seconds, staring at me over the tops of his dark glasses. Finally, he seemed to reach some kind of decision.

'Artemis reckons that Mach5 and OmegaBomb were just stepping stones on the way to something else. Whoever was manufacturing the stuff was making damn sure they kept the whole deal at arms' length, and they went to a lot of trouble to make it look like amateur night. But whoever lifted those records from the police did it real professional. And those drugs didn't come from any kitchen-sink lab.'

Artemis. I gazed at Gabriel blankly, snatched straight back to this afternoon, and Bowman's low, gasping voice: *Tell Artemis they . . . did it. Everything—everything . . .* I blinked, and drank a mouthful of beer to cover my confusion. It tasted like dishwater suddenly. 'Sorry. Uh . . . stepping stones. What to?' I didn't really care; I just wanted a breathing space. Gabriel obliged.

'They were too complex to be street drugs. I mean, most of the crap that you can get in the clubs is one active substance, right? If you're lucky. But these were a whole bunch of chemicals spliced together. Synthetic alkaloids, some pretty weird-looking hormone derivatives. There was even a psychoactive or two in there, we know they were trying to design some kind of psych element called PSA—that's one of the only pieces of hard data Bowman got out to us—but we don't know what it is. Complicated stuff, anyways. Dangerous stuff,' he added with a wry face. 'Even if you forget the psych bit. A designer drug that jacks up the whole body system—muscles, nerves, brain activity.' He peered over the tops of his glasses again. 'Now you tell me, Robin. Where would you find a customer for a drug like that? Who needs strength, stamina, speed?'

'Hell, I don't know.' I shrugged. I hate guessing games. 'Athletes?'

'Not athletes. Closer to home. Think about it,' Gabriel instructed.

I didn't need to think about it. Anger made my voice small and tight. 'The military? How in the hell do you know that's close to home, huh? Did you do a background check on me, too?'

Gabriel ignored the jibe. 'We're talking about military-spec designer drugs. I think the current jargon is 'battlefield pharmacology'.'

I shook my head in disgust. 'You seem to know an awful lot about me, so you'll know I grew up as an Army brat. And I know this: the military wouldn't farm out something this sensitive when they could develop it themselves, in perfect secrecy.'

'Credit 'em with a bit of sense,' Gabriel said. 'Nothing's ever really secret, not for long. Even the military have to think about politics these days. No democratic country wants to be caught dead mucking about with designer drugs, especially ones as dangerous as these. It's called plausible deniability.'

'Someone else takes the risks for them.'

'Bingo.' Gabriel pointed his finger at me like a gun. 'If something like this drug is already in use—say in guerilla warfare, mercenary troops, that kind of thing—the big countries will be able to hold up their lily-white hands in horror at such an obscenity. Then they bow to the inevitable and—Bob's your uncle, Fanny's your aunt—they've got what they wanted and more to the point they have a clear conscience about it . . . publicly, anyway, which is the only thing that counts to them.'

'I came here to talk to you about Cary Bowman. Are you telling me that someone's dosed him with—what? Mach5?'

'Something different,' Gabriel said. 'Something new. That was just a stepping stone, remember? Nemesis is the real thing, the killer app—'

'*Nemesis?*' The name made me flinch. I scowled at my beer, mind racing. How far could I trust this guy? How far had Cary trusted him? Damn it, I had no time, I had to find out what these people knew. I took a sip of beer to undo the knot in my throat. 'Cary, uh, gave me a message for Artemis.' I looked at Gabriel. 'You can get a message to her?'

''Course. Go on.' Gabriel took his dark glasses off. Naked, his hazel eyes were watery and almost comically unthreatening. I moistened my lips.

'It's not much. He said to tell Artemis that they had done it—don't know who *they* were, he didn't say—uh . . . they'd done it—sorry if this isn't making sense, he was pretty hazy—then he said 'everything'.' I shrugged, embarrassed by how lame it sounded. 'That's it. Mean anything to you?'

'Yes,' Gabriel breathed. His Adam's-apple bobbed. 'Oh, sweet baby Jesus, they did it.'

'Who did what?' I was regretting telling him already.

'They're ready to go,' Gabriel said. He jammed the dark glasses back on to his face, agitated. 'Back in April when we first got wind of this, they were stalled because they couldn't develop an essential component. They've done it, they've cracked it. Damn.' He shook his head, and drained the last of his beer in one gulp. 'I'd better be getting back. Artemis has got to know about this *now*.'

'Hey, wait a second!' I grabbed his wrist to keep him in his seat. 'You can't just leave. What—what about Cary? He said that the hospital didn't have what he needed. What did he mean?'

117

There was a long pause. The noise of people talking washed over us as we sat silent. Normal conversations about football and the weather and somebody's girlfriend's tits. Laughter, and the clink of glasses. It all seemed to be happening on another planet.

'There's a second drug,' Gabriel said eventually. 'Nemesis is addictive, right? And we suspect that it's cumulatively toxic. When I said they were stalled—they were developing something else—an antidote, I guess you'd call it. Maybe more like a vaccine. Something that can remove the Nemesis toxins from your system and nullify the addictive components. That was what Bowman meant. That's what he needs.'

I leant forward. Under the table, my fists were clenched.

'What happens if he doesn't get it?'

'We're not sure,' Gabriel hedged.

'Take a guess,' I snapped. Gabriel flinched.

'Nothing good. I'm sorry.'

Toxins. My mind had snagged on the word. 'Cary said I had to find Kris de Haan. He said that he had something—maybe De Haan has this antidote.'

'De Haan went missing months ago,' Gabriel pointed out. 'He's most likely dead.'

'He's not dead,' I said. 'Damn it, Gabriel, you got Cary into this, it's your responsibility to get him out. You've got to help me find De Haan, before—' Dread, like a lead weight in my chest. Gabriel looked away.

'I'm sorry.' He stood up again, awkward. 'Look, we're doing our best, all right?'

I wanted very badly to grab him by the front of his coat and yell *But your best isn't good enough, is it?*

Instead, I sat clutching my beer glass, and watched him leave.

I don't believe in omens, as a rule. It's not a coincidence that they put the horoscopes next to the cartoons in the newspapers, you know. But that slip I'd made earlier, combined with what Gabriel had just told me . . .

No. I clenched my fist over the Family Curse. *I made a promise.* I was going to find Kris de Haan if I had to turn Amsterdam upside down and shake it till all the whores fell out of their windows and the canals spilt water on the floor.

I'd find him, and then we'd all live happily ever after. Or something.

❖

What have they done?

Wolf looked at the dark flowing past his window and bit down on panic till his jaws ached.

Under him, the tram bumped and swayed. Wolf pressed himself into the corner of the seat, screwing his eyes shut. Slick bulging colours ringed and quivered around everything. Even with eyes closed, his vision swarmed with bright motes and sparks of colour that made his nerves cringe.

What have they done to me?

His legs were numb and heavy from his aimless running, soaked to the thighs with melted snow. He smelt blood, sharp like tin, matting in his coat. He had scrubbed his hands clean in a drift and his fingers were pink-white, raw with cold.

He wasn't sure of the time. Common sense told him it must be sometime before midnight or there wouldn't be a tram to ride in.

He'd been crossing the road near the huge flat sheet of the Slotermeer when the stinging clang of the tram came behind him. The driver had cocked a jaundiced eye at his agitated state but he hadn't told him to get off. Now Wolf leaned his face against the chill plane of glass and tried to slow his breathing, hardly able to believe that he had escaped. If he had.

He could see the Frenchwoman's face even through the pyrotechnics in his mind. She lingered like a pain in his head: a cruel angel, mercurial, deceitful, smiling. *Tendre Poison.* Her hands flourished sharp needles, wings folded secretively in her sleeves. The wide steady gaze of her eyes, a mouth like some painted icon of the Madonna, small and perfect and recurved in a tiny sardonic smile like a steel-strung bow. Just as dangerous.

Wolf shut his eyes, feeling sick again.

It had happened so fast, there had been nothing he could do.

The gamble seemed to have paid off. It had been almost funny, seeing the Black Coats scurry backwards as they advanced up the corridor towards the lift. Wolf edged into the lift cage, still clasping the Frenchwoman to his chest as if she was his best friend—in the circumstances, she probably was. The American, Mulder, was closest.

'You're not going to make it. We'll get you.' That hot little wick of sadism glowed up in his pouchy brown eyes. Wolf bared his teeth past the doctor's small pink ear.

'You can't stop us.'

'What do you plan to do with her?'

'I'll turn her loose when we're well away,' Wolf said. 'Now punch in the code.'

'No—' In Wolf's arms, the doctor stiffened in alarm.

'Shut up. You!' Wolf jerked his chin at Mulder. 'Do it.' The man reached out and pressed the buttons, lips compressed and eyes averted as if he was being forced to perform an obscene act in public. Wolf hitched his arm a touch higher. 'Now back off.'

The lift doors slid shut on a mute gallery of taut, reproachful faces. The cage jolted against the side of the shaft, and started to move upwards. Wolf sagged in relief. The doctor spat something with a lot of savage 'r's in it.

'Jan, we did it!' Maartje lowered the Uzi and took a step towards him, smiling in relief.

That was when the speck appeared near the base of the right-hand lift door. A tiny hole, no bigger than a dried pea.

Maartje uttered a choked-off sound. The gun dropped from her fingers. Something dark sprayed from the back of her white doctor's coat and made a random pattern of dots on the carpeted wall and the mirrors.

Wolf had stood there like an idiot. Maartje staggered sideways, a look of surprise on her face. The doctor shrieked in French and tried to bite Wolf's arm.

He clouted her hard enough to make her sit down, and left her whimpering in the corner. Maartje had fallen to the floor. There was blood everywhere.

When Wolf lifted her up and cradled her in his arms, he found out why. The bullet had made another neat, pea-sized hole just under her right breast, and wasted its force blowing a fist-sized hole in her spine. There was no time for any pain. Wolf felt the paralysing numbness in his own body and knew what it meant.

Maartje died before they reached the ground floor—just a flicker of the long lashes and she was gone, quick and quiet as a little bird. Wolf touched her closed eyes with his fingertips, just once. Her skin was already cold.

He had thrown up, he recalled. Outside in the snow, staggering and retching like a drunk, repulsed by the hot slaughterhouse stench of her blood on his hands and clothing.

There were two black cars parked in front of the derelict building. Wolf pried up their bonnets with a piece of steel piping and wrenched free any number of important-looking bits of metal. He threw them as far as he could. Smears of sticky blood on the pristine paintwork.

Then he ran away. They would be after him. Clever black bloodhounds on his trail.

A jerky clanging. Wolf's eyes sprang open as the tram lurched. He peered out, clinging to the back of his seat. They were just turning on to the wide white line of Overtoom across a black ribbon of water. More traffic, cars and buses crawling down parallel tracks of grey-black ploughed through the snow. Over the roofs to his right, he could see tree-tops, and side streets slatted him glimpses of snow-covered benches and trash cans, white-mounded grass and wrought-iron. The Vondelpark.

He swung into the aisle, finger jabbing at the nearest call button. Twenty metres. The tram was slowing. Wolf walked to the doors. Ten metres.

Wolf hit the button and jumped out as soon as the doors were wide enough. He looked back at the tram as it pulled away. The driver was scowling at him.

Wolf turned to his right and jogged down to the narrow slot of Kattenlaan, shaking his head. Getting the terrors over nothing. Surely he'd lived with nightmares long enough to know better than this?

He slowed to a walk. The sky was clear above the crowding roofs, stars dimmed into a milky blur by the city glow. Only the swollen moon watched over him, a baleful, cataracted eye.

Wolf thought of the Frenchwoman's blue-grey eyes, and balled fists inside his pockets with a shiver. He had almost lost it tonight when Maartje died, had almost stayed there with the doctor and let them take him. And that had been real.

Reality could be a problematic concept, he thought. He felt vividly alive. He was warm, hot even, and the heavy feeling in his muscles was gone. He felt strong, tireless— and utterly confused.

Maybe I really am crazy, maybe I'm . . . I'm a bank clerk, or a brewery worker, maybe I work in a cookie factory—I got food-poisoning and I'm safely tucked up in a hospital bed, and I'm dreaming all this.

Hell of a long nightmare, he added.

At the end of the little street, the park was a broad, abstract canvas behind its railings: winter shells of trees and shallow curves of paths and empty flowerbeds, soft shapes of snow with hard edges.

Wolf hauled himself up by the gateway and kicked clumsily off the slippery metal to land on all fours in the snow. His breath glittered in an iridescent cloud about his head. He clambered up and hurried down the blank white line of the first path, away from the incriminating glare of street lights.

He wanted quiet and dark, and above all, no people. Not many stuck it out in the parks in winter, and the police were mostly happy to let alone the ones that did, provided they kept away from the buildings and didn't abuse the animals.

Wolf headed south on the lake path. Nobody else was about. The snowfall he'd run through hours ago lay here in a pristine layer a couple of inches deep, and made funny little grunting noises under his boots as he walked. There was nothing to be done about footprints, but he'd feel safer when he was down in the dark slice of shrubs and trees past the end of the lake.

A swarm of dizziness overtook him and he squatted down beside a white-striped bench, clutching the wooden slats for support. Snow melted under his hand and ran down inside his sleeve. The bench was cold and solid. His handprint was a vivid black starburst interrupting the neat white parallel lines.

Somewhere, he remembered a girl's voice asking him *do you dream in colour?* Questions like that always used to make him angry, they teased at him from the far side of a closed door. Pity she wasn't here now, Wolf thought, because hand on heart, he could have said—Yes, including some colours that don't even have names.

He looked at them with a new disbelief as he walked.

The snow was a jigsaw of white light, black shadows, all lit luminous at the edges with crystalline rainbows, glass-sharp splinters of colour that rolled and broke like the never-ending splay of surf on a beach.

He found a dry place in the centre of a rhododendron bush and lay down, curling around his pain. The rank loamy scent of earth and rotting leaves surrounded him.

In an odd way, after the chemical stinks of the Hole, it was reassuring. Wolf lay for several seconds gazing at the green-lit hollow while he breathed in and out. The clamour of mind and body quieted a little, enough for him to realise that he was shivering again.

The collar of the coat, turned up, warmed his face. He closed his eyes, grateful. Traffic was a distant, intermittent grumble. He could hear music, magnified by water and ringing frost—some classical stuff that tinkled in faded spurts and conjured pictures in his mind of spindrift tumbling over swollen green-white Atlantic waves. He fell asleep with the music moving in his head.

❖

He knew immediately that it was a dream. It must be a dream because when the man lifted his arm to point at him, he saw the black eye of the gun spit fire—damn big black eye, and the spark like a wink—saw the bullet streak towards him out of the dark, a small bright fingertip. It punched him backwards into the brick wall.

Yes, it had to be a dream: you don't see it coming, not like that.

There was no pain yet. He watched his body fall and felt nothing except the jarring cold blow as his head hit the concrete. His camera was gone. He heard it clatter on the rubble but he could not turn his head to see.

Someone was making desperate, bubbling noises. It took a second to realise that it was him. His mouth was full of something warm and wet and salty. Sticky warmth spread up his spine.

They just don't make the quality of air these days. It was thick and cold and hurt his teeth, like those little lightning-strikes in an ad for sensitive toothpaste.

His eyes seemed to be fixed open as if he was a roving reporter and they a sort of futuristic stereo camcorder. He remembered reading something like that in a science fiction book. Gibson—yes, he was sure that was right. A girl with Zeiss Ikon eyes. Maybe this was a sequel. Murder, from our on-the-spot correspondent.

He moved the camcorders in a jerky arc and wished he hadn't. Everything was upside-down—scabby brickwork and half-demolished floors, all going up and up at angles that made him feel sick.

Sky up there, through the criss-cross rafters. Pale blue as a bird's egg. It was almost morning. Trash compactors growled and whined in the street outside.

Voices clattered around his head.

'Is he dead?' Hands pulled at his clothing, and someone grabbed his face with cold fingers. He gagged. The hands released him with an expression of disgust.

'Ach, he's spitting blood. Why didn't you take a head shot. Nice and simple.'

'What, brains all over the place? Huh, no thanks. Ah, he'll be dead soon enough, what—you think he's in a hurry?' A foot nudged his leg. The voices swelled and faded in the chilly shadows, and one of them laughed.

He smelt the sour ash as one of them dropped a smouldering cigarette butt and ground it out with his heel. It conjured things in his head: the stiff spiky skyline of Amsterdam. A smell of tobacco smoke and autumn rain in the elms.

Elms all dead now. Sycamores and limes instead, they smelt different. Sweet and bitter.

Snotty bloody Rotterdammer Erasmus, wasn't it, who said Amsterdammers lived like rooks in the tops of the trees.

Rooks, or crows? Crows, or rooks? It bothered him fleetingly that he couldn't remember.

Steps echoed. A new, deep voice spoke—a dry, clipped drawl that silenced the breathy chuckles of the other men.

'Strip him. We'll put him in the canal.' He remembered that this place had loading doors that opened directly on to the water. He could taste the wet salt tang of it in his mouth already—or perhaps it was the blood.

The shocked absence of pain did not last. They rolled him onto his side carelessly, as if he was meat. His voice betrayed him into a whimpering moan.

They were efficient. They took everything, even down to the wedding band that he still wore, and the gold ring in his ear. There was a short but heated debate about his tattoos.

The pain when they hoisted him to his feet was indescribable. Only the crazy weakness stopped him screaming. His legs gave way. They had to more or less carry him over to the loading doors. By the time they lowered him to the ground they were panting and swearing.

Everything looked clear, but distant, as if seen through the wrong end of a telescope. His cheek was pressed against the rough pebbled concrete of the door sill. His horizon was crowded with feet and legs. The men's voices had dimmed to a muffled burring, a radio play heard from another room.

He was cold, despite the warm air. His innards trembled. They were killing him. They were going to dump him in the diesel-tainted waters of the canal and let it finish the job for them.

Detached somewhere, a familiar voice told him that there was too much blood, he would be too weak to swim far, if at all. He wondered how long it would take for him to drown, and whether it would hurt.

The forest of legs shuffled and parted. Someone bent over him.

A broad, hawkish face stared into his. The muscles along the man's jawbone were tense, twitching. Someone had turned the sound right off. There was just this white-noise hiss, right on the edge of hearing.

The man had sharp eyes, blue as chips of sapphire. They were creased into a hundred smiling lines at the corners. They evaluated you. *Are you going to die now and save us the trouble of drowning you? Huh?*

Light fell over them. Doors were pushed open with a squeal of protesting metal. Close by his head, water slopped placidly.

Something broke, crushed into powder under the calm pressure of the man's gaze. Dizzy fumes of panic in his throat. His eyes welled chilly tears that ran down on to the hand that gripped him. Names . . . there were no names in his head. Nothing. His lips quivered against the other man's fingers, but no words came out.

Just a few seconds ago, he had been—had been *someone*. The fear almost made him sick. He heard his own voice sobbing, 'No, no please I can't—I can't—' but the hands released him. The words choked on the blood in his throat. The man rose and walked away without a backward glance, wiping his blood-smeared hands on a clean white handkerchief.

'Do it.'

They lifted him by legs and arms, hoisted him up between them, swung him like a sack.

A fleeting moment of vision as he fell. The black waters of the canal rushed towards him like a wall. The morning sky swivelled above like a fairground ride and flew into splinters of coloured light.

He hit with a splash that thundered in his head, and sank.

And of course drowning did hurt, a lot. But not as much as the screaming grey absence in his head.

❖

Wolf woke with a start and found frost on his eyelashes. Dirt and bits of twig dug into his cheek. He sat up, shivering and stiff. He could not feel his hands or feet at all.

The traffic-noise had swelled into a steady roar. There was a streak of dull grey behind the zigzag of roofs to the east. Wolf squatted on the iron-hard ground and stuck his hands into his armpits to try to coax some feeling back into them.

Ever since the hospital, he had never been able to recall a dream, not a single image; and now this. The maze was breaking down.

Last night. It crept back to him. The Hole—that bitch of a doctor—and Maartje. Maartje dead. Pete dead too, rubbed out like a bookmaking error.

Wolf sat with his head in his hands then and cried for sheer self-pity. The tears and the puny trembling of his chin surprised him by hurting his pride. He hadn't thought he had any left. *It just goes to show.* But for once, even sarcasm did not do the trick.

Wolf pressed his hands together in front of his face and the warm tears ran down his fingers. *Sweet Jesus, is this how it's going to be? I'm going to die, shot or poisoned or drowned like a bloody kitten, and I don't know why, or who my killers are or even who I am . . . ? Please God, no. I don't want to go like this, not knowing. Please . . .*

'Not like this. Please.'

So it's true that everyone comes to it, Wolf thought with a stab of black humour. Prayer, muscling in like a failsafe mechanism. Damned unruly impulse.

Question is, he thought, if God is just a toothache of the psyche, what does one have to extract to make Him go away? He found that he was laughing into his cupped hands, a shaky honking that subsided into giggles and coughing. Silly really; it hadn't been that funny. A different kind of release.

Wolf frowned at the earth between his feet. He had to do something sensible before they caught him. Yes. He should go to the cops. The police would know what to do, they'd protect him. He would wait until it was light, then he would present himself at the nearest police station and tell them everything. That was sensible.

God, I need a cigarette. He fumbled in his coat pocket. No lighter.

Wolf sank back down on his haunches and occupied himself by trying to blow smoke-rings with his own breath. Hurry up and wait. Some things never change.

11

THE POLICE STATION was warm inside, and quiet, with an institutional smell of floor polish and cigarettes.

Wolf took a deep steadying breath as the double doors swung to behind him. He had walked past the place three times before he got up the nerve to come in.

'Yes?' The woman sitting behind the high counter on the far side of the lobby looked up from her newspaper. Shiny dark hair and brown eyes, minimal make-up. She wore a police uniform. Sergeant's stripes. Wolf stuttered.

'I—I—' His bad eye flickered and he rubbed at it, swallowed and tried again. 'I want to report a murder.'

'A murder?' The desk Sergeant slid her newspaper aside and picked up a pen.

'Two murders,' Wolf amended. The policewoman raised one sleek brow. Wolf licked his lips, and repeated, 'two.'

'Everything all right here, Sergeant Gonggrijp?' A bulky man in a white uniform shirt poked his head round a door behind the counter. The policewoman cast a grateful look at him.

'This gentleman claims to have witnessed two killings, sir.'

'Not witnessed,' Wolf corrected. 'I—well, I—I saw one, the girl. Maartje Rijk. They shot her.'

'Shot . . . her,' murmured the woman, scribbling. Wolf glanced at the older man and found himself under close scrutiny.

'How about the second victim?'

'No, she was the second one.' Wolf blinked, confused. 'Maartje was the second one.'

'Who was the first?' The officer leaned on the desk. He had the shiny, worn look of old furniture. 'Before Marni—'

'Maartje,' Wolf muttered. He collected his scattered wits. 'The first . . . uh, the first victim was called Pete. Peter Susskind, he was an American citizen.'

'And did they shoot him too?'

Wolf floundered, thrown by the question. 'I—don't know. Maartje said they killed him . . . '

'Did you see the body?' pursued the policeman.

'No,' Wolf admitted. This wasn't how the conversation had gone in his imagination. 'No, but—'

'So it's only hearsay.'

'You're not listening to me.' Wolf took a step towards the desk, breathing hard. 'My friends are dead, I would be dead too if I hadn't escaped. I need help.'

'Ye-es,' agreed the policewoman after a pause. Wolf saw the sceptical look in her eye.

'You think I'm crazy.' Wolf ran his hands through his hair. His fingers trembled. 'Look, at least take a statement, check out the names. I can give you descriptions . . . please,' he said helplessly. 'I'm telling the truth.'

'Give me the names,' the policeman said after a short pause. He looked irritated and weary. 'I'll run 'em through the computer, see what comes up, we can't say fairer than that, can we?'

'Thank you,' Wolf said. He closed his eyes for a second. 'Thank you.'

'The names?' prompted the woman. Wolf opened his eyes.

'Maartje Rijk, that's R, i, j, k. And Peter Susskind—'

'Two esses?' inquired the man, jotting on a scratchpad.

'Yes,' Wolf said. 'He was an American.'

'Address?'

'No—uh, n-no fixed address,' Wolf stammered. 'Not for either of them. Maartje . . . I think she came from Limburg, somewhere down there. I heard her people were farmers . . . '

'OK. Sergeant Gonggrijp, take his statement upstairs in Room Three. I'll go punch this into the system and see what happens.' The door banged to behind him.

'This way.' Gonggrijp bustled out from behind the counter. She was tall even in the regulation flat black lace-ups, and athletic. Wolf followed the sweet curve of her rear end docilely up the stairs.

❖

Taking his statement was a task that seemed to take forever. The sergeant wrote with excruciating slowness, and had to stop every few minutes to answer the telephone that stood on the bare wooden desk. The lines of completed text that crept down the page were maddeningly few.

After twenty minutes, Wolf had to ask for a break to use the lavatory.

'Turn left out of here,' Gonggrijp said without looking up from her snail's-pace scribing. 'Third door on your right.'

'Thanks.' Wolf followed her directions to a white-tiled restroom where everything was constructed from galvanised steel. The dimpled surface of the metal pinged and sparkled with colour as Wolf walked past. Someone had abandoned a half-crushed cigarette butt on the tiled windowsill.

Wolf locked himself in a cubicle and put his head in his hands. Why was this all taking so *long*? Surely it shouldn't take half an hour just to get the first few lines down on paper? It occurred to him, a bit late, that he was being jerked around. They were stalling. But for what?

The sense of wrongness redoubled when he got back to the little interview room. The bulky police officer was there, talking to Sergeant Gonggrijp. They broke off as Wolf came through the door. The policeman forced a smile on his face. There were circles of sweat under the arms of his crisp uniform shirt that had not been there half an hour ago.

'There you are, Menheer Wolf! Er, if you'd just like to sit down again, Sergeant Gonggrijp will get you a cup of coffee, and then she'll finish taking your statement.'

Wolf stayed where he was. 'What about the names? What did the computer say?'

'I'm waiting for a response on the American male,' the policeman replied. His gaze flicked away from Wolf's, and he turned on his heel and left the room.

That was a lie, Wolf thought. One minute they're treating me like a worthless nuisance, the next they're offering me cups of coffee and telling me lies to keep me here. Why?

'Great,' he said out loud, and sat down opposite the sergeant. 'Milky coffee, please.'

Gonggrijp smiled manfully back at him and got up. 'Would you like sugar, Menheer Wolf?'

'Two,' Wolf said. 'Thank you.'

The sergeant closed the door behind her a little more forcefully than might have been deemed necessary. Wolf guessed that she was not used to the role of tea-lady.

He slid the notepad round so that he could see what she had written so far. Her handwriting was small and crushed into unnatural shapes by the weight of all the empty space left above it on each line.

The telephone rang.

Vivid colour sizzled at the edge of Wolf's vision. He stared at the phone, mouth gone dry: was this part of the puzzle? Was he supposed to pick up? Almost of its own volition, his hand went out to the receiver. He put the handset to his ear.

'Yes?'

'Who is this? I want to talk to Kees van der Brugh *right now.*' An American voice, rich with impatience. Wolf froze with the receiver clutched to his cheek. He could not utter a sound. His legs felt as if someone had just filleted them. It was the man from his dream.

There was a short pause on the other end of the phone. Then a gentle chuckle. 'It's you, isn't it? How'd you get a hold of the phone?—Dumb cops, they left him alone—' Muffled, as if he was commenting to someone standing beside him.

Wolf's lips shaped sounds, but nothing emerged. His fist shook. In his ear, the American said, 'Hell, Kris, they were right about you. I should have finished you when I had the chance. Later.' Click. The flat bleat of the disconnect tone.

Wolf banged the handset back into its cradle and bolted to his feet. The pale grey morning light was suddenly white-hot lava that stung tears to his eyes. His skin prickled.

They were coming here, now. That must be why the police were spinning out his visit as long as possible. He might only have moments before the Black Coats got here.

Wolf inched the door open and peeked into the corridor. Nobody yet. He slid out and eased the door to behind him. Heart trampolining in his throat.

He hurried down the corridor to the restroom, holding his breath. Any second, and someone would shout—someone would realise that he was getting away and they would come running to stop him.

Nobody did. The restroom was empty. Wolf hesitated, then grabbed the waist-high steel pedal bin from the corner and jammed it between the corner of one of the cubicles and the door. If he could make them think he'd barricaded himself in here, all the better.

He strode to the window and tried the handle. Locked. He peered closer. It wasn't just locked—someone had fastened a shiny screw right under the catch.

Wolf growled in frustration and cast a look back at the door. There was no way he could walk out there now. The Black Coats might be here already. He would walk right into their arms. The thought of being their prisoner again made him dizzy with terror.

He turned back to the window with renewed determination. There had to be some way to open the damned thing. He ran his hands over the metal frame. The top corner stuck out a little. He wriggled his fingertips into the gap. It was too high.

Wolf dragged over a broken plastic chair and clambered up. The chair wobbled. He braced himself as best he could, and squeezed his fingertips back into the crevice. Quick but quiet. He pulled as hard as he could.

The window rocketed out of its frame. Wolf went sprawling. The noise was incredible. He sat up in a mess of broken glass, dazed. Someone rattled the doorknob.

'What's going on in there?'

Wolf struggled to his feet. 'Just a minute!' he shouted. 'The door's jammed.'

He threw one leg over the windowsill and peered down. There was a drop of about ten feet to a pile of bulging garbage bags covered with a thin crust of snow.

He got both legs out and jumped. His landing in the garbage made a surprisingly loud noise.

Wolf rolled to the ground, gagging at the stench from the burst bags. No face at the open window yet. No shouts of discovery.

Wolf ran for the street. There was a bus stopped just a few yards away from the alley mouth. He grabbed the half-used ticket from his coat pocket. Five units left. He got the driver to stamp three of them, and pushed his way to the back of the bus. There was a free seat, and he swung into it, ignoring the fastidious glances from the people around him. His bad eyelid fluttered, as if trying to keep time with his pounding heart.

The bus lurched and swung away from the kerb. Wolf released a shaky breath. That had been close. Too damn close.

He gazed at the ticket still clutched in his fist. Three units—where would that take him? He had had no time to see which bus he had jumped on to. Still. Whatever direction he travelled in, he was leaving the man from his nightmare further behind every second.

❖

I caught a tram at the end of my street, and rode into Weesperplein on the last stub of my ticket, yawning.

There was a stall close to the tram stop selling hot baked potatoes. The thick fragrant steam mugged my senses the moment I stepped down to the sidewalk.

I swallowed the water that flooded my mouth, and passed my tongue over my lips. If I bought breakfast, I'd have to walk home when I got through at the hospital.

A little walking never killed anyone, I told myself, ignoring the fact that it must be at least two miles. At least I'd had the sense to wear my Docs today instead of the leaky cowboy boots.

I scooped the loose change out of my coat pocket, and stepped up to the stall.

❖

A bag of fried potato skins—the cheapest item on the menu—lasted me almost the whole walk to the hospital. The last bite left a burnt crunch on my tongue. I grimaced at the acrid taste but swallowed it anyway. Charcoal's good for you.

Al fresco eating seemed to have become a regular feature of my life. It would be nice, I reflected as I turned the last corner, to be civilised and eat off a table sometimes. Even use a knife and fork. Hell, I added, nice to eat food that *needs* a knife and fork. I seemed to have eaten an awful lot of falafel lately. Spring rolls, burgers, hot dogs, I added mentally. Cheap food, eaten on the hoof. *Junk, Carlson,* I corrected myself. *It's called junk.*

I picked my way across the road towards the main entrance of the hospital, and had to wait for an ambulance to pass.

Before I could reach the sidewalk, there was a sudden slap-slap of feet in the slush behind me and a hand grabbed my sleeve.

'Robin! Wait up!'

'Hey!' I wrenched myself free and whirled to confront my assailant. 'What in the hell—'

'Calm down!' It was Gabriel, flushed and puffing with exertion. 'We need to talk, Robin.'

'I've got nothing to say to you.' I walked away. Gabriel followed.

'But Artemis—'

I spun round so fast, he almost sat down in the gutter. 'Artemis nothing! If you're not going to help me find Kris de Haan, just leave me the hell alone.' I stalked away from him across the hospital car-park, kicking snow out of my way as I walked. Gabriel uttered a breathless curse and plunged after me.

'We have to talk—'

'No, we don't.' I walked faster. Gabriel seemed to realise that he was fighting a losing battle, and fell into step beside me.

'Can I at least come with you?'

I compressed my lips in a straight line. 'It's a free world. Excuse me,' I added, and eeled through the main doors of the hospital, leaving Gabriel to make his own way in.

It was very warm inside the building. Perspiration prickled between my shoulder blades.

I hesitated, looking around. The few people I could see all looked as if they knew where they were going. Tom had brought me in through the Emergency Room last night. I realised suddenly that I had no idea even of the right ward number.

There was an information desk. The woman behind it looked put-upon when I explained the problem.

'Wait, I'll check. What's the name, please, and when was he brought in?' She manoeuvred a mouse and poised her fingers over a keyboard, still not looking at me.

'Bowman. Cary Bowman, that's B, o, w, m, a, n. And he was brought in yesterday afternoon, I'm not sure what time.'

A pause, during which the woman tapped her manicured fingernails on the mouse, her attention on the screen. I saw Gabriel fidgeting with his cellphone over by the doors. He wasn't crowding me, which was a relief.

'I'm afraid I can't tell you where Menheer Bowman is,' the woman said. I frowned.

'I don't understand, I saw him last night. He couldn't possibly have been discharged already, he was too sick—' My brain caught up with what my mouth was saying. 'Wait—what do you mean, you can't? Do you mean you don't know where he is?'

'I can't discuss Menheer Bowman's case with anybody except immediate family. I'm sorry.'

'Is he all right?' I felt as if I was floating somewhere close by, watching the conversation happen. The woman was starting to look dogged.

'I can't discuss Menheer Bowman's condition with anyone except immediate family. I'm sorry.'

'This is stupid.' I placed my hands flat on the counter-top. 'Look, Cary doesn't have any immediate family here. His mother's ninety-three, she lives in England. His father died ten years ago. There is no family. Just me, I'm, uh, I'm his fiancée, and I want to see him now.' I stuttered over the lie, and saw the woman's eyebrows elevate. She reached out to press a button.

'I think it is better if you speak to the doctor. Could you wait over there, please?' She gestured towards a square of seating nearby.

My head was filling up with the noise of the sea. Why would I need to talk to a doctor? What was going on? 'Is he worse? I—I saw him just last night, I promised I'd come back today! I have to see him!' I had spoken too loudly. Gabriel was jogging in our direction looking worried. I saw a white-coated orderly down the hall change his trajectory.

A woman in a blue skirt suit came out of a door behind the desk. The receptionist beckoned her over and a murmured exchange took place. The doctor glanced up at me and nodded, then came out from behind the desk.

'I understand you are Menheer Bowman's . . . fiancée?'

'Yes. Look, I have to see him, I promised—'

'Please . . . ' The doctor took my sleeve and tried to lead me off to one side, but I broke her grip and stayed put.

'Why can't I see him?'

The doctor looked me in the eye, but she spoke softly. 'Menheer Bowman's condition is worsening, he has been placed on a ventilator. Visiting is not permitted. I'm sorry.'

'Sure you are.' I glared at the woman. The ersatz sympathy was meaningless. It infuriated me. I banged my fists on the desk. 'I have to see him! I promised him—'

'Robin, cool it.' Gabriel interposed himself between us. I aimed a blow at him and he dodged. 'Will you calm down?'

'I am calm,' I spat. I couldn't breathe properly. As if from another room, I heard the orderly ask if there was something wrong.

'No,' Gabriel said. 'Everything's going to be fine, she's just had a bit of a shock. Robin, come on. You can't do anything here now.' He tried to put his arm round me and guide me away from the desk.

'Get off of me!' I pushed him so hard that he staggered. My face was wet. I backed away from Gabriel, fists clenched. 'Haven't you freaks done enough already? Just leave me alone!' I whirled and ran for the doors, slammed through them.

The air outside stung like a slap. The tears on my cheeks suddenly cold as ice. I smeared them away with my jacket sleeve as I ran.

Behind me, someone shouted my name. Gabriel. I put on a spurt of speed and made it across the road just before a stream of traffic got loose from the lights.

Gabriel's voice was swallowed in the roar of engines and swish of tyres. I pounded away down the sidewalk that ran alongside the Oosterpark railings. My bag bounced at my side but I barely noticed it.

I had to keep running. It was an article of faith. I clung to it. People were a moving maze that I wove through without seeing individual faces. Roads were more problematic: one taxi barely stopped in time when I slipped on the compacted ice. The driver hopped out of his door yelling, torn between fury and anxiety. I climbed to my feet using the front of his car as a crutch, and ran away again.

In the end, a fierce stitch forced me to drop to a jog, then a limping walk. A taste of bile and ashes in my mouth. I hung my head and clutched my ribs but kept moving. Gabriel mustn't catch me. If he caught me it would make it real. If I just kept going, kept walking, nothing bad could happen.

I was almost home. I quickened my pace as I turned the final corner. I would lock the door and disconnect the phone and close the drapes. Nobody could get in. Nobody.

I drew a deep breath of the icy air, and looked up at the window of my bedroom, just as it exploded outward in a bright bubble of yellow fire.

Tick. That was the first second—just the flash, magnesium-bright. Fragments of glass splashed out, glittering surf on the crest of a billowing breaker of flame.

Tock. That was the world, catching up on events. A hail of debris and glass splinters. A sound like canned thunder. It punched me backwards off my feet. Something came up in a terrific hurry from behind and bashed me on the head (the ground, as it turned out).

❖

I opened my eyes—it seemed only a second later—on a confused scene of faces and bicycle wheels. My head was cold, and it hurt.

I groaned and blinked until things came into proper focus, and discovered that I was lying in the snow beside the cycle rack with several people bending over me. There was a lot of shouting going on. A terrible smell, like sausages left too long on the barbecue.

I sat up, coughing. A woman whom I vaguely recognised pressed a glass of water into my hands. I sipped. Water spilt down my chin. I wiped at it with my cuff, feeling foolish. My ears seemed to be full of cotton wadding.

The woman was speaking, I realised. I recognised her now from the next building but one. Her voice seemed to come from a couple of blocks away.

'Are you all right?'

'I'm fine. I'm OK.' My own voice sounded almost as muffled, and I patted at my ears with numb hands. There was snow caked in my hair.

I did a quick inventory of body parts and was relieved to discover everything in working order. There was a big lump on the back of my head. I fingered it tenderly.

A fire engine was slewed across the roadway. A couple of police cars stood just beyond it. Uniformed figures hustled about, stringing striped tape from one side of the street to the other. Grey snake-shapes of hoses coiled across the ground.

A few yards away, two firemen held a bucking nozzle between them. I blinked at the huge jet of water they were aiming at a third-floor window. There really wasn't a window there any more—just a shattered hole that spewed orange flames and thick, greasy smoke.

The third floor.

'My apartment . . . !' My voice cracked. I scrambled to my feet and launched myself at the surprised firemen. 'That's my apartment, stop it, what're you *doing*—?' The finger of water waggled as I shoved at the nozzle. One of the firemen gave a warning shout.

'Robin!' Someone grabbed me and spun me around. It was Tom Barnabas.

'Tom!' My voice cracked again, and set me coughing. I grabbed him back, hard enough to hurt. 'Tom. My—m-my ap-partment—'

'Are you OK?' Barnabas' mouth was a grim line as he looked me over. He touched my face, and the place stung. 'You're cut.'

'It's the glass. The, the windows . . . *OW!*' I yelped as he tweaked something free and flicked it away. Warmth tickled my cheek. I touched it with cold fingers and they came away red.

'Press on it.' Barnabas handed me a folded white handkerchief. I obeyed, staring across the street at the burning house.

The floor above my own looked as if it had collapsed: the roof had sunk in and wooden rafters stuck out like shattered bones. The first and second floors were burning almost as fiercely as the third. Smoke poured from every opening.

On the sidewalk just outside the front door, two paramedics knelt over something. Some charred thing, that was all I registered. It looked like a bundle of black sticks and rags. Barnabas placed himself squarely in front of me.

'You're comin' with me, young lady.' He put an arm round my shoulders and steered me away from the heat and stink of the fire. 'We'll get you fixed up, OK? Good as new. Here we go.'

I went where I was led. My bag was still slung across me and I clutched it tight. My legs seemed inclined to go in different directions. Barnabas made an impatient noise and scooped me up into his arms. Beyond the hastily-erected police barriers, I saw his Jeep stopped in the middle of the street with the driver's door standing open.

'D-did you see—?'

'Nope. Heard it, a few streets back. I was just coming to pick you up, you can imagine what I thought when I turned the corner. Can you get the handle—? There you go.' He elbowed open the passenger door of the Cherokee and lifted me into the seat without apparent effort. 'Sit there, OK? I'll just go talk to the cops, let 'em know where you are. They get kind of picky about stuff like that.'

'OK.' I leaned my head back against the rest as Barnabas walked away in the direction of the police vans. He had left the door open, but I was grateful for the blast of cold air.

Stupid how the mind works. All I could think of was how I was still paying for the fridge. The insurance had lapsed months ago. And what about my best pair of jeans, the 501s? I'd left them stuffed under the bed.

That smell, of seared meat . . . I struggled to push away the sight of the bundle of charred sticks, and failed. Who'd be in there at this time of day? Only old Schama, in his downstairs room with the TV on too loud as usual. *MAN BURNT ALIVE IN DAYTIME SOAP TRAGEDY?* I didn't know whether to puke or laugh. I gulped air, and got hiccups instead.

'Robin Carlson?' The car moved as someone leant in at the door. I opened my eyes, startled. A man stood there, frowning at me. 'Robin Carlson?' he repeated. He had blow-dried dark hair and a neat beard.

'Uh—yeah. Yeah, that's me, uh . . . what—' I struggled to sit up straight, still holding Barnabas' handkerchief to my face. Hell, this guy looked like police or something— dark suit under a black overcoat, leather gloves which he stripped off as he spoke.

'You seem to be getting into trouble, Robin.' A utilitarian American-English accent. The familiarity jarred. His smile was wide and white and perfect. It failed to ignite any warmth in his eyes.

'Didn't my friend talk to you people already? Tom Barnabas, he, he went to find someone . . . ' I muffled a hiccup and got a sharp pain in the chest for my trouble. I pressed my fist to my sternum and held my breath. Where was Tom? I tried to peer past the man, but he was in the way.

The bearded man reached into his coat and flicked something on to my lap: a little pack of photographs. 'Take a look, Robin.'

I opened the flap and pulled out a slim wad of prints. They were all pictures of me. I leafed through them, numb. They'd taken pictures of me everywhere—through the window of Sunny's office, coming out of my front door, at Dvaar's after work with a Danish in my hand . . .

'What's this?' I peered from the photograph to the man's face, bewildered. I shook my head. 'Wh-what *is* this?'

'It's a warning,' the man said. He had moved close enough for me to smell his breath, sour under a miasma of breath-fresheners. I watched his smiling mouth, hypnotised by the sight of so much dental work this far from LA. 'You've been concerning yourself with other people's business, Robin. It's very unhealthy.' A pained look. He pulled a little book of matches from his pocket and tore one out, struck it deliberately close to my face. The sizzle and flare made me flinch. 'Accidents will happen, Robin. It's amazing what a little gas leak can do, isn't it? I hear the landlord didn't get out. Cooked in his armchair. Shocking. Could've been you.' He picked the photograph out of my unresisting hand, and set the flame to the bottom corner. The emulsion twisted and bubbled before the flame licked the piece of paper to white ash. The man retrieved the other prints, and tucked them into his coat, brisk. 'Now. I'll tell you how it's going to be. You are not going to pursue this any further, Robin. Go back to the States before you get hurt. You saw what happened to your boyfriend.'

'Cary—?' I jerked as if he had hit me in the face.

'He knew exactly what was going to happen to him,' the man said. The smile widened. 'That's what made it so . . . poetic. I guess you realised he was getting a little confused? He never regained consciousness after you left him last night, you know. Coma. Then convulsions as the brain damage really started to bite. Then, well . . . it's just a matter of what gets him first. I've seen the test figures. Real educational. Sometimes it's heart failure. Sometimes the brain damage just gets too severe and they flatline. But you know, your man's a real strong healthy guy. He could fight it all the way down to the terminal stage. That's respiratory paralysis. The lungs gradually cease to function. Of course, they might put him on a ventilator, but there isn't much point. His brain'll be too severely traumatised by then. So they'll just let him suffocate. Not a pretty way to go, Robin. And you know what he'll have died of? Huh?'

A bare shake of the head. I kept blinking—like the frames of a film moving past—flick, flick, flick. As if the sordid images he conjured in my mind were specks of dirt and I could blink them away.

'He'll have died of curiosity. He didn't know when to leave well enough alone. You have a responsibility now,' the man said, and touched my cheek with one ash-smeared fingertip. His eyes were grey, and set too close together, like conspirators. 'You're a smart girl, Robin. You know what'll happen if you try to involve anybody else, don't you? Your kick-boxing friend with the Harley, for instance?' Waiting for my stiff nod. The finger stroked again, approvingly. 'That's the girl. No heroics, no cops, no calls for help. It'll be our little secret, hmm? Just between us.' He stepped back from the doorway, tugging on the gloves, buttoning his coat. The smile gleamed like a dagger. 'Don't forget now.'

He walked away. I brushed at the pale feathers of ash on my knees, numb with shock. He had cured my hiccups.

Tom Barnabas ducked under the stripy police tape, hauled himself into the driver's seat with a sheepish look, and banged the door.

'Sorry I took so long, Birdy. Nobody knows nuthin' until it's been cleared, blah blah. Looks like it started on your floor, though. Probably a gas build-up. You get your fire tested lately?'

'No.' I said. 'Not lately.' I was distracted by the normality of my voice. It was as if what had happened was contained inside a hard, tight bubble. My chest ached with the strain of holding it in. *Just between us. Don't forget now.*

'Ah, what the hell, they'll figure it out. Damn, you look like you've seen a ghost, kid. What you need,' Barnabas said, 'is bed, young lady, and something warm inside you. I mean soup,' he added, with dignity. 'You're coming back to my place, Carlson. No arguments.'

'No arguments,' I agreed in a whisper. My throat kept closing up as if I was going to cry, but my eyes were bone-dry. My thoughts battered back and forth like a moth inside a glass light-shade. *TELL him, he'll know what to do—I can't tell him, it'd put him in danger too—what am I going to DO?—I'm on my own, they've made good and sure of that. I can't even go to the police, they'll know and then it'll be worse than ever . . .*

I found myself staring at Barnabas' hands on the steering wheel. They were slender, for all the wide build of him, scrubbed clean as a surgeon's, nails trimmed. A gold chronograph peeped from beneath his coat cuff.

Whatever he's doing these days, it seems to agree with him, I thought, and added, *it sure looks as if it pays better than an Army pension, too.* Well, good for him.

I snuck another sideways peek, and caught him looking at me. He flashed a grin. 'Okay, Birdy?'

'Sure. I think.' I tried to smile. Barnabas returned his attention to the traffic. It was appalling, as usual. He bumped the big Jeep up on to the path, and hung a tight right turn down a narrow street.

'Well, you just tell me if you start feelin' weird or sick or anything, OK? Shock's a funny thing.'

'Hilarious,' I murmured in a small voice, and lifted my shoulders at his frown. 'Joke. I'm OK, really.' I thrust my hands into my coat pockets and hunched deeper into the seat. 'Hell, I mean, it could have been a lot worse, right? That could have been me back there.' I closed my eyes, then opened them and tried another smile. It still didn't work properly. 'I lost my best jeans, all my underwear, a fridge I didn't even pay for yet, a TV set and a broken microwave oven . . .' A sudden stab of nausea: I clapped my hand over my mouth. 'Oh my God no—'

'What? *What?*' Barnabas looked at my face, braked hard and swerved in to the kerb. I flung the door open and vomited neatly into the gutter. Barnabas let me get on with it. When I'd finished decorating the street, he handed me tissues and waited while I cleaned up.

I was trembling as though every cell of my body had motors fitted, I couldn't stop crying. It was a few minutes before I could articulate clearly enough to explain.

Barnabas reached across me to slam the door shut. 'Who the hell's Ziggy?'

'*Zbiggy.* Zbigniew, he—he's . . . was, uh, my—my f-fish.' I dragged my coat sleeve over my eyes and blew my nose on another tissue. Barnabas looked at me for a long moment.

'Your fish. Zbiggy—' he pronounced the name carefully, 'was your fish, and he was in the apartment, is that what you're telling me?'

'Y-yes. He's de-*dead*.' I couldn't control my breathing. It was all jerky and painful, as if I was being beaten up by the Invisible Man. I mopped at my face and wondered where the hell all the tears came from.

Barnabas peered over his shoulder, and pulled away with a scrape of tyres on the gritted road.

'Buckle up, Birdy. Not far now.' As I fumbled the seatbelt across my body and stabbed the clip at its slot, he added, '—and the next time you tell me you're OK, remind me not to believe you.'

'S-s-sorry. Damn.' I had the hiccups again.

12

BARNABAS' HOUSE stood on the town end of the JM Kemperstraat, within traffic-vibration distance of the Haarlemmerweg. I teased him sometimes about the kind of money he had to be making to afford a whole house in Amsterdam, but he didn't rise to it, just hiked up one shoulder and smiled, and changed the subject. Ex-forces guys can be cagey like that, especially if their CV hasn't been what you might call orthodox; I knew better than to stick my nose where it wasn't wanted.

The house was constructed from those greyish-black bricks half the city seemed to be made of, and had a very modern alarm keypad just inside the front door. The rest was a blur of lace curtains and pastel-tinted walls and paintings of flowers, some of which I recognised as Tom's own work. Not your average guy place. Like always, it smelt very clean.

Barnabas sat me at the kitchen table (limed oak, scrubbed) and bustled around with all the cosy domesticity of the lifelong bachelor. He switched the little portable TV on as he passed, and punched the start button on the kettle.

While the water heated up, Barnabas fetched a saucepan out and opened a tin of tomato soup, set it on the hob and ripped open a pack of soft white rolls.

I drank the disgustingly sweet tea he made, and felt a little better. The cup was whisked away and refilled. I sipped obediently and stared at the newsreader's lipsticked mouth opening and shutting. The woman had an irritating habit of crinkling her eyes at the camera at the end of an item, as if to demonstrate her empathy with the viewer. It made me want to punch her.

Barnabas straightened up from a cupboard holding a green plastic First Aid box. 'Come on over here by the window, I want to check that cut. Glass is a bitch to get out. That's it. Huh. Uhh-huh . . . Chin up, OK . . . Turn your head—no, the other way, dummy. Umm, looks like I got it all. All right, just hold it there a second. This'll be cold—' I jerked and uttered a squeak of surprise as he squirted the wound with something citrussy from a tiny aerosol. Barnabas grinned. 'Told ya. Antibiotic spray. Now keep still.' A moment's concentration while he snipped up bits of micropore. 'All right, now we're cookin' with gas. Just put your finger here and push up a little, that's it—' Another pause while he stuck strips of tape across the gash.

'Tom—'

'No talk,' Barnabas said, releasing my face and packing the medical supplies away in their box.

'But I—'

'Soup first,' Barnabas said. 'Sit. I'm not havin' you pass out on me, kid. First we get you fixed up. You can talk afterwards.'

'I'm really not hungry.' The warm aroma of the soup was making my mouth water, but my insides still quivered. The thought of throwing up tomato soup was distinctly unattractive. Barnabas seemed to read my mind.

'Trust me, you won't puke again. That was just the shock. Come on, sit. Eat. You'll feel better.' He planked two china bowls on to the table and poured neatly from the saucepan, scooted a bowl across in front of me. 'Get it while it's hot.' Barnabas scraped back his own chair and sat down. He reached over to tweak the volume on the television, then started spooning soup into his mouth. I hesitated with a hand on the chair back.

'I'm not taking any more of those pills, Tom.'

'Won't have to if you just eat sump'n, get a little sleep later on.' Barnabas tore a roll in half, dipped it into his bowl and engulfed it, making *mmm*ing noises. 'I tell you what,' he said through a mouthful of bread. 'I didn't want to bring this up, but you're filthy and you stink of smoke. Whyn't you go take a shower after you eat your soup, then you can get right in the guest bed. Do you good.'

'I don't want to sleep,' I objected. Barnabas rolled his eyes.

'Just humour me, will ya? You gave me the shock of my life back there. I thought you were dead.'

I lifted my hands in surrender. 'OK, OK. Sorry.' I sat, and pinched off a hunk of bread. 'Look, Tom, I don't want to get under your feet here. I'll ring Sunny and see if she can put me up—'

'Your friend from the Fight Club?'

'Yeah.' I nodded, chewing. 'We're pretty close. If she sees this on the news, she'll freak.'

'Well, it's up to you, Birdy, but you wouldn't be under my feet,' Barnabas gestured with his third bread-roll. 'Be good to have the company, tell the truth.'

I was touched at the admission. 'Tom, that's really sweet. You're about the only family I have now.'

'The only family you're speaking to, you mean.' Barnabas' blue eyes were very shrewd. I shrugged.

'I guess.' I dabbled my bread in the soup, chewed and swallowed. 'Tom, I just came from the hospital.'

'Oh yeah?' Barnabas picked up another roll and tore it in half. 'How's he doin'?'

'He, uh . . . ' A fierce ache in my throat. I put down the piece of bread. 'He's getting worse. They wouldn't even let me see him, he's on a ventilator.'

Barnabas stopped, spoon poised. 'Life support?'

I nodded and stared at my soup. Barnabas pushed his own bowl away, and reached for my hand. Regret on his face.

'Aw, Birdy . . . '

'It's OK.' I shook my head, and folded my arms. Barnabas got up and came to put his hands very gently on my shoulders.

'If I'd a known . . . '

'Yeah, well, we did kind of get overtaken by events.' I leaned back and squinted up at him. 'I guess I'll take that shower now.'

'Want to talk?' Barnabas gazed down at me. I closed my eyes at the flood of need. 'No. Thanks, but no.'

❖

Barnabas rapped on the bedroom door while I was getting dried. I shouted, 'Wait a second!' and grabbed the oversized bathrobe from the back of the door. There was enough of it to wrap round me twice, and it swept the floor as I walked. I opened the door towelling at my hair.

'You smell a whole lot better,' Barnabas said. He dodged the towel. 'Not quick enough, kid.'

'I'll get you next time,' I promised. I fingered the collar of the bathrobe. 'Yours?'

'Spare,' Barnabas said. 'Keep it, it makes you look cute again.' He grinned at my martyred expression. 'Look, I just came up to tell you there's a washer-dryer and detergent and stuff in the utility if you want to get your stuff clean later.' He sighed and looked at his watch, running the other hand over his buzz cut. 'I've got to get back to work. You sure you're going to be OK?'

'Sure I'm sure.' I kissed his cheek. 'But thanks for being worried.'

'Be good, Birdy.' Barnabas glanced at his watch again. 'Oh-oh, gotta run.' He pulled a little cellphone out of his inside pocket, and stabbed a button, spoke after a second's pause. 'Barnabas. I'll be there in twenty.' He pocketed the thing again, and scowled at me. 'Just take it easy, OK?'

'Yes, Uncle Tom. I'll be a good girl. See you later,' I added pointedly. Barnabas grunted and rattled off down the stairs, mind already elsewhere. The front door slammed.

I flopped over backwards on the bed and lay for several minutes, staring at the ceiling.

My thoughts were an exhausted tangle—of going to the police, or the US Consulate—of finding someone who could handle these hit-men or whatever the hell they were—of going to Sunny and Marik for help—all broken threads, no beginning, no end. I had to do what the man with the beard said. It was the only course open to me now. I couldn't take the chance that anyone else would get hurt.

It occurred to me with a jolt that someone was already helping me. How were the bad guys to know that I hadn't told Tom everything? They might hurt him.

My eyes spilt scalding tears. No, you stupid bitch, they might *kill* him.

The enormity of it crushed me. I curled into a ball and pressed my trembling hands to my face. Tears dripped through my fingers on to the neat white bedding.

My mind skipped from thought to thought. *Got to call Tom, got to warn him—but I don't have a number, I don't even know where he works—how can I warn him, he'd ask why and then—Oh God, they're going to kill him and it's all my fault—shouldn't have let him bring me here—this is all down to me, why didn't I listen to Cary when he tried to warn me off?—had to be so tough and independent—dumb bitch, it's all my fault—*

Even after the storm of tears dried up, I lay shivering for a long time, staring at the wall. What was it I'd been telling myself? That one unspecified day soon, there would be an ordinary way of things again, a normal life where I didn't have to tough it out all by myself? No more bad dreams? The tantalising possibility of (admit it, Carlson) *love*?

I crushed my lips against the cool hard shape of the Family Curse and shut my eyes. It had all been poised to happen. And then the tidal wave had crashed over us. Other people's secrets, other people's desires and hatreds and lies. Intangibles, all of them, whispers in the dark. Whispers that had left Cary Bowman on a life-support machine.

Maybe not so intangible after all.

❖

Wolf swept snow from the edge of a bench in Leidseplein and tried to sit on the hem of his coat. As efforts to keep warm go, it was pretty pointless. His jeans were soaked through. He muttered a bad word, and hugged his arms round himself inside the coat.

Underfoot, the snow had been trampled to two inches of translucent grey slush. It seeped through the cracks in his boots and turned his socks into ice-packs.

Wolf cradled his head in his hands, and tried to think. It was difficult—not least because he was out of the habit. Life on the streets encourages a Zen approach to existence: go with the flow, embrace the chaos. It dignifies a certain lack of options.

Things had changed. Go with the flow today, it could get him killed. Wolf wasn't sure he was ready for that much chaos.

How could the Black Coats have suborned the *police*? Wolf pressed cold fingers to his temples, and stared out over the square. *There are other explanations*, he thought. *Maybe I'm not a factory worker after all, maybe I'm an escaped lunatic.*

The huge Christmas tree in its prim little enclosure of steel fencing nearby crackled merrily, ablaze with spitting amber and green flames that only Wolf could see. The sky was worse—it swelled and shrank and billowed like a vast soap bubble above his head.

The Salvation Army silver band started up at that moment. It cut his thoughts into shiny ribbons of nonsense. *Siii-lent niiight, Ho-oly niiight* . . . .The plump, piercing sound made Wolf shiver.

. . . *aaall is calm, aaall is bri-ight* . . . The french horn dragged a little behind the rest, and gave rise to some disturbing harmonies.

Wolf ducked his head deeper into his collar. He wished he had some control over the memories that were coming back to him.

He squeezed his eyes shut and summoned the latest one again, like a talisman: wooden walls painted sunflower yellow. Books crammed on to shelves. Many, many books, and a comfortable old chair by a pot-bellied stove. A low ceiling with tiny owl faces painted on the studs where the wooden panels met. Hollow clucking noises of water in the dark as he slept. A door that locked on the inside. And a name, a special name . . .

Wolf rubbed hands over his face and sighed. If only it would all come clear. The details were tantalising, they tugged at his heart, but they did not help him at all. No use remembering how the springs sagged in his old chair if he did not know where to find the boat it sat in. Three thousand plus moorings in this damn city, Wolf thought in despair: I can't look over all of them.

Leidseplein was a circus this time of year, a constant shifting mob of shoppers. Clumps of passers-by stopped to gawk at the swirl of movement on the temporary ice-rink. Little square trailers sold roast chestnuts in paper cones, and styrofoam cups of hot chocolate. There was even a calliope stranded on the fringes of the square pumping out *Have Yourself A Merry Little Christmas* in brash counterpoint to the band. Figures made bulky by brightly-coloured winter clothing darted by, circling the ice.

Wolf trawled through his pockets and turned up not much: his tobacco-pouch, folded tight around a pack of Rizlas, an almost-empty matchbook that he had picked out of a trash can, the last stub of his transport ticket, a wadded-up paper tissue and a single coin. He turned the coin in his fingers and cursed whoever had gone through his pockets, back in the Hole.

He laid the folded pack of tobacco on his knees and fumbled for papers. His fingers shook and wouldn't behave. It took a ludicrously long time to get the tobacco rolled to his satisfaction.

The flare of the match made Wolf wince. He inhaled the smoke in a blissful gasp, hunched over his own warmth.

The hit of the nicotine made his head spin a little. He slitted his eyes and stuck the cigarette into his mouth, pulling the hot smoke deep and letting it trickle out without his help.

Anything to disoblige, he reminded himself: he was still breathing in and out, which was more than Mademoiselle and her Black Coats had planned for him today. He drew in a luxuriant lungful of oxygen and wondered what came next. Being a hero was more tricky than it looked on the TV.

The low afternoon sun stabbed white pins at his eyes. A sudden surge of pigeons, speckled grey bodies like hail falling. Multi-coloured trams sliced and swished across the centre of the square.

From behind the Christmas tree, a man in a black coat hurried towards him.

The cigarette dropped from Wolf's nerveless fingers on to his jeans leg and burned him. He swore and leapt to his feet, heart jackhammering. It was Mulder.

Wolf bolted across the road. He slipped on ice and crashed down on his back. A tram clanged, right on top of him. Wolf saw only a blurred wall of yellow. The draught of its passing brought water to his eyes. Almost brought water to other, more embarrassing parts.

Wolf shook off hands that reached to help him. He scrambled up, panting. The black coat had vanished in the crowds. Wolf craned his head round like a startled owl. *Where the hell is he?* Panic scraped sharp fingernails down his brain.

Police uniforms in the crowd. Wolf ducked his head and tried to look unobtrusive. They were coming this way. He should keep moving. Walk, don't run.

He turned to his left. More uniforms. Panic overruled. Wolf pushed through the shoppers in a heedless straight line, snatching at shoulders. He stumbled into a fat woman in a raincoat. She shrieked. They fell in a slippery mound of carrier bags. Eggs smacked to the floor. Apples and oranges scattered, bowling across the cobbles.

Wolf gabbled some kind of apology. He struggled away from the mess. Broke into a run as soon as he got his feet under him. Panic roared in his head. A craggy-faced man with white hair and a ski jacket grabbed at him. Wolf shouted something—don't know what—and twisted away, frantic. Angry noises behind.

Mulder was still coming. Walking fast, purposeful. He was close enough for Wolf to see anticipation in the wrinkled brown eyes. One gloved hand reached inside the breast of the black coat.

Wolf vaulted over the steel fencing on to the ice. He lunged for the centre of the rink. Squeals and whoops swept over him. He felt rather than saw bodies fly past, cutting around the unexpected obstacle in a spray of ice crystals.

'Look *out!*' A female yell. Wolf jerked round and collided with a Lycra-clad skater. The impact knocked him off his feet. He lurched up again, stammering. 'Sorry, I'm sorry—' His hand was bloody but he didn't feel a thing.

'It's OK.' She was pretty and dark, impossibly slender in the figure-hugging suit. 'Here.' She held a hand out for him to help her up.

Got to keep going . . . Wolf staggered past her towards the far side of the ice. The skaters were a multi-coloured skein whirling past. The roar of their steel blades drummed in his head. He was dizzy, sick with fear as he half-fell over the barriers at the far side. Annoyed faces, amused faces. He staggered away.

He could no longer see Mulder, but it was only a matter of time. He had to get away.

Sweat trickled over Wolf's scalp. He was shivering again. Car-noise and music battered at his head. Unbearable pressure. He whimpered out loud, 'Stop it . . . stop it—' A woman glanced and edged away.

Wolf thrust through the crowd with his arms out, fending off bodily contact. Leather, and canvas and plastic and skin, all warm and rough and horribly intimate under his fingertips. Ripples of cold over his skin. He was going to pass out. He could feel it.

'Hey, you there!' A heavy hand clapped on to his shoulder. Wolf jerked round and almost yelled in terror at the black face inches from his own. All that came out was a strangled yelp.

The face was shiny under a floppy red hat. Black greasepaint smeared at the blue eyes into crows'-feet crinkles of pink. A stiff white ruff gave the momentary surreal impression of a man's head on a plate, complete with paper doily.

The man grinned and hefted a bulging black sack at his side. 'Have you been a good little boy, hey?' A scatter of laughter. Wolf twitched and gulped. His throat was a tangled knot of panic.

Black Pete. If you hadn't been good when Sinterklaas arrived, Zwarte Piet took you away in his sack.

The amusement of the onlookers gusted over Wolf like a blast of hot air. Zwarte Piet took advantage of his confusion to pull him closer. The man's breath was a warm mist of *jenever*. 'Can't have naughty boys about when Sinterklaas comes, can we?'

Wolf clung to the man's garish waistcoat. 'Please—please, leave me alone . . .' A gold button came off in his clutching fist and he held it out, stuttering, 'I—I'm sorry . . .'

Zwarte Piet tutted and released his grip. 'Get back in the bar, *jongen*, and stay there, eh?' He had to shout to make himself heard above the tooting of the calliope. Then he relented, grinning. 'Here, mate, have a sweetie.' He dropped something into Wolf's outstretched hand and brushed past, gone in search of more amusing prey.

Wolf gazed at the sweet in its crinkly wrapper. He blinked, and thought *I don't even like these.* He stumbled on numb legs across the square, narrowly missing another incarnation of Black Pete. The man dodged around him and was gone.

Wolf headed down the side of Leidsestraat, clutching at the Amsterdammatjes, wonky iron posts stationed at irregular intervals to emasculate the unwary.

No cover here. Panic grabbed Wolf by the throat. Lots of plate glass and chi-chi clothes.

An alley mouth. Wolf fended against the wall with one hand as he stumbled away from the noise of the street. Away from Mulder. Away from Zwarte Piet. His heart thudded in his throat. His feet made a hesitant dotted line in the drifted snow.

Zwarte Piet. The Sint Nikolaas Parade. Wolf made a sound that was somewhere between laugh and sob; get a grip, *stommeling*, there must be dozens of Black Petes out on the street with their politically-incorrect blacked-up faces and bulging sacks. It happens every year, remember? But of course, he had forgotten. Christmas and St Nikolaas weren't a part of his world. He didn't even know what day of the week it was.

Wolf tried to stop laughing but he couldn't. The helpless hysterical giggling appalled him.

His legs folded. He grabbed at some iron rails. A buzzing in his ears.

So strange, to be looking up at sun-dappled snowy rooftops and a steel-blue sky, and feel the inimical air of the Hole close around him. Ammonia stink in his nostrils. Memory jabbed at him—the moment when Maartje stepped into the path of the bullet. Overlapping images reached for him, saying his name. Falling. Shadows blotted across the sky.

Mustn't black out—not here. Wolf scooped up fistfuls of snow and rubbed them on his face, gasping. The icy shock drove him back to his feet, but it was long moments clinging to the rails before he trusted his legs to carry him.

He walked. He had no idea where he was going. Away from Leidseplein and uniforms and Black Coats.

By the pilings of a bridge, a huddle of teenage boys were testing the canal ice. Wolf heard it squeal under their feet, and shivered at the purply-iridescent bloom of the black water just beneath. *Idiots. Don't they know it's always thinner under the bridges?* The memory of that cold black kiss in his throat almost made him retch.

On Prinsengracht the plant market was a mass of forced winter colour. Armies of Christmas trees bristled, held to attention by orange plastic netting. Wolf hunched into his coat and tried to be invisible.

Street people see the world from behind a transparent partition. Unexpected contact is a door snatched open on loud voices and bright light and then slammed in one's face: unnerving. For Wolf, it pressed on unspecified wounds.

For what seemed a long time now, he had been grateful for that partition, but the purposeful figures busy with their own lives, oblivious of his, today filled him with a kind of restlessness. He fretted at his own failure to pin it down. The emotion jolted free coloured fragments of thought. It was as if his head was a broken kaleidoscope that never quite made a pattern any longer, no matter how hard one shook it.

Until all this started, the whole breathing, enveloping city had been his, walking in it like inhabiting a toy map of pirate waters alive with friendly sea-monsters, marked playfully 'Here Be Dragons'.

The dragons had pulled themselves free of the page. Wolf sensed their glowing eyes watching him from the trees, felt the wind of leathery lizard wings on the back of his neck.

Paranoia ticked in his skull. Every darkened window and alley mouth yawned at him with lazy menace, spilt moving shadows. Wolf heard his own voice muttering dully, *'Oh God, oh God, God—'* and he knew he was losing it because he could not stop, and he was walking faster in the strange-familiar maze of streets, stumbling, glancing over his shoulder. He did not belong here any more.

A Metro station. Wolf darted down the steps, gasping. He had the *strippenkart* out of his pocket, punched the last units through the steel barrier, and was half way down the moving stairs into the warm cavernous belly of the city before panic caught up with him again. His knees went watery.

Wolf clung to the rubber handrail, and swallowed a whimper. What was he *doing?*

The downwards movement and the slick tiled tunnels gave him the feeling of being pressed, hustled into a trap. He stumbled over the end of the escalator and hesitated— where now? The impetus that had propelled him thus far seemed, just as arbitrarily, to have deserted him.

Steps clattered to his right. He jerked round. A security guard was walking his way, head bent to speak into the two-way radio clipped to his uniform jacket.

Wolf turned on his heel and hurried in the opposite direction. He half expected to hear shouts, sounds of pursuit. None came. He slowed as he emerged on to the north-bound platform, rubbed one trembling hand over his mouth and crammed it back into his pocket wishing for a cigarette.

The black mouth of the tunnel boomed and extruded a hard moving column of warm air that smelt of stale water and unnameable waste.

Wolf held his breath. He moved forward with the scatter of other passengers to the platform's edge. The train rushed suddenly out of the dark, a squat live thing that hissed and squealed to a halt with a stink of hot oil and iron filings.

Wolf got on and sat near the doors, hunched over with his gaze on the floor. He was shuddering as if he had the 'flu. As the doors jerked shut, he closed his eyes, so that he wouldn't see the dark rushing towards him.

❖

'Hey, you. Jan. Wake up.' The train still clattered and swayed under him. Wolf didn't want to open his eyes, but the voice was insistent, close to his ear. A hard finger prodded his shoulder. He twitched away from the intrusion, and blinked at the figure seated beside him.

The young blonde girl who had been sitting there was gone. In her place, gazing at him with black eyes like two burnt currants in an over-cooked bun, was a plump man with pockmarked brown skin. When he saw that Wolf was awake, he smiled benevolently—a flash of small, impressively white teeth in his broad, stubbled cheeks.

The Fireman. Wolf closed his eyes again and uttered a faint, whimpering groan. Of all the people to meet when one was in a slightly flaky state of mind, the Fireman was the one to avoid. On a scale of one to a hundred, he wasn't as out-and-out barking mad as Pete Susskind, but the superficial lucidity lent his madness a certain shock value.

His street name was *Le Sapeur-Pompier*, although as far as Wolf had ever been able to tell, the man was no more French than he was. He spoke English with a curious accent that a man in a bar had once identified—violently—as Iranian. He was supposed to have come over as a refugee from the Iran-Iraq war, years ago, and had just never gone back. Wolf supposed that was at least as credible as any other explanation. He had certainly never been a Sapeur-Pompier, the French firemen. It was a moot point, really. He didn't get the nickname for putting fires *out*.

His blunt forefinger was still jabbing into Wolf's shoulder, like a naughty child at a doorbell. Wolf swallowed the groan and did his best to smile.

'*Bonjour, mon ami. Ça va?*'

'*Oui. Ja.* Not bad. On the edge, you know how it is.' The Fireman narrowed his eyes, International Man of Mystery, then smiled in delight, slapping Wolf on the back. 'They nearly got me, you know, two days ago up at the Dam. Had to hide underneath a music-box, man, I was under there for nearly half an hour, it's true. *Rudolph the Red-Nosed Reindeer.* I nearly chucked a grenade in just to make it shut up.'

Wolf made some kind of sympathetic face. Speech wasn't really necessary. All the guy needed or wanted was a pair of ears into which to pour his latest tale of the grand conspiracies that—according to him, at least—riddled the democracies of the Western world.

Wolf had never yet been able to figure out exactly what role the *Sapeur-Pompier* played in the endless reel of paranoia, but it was obviously pivotal, if the number of sinister pursuers was anything to go by. Spending half an hour hiding underneath a calliope was a normal way of passing the time, if you were the Fireman.

He was dressed as always, in layers of ancient military cast-offs, with the addition since Wolf had last seen him of an eye-catching Peruvian woolly hat with ear-flaps. A pair of red-tinted tank-driver's goggles hung round his neck, and his stubby dark fingers protruded from ragged mittens.

All around him, simmering away into the surrounding air, was a dim yellowish *something* that eddied sluggishly as he moved. Like an aura, Wolf realised. Probably his BO.

People who live on the streets smell. It's an unavoidable result of a life spent dressed in the same clothes, sleeping rough, a certain paucity of washing facilities or money to buy soap. Wolf had become more or less inured to the aroma of his fellow derelicts, but some bodily odours went the extra mile. The Fireman's was one of these. Wolf couldn't escape it.

The scent of a madman, Wolf thought, and wanted to laugh. Politeness made him turn it into a coughing fit. To make matters worse, the Fireman leapt up from his place and patted him solicitously on the back.

'Hey! Take it easy, Jan. Big breaths, yeah? Take it easy. That's it. That's good, yeah. Ver' good.' Stroking the back of Wolf's neck now, arm round his shoulders. The sensation set Wolf shivering again. The Fireman's voice seemed to come from far away and uncomfortably close to his ear, all at the same time. He had killer halitosis. 'You're running, *mon ami*. Who are you running from, huh?'

'How—' Wolf jerked his head round to stare into the bloodshot black eyes. The Fireman grinned, pleased at having surprised Wolf.

'A fox recognises another fox, huh. You have the look in your eyes. The question is, who are the hounds? Police?' He seemed unsurprised when Wolf shook his head. 'Military, then?'

'I don't know who they are.' Wolf shut his eyes and rubbed at his forehead. His head felt numb, his wits muddy. Sharing the knowledge of his predicament with someone else felt like a bad mistake, but the compulsion to share the burden was overwhelming. He comforted himself with the thought that, even if the Fireman were to tell anybody, they wouldn't believe him. He moistened his lips, and wished his voice sounded stronger. 'They wear black coats, carry guns. They tried to kill me but I escaped.' *Look at me*, he mocked himself, *mumbling to a madman on a tube train, as if he was a priest. Bless me, oh bless me father.* 'Look, I know it sounds crazy . . . '

'*Au contraire, mon ami. Au contraire.*' The Fireman's eyes glittered. He nodded. 'You've seen it, the truth, the skull beneath the skin. The MIBs, the men of violence, the new enforcers of the laws of the Medes and Persians. Their smiling mouths drip lies to trap the innocent. Their clean hands are full of the blood of those who stood in their path.'

'Yes,' Wolf whispered. It was the Fireman's standard paranoid pseudo-Biblical garbage—the man could spout like that for hours on end and link up anything from the Tokyo subway bombing to the Kennedy assassinations. Hell, probably take in Mary and her little lamb en route. Wolf knew all this. He just hadn't been prepared for the sheer scary emotional force of being caught up in it. Tears pricked his eyes. The hairs on the back of his neck bristled.

'You need a guardian angel,' the Fireman said, and grinned again. 'Need to rest? Sleep?'

Wolf managed a nod. The train was slowing. The Fireman tugged him to his feet. 'Hup. Come on, *mon ami*. I know a place, not far, you can sleep there. Safe, I swear. I'll stand guard myself, me and my partner here.' He twitched the layers of khaki aside.

Wolf found himself staring at the biggest, rustiest Bowie knife he'd ever seen, secured inside the Fireman's garments by a length of old red electric flex. 'Jocasta,' the Fireman murmured, and buttoned his coat over, patting the place fondly. 'Been in a lot of fights together, we have.'

Bet all the other guys died of blood poisoning, Wolf thought. He staggered as the train hissed to a halt. The Fireman gripped his arm, bracing him up against the steel.

'You trust me, huh? Trust the old *Sapeur-Pompier* do you, hoy?' The whites of his eyes were a road-map of tiny red veins. The irises were black with a silvery bloom to them, like olives.

Wolf stared into the Fireman's disconnected gaze from a distance of a few inches. He nodded again, numb. Not much choice, in the circumstances.

The white smile flashed at him, and the Fireman took a proprietorial grip on his sleeve. 'Right. You come with me. Best choice you make all day, *mon ami,* and that's the damn truth. They won't find you, not while you with me. Come.'

Wolf allowed the Fireman to lead him—tagging behind like an orphaned lamb—through the jostling lunchtime crowds. He felt drunk with tiredness. The prickly, panicky sensitivity had returned. Without the imperative grip on his sleeve, he would have frozen, or run. Lost, either way.

He stumbled in the Fireman's wake, up the rush of the escalator and out, dazzled, into the bright cavern of Centraal Station. It smelt of stress and wet coats. The Fireman forged a path through the single-minded rush of commuters and out into the street.

Snow flurried down and brushed Wolf's cheek.

'Wait.' The fresh air was making his head spin. He leant against a wall, forehead pressed to the bricks. It seemed all wrong to be sweating when it was this cold. The paving slabs beneath his feet swelled and dipped. He kept his eyes screwed shut until they stopped.

'OK, *mon ami*? We go now, yeah?'

Wolf opened his eyes at the familiar touch on his shoulder. His mouth was dry, and he couldn't summon the energy to speak. He shook his head. The Fireman tugged at his coat, anxious. 'We go now,' he repeated.

'I can't . . .' Wolf grabbed the man's mittened hand. 'I . . . just—get me—where I can sleep.'

'Sure thing.' The Fireman pulled Wolf's arm over his shoulders, started him walking west across the square. Masts and ice-crusted rigging poked up from the tourist boats moored in the dock. They halted to let a convoy of buses belch past. The Fireman patted Wolf's hand. 'Didn't I tell you already, I'm your guardian angel.'

'That's right,' Wolf nodded, then uttered a cracked laugh at the picture they must be making. 'Yeah, that's about right.'

'You bet,' the Fireman said. 'Come on, nearly there.'

Nearly where? Wolf had time to register a clutter of bikes around a painted kiosk. The Fireman led him round the other side, and stopped. 'Here.' He indicated a stack of folded trestle tables chained to the kiosk. 'Dry in there. Go on.'

Wolf realised that there was a triangular gap between the tables and the back wall of the kiosk. The Fireman looked about, anxious, and made shooing gestures. 'Quick, *mon ami*. I cover you. Quick.'

Wolf crouched down and crawled on hands and knees into the space. It smelt of cat's piss. He tried to back up and bumped into the Fireman. Wolf nudged him. 'Let me out of here,' he hissed. The Fireman patted his boot.

'You be safe in there till it gets dark. Nobody sees you. I stand guard right here, no problem. Get some money too, huh.' He had seated himself cross-legged on a scrap of carpet, right in front of Wolf's hiding place. Now he dragged up a clay ocarina on a piece of string round his neck, and began to play a squeaky, plaintive tune.

Wolf groaned. There was not even enough room to curl up and keep himself warm. He lay down on the freezing tarmac. It was incredibly uncomfortable. Outside, the asthmatic tootling of the Fireman's ocarina went on against a background of traffic and trams.

Wolf wrapped his arms round his head in lieu of a pillow, and tried to ignore the sound of folk-music being murdered by numbers.

13

COINS PINGED and twinkled on the ground. The music had stopped. Wolf opened his eyes and blinked, shivered. The light was almost gone. He must have slept again. No dreams this time—not that he could recall anyway—just a bleak, hung-over dullness. He could not decide if that was good or bad. His hip-bone hurt and he rubbed at it with numb fingers.

'You still asleep?' The Fireman's voice echoed as he stuck his head into the cramped space. Wolf got up on one elbow.

'No.' He shuffled himself backwards out into the snow and straightened, groaning. He did not feel rested at all—if anything, he felt worse than before. Stiff and exhausted.

The Fireman was in good humour. He danced around Wolf, brushing snow from his back and sleeves. 'Didn't I tell you I keep you safe, huh? Now we got money too. Come,' tugging at Wolf's arm and jingling coins in his mittened hand. '—come! We go get something to warm us up.'

'Sounds good to me,' muttered Wolf. He tried to follow and almost fell over. The Fireman grabbed his arm. Wolf leaned on the smaller man's shoulders, feeling ridiculous. 'Thanks.'

'Hey, is no problem. You need a drink, that's all.'

I'm not going to argue with that, Wolf thought. Except maybe I need more than one drink.

The Fireman was navigating eastwards. Nurse-tender, he steered Wolf away from the glare of street-lights and the gliding trams, into an echoing brick tunnel that must be an alley. They staggered between fire-escapes and overflowing dumpsters, feet slipping and sliding on loose trash hidden beneath the snow, like participants in a drunken three-legged race.

Wolf clung to the Fireman's coat. He felt clumsy and gangling, as if he didn't belong in his body.

No, that wasn't right. It was more like the feeling he'd had after that last blackout: someone had let themselves in by a hidden door. His body felt big and solid and capable, but Jan Wolf wasn't the one at the controls. It was like looking at one of those 3D pictures: the more he struggled to regain some sort of focus, the worse the feeling became. *Like wrestling fog.* The familiar warning tic of pain started behind his left eye, and Wolf cupped his free hand over the spot. *God, not again.* Maybe the drinks would help.

Beside him, the Fireman baulked, pulling on his arm. 'Whoa.'

In the pale rectangle of the alley mouth ahead, three figures stepped into the shadow of the buildings. Wolf saw them come sidling, outlined in crawly green fire like flames licking coal.

Adrenalin made his heart lurch. The pale, colour-tinged grey bloomed as if someone had turned on an invisible floodlight.

The Fireman tugged Wolf backwards. 'We better go back, *mon ami*. Those guys are bad news. Come. Come *on*.' Alarmed when he could not get Wolf to move.

Wolf shook his sleeve free. 'No time.'

The three men advanced more boldly now that they were away from the street. Their teeth and eyes glittered. They might be Filipinos. The nearest pointed a threatening finger and yelled something that was almost certainly not a friendly greeting.

Behind Wolf, the Fireman whimpered. Wolf spoke over his shoulder. 'Who are they?'

But there was no time for explanations. The men came briskly on, as if hurrying to an appointment. They halted a couple of metres away.

Just in case there was any doubt of their intentions, one held out his hand, palm up. He made a short impatient movement as if trying to snap his fingers: a knife appeared in his hand.

He must have cut his fingers to ribbons practising that move, Wolf thought. It had to be a spring-loaded arm sheath of some kind. Fancy. Too fancy, perhaps.

The third man, more smartly-dressed than the others, had halted a pace to their rear. He pointed straight at Wolf.

'You. Get out of the way.' The finger shifted. 'We want *him*. You can go.'

'Sorry.' Wolf shook his head and shrugged. A panicky fluttering in his guts. 'Why don't you leave, before someone gets hurt.'

He did not have time to be impressed at how calm he sounded. The leader jerked his chin up. The man with the fancy knife reversed his grip and flung the knife straight at Wolf's head.

The world changed.

Brightly-coloured flames blazed suddenly from every surface, gaudy as a Chinese lantern. The knife grip was yellow-green, hot from the man's hand. The blade was black. Its edge spat a trail of silver sparks.

The knife somersaulted through the air towards him—slowly, it seemed to Wolf. It was easy for him to duck aside. It passed by his shoulder. All in an echoey drawn-out moment of hissing wind-noise. The Fireman uttered a surprised yip.

The knife-thrower's eyes widened. Wolf flung himself at the man and threw a wild punch. Surprised himself by connecting. The man buckled.

Wolf stepped over him. The leader was groping inside his jacket. Wolf grabbed his arm, yanked and twisted. Bone and gristle popped under his fingers. The man's mouth gaped in a slow-motion grimace of agony. He fluttered into the drifted snow.

Wolf whirled towards the third man, teeth bared. The man windmilled backwards. There was a look of terrified revulsion on his face. He moved so slowly—Wolf couldn't understand it. He punched a fast one-two into belly and jaw. Hammer-blows. The man seemed to spring off the ground. A gymnast or an ice-skater, spinning. He had long hair—Wolf recalled that, later. Black, silky hair that streamed in an unseen wind.

The muffled fullstop of his landing seemed to do something inside Wolf's head. Colours sputtered into grey ash. Sound and movement returned in a rush.

The man whose arm Wolf had broken was screaming incontinently. The would-be knife man dragged him away at a staggering run.

Wolf took a step backwards, shocked. His hands hurt. A sour aftertaste of burning in his nostrils and mouth. Pearl-grey light everywhere, and muddy traceries of movement. Like being drunk only worse.

He was bleeding. Wolf put his hand to his mouth. His knuckles stung. The salty, rusty taste of the blood made his head swim.

He stood in the snow, swaying. The third man lay sprawled across the steps. Snow was already sifting on to him, like icing sugar on to a cake. He was horribly still.

Wolf twitched, and shuddered. There was a voice at his side, saying urgent things that he could not understand. Hands plucked at his coat. The Fireman. Wolf grasped at him.

'Gone? They're gone?'

'Yes, yes, my God yes. Come, come on. We've got to get out of here.' More tugging at his coat. The voice a little panicky. Wolf pushed the Fireman back against the slimy brick wall with hands that trembled.

'Who were they?'

'Just guys, they—I owe them money,' the Fireman admitted wretchedly. 'They get me some sweet gear, man you should see it, napalm grenades, blast radius like you wouldn't believe—' He broke off, some tendril of that paranoid sensibility telling him perhaps that this was not a good moment to rhapsodise over munitions. 'You saved my life, man.' He touched Wolf's fist, wrapped in the lapels of his coat. Fear in his eyes. 'Hey, come on, Jan. I'm your guardian angel, remember?'

'Sorry.' Wolf released him, confused. 'What the hell happened?'

'Happened?' The Fireman eeled past him. The white grin flashed again. 'You took them apart, man, where'd you learn to fight like that? You a cop or something?'

'I don't think they teach that sort of thing at the police academies,' Wolf said. 'People would complain.' He blinked at the body of the third man with its morgue-sheet of white. 'We'd better . . . better move.'

'You won't get no arguments off me.' The Fireman beckoned. 'Come on, this way.' Wolf allowed himself to be shepherded back the way they'd come. His limbs felt heavy as sandbags.

Wolf grasped after the Fireman's sleeve again, and pulled him up just short of the alley mouth.

'I have to find a place.'

'Sure, sure, com'on, not far now, we find another place, you can hide, sleep. Come on.'

'No.' Wolf shook his head. 'We have to split up. Safer.'

The Fireman nodded, already backing away towards the street. He looked relieved.

'Hey, take care, man. Don't let the sons of bitches find you, hoy? You need any more help, you know where to get me. I owe you one.' Another nod and he was gone, threading neatly into the street.

'Sure.' Wolf passed one hand gropingly over his forehead and leaned back against the bricks. His teeth clattered. *I just killed a man with my bare hands.*

He held them up to see what the hands of a berserker looked like. They looked just like they always did. He clenched them and stuffed them into his coat pockets. The wind threw snow round the corner into his face.

*I've hit people before. None of them ever **died**.* Wolf banged his head back against the wall and groaned out loud, 'What's happening to me?' The sound smacked back and forth between the walls. No answer. He swore, feeling wretched.

He had to hide. The boat. That name . . . what was it? He fumbled for the memory. *Questor.* Wolf turned up his coat collar and limped towards the end of Geldersekade hunched against the wind and the snow.

He had to find *Questor.*

What the hell was a Questor?

❖

Nobody can cry forever. The mundane always gatecrashes sooner or later, like a tactless acquaintance. I was no exception to the rule. I cut my toenails, flossed my teeth, brushed and braided my hair. I called in sick at the Fight Club, got a lecture from Sunny and made her promise to look in at the hospital later. I sat in Tom Barnabas' kitchen for a couple of hours, watching my stuff go round and round in the window of the washer-dryer and reading an out-of-date car magazine. I don't think I took a single word in, but the simple act of reading calmed me.

I must have eaten—there was a plate on the kitchen table with a few crumbs left on it. My belly wasn't rumbling any more. I just didn't recall actually biting, chewing and swallowing.

Things seemed like that today: disjointed, as if my life had been smashed into pieces and I had somehow failed to sweep up some of the smaller bits.

The emptiness of the house buzzed in my head. By the time the kitchen clock showed six p.m., my anxious self-flagellation had given me a belly-ache. Maybe I should make dinner. If only Tom would call.

The dryer cycle had finished, so I opened the round glass door and started to get dressed.

My cellphone chirped.

My hand shook so much, it took three goes before I managed to hit the right button.

'Hello? Tom?'

'No,' a woman's voice said, 'it's me.'

A blank pause. *Who*? I realised I was leaving it too long, and said, weakly, 'Oh, uh, hi. How're you doing?' I shuffled back to the washer-dryer and tugged my bodywarmer out. It was crumpled all to hell. I put it on anyway.

In my ear, the voice said, 'Robin, it's me, Zia. Are you all right?'

'Zia?' I flopped into a chair and began to pull on my socks. 'Whew, sorry. I didn't recognise your voice for a second.'

'I saw your place on the news,' Zia said. 'Are you OK? I mean, were you hurt?'

'No, I'm OK. Just one little cut but Tom fixed it.'

'Tom?'

I know what it was, I realised. *Her voice sounds different today. Usually it has all these .. . squeaks in it, little breathless Valley-girl kind of noises. They're not there. She sounds like someone else.* 'Tom Barnabas,' I said aloud. 'You might have met him, he served at Fort Polk with Dad? He's sort of a family friend, he's been really terrific.'

'Are you at his place now?' Something odd in Zia's tone. I frowned.

'Yeah, he's letting me stay in his guest room. Why?'

'Are you alone? I mean, is Tom in the house with you now?'

'No,' I said. She was creeping me out. 'He had to go to work. I thought you were him. *Why?*'

'Robin . . . ' Zia hesitated, then went on in a firm tone, 'Red, listen to me. You are in a very dangerous position. You understand what I'm talking about?'

I said nothing. My mind seemed to have stalled. How could Zia know? The complicity in her tone reminded me of the bearded man, the false white smile. *Don't forget now.* I could not speak. In my ear, Zia's voice went calmly on, 'You met an associate of mine yesterday. Gabriel? You gave him a message for me.'

'But I—' I stopped myself. '*You're* Artemis?' A rabbithole feeling. I got up and paced the cold floor. My voice wobbled. 'Chili, what the hell are you trying to do to me?'

'Gabriel told you about the Nemesis project.'

'Yeah.' I could not think. My brain was a numb exclamation-point of shock. Does anyone ever expect their schoolmates to do anything startling? Zia—Artemis—sounded calm, controlled, as if we were discussing the weather instead of the illegal activities of her own personal hacker group.

'Gabe didn't tell you who is behind the actual development of the drug.'

'Uh . . . n-no.'

'Red, I'm sorry to have to tell you like this, but things are moving, like, really fast.' Zia heaved a short sigh. 'Thanks for the message, by the way, hon. If you hadn't told us that . . . well. OK. Getting ahead of myself. We think that the company manufacturing Nemesis is DCI.'

'DCI? You mean, like *Michel*?' I sat down with a bump. Fortunately there was a chair in the way. 'No way, Chili. DCI are gunning for a business ethics prize, you know that.'

'Way,' Zia said. 'And this whole social-conscience bit's part of it. We think they set NERVE up to be a clean resource base for Nemesis. Think about it, Red, it's an R&D outfit. They're developing drugs to treat nervous-system malfunctions like MS. A lot of the chemicals and equipment used would be identical. You remember the break-in a few months back, the one that dumb reporter brought up at the launch?'

'Uh-huh.'

'There was no break-in,' Zia said. 'We've been through the computer records at DCI, and at NERVE and the police HQ. There are discrepancies. You saw the pics in the papers—labs smashed up, anti-biotech slogans sprayed everywhere. A lot of very expensive, specialised equipment was listed as destroyed or damaged beyond repair. DCI replaced the lot, but Red, get this—they never claimed on their corporate insurance. That's unthinkable, we're talking multiple millions of dollars for the stuff that's listed. The reason the assessors weren't brought in was that there was no broken machinery for them to see. It had already been taken to equip the Nemesis lab, wherever that is. Michel is using Dominique's work to cover up illegal research. Hell, we're pretty sure she's involved too. Thanks to Cary, we have a chance to expose them, and we're going to take it.'

'Chili, why are you telling me all this?' I sat clutching my head. The same nauseating whirl of conflicting thoughts. Zia sounded grim.

'NERVE has its own security team. After the break-in, Michel insisted that DCI would look after its own. Basically he foisted this team of grunts on to Dominique and her people to make sure things went the way he wanted. His own personal men in black.'

'Men in black . . . ?' I sat up and clawed a hand through my hair. 'Chili, don't be funny. I was threatened by a man in a black overcoat this morning. He knew about Cary. He, uh, he said if I went to anyone for help they'd end up like him.' I sniffed and tried to steady my voice. 'I think I should leave here. Tom says I can stay but I'm scared they'll think I've told him things and they'll kill him.' Tears again. I rubbed them away. Zia's voice in my ear was calm.

'Robin, I agree that you should leave, but Tom isn't in any danger.'

'You don't know that—'

'Yes,' Zia said soberly. 'I do know.'

'Will you quit that?' I started pacing again. 'Why isn't Tom in any danger?'

'Because even a scumbag like Michel Rancoul doesn't kill his own employees,' Zia said. 'Tom Barnabas has been working for Michel Rancoul for the last two years. He's the head of the NERVE security team, Robin. The men in black.'

'He can't be,' I said. 'He, uh, he—' *He what?* A cold feeling slid through me. It couldn't be true. Not Tom.

'Red, you have to trust me on this,' Zia said. 'He had your apartment blown up this morning. He probably had Kris de Haan killed. He had Cary Bowman beaten up and dosed with a dangerously toxic drug. He's been watching and manipulating you ever since he found out you were involved with Cary. And now he has you right where he can find you.'

'No.' I shook my head. 'I don't have to trust you on anything. You're wrong. Tom's my friend, he took care of me. Why would he do that? He wouldn't do that, why would he—?'

'Red.' A warning in Zia's tone. 'He's going to try to get you to leave—'

I cut her off, my voice rising. 'I, I can't believe you're doing this to me, Zia! My best friend is dying because your asshole *associate* refused to help me find Kris de Haan. Now you're asking me to believe that a man I've known all my life is going to harm me. I'll see you around, *girlfriend*.'

I cut the connection, and turned the phone off with fingers that trembled. Tears welled up again. It couldn't be true. It wasn't true. Tom had been around for so long, he was like a part of me. I knew him. And I knew he couldn't be involved in this.

Well, whatever the hell kind of game Zia and her merry hackers were playing, those guys in black were still out there. I couldn't make Tom a target any longer. I had to leave, now, before he got back. The decision steadied me.

I stuffed the phone back into my bag, slung it on my shoulder, then stopped, staring at my stockinged feet. My boots. They were upstairs in the guest-room. I scampered for the stairs, heart thumping, and went up two at a time.

The boots were where I had left them. I sat down on the edge of the bed and pulled them on without bothering to do up the laces. I heaved a shaky breath and made for the stairs again.

Tom was just closing the front door.

I froze in the doorway of the guest-room. I felt horribly hot and wobbly. If he looked up the stairs he would see me.

Barnabas puttered off down the hall towards the kitchen, humming. He dropped scarf and gloves on the hall table and draped his long black overcoat over the end of the banister rail. I stared at it as it hung there, dripping bits of half-melted snow. *This is crazy. He can't be one of them. A black coat doesn't mean anything.*

The telephone on the hall table rang. I shrank back into the darkened doorway as Barnabas came to answer it.

'Yeah?' He sat down on the bottom of the stairs to unlace his shoes as he listened. He made a disgusted noise. 'Mulder, you moron. Didn't I tell you he was a slippery sumbitch?' He placed his shoes side-by-side under the table and leaned back on the stairs, massaging at his right foot. 'The boss wants him under wraps by tomorrow at the latest—' A pause for whoever was on the other end, then Barnabas cut in. 'No, you listen, Karel. You can't handle the job, I'll replace you. How does that sound?' He grunted at the other man's response. 'You better, that's all.' He slammed the phone down. I stepped soundlessly backwards into the bedroom and eased the door shut.

No time to get undressed. I dropped my bag and coat in a heap on the chair and wrenched my boots off. I grabbed the enormous bathrobe off the floor and thrust my arms into it, bundled the thing round me all anyhow, and slid into bed.

I was just wriggling into what I hoped was a relaxed pose when I heard the bedroom door-handle squeak.

I froze, heart pounding. I had expected to hear Barnabas come up the stairs. Had he seen me move? I groaned in what I hoped was a convincingly sleepy way and opened my eyes.

Barnabas stood in the doorway, looking tired. When he saw that I was awake, he smiled and came to sit on the bed. 'Hey, Birdy. Just checkin' up. How do you feel?'

'Tired,' I mumbled.

'You hungry?' Barnabas asked. 'I got take-out,' he coaxed. 'Thai stuff—jasmine rice and everything. Beer too. There's a UEFA Cup qualifier on TV tonight, starts in a minute, what'cha say?'

I shook my head and tried to look wan. 'I ate already. I don't feel too good. I guess I'll come down later.'

'Sure, sure.' Barnabas mussed my hair in the same annoying way he had always done. Then he frowned. 'Baby bird, what'n'hell are you wearing your clothes for?'

I hunched my shoulders up round my face. 'I can't get warm.' At least that was true. I felt chilled.

Barnabas put his hand on my forehead. I tried not to flinch. 'You feel pretty warm to me,' he said. 'Give me your hand.' He timed my pulse for a couple of minutes against the big gold chronograph, and let me pull the arm back under the covers. 'Bit fast there. I think the shock's still got you. Why'n't you get some sleep, you'll feel better in the morning.'

'OK.'

Barnabas hesitated. 'Kid, now don't take this the wrong way, all right . . . I think you could use a break.'

'A break?' My voice seemed to have faded away to almost nothing.

'I think you should go back to the States for a while,' Barnabas said. 'It's about time you and your Daddy got yourselves sorted out. Even if you can't bring yourself to go see the old man, the holiday'll do you good.'

'Right,' I said. Something inside me had shrivelled at his words. I tried to smile. 'I'll think about it, OK? I don't have the money for the air fare—'

'Don't worry about it,' Barnabas said. 'You can borrow the cash off of me, let me have it back as and when.'

'Thanks,' I managed. 'I guess I'll do that.' I mimed another yawn, and closed my eyes. 'G'night.'

A slight pause. I sensed Barnabas lean over me. He smoothed my hair. His lips brushed my ear. ''Night Birdy.' He got up and walked out of the room. I heard the door shut, then his muffled footsteps going down the stairs.

I shot upright in the bed and hugged my knees, shivering. My mind was a welter of confusion; I was too shocked even to cry. Zia had told me the truth.

I had to get out. But how? Barnabas was downstairs, I couldn't just waltz out the front door. The back door was locked—I'd tried it out of curiosity when I'd been wandering round the house earlier. Anyway, he'd hear me. I buried my head in my hands.

Think, Carlson.

I opened my eyes. Shouldn't there be a fire escape? I slid out of bed and tiptoed over to the window. The glass was misted up and I had to wipe at it with the bathrobe sleeve before I could see out.

Iron railings, caked with snow. I cupped my hands round my eyes. It *was* a fire escape, I could see the steps criss-crossing down to the garden. Hope skipped in my chest. Thank God the guest-room was at the back of the house.

I ran my hands over the window-frame. It was an old sash window with a little swivel-lock in the centre. It was going to make the most almighty noise if I tried to open it.

I'd have to take the chance. I padded over to the bedroom door and pressed my ear to the panel. TV noises downstairs, some commentator getting over-excited. I almost smiled: Tom and his soccer. *I never would've thought I'd be grateful for that one day.* I heard the pop of a beer-can being opened. I couldn't be sure, but I thought the noises came from the lounge at the front of the house.

I'm not going to get a better run at it than this. I sat down on the bed and tied my bootlaces.

The key was in the lock of the bedroom door. I turned it, grimacing at every tiny rasp or click.

The window was worse. The lock dragged open with a miniature screech of rusty metal. I froze, listening for sounds of discovery. The cheering and honking of the football crowd carried on unabated. After an anxious minute, I turned my attention back to the window.

There were lifting hooks on the frame. I slid my fingers into the curved shapes and pushed upwards. No movement. Harder. Still nothing. I crouched, got my shoulders underneath the movement, and heaved.

The window shot upwards with a shriek of tortured wood, and stuck fast. A gust of cold air made the curtains billow.

I did not wait to find out if Barnabas had heard my unstealthy exit. There was a gap of about a foot. I threw my bag out on to the landing and crawled over the sill on my belly, gasping in fright.

The window would not close. I abandoned the attempt and slung my bag across my body. *Down, quick.* I gripped the iron handrail like a lifeline as I crept down the steel steps. The fire escape creaked like a nightingale floor. Every second, I expected Barnabas to jump out of the back door below and grab me. My legs wobbled when I stepped down to ground level.

I crouched for a second under the lighted kitchen window, listening. A splash of beery cheering went up from the other side of the house. I crunched my way across the white square of the yard with aching care, and slipped out through the gate.

I stood in an unlighted alley. I jogged along the path to the end of the row. Somebody had left a bicycle leaning against their back wall. There were no locks on it. I wheeled it away, heart flopping about like a landed fish. I'd never stolen anything before, *ever*. The ghosts of ancient outraged Carlsons were going to haunt me for the rest of my life.

The bike was ancient and pigheaded. It was also constructed for someone with legs at least three inches longer than mine. I hoisted myself up with as much panache as I could muster, and pedalled furiously, hoping like hell that I wouldn't have to stop. The bright lights of the Harlemmerweg were close. I veered on to the big road with barely a wobble.

The lights on Nassauplein were green. I sailed through, grinning like a madwoman. *I made it!*

I hung a hard right on to Brouwersgracht. The canal street ahead curved sharply. There were people around. Cars, trees, streetlights. I braked hard. Nothing happened.

I dropped on to the crossbar with a yelp, and tried to use my feet as brakes. My boots sliced through the slush like water-skis. My knuckles gripping the brake levers were bone-white. I was still travelling too fast. The corner raced at me like something in a video game.

I dug my heels in. The bike veered to the right, narrowly missing a tree. The front wheel rebounded off the rutted ice at the kerbside. I elected to fall off. The bike disappeared over the edge of the wharf.

Instead of a splash, there was a noisy clatter, as the bike hit the ice. Then silence. Somebody cheered. I picked myself up, brushing off snow. A group of young men were peering down at the bike from the far bank. One of them shouted something to me in Dutch, grinning. I lifted my hands, and shook my head.

'It's OK, guys, I'm walking from here. That'll teach me to take other people's stuff,' I added for the benefit of the ancestral ghosts, and walked briskly away. Or as briskly as I could when my knees felt as if they were made of marshmallow.

❖

I hid myself at the back of the first bar I came to, a dingy little place that was obviously short on money for lightbulbs. I chose a table where I had my back against a nice solid wall, and a good view of the door. How many times must I have seen that on TV when I was a kid, to do it like that without thinking? After my second bourbon, it struck me as funny: the etiquette of spies, the lore of the desperate. I felt underdressed for the role of desperado. I wanted to put on a pair of dark glasses and cuddle my gun.

Tom would most likely have discovered my absence by now. They'd be looking for me. The thought of faceless black-coated men cruising the streets sent a quiver of panic through me. I was going to need a hiding-place. I couldn't just book into a budget hotel or something—they'd expect that, and anyway the glass of bourbon in front of me represented the last of my cash. But what else was there? Tom had made damn sure I was as isolated as Neptune's frozen moons.

The impulse to just call Zia and let her sort things out was almost irresistible. I'm not sure why I resisted it, except that the Tekno-G made me think of the Fair Folk, heel-and-toeing it into my life with their esoteric knowledge without so much as a by-your-leave. Right then, I had a strong inclination to keep one foot planted firmly outside of their aetheric fairy-ring, Zia or no Zia.

I fumbled in my bag for my notebook. Lime-green fur fabric didn't seem a very serious choice for a lone fugitive. I felt down to the bottom of the bag for a pen, and flipped the notebook open.

The little passport photograph of Kris de Haan stared up at me. I tapped my finger beside him. 'C'mon, you were a PI, what would you do?' The faint smile on his face seemed to suggest that I would have to do my own thinking. Thanks, Kris.

I cupped my chin in my hand and looked over the list of facts I'd printed under the picture.

KRISTIAN DE HAAN.
BLOND; 6'?; BLUE EYES; BEARD?; EARRING?
FORTYSOMETHING?
TATTOOS—COLOURED COMPASS STAR WITH DOLPHINS ON CHEST,
WHALES AND DOLPHINS ON ARMS AND BACK, MONOCHROME (ARTIST:
KURT HELLER)(DESIGNS: K. DE HAAN.)
EX-FORCES (NAVY)(DIVER?)
WORKED IN FINE ARTS, MUSEUMS (CERAMICS RESTORATION?)
LAST JOB PRIVATE INVESTIGATOR, 'FIXX', KERKSTRAAT.
DRAWS AS A HOBBY—TALENTED (VERY).
EIDETIC MEMORY.
MARRIED IN 1977, TO LISETTE BRAUN (GERMAN CITIZEN).
DIVORCED IN 1980, NO KIDS.
HIRED BY CARY BOWMAN IN MAY THIS YEAR TO INVESTIGATE—???
DISAPPEARED AT BEGINNING OF JUNE
POSING AS A VAGRANT??? WHY???

The number of question marks was depressing. Snippets of information were worse than no use. It was like those stupid logic puzzles that I'd never been any good at: 'Kris got married in 1977, but not to Gerda. He is no less than six feet tall, but he has an eidetic memory and a compass star on his chest. Why is it dangerous for him to pose as a tramp?'

I snapped the notebook shut, feeling more inadequate than ever. A ripped manila envelope was stuck among the pages. I pulled it out with a sudden bump of the heart. It was the rent demand. I never had gotten around to looking at it. I pulled out the flimsy paper sheet and pinned the corners down with a couple of empty glasses.

Talk about grasping at straws. I took a hefty swig of bourbon and peered at the officialese in the dim lighting.

My spoken Dutch wasn't too bad, but reading it was something else again. I skimmed down the page. A meaningless word-blur.

What was that? My eye tripped on something scrawled in one of the boxes. I lifted it close to my face and squinted at the print: *Boot?* That was Dutch for 'boat', I knew that much. And *Namen*, that was easy—'name'. Boat name.

This was a rental demand for a *houseboat*?

The fainter pen scrawl was hard to make out, but it began with an 'O'. I twisted my head at various angles. Could it be a 'Q'?

I scrabbled in my jacket pocket, and came up with the little brass key. I turned the label over, fingers trembling: '*QUESTOR*'. It was a houseboat, and I had the front-door key. Just in case. Love, Cary.

He knew I'd need somewhere to hide, I thought. My throat closed up, and I pushed the glass away. *He knew they were on to him, and he hid it where he knew I'd find it.* I shut my eyes at a sudden stab of memory.

'A promise is a promise,' I whispered. I picked up the glass of bourbon and drank it down like a toast. *Hang in there, Cary. Just a little longer.*

14

QUESTOR didn't seem the right name for such a squat, black-painted lump of a boat. It looked like the offspring of a river barge that got off its leash and mated with a garbage scow.

I had almost walked past it when I saw the name, half-hidden under a snow-caked loop of rope.

I clambered over the slippery iron railings, and dropped to the deck. The metal plates boomed. I glanced about and tried not to look guilty.

My luck seemed to be in—it had begun snowing again while I was still in the bar. Pedestrians were fleeting, hunched shapes that scurried through the puddles of streetlights. Nobody was hanging about tonight to observe strangers. I relaxed, a little, and turned my attention to breaking and entering. Well, entering anyway.

The key fit the padlock on the main hatch. The padlock went into my coat pocket. I slid back the top hatch and dislodged a shelf of snow. Ice down my sleeve. I felt about inside for the bolt that held the wooden double doors closed.

The doors opened to reveal a black oblong. I poked my head inside. A musty smell of neglect greeted me.

'Anybody home?' No answer. I felt a switch under my hand, and snapped it back and forth without result. My heart sank. Of course, if the guy hadn't been here, he hadn't paid his bills either. The power must be cut off.

I felt further along the bulkhead. A wooden lip, and a handle. A cupboard door? I took an awkward step down on to the rungs of the companionway to reach inside.

My groping fingers knocked over something that rattled. Aerosol cans, and a wad of rags that smelt of polish. A bunch of small keys, and some kind of hinged control panel with rows of little buttons. A squashed roll of kitchen towel.

My heart went thud. A torch—the big boxy plastic sort with a handle on top. *Please God, don't let the batteries be dead.* I pressed the switch. A sickly circle of light appeared on the opposite wall.

Good enough. I pulled the doors shut, and clambered down backwards into the belly of the boat. The torch beam bobbed across wood panelling, dusty light fittings.

Bookshelves was my first impression: lots of them, crammed with books and papers. Framed pictures, propped against the books. A wooden drawing-board covered with a piece of cloth. It all looked dim and grimy. Nothing moved apart from a lopsided mobile that dangled on a piece of fishing-line from the ceiling. It was one of those plastic children's science toys with interlocking rods and balls in primary colours. It gyrated unsteadily in the breeze from the street.

I played the torch-beam slowly across the wide room, left to right. Segments of light slipped, ghost-like, over a neat, bare kitchen nook, pans and tools hanging on a rack on the wall. The light glanced off the screen of a computer monitor, perched on a narrow worktop in a corner.

A refectory table took up almost a quarter of the room, benches stowed underneath. In the centre of the room stood a big black wood-burning stove. A round chimney pipe went up through the ceiling. A dusty little portable TV sat on a shelf in the corner.

In the light of the torch, my breath clouded up. I shivered. It was freezing in here.

Satisfied that I was alone, I scouted the perimeter of the room, snapping open wooden doors. I discovered a wardrobe half full of men's clothing, a shower, a chemical toilet with a tiny wash-basin squeezed in beside it, and a set of steps, leading down into more darkness. Past the shower and the toilet, a heavy curtain patterned like a Turkish kelim pulled back to reveal four bunks.

The urge to lie down and sleep was seductive. I stifled a cavernous yawn. I prodded the pillows on one of the lower bunks. Soft, but faintly dank. I wiped my fingertips on my jeans leg, gazing around.

The drawing board caught my eye again. I lifted it on to the table and pulled the cloth away.

A pencil drawing: in blue and gunmetal-grey—fantastically grooved and barnacled— a humpback whale's tiny kindly eye and the patient, enigmatic curve of its mouth. It was not finished. I stared at it in the wan yellowish torchlight. If there had ever been any doubt whose place this was, it was dispelled in that instant. De Haan's style was instantly recognisable. I let the cloth drop back over the board.

I couldn't stay here with no light, no heat. But there wasn't anywhere else. Defeat thickened my throat.

I placed the torch on top of the stove, sat down on one of the frayed bench seats and unzipped my bag. My fingers, searching for the little cellphone, encountered the forgotten half-bar of chocolate I'd been saving for when I felt peckish.

If ever I needed comfort food, it's now. I broke the chocolate up into small pieces and ate them one at a time, wishing for a cup of hot coffee. It must be really cosy in here with that stove lit, a crackling-warm fire glowing out of the little glass doors, curled up on the rug with a good book, or better still with someone warm and companionable, someone you could read a good bit out loud to, or talk about movies, and laugh . . .

I gathered my wits, and dialled the number. As usual, he picked up on the first ring.

'Yep?'

'Gabriel, it's Robin Carlson.'

'You had us worried!' Gabriel exploded; then, calming himself with an audible effort, 'You OK? You got away?'

'Sure,' I said. 'No problem.'

Gabriel snorted, then cleared his throat. 'So, what can I do you for?'

'You can fix stuff, right? Computer stuff?'

'Sure, sure. Shoot.'

'I, uh . . . need you to hack a computer for me.' I heard him chuckle. I held the rent demand up into the torchlight. 'OK, got a pencil? It's the local government computer—uh, the Gemeente . . . belastingen . . . Amsterdam? There's a boat called 'Questor', registration number 6795, Oude Schans t/o 43, Stadsdeel Centrum. Owner K. de Haan. The, uh, precario—is that right?—it hasn't been paid. Oh, uh . . . and I don't have lights or anything. Can you fix that as well?'

'You don't want much, do you?' Gabriel made a disgusted noise, but I could tell he was amused. 'I'll get the *geister* on to it straight away.'

'The what?'

Gabriel sighed. 'Tekno-G is short for *Teknogeister*—machine-ghosts. That's us. We're the good guys. Try to keep that in mind, all right?'

'I'll call you.'

I switched off the phone and drew a deep breath. I hugged myself inside the heavy jacket: Gabriel and his ghostly buddies had better get that power on quick or I'd freeze to death right here.

Caution made me stir myself to turn out the torch. I still couldn't shake the creepy tingle of paranoia. I felt my way back to my seat, and sat down, yawning. I rested my head back. Really, it was pretty nice here. If I closed my eyes, I could imagine the soft glow of the stove, could almost remember what it felt like to be warm . . .

❖

I opened my eyes with disorienting suddenness on musty darkness. It came back to me in bits. The rent demand. Gabriel, and Tom. The boat . . . I groaned. I'd only meant to rest for a while, and it must have been *hours*. I was stiff with cold. My feet were numb blocks of ice inside my boots.

I was leaning down to massage some life back into my legs when the sound which had awakened me came again: a sharp creak, just overhead, followed by a thud. A man's voice muttered something.

I froze, terrified. Someone was on the boat.

Heavy footsteps crunched over the deck. I jammed my fist against my mouth to stifle a yelp as the hatch doors banged back against the bulkheads. There was the creak of weight being placed on the first rung of the ladder.

Move, Carlson! I slid off the bench seat. I felt with clumsy, trembling movements for the stove. The torch was where I'd left it. I clutched it in one hand and eased back towards the seat. My bag was just here . . .

The zip of the cosmetic compartment stuck. I yanked at it, and felt a fingernail snap. The Glock was smooth and cold against my palm as I slid it out.

Now what? My brain freewheeled.

There was nowhere to hide. The man was already coming down the companionway. I could just see him, a bulky figure outlined in the faint wash of light from the street. He tripped as he turned from the ladder, and grunted something irritable in Dutch. I steadied myself, and snapped on the torch.

'Stop right there! I've got a gun!' Voice a little too quavery for my liking. I thrust the Glock forward into the torch beam.

The man had frozen in a clumsy crouch. One hand was up in front of his face as if to ward off the light. He made as if to rise. I yelled at him in fright.

'Stay down! *Down!*' The man dropped back into the crouch, huddled against the bulkhead. He held up his hands in a conciliatory gesture. His voice was a husky whisper.

'Don't shoot—'

'Let me see your face.' I moved a step closer. The man shrank away, shaking his head.

'Please . . . the light . . . '

'Don't move.' I played the beam over his face. He winced, eyes averted.

'Leave me alone.' A hoarse thread of a voice. He had blond hair, I'd guess. It was plastered to his face and neck just now, dark with moisture, but the scraggy beard was fair. He was shivering, hunched into his snow-crusted coat. He looked about as wretched as any human being I'd ever seen. I jerked the gun, as punctuation.

'What's your name?'

'N-name?' He looked down, darted glances to the side—anything except look at me. 'Wolf,' he said eventually, without conviction. 'Jan Wolf.'

'That's not your name,' I countered. 'You're lying, I can see you're lying.'

'God's truth, lady. I'm Jan Wolf.' The man rubbed one finger into his left eye, blinking. 'Please, just put the gun down . . . '

'You're Kris de Haan, aren't you?'

I had been prepared for a lot of things, but not the speed with which he moved. One hand flicked out at me, quick as a snake. Torch and gun went flying. I fell on my backside with a spine-jarring thud. The light went out.

'Hey!'

The man was up the ladder in a flash, scrambling through the hatchway. I went after him—running on pure adrenalin, for sure, not common sense. Common sense never has been a strong Carlson trait.

'Hey, come back! I don't want to hurt you—' I was talking to myself. The deck was bare. I peered up and down the street. Apart from a couple of cars crawling through the slush, there was no one in sight. The wind threw snow in my eyes.

A clatter jerked my attention to the stern of the boat. I took a step around the side of the deck-housing and peered into the mosaic of black shadows and white snow. Something was moving back there.

'Mister?' I lost my footing and had to grab at the deck-house roof.

The man was just lowering himself over the side of the boat. When he heard my voice, he gasped a curse and let go. There was a hollow thump as he landed on the ice below the hull. I hurried to the side, slipping on the icy deck-plates. 'Hey! Wait, stop! It's dangerous down there, come back!'

'Please.' He was backing away, steadying himself on the hull of the next boat. His face was a pale blur in the shadows. 'Please, just leave me alone.' He turned away, and began working his way further along the hull.

'Goddamn it!' I flung a leg over the gunwale, hesitated a second, then stepped down and ran back to the hatchway: no way was I going after him without some light. And a gun. Definitely, a gun.

I found the Glock first, by dint of stepping on it. I ran fervent fingers over its cold shape. The torch was more elusive. I must have scrabbled about the dust-smelling floor for a minute or more before my groping fingers knocked against plastic.

No light. I snapped the switch back and forth a couple of times, then shook the thing, hard. A small, flickering glow, like an embarrassed fire-fly. I groaned aloud with frustration: I might just as well light a match. I hit the torch hard with the heel of my hand. The beam bounced into being, as if I had jolted it out of hiding.

I hesitated. I couldn't take the shoulder bag with me, but I didn't have time to lock up after myself.

I settled for stuffing it under the bench seat. It would have to do. The number of stupidly flukey things that had happened already today surely must mitigate in favour of there not being a burglary before I got back? I mean, *please*?

The wind had got up. It lashed tiny needles of ice into my face. I slipped and slid towards the stern, and found the broken crust of snow where De Haan or Wolf or whatever he called himself had gone over the side. I leaned out and peered into the mess of shadows and whirling white specks. Nothing moved on the ice.

Dammit, why had he lashed out like that? Why had he run? Didn't he know what kind of danger he was in?

Ah, an unhappy part of me admitted, but perhaps he thought a strange woman pointing a gun at him was in some way dangerous. Just a thought.

I found handrails, half-buried. There was a ladder. I stuffed the Glock inside my jacket, then dug gloved fingers under the metal and swung myself out, feet stabbing clumsily for a hold.

'Well, congratulations, Carlson,' I mouthed, clinging. 'This may be the stupidest thing you ever did. Oh, shut *up*,' I added, and dropped.

I landed as lightly as I could. The ice squeaked and flexed under my feet. My heart took up temporary residence in my stomach.

The moment passed. I shuffled warily the way I'd seen De Haan go, fending off the rust-streaked hull of the next-door boat. My woollen gloves were soaked already, my hands clumsy with cold.

The torch beam was just strong enough to pick out footprints in the shallow drifted snow. He seemed to be hugging the edge of the canal as much as possible.

I followed the straggly dotted line, grateful for his good sense. Oude Schans was wide as well as long, a stubby extension of the docks poking south-west into the city streets. Even with houseboats clustered three deep along its edges, there was a broad swathe of ice out there, and it would be thinner towards the middle of the canal, weakened by the passage—yesterday or the day before—of tourist boats and other water traffic.

The city up above carried on with its winter-evening amusements, heedless of snowstorms or incipient murder. Music gusted past my chill-numb ears with the flurrying snowflakes. Jazz closest to, a heavier house beat stabbing out from a club somewhere in the nearby streets. In one of the boats I passed, someone played the guitar, a rich dancing sound, and I heard laughter.

I peered out from beneath the prow of yet another steel-built scow. It was like a city within a city down here. A tight-packed, unplanned town of squat black walls and clusters of lighted windows like strings of coloured lanterns. The snow heaped along gunwales and deckhouse roofs only added to the sense of cosiness.

I sneezed and wiped water out of my eyes. The snow was falling fast now, big wet flakes. My hair was soaked. I turned my jacket collar up and gripped an ice-crusted rope with one hand to steady myself.

There were too many places down here where he could just stand still in the dark and I'd never find him.

Or—which sent a sudden quiver down my spine—he could stand still and just wait for me to tippy-toe past peeking hither and thither with the ridiculous little flashlight, and he could twist my neck. The way he'd gone for me, back on the boat . . . it had rattled me more than I liked to admit, even to myself. His speed was uncanny.

Shadows slid towards me between the boats. I choked down a yell. The torch beam wavered at nothing. I relaxed with a gasped curse, heart hammering. It was just a car, crawling past on the road above, its headlights throwing magic-lantern shadows downwards as it moved.

I squinted up at the iron railings that fenced the wharf off from the footpath. The relentless downward motion of the snow confused my eyes. There must be steps of some kind somewhere. It might be easier to spot him from up there. I'd certainly feel a whole lot safer.

Uncanny. I shivered again. I wished I could un-think the word. It set off all kinds of nasty primal, hind-brain impulses that clamoured for my attention. The biggest had flashing neon letters of adrenalin that read: *RUN AWAY*.

A close second added—*QUICKLY* . . .

I looked back the way I had come. To my surprise, I could not even see the *Questor*. On the far side of the canal, further back, the big brick tower of the Montelbaanstoren was no more than a backlit shape in the driving white. I turned back towards the harbour.

A dark figure stood in the swirling grey-white barely ten yards away. I froze. The man was making strange backward swooping motions with his arms. His fingers plucked at the front of his torso.

A dark mass fell to the ice behind him. I realised that all I had seen was the man struggling drunkenly to take off his coat. I muffled a gulp of nervous laughter, and switched the flashlight off. I backed away, taking care not to make any noise. Not that I really needed to be careful: in this blizzard, with the wind whipping past your ears, you couldn't even hear yourself, let alone anyone else.

My right foot slipped. I went down on one knee with a hollow thump. The man whipped round. I shrank into the shadow beneath the hull of the nearest boat, fumbling for my gun. My hands shook so hard, I could barely grip it. *Damn. Oh, damn.*

The man shuffled closer. I breathed shallow behind my folded arms. Just my eyes and the shaking muzzle of the Glock were exposed. I was on a level with his feet. He moved another step towards me, then stopped. A smaller step. He stopped again, maybe five paces away.

I heard him sniff, and cough, as though his throat hurt. His breathing was fast, fevered. He couldn't possibly see me in the deep shadows, but he was so close I could see the ragged knees of his jeans, little white whiskers of broken warp waving in the wind.

Why in hell had he taken off his coat?

I forced my gaze up the man's swaying body. He was dressed just in jeans and a thin shirt. He wasn't shivering at all. Hell, that sounded like hypothermia. I remembered Dad telling me about people going crazy and stripping off at thirty degrees below because they thought they were burning up. We'd had lectures about hypothermia in boot camp. Shame I hadn't listened. *Private Carlson, at what stage of hypothermia does the shivering reflex stop?* Drill Sergeant Cahill's face in memory had its usual expression of apopletic disbelief at my stupidity. My weary brain rebelled. I let my gaze carry on up to the man's face.

He was looking straight at me. My pent-up breath exploded out as if he had kicked me. He could not possibly see me down here in the shadows—but he had.

'Go away.' Bewilderment in his voice. 'Go *away*.' He whirled, arms stabbing out for balance. Then he was gone past the last of the boats, into the blinding scribble of white.

'Hey!' I crawled out of my hiding-place on hands and knees, fumbling for the flashlight.

He wasn't moving fast, thank God. I could see him, a shadow-figure visible in fits and starts as the wind rippled the white curtains. If I was quick, I could catch him. Except . . .

'Damn! Wait! Hey, wait, come back!' I tried to run and fell with a breath-stealing thud. Moving quickly was almost impossible here. The ice was swept clean of snow by the wind and it was horribly slippy. It was like trying to run in a bad dream—too late, too slow . . .

There was a crossroads ahead, a canal junction. That was why the wind swirled the snow away. And he'd have to cross, to get away from me. But which way?

I stepped out from the cover of the last houseboat. I sensed the wide open space even through the maddening snow. Faint globes of sodium light marked the bridge arch of the left-hand canal. A taxi crept over the bridge, headlights like yellow streamers. It all looked a million miles away.

I glimpsed the man ahead of me. His legs were straddled, arms out. He was more than half way across the Rapenburgwal and keeping his line, still heading up Oude Schans towards the docks. As I hesitated, he made the last few scrambling steps that took him to the dark wall on the far side.

I had to go after him. I tucked gun and flashlight inside my coat again and shuffled out on to the open ice. The faint sensation of responsive movement under my feet returned. My deep calming breaths threatened to turn into hyperventilation.

Keep your cool. It held him, it'll hold you. You're half his weight, easy. Just take it nice . . . and slow . . . one foot at a time. Slide, don't stride.

Who the hell coined that stupid line? I had a suspicion it had been my father. Serve me right to be forced to take his advice for once.

The ice squealed and groaned a beginner's easy piece for human nerve-endings as I inched across. I fought a compulsion to shut my eyes—as if the ice would be tricked into not perceiving my weight if I couldn't see it. Despite the cold, my back was damp with sweat by the time my outstretched fingers bumped brick.

How long had it taken for me to cross? Subjective time said a couple of hours. Real-time—well, two, OK, maybe four minutes if I wanted to be pessimistic. How far ahead could De Haan have gotten in that time?

Too far, that's how far. I just better stop him before he hits the real thin stuff out in that dock. I slipped on my behind again rounding the corner. I had to crawl over and pull myself up by a narrow flight of brick steps that led straight down into the ice; surrealist installation just for me.

I hesitated, peering up the steps, but they were crusted with unbroken snow. De Haan must have blundered straight past on his single-minded straight line to the docks.

The bridge was just up ahead—in fact, it was the only thing I *could* see up ahead. A flat dark cutout shape at the end of the last brick-walled corridor, topped by the tall stalks of street-lights. Prins Hendrikkade.

Snowflakes jerked and tossed in the orange spotlights, fairy-lighted oblongs of trucks rumbled past. A snow-plough whisked westwards towards the railway station, blades gouging two perfect arcs of glittering powder.

Beyond the deep blue shadow of the bridge, everything was white: a portal to the North Pole. Fragments of ice stuck up, broken and trapped, re-frozen. Through the whirling storm I could just see the blue-green, floodlit shape of the newMetropolis, sticking up like a failed attempt to raise the *Titanic* in the middle of Oosterdok.

Nothing moved on the rumpled plain. The man had vanished. My eyes ached from searching. I pulled off a glove to rub cold fingertips over my closed lids.

'This is stupid,' I repeated aloud—as if I needed reminding. 'Stupid, stupid, *stupid*.' I'd lost him.

I walked up the white trough towards the bridge. I couldn't go any further, the ice wouldn't be safe underneath. It never froze properly under cover like that.

Stupid was right, Carlson. You were so close, and you blew it. My throat tightened. I should just go back to the boat.

The ice under my feet thrummed. The sharp tang of snow was overlaid down here with algae and rust and brackish water. The wind had tidied the snow into smooth, concave drifts.

I went the last few steps to the shadow's edge—just so that I could tell myself, later, that I had done everything I could do.

My right foot kicked something heavy. I jumped back with a yelp of fright, slipped, pirouetted in a flurry of limbs, and headbutted the ice.

Light shone through the fat whirling flakes. I groaned and spat snow. *Must've passed out for a second*. I levered myself up on to hands and knees, shivering. The flashlight had fallen behind me.

I sat down to explore the damage. Limbs all intact, thank God. My face was numb when I touched it with my gloved fingers. A fat lip and a lump on my forehead. Could be worse. I twisted round to look for the flashlight.

The stupid thing had half buried itself in a drift. Its beam sliced across the grainy surface of the snow. The pointing finger of light threw what I had tripped over into sharp relief.

I sat there for several seconds, gaping like a dummy. I had found him.

De Haan lay on his side, stretched on the ice as if he had fallen asleep there. It was his outflung arm that I had kicked as I stepped into the dark.

I scrambled for the torch, and set it down gently. It wouldn't do for the thing to give out now. I knelt close to his head.

'Mister?' My whisper racketed off the concrete walls. Snow lay on him like a shroud, over his hair and skin and closed eyelids. 'Mister, are you OK?' *Oh God, please don't be dead.*

I stripped off my gloves. I hesitated a second, then brushed the snow away from his face. His skin was clammy and slick. The parted lips and the hollows of his eyes were greyish blue. 'Can you hear me?' My voice was a quivery whisper. My hands shook. I wound my fingers in the folds of his shirt and hauled him over on to his back.

The ice squealed in protest. There was an ominous splashing noise. I froze. My heart drummed 120bpm in sudden comprehension: he'd gone through. I sneaked out one hand to touch his jeans leg. It was sopping wet. I slid backwards and reached for the torch, shone it towards his feet.

Black water rippled in the stiff breeze. Under the shadow of the bridge was the same pearly skin of ice that we had crossed in the centre of Rapenburgwal, but thinner— much thinner. The broken black mouth lapped at its lost prey. De Haan must have dragged himself out, because only his feet still dangled in the water.

I shuddered: how could anyone haul themselves out of freezing water on to ice, especially in the state he was in? The guy must have the constitution of a buffalo.

I hooked my hands under his armpits, and hauled. A nasty splintering sound from the ice. I gritted my teeth and heaved. He slid free suddenly and I fell on my backside again.

I dragged De Haan twenty dogged yards from the bridge to the foot of the steps. Then I slumped on to the ice at his side, panting. How the hell was I going to get him back to *Questor*? There was no way I could carry him up the steps.

I bit my lips in frustration. Time was a big factor in hypothermia cases. If I didn't do something, and quick, he was just going to slip away.

I slid my hand inside his shirt, grimacing. I couldn't find a heartbeat, but I recognised the compass-star tattoo from the wad of sketches. Its vivid colours stood out stark against his milk-white skin.

An unpleasant possibility occurred to me. Sudden immersion in below-freezing water is enough to stop a human heart. De Haan's body had been cool and limp when I turned him over. Maybe he had already slipped away. Maybe what I was taking such great pains with was a corpse.

I brought the flashlight very close, and bent over him, holding my own breath. I found I was clenching my teeth together. *Come on.*

Vapour lingered in the chill air above his face.

'Oh, thank God.' I leaned down with my face almost touching his, and slapped at his cold cheeks. 'Come on, mister.' His breathing was tiny, desperate gasps. *Sheep's breath,* I recalled in a distracted aside. I had giggled along with the rest of my rookie class when Sergeant Cahill had uttered that immortal phrase. Funny, I didn't feel much like laughing now. I gripped his shirt and shook him. 'Please wake up. *Please.*'

On an impulse, I blew hard into De Haan's face. I was unutterably startled when he coughed and half-opened his eyes, mumbling something that I didn't catch. I shook him again, hard.

'Wake up! You've got to stay awake, come *on!*' The bruised eyes flickered open. I spoke loud and slow, as if to an idiot.

'Listen, mister, I don't know if you can hear me, but I'm trying to help here, OK? Now, I've got to get you back to the boat, the *Questor,* but I can't carry you, right? *Ik . . . kan . . . je . . . niet . . . dragen.* Understand?'

He didn't seem to have heard me, but after a moment, his lips moved. '*Questor . . . ?*'

'*Yes!* Yes, your boat. I've got to get you warm, understand? You're hypothermic, if we stay out here you'll die. You've got to help me.'

De Haan groaned, and coughed. 'Leave me . . . leave me alone.' He closed his eyes, and his head lolled to one side. For a stultifying second, I thought he had died. I straddled his body, shook him by the shoulders.

'You can't die!' I slapped him, full force, across the face. 'You've got to come back, you've got to, now come *on!*' Logic had fled. I pounded on his inert chest, sobbing. Tears mixed with the snowmelt on my cheeks. 'You're not going to give up—I won't let you give up—you're not going to die—you're NOT—'

Something caught my wrists mid-air. I yelped and tried to jerk away, couldn't. Fists the size of bear paws clamped tight on my arms. His eyes were narrowed.

'You hit me.' The hoarse thread of a voice again. He released my hands. I scrambled off him, trembling. *Nobody should be able to grip like that when they've just been half frozen.*

The man was on all fours now. As I watched he rose unsteadily to his feet.

If I had been the sort of person to take sensible advice—*well,* I thought with resignation, *I wouldn't be here at all, would I?*

I stepped in to his side, and dragged his arm across my shoulders. He gave a funny little growl of surprise, then leaned on me. He was very heavy. I tried to sound calm. 'Come on, Mister Nobody, we gotta get you back to that boat, get you warm. Up the steps. That's it, one foot at a time. Whoa, careful. C'mon, it's not far—'

❖

The coaxing and hauling on his hand (which felt like a lump of frozen meat), and drunken staggering and heavy breathing seemed to me to go on for about a week.

Then we were out of the wind. The constant flurrying attack of snow had stopped. I was taking the last step down off the main companionway into *Questor*'s saloon. And there was a polar bear sitting hunched over at the bottom of the ladder, getting in my way.

I wiped water out of my eyes, and blinked. It was only De Haan—or whoever the hell he was—slumped against the bulkhead covered in snow.

I reached back up to push the doors together. The muscles in my arms and legs quivered. *And I thought I was fit.* I pushed the bolt home, wheezing, and reached out to touch the light-switch. 'C'mon Gabriel. Gimme that power . . . '

With a rapid succession of flickers, light bloomed overhead. I stepped down—careful not to tread on the man's limp hand—and moved through the saloon flicking switches. Light, wonderful light, from reading lamps and spotlights. The place was even cosier than I'd imagined. Polished wood, and golden-yellow paint edged with patterns in crude chalky blues and greens.

From beneath the wooden settle by the stove, my phone rang, muffled. I ran to answer it.

'Hello?'

'Told you I'd get you fixed up all right,' Gabriel said, smugly. 'You've got electric, gas, water, the works. Phone's connected. We even paid his taxes for him.'

'Thanks.' I hesitated, and lowered my voice, gazing over at my unconscious visitor. 'Gabe? I, uh . . . I found him. I found De Haan.'

'Get outta here.' Gabriel's voice went high with disbelief. 'How did you manage that?'

I paused before answering. 'That might take a little explaining.'

'Well—is he OK? Can I talk to him, this is terrific!'

'He's asleep,' I lied.

'This is incredible!' Gabriel was bubbling. 'Robin, you little genius. Artemis was right about you. This changes everything!'

His enthusiasm grated. I sighed. 'Look, just tell Zia I found him. You've got my address here, don't you? Come here tomorrow about twelve, you can talk to him all you like.'

'That's not a good idea,' Gabriel said. 'You know what it's like with Zia, she can't go anywhere without the paparazzi following her. No, you bring him to us. I'll put the address for you to pick up in Zia's V-Zone room, OK?'

'OK,' I said. 'See you tomorrow.' I pressed the off button before Gabriel could object.

Time to see how much of that survival training you really took in, Carlson.

I squatted down in front of the stranger, and pushed the wet hair off his face. Whatever reserves of strength had got him this far seemed to be gone. His skin was very white under the saloon lights, and there were still those awful blueish shadows around mouth and eyes. His breathing was very shallow. 'You're going to be all right,' I told him. I wondered if he could hear the uncertainty in my voice as clearly as I could. I cleared my throat and tried to inject some authority into my tone. *Just pretend Drill-Sergeant Cahill's standing behind you with a clipboard.* 'Gotta bring your temperature up just a little at a time. That's important.' I sighed, and patted him gingerly on the chest. 'I wouldn't like you to think that I didn't know what I was doing here.'

15

LIGHT was the first thing that Wolf was aware of: flickery yellow light. It snapped and creaked and sang to him in a chorus of wheezy voices. He drifted, listening to the light.

His drowsy solitude was interrupted by fierce scrapings and rattlings. Wolf blinked, and found that he was looking at the crouched silhouette of a woman. Stoking a fire, from the sounds that accompanied the vigorous movements of shoulders and arms. Iron banged on iron, and she sat back on her heels with a satisfied noise.

Wolf gazed: there had been a woman like this in his dreams. An American. She had been angry—he remembered that, though he did not remember why. So fierce . . . perhaps he was still dreaming. His eyelids slipped a notch. The woman was gone again. The yellow light sang him back to sleep.

❖

The next time Wolf awoke, it was darker. The yellow light had dimmed to a glowing orange rectangle. He moved his head a little, and discovered it lay on a soft pillow. Why was he so cold? He was shivering all over despite the blankets that wrapped him, and there was a foul taste in his mouth. He tried to cough, but his throat stuck together. All that came out was a truncated croak. He lay still, and tried to gather some sense of where he was.

Shapes teased at the limits of his vision. The glowing rectangle was the fire-door in a pot-bellied iron stove. He was lying on the floor in front of it. If he swivelled his eyes the other way, he could see benches lining the wall behind him. There was painted wood panelling, striped with shadow. A frayed old armchair.

Wolf craned his head off the pillow, confused: he could not see anything except what the faint brushstrokes of orange from the stove revealed. What had happened to the pearly light, the foreign, crawly colours? He had become so habituated to them that their absence shocked him. He felt so weak and dizzy that he had to lie down again. Was this what withdrawal was like? He could not seem to concentrate.

There was a bang of wooden doors, a whisk of cold air.

The woman was there again, a flashlight in her hand. She knocked snow off the front of her jacket, and dumped a dark bundle on the floor. She kicked her boots off, and padded over to bang open the fire-door.

She stirred at the glowing mass inside with a blackened poker. The result did not seem to satisfy her. She went off and came back with splintery chunks of wood. She fed them to the stove one by one, blowing on the embers, holding her coppery hair back from the flames with her free hand. She had a jaw you could crack rocks on.

When the fire was snapping primrose-hot again, she turned to look at Wolf. 'Awake, huh.' In an American drawl. She placed the back of her hand on his forehead, then his cheek. A nurse's touch, impersonal and brisk. 'You're a little warmer. How'd you feel?'

Wolf tried to speak but only the ridiculous croak came out. The woman got up. Water drummed into a steel sink. Then she was back, slipping a hand under his head. 'Here.' A cup touched his lips. His teeth clattered against the china as he sucked at the tepid liquid. He would have drunk it all, but she took it away. 'That's enough for now.'

'Cold . . .' Wolf gulped. He had to clench his teeth to keep from biting his tongue. His voice came in a series of grunts and gasps. 'Why'm I . . . so . . . *cold?*'

'You went through the ice,' the woman said. 'Don't you remember?' She leaned over him, doing something to the blankets. 'Hope you don't mind me using your place like this, I needed somewhere to hide, and then—' She quirked one shoulder. 'Well, you were pretty sick. Still are,' she added, sitting back on her heels. 'Don't worry about the shivering, OK? It's good. Your body's trying to warm itself up. You weren't shivering at all when I found you. I thought you'd given up on me.'

Memory tweaked at Wolf: the cold lying over him like a feather quilt, and all he'd wanted to do was sleep, just for a moment . . .

Wolf tried to focus on the serious, intent face that hung over him. 'You wouldn't let me sleep.' Another twinge of remembrance. 'You *hit* me?' He moved his jaw experimentally. It hurt. 'You hit me,' he confirmed idiotically. Surprised at how small and shaky his own voice sounded.

'I couldn't just leave you there,' the woman muttered. She looked away from him. 'I couldn't carry you, I didn't know what to do . . . Look, I'm sorry, all right,' she said abruptly. 'I'm sorry I hit you.'

She jumped to her feet and went to rattle things in the sink. Wolf could hear her moving back and forth, small busy noises. An odd feeling crept over him, so unfamiliar that he had to grope for the word: *safe.* He could not recall the last time he had felt safe.

'Here you go.' She was kneeling beside him again. 'Want a little more water?'

Wolf nodded stiffly. This time, the water was warm. The woman chuckled at the grimace he made. Her voice was deep but not mannish, with a throaty catch to it.

'Sorry, pal. You've got to take it one step at a time. Too much heat too quick, you could drop dead from shock. And there's no way I'm going to let *that* happen,' she added, and took the cup away again in mid-drink. Wolf groaned and wriggled his stiff neck against the pillow. The woman frowned at him, upside-down. 'Try to sleep, OK? It's what you need right now.' She turned away.

'Wait,' Wolf croaked. She looked back at him, frowning. He cleared his throat. 'Who—who are you?'

A small silence. Then the woman uttered a snort of laughter. 'I'm your guardian angel. Go to sleep.'

Wolf could not have disobeyed even if he had wanted to. He slept, and dreamed confused dreams of sleek-feathered wings and guns and snowflakes.

❖

The woman woke him at some point during the night with a cup of hot black tea. This time she let him drink it all. Wolf's throat felt better when he had finished. He sank back into sleep so quickly that the brief, silent interlude seemed like just another dream.

If it was, it was not the only one. Wolf bolted awake in the early hours with the familiar gut-jolt of a nightmare. His hands were pinned down at his sides. He fought them free of the rat's-nest of blankets and lay, shuddering, until his heart stopped rabbitting in his chest.

Wolf sat up with a groan, clutching his head. He felt all wrong. Every damn joint and muscle in his body hurt. His back was an articulated column of aches and pains. Pins and needles handily filled-in where all the other discomforts left off.

Wolf rubbed at his tingling legs, and found that he was naked under the blankets. He looked around for his clothes. After the humiliations of the Hole, hanging on to them by choice felt important.

In the faint glow from the firebox, he saw a door.

Recognition was instant: it was in there. The thing he needed was behind that door, he just had to go and get it—had to go and get it now. *Now.*

Wolf got to his feet, dragging the topmost blanket around himself, squaw-style. His legs wobbled. The floor looked far away and close to simultaneously.

He misjudged his grab at the door-handle and the panel rebounded off the wall with a bang. Steps, leading down into darkness. He set one bare foot to the metal tread.

'Hey!' Rapid footsteps behind him. The woman had him by the shoulders, tugging him backwards. 'Whoa there, where're you going?'

'Got to find it,' Wolf managed. He clung to the steel rail, swaying. What was he doing? For a second, he couldn't remember.

'Find what? What're you talking about?' She'd eeled past him somehow in that instant of blankness. Now she blocked his way down. Wolf tried to side-step but she was nimbler and not encumbered with blankets. 'Find what?' she repeated, then frowned. A flicker of her cool hand on his cheek. 'You're burning up, you're sick. What—'

'Not sick,' Wolf said. Rising urgency. His mouth felt swollen and stiff. 'Hid it—down there.' He nodded down at the dark stairwell. 'Please . . .'

'What're we going to find in the engine compartment, for Pete's sake?' Caustic. She scowled, then relented. 'Just wait while I get the lights.'

The striplight stabbed at Wolf's aching eyes, but perversely failed to illuminate much more than a puddle of steel decking at the foot of the steps. The woman had wriggled in below his arm again, and she supported him down into the diesel-smell of the compartment. Wolf trusted his weight to her shoulder with a twinge of surprise. He'd forgotten how strong she was.

At the bottom, she stepped away from him, flipped back her hair, folded her arms and peered around the damp-smelling space with obvious distaste.

'OK, what're we looking for?'

'Need—' Wolf gestured and had to grab for the handrail again. His breath wheezed in his throat.

'What is *wrong* with you?' The woman again, in his face, peeling up his eyelid with her thumb. Wolf batted at her hand.

'Get off. I'm all right.'

'Sure, and I'm Mother Teresa. You're sick, you should be in bed, not staggering round in the cold with nothing on. Come on, come back up in the warm and lie down.' She patted and pushed at his shoulder like a mahout with a reluctant elephant. 'You need a couple of paracetomol—'

'No.' Wolf clung to the rail. 'I know what I need. S'there . . .' He nodded at a steel hatch-plate in the floor. His teeth were chattering now. 'In there . . .' His fizzing, distant legs wouldn't hold him, so he slid to his knees beside it.

The catch was stiff. Wolf's fingers were clumsy bananas that seemed to belong to someone else.

'Here, let me do that.' A warm body leant beside him, quick strong fingers turned the rusted metal. 'There, it's free. Look out, I'll get the plate up.'

Wolf crouched backwards, blinking in the confounding darkness, while she heaved the plate up and scraped it off to one side. A stink of diesel and stagnant water. Wolf leaned over the side of the hatchway. Black greasy water, still as a mirror. His breath disturbed the surface. The stink of diesel filled his nostrils and mouth.

Very close now, he could almost remember. Had to remember, had to find it quick now, quick—

Wolf leaned down and plunged both arms into the black water. His knuckles jarred against metal. Soft silt tickled his fingers.

What was he doing? He couldn't remember. The freezing water frightened him. Exhaustion surged in his limbs like molten lead. Wolf gasped a curse. *Black water that stank of diesel fuel, water in his eyes, his belly, his mouth* . . . He jerked his arms out of the bilges all slimed with grey oil, dripping.

'Kris? Are you OK?' The woman. Why did she keep calling him that? He'd forgotten her, crouched intent beside him.

A couple of deep breaths. Wolf closed his eyes, frowning, and let his fingertips touch the surface of the water. Icy water, and the smell of diesel fuel . . . He just needed to remember what these things meant *before* . . . Wolf's eyelids flickered. His breathing became ragged. A dreamlike certainty: he had hidden something down here, something important. He would find it . . . *here*.

He reached out under the water. His fingers brushed plastic.

Wolf groped at the slippery shape. A small hard rectangle, covered in thick polythene. He barely had the strength left to bring it to the surface and dump it on the metal plates at his side.

Wolf dragged himself away from the open bilges and collapsed against the bulkhead, wheezing. The mess of oil and grime on his arms disgusted him but he seemed to have used up his strength. The air felt too thick, it was a constant struggle to suck it in and push it out.

The woman's throaty voice belled around him in the ringing metal space. Wolf could not make out words from the stream of sound. He was so tired. His chest hurt inside. Wasn't there something he had to do? Nothing would stay in his head, thoughts dribbled away like the water droplets that ran off his fingers.

A white shape jiggled in front of his eyes. She was holding up the little package, turning it over and over as if it was a bloody Chinese box puzzle instead of—'Give,' Wolf managed to whisper. 'Give . . . it . . . me . . . '

The effort of speech took the last of his energy. Footsteps scuffled right by his head, then receded. Someone must have turned the lights out. Why didn't she put the blanket over him at least?

Wolf stared at a grey rectangle, somewhere above him. He could no longer see or even hear the woman. He struggled for a moment to understand what that meant. Had she left? Was she hiding from him? Nothing made sense. Everything cold and dark as the inside of a sack.

Zwarte Piet. Wolf's eyelids fluttered. His ribs were steel bars around his lungs. He tried to breathe shallow so it didn't hurt, but all that happened was that he felt tired, and the shadows in the corners of the room crept towards him, sucking the last tiny glow of light away until he could no longer see anything.

Wolf lay smothered under the weight of the dark. Tears pricked his eyes. She said she wouldn't let me die, she *promised* . . . Some lucid part of his brain demanded to know when exactly he had begun to trust the promises of complete strangers. Wolf could not summon a coherent answer. Dark covered everything now. Only the pain was bright and sharp. He clung to it.

Warm fingers pressed his neck. The woman's hands shook as she tilted his head back. Wolf felt her breath on his cheek, then a cold kiss of metal on his throat.

His heart stuttered. The gun, that fancy 9mm of hers. She was going to shoot him. He forced his eyes open. She was bent over him. When she saw that his eyes were open she smoothed his hair and twitched a tight, unhappy smile down at him. 'Here goes nothing.'

A dull thud of noise. The metal kicked against his flesh. It felt as if she had flicked his neck with her fingernail. It stung.

Wolf recognised the sensation with a flood of relief: not the 9mm, but a hypo-gun. The white package. Memory ghosted through the ruins of the grey walls: he had stolen the gun ready-loaded. The drug in the plastic vial was a delicate pale blue.

A sliver of ice slid into his heart. Wolf shuddered. A dizzy lurch, like the moment at the top of a roller-coaster. His skin felt a size too small. She had banged the stuff in right over his carotid artery.

Wolf clenched his teeth and groaned. His skull felt as if it was filling up with iced water. Cold lapped over him as if the intervening time had been a delusion, and he was still lying out there on the canal with snow falling on his skin.

The woman was kneeling beside him, gripping his hand in both of hers. She was bent forwards like a squire at prayer beside a fallen knight. Her fingernails dug into his palm. She looked scared to death.

Wolf wanted to say something reassuring, but his lips and tongue seemed to have forgotten the mechanics of speech. Besides, he was scared to death as well.

He took the fierce grasp of her hands with him into the dark.

❖

'Home.' The word lacked conviction. Wolf braced his arms on the sides of the tiny washbasin, looked himself in the eye and tried again. 'I'm home. This is . . . my . . . home.'

Wolf squeezed his eyes shut and tried to ignore the knot of panic in his stomach. It was no good. He might as well be speaking a foreign language.

He'd hoped that getting showered and shaved and dressed in clean clothes—like a real person with a real life—would help bring things into focus. It didn't seem to be working.

Wolf stared at his reflection in the water-spotted bathroom mirror, and ran a hand over his jaw. Wet-shaving was obviously something that took practice. He'd made a real dog's breakfast of his face.

If it *is* my face, he grumbled. Something else that didn't feel real. Apart from the eyes and the familiar beak of a nose, the man gazing back at him was a stranger.

There was something about the set of the jaw and the mobile, mocking mouth that belonged to someone else. Kris de Haan. Wolf didn't like him. He wasn't even sure he trusted him.

It was as if the person he had been had fled, capriciously abandoned his traumatised flesh until such time as he—they? (the etiquette of addressing one's own absent person vexed him)—deemed it safe to return. Any attempt on Wolf's part to hasten the process had been met with resistance bordering on aggression.

Now, that person wanted his body back. The only trouble was, in the interim, Jan Wolf had made himself at home here, and—in traditional Amsterdam style—asserted squatter's rights. A certain amount of mental squaring-up and unfriendly staring was going on.

Wolf blew out his cheeks in a sigh, and shook his head at himself in the mirror. He'd pulled his hair back in a ragged ponytail, and it tickled his neck. *I'd better figure out who exactly I want to be, before I really do go crazy.*

'You ready back there?' The woman's voice snapped Wolf back to the present. He stuck a finger in his eye before it could twitch. Somehow, he'd expected his guardian angel to be bigger. She made him more nervous even than the man in the mirror.

The changes had begun the second he opened his eyes, some time in the early hours. It wasn't that he was averse to clean clothes, but it's an altogether different kettle of fish when a woman tells you she's burned your stuff, and points you at the shower.

Wolf smoothed at his new clothes and scowled. There were jeans, and a thick flannel overshirt that did in place of a sweater, and socks and underpants thank God. Even an old pair of work-boots.

They were good clothes, they fit just fine. Wolf still felt as if he was being washed and brushed and dressed-up to act in a play for which he hadn't learned the words.

He opened the bathroom door: food smells, and a tantalising whiff of coffee. He hadn't had a cup of coffee since—well, for too damn long.

The steel-capped boots clumped as he walked into the saloon, and made him feel twice as big and clumsy as usual. Grey daylight bled from behind the closed blinds.

Wolf ducked his head to avoid the mobile dangling in the kitchen nook, then reached up to touch the silly plastic thing with one finger. *I must have put this here.* He couldn't remember why.

'Don't know if you like beans,' the woman said, as Wolf scraped back a bench and sat. 'It's all I could find.'

Wolf stared at the steaming dish of baked beans in front of him. They had been cooked into a dark orange mush, flecked with black. He swallowed. 'Thanks.'

''Scuse me if I don't stop. I'm kind of hungry.' The woman pulled a guilty face, and filled it with forkfuls of beans. Wolf watched her pack away the contents of her dish.

She ate with a single-minded concentration that he recognised. After a minute, she looked up with a frown. 'You're not eating.'

'I'm not hungry.' Wolf put down his spoon. 'I'm sorry—'

'No problem.' She grinned at him, a bit shamefaced. Wolf noticed that she still did not quite meet his eye. 'Push it over here. Waste not, want not.' She seemed to see him for the first time as he leaned over with the dish. Her brows went up. 'Say, you clean up pretty good.'

'Well, thanks.' Wolf shoved the bench back, hard. 'I bet I smell better too, don't I?' He stamped over to the sink and opened a drawer, pulled out the tobacco pouch and matches he'd seen there earlier.

When he sat back at the table, the woman had put down her fork. Wolf pinched up tobacco, stopped with raised brows.

'I'm sorry.' She was crimson. A part of Wolf noted with interest that her face clashed with her hair colour. She bit her lips together, then sighed and lifted her hands. 'I really am sorry, OK? I don't have any right to be rude to you.'

'You didn't have any right to burn my clothes,' Wolf pointed out darkly. He ran his tongue along the edge of the paper, then picked strands of tobacco off his lips. 'Didn't seem to stop you.'

'I needed fuel for the stove, and anyway they stank. What do you want from me?' Definite sore tone there. Wolf lifted his eyes to meet hers. She flinched at the eye contact, but there was a mulish set to her mouth.

'Nothing,' Wolf said. 'I don't want anything from you. Well . . .' He scratched at the nape of his neck, stuck the unlit cigarette in the corner of his mouth. 'Maybe your name?'

'Oh.' She hesitated. Wolf could see her thinking back along the short but convoluted line of their acquaintance. It had been packed full of incident, certainly. Odd intimacies, even. Introductions, no. She moistened her lips, hesitated again.

'I'm not holding a gun on you,' Wolf snapped, obscurely irritated by her reticence. 'You don't have to tell me, all right? Don't have to stay if you don't want to, either.' He struck a match, and puffed on the slender cigarette, affecting not to watch her from the corner of his eye.

The reminder of his ownership of the boat had knocked the wind out of her. Her face had gone very stiff, and she was having trouble swallowing something. Her pride, maybe. Wolf felt ashamed. He'd been away too long, he'd forgotten his manners; or maybe this was how Kris de Haan always spoke. Wolf made a sudden, silent resolve that he was not going to do the same.

'Robin.' The woman stuck her chin out at him. It had a little white scar on it. 'My name's Robin Carlson.'

'Jan Wolf.' He stuck out a hand across the table. After a tiny hesitation, she shook.

185

She had a small slender hand, and a grip like steel pincers.

She let him have his hand back, and poured coffee from a pot. 'Do you drink it black? Only there's no milk.'

'Then I guess I drink it black,' Wolf said, deadpan. He grinned at her startled look. 'What—didn't you expect a tramp to have a sense of humour?' He blew a smoke-ring and drank coffee. The woman looked uncomfortable.

'But you're not really a tramp, are you?' She flickered a look at him over the top of her coffee cup as she sipped the hot liquid. Green eyes, direct and cool as a cat's.

'Oh?' Wolf kept his tone light. 'Do you have another word for it?'

'You—uh, y-you were undercover.' The woman stuttered under Wolf's uncomprehending stare. She ploughed on. 'Carrie told me you'd discussed it, it was something to do with the Nemesis project. You decided it was too risky. I mean, you're a PI, not a cop, right? You were supposed to try to get the information some other way. Then you disappeared, everyone thought you'd gone off to Germany or something, but you didn't, did you? You stayed right here in Amsterdam—'

'Germany?' Wolf held up a hand to fend off the dizzy flood of words. *I'm a PI? Like Mike Hammer or something?*

Merciful heaven intervened on his behalf just then: the little cellphone on the table rang. The woman started, then picked it up.

'Hello?' A pause in which she fiddled with her hair. She glanced at Wolf, then away. 'Yeah, he's here. . . . no. Look, Gabe, I don't want to—' She broke off and chewed the end of the lock of hair, rolling her eyes at nothing. 'Gabriel—*Gabe*—look, all right, tell her we'll come. What time?' Another short pause. 'Ok, got it. See ya later.' A brittle, unhappy laugh. 'Hey, I'm always careful.' She punched a button and placed the phone back on to the table between them. 'Damn it.'

The expletive did not seem to be aimed at Wolf, but she still seemed disinclined to look at him. He dropped the cigarette into the dregs of his coffee with a tiny sizzle. 'Who was that?'

'Friends.' A flicker of assessment from below guarded lashes. 'The TG. They want to meet.'

She obviously expected the letters 'TG' to mean something to him. Wolf shrugged shortly, and looked away. 'Whatever.' How was he supposed to explain to this Valkyrie that he had no idea who or what she was talking about? If he just had more time . . . it was like having someone's name on the tip of your tongue. The more he tried to force the memory to come clear, the faster it faded away. Infuriating. Scary.

He got to his feet and walked over to pull the dust-sheet from the drawing-board in the corner. It was like looking into the face of an old friend. 'Humpback whale,' he said. 'I didn't finish this.'

He peered at the sketch, then ran his fingertips over the paper's surface, absorbed by the textures of pencil and wash. Gritty fragments of graphite sparkled on his skin. He cast about for a tool, distracted: how could he have left a drawing like this? It was flat as a plate of glass. The balance of light and shade was all wrong, any idiot could see that . . .

'Here.' Robin was at his elbow again, proffering a stub of soft pencil. That cat-curiosity in her eyes again. Wolf took the pencil from her fingers and bent close to deepen the shadow of the corrugations that swept the whale's jaw, changed the texture of the mouth's line, pricked out hard detail in the white crust of barnacles. Finally he changed the eye itself, so that one could see the membranes of the cornea and the way the light slid over it—

'Kris. Hey, Kris, snap out of it. Kris?' Gentle, coaxing words, and a sardonically-snapping finger and thumb between him and the paper. Wolf straightened with a deep intake of breath, blinking gritty eyes. His back ached and he rubbed it, groaning. The woman looked torn between amusement and exasperation.

'Do you realise how long you've been bent over there scribbling?'

Wolf shrugged. 'A few minutes, I suppose.'

'Try half an hour, pal.' She looked past him at the drawing, and there was unfeigned wonder in her voice. 'It's beautiful. I can't believe you did that—'

'You know, you have a real way with words,' Wolf interrupted. He brushed past her to the table where he had left his tobacco. He wanted a cigarette. Half an hour gone. To lose track of time so badly frightened him, it seemed to send him slipping backwards into the nonsense world of the summer. He had his life back now. He had a home. Wolf felt as if he would fight to the death for the chance to keep them. He sat down and tried not to think about it.

The woman was talking at him again, he realised. She had a mouth on her like a freight train. Well, he didn't have to listen.

Wolf tapped tobacco out of the pouch on to a paper. His fingers were steady, which pleased him. Moisten the paper's edge with his tongue-tip, then roll it on the table-top.

'Kris!' The woman's fist banged down on to the cigarette with the force of real anger. She faced off at him, hands on hips. 'I don't believe you even heard a word I just said!'

'You're right,' Wolf said. 'I didn't. And my name's Wolf. Jan if you like. Kris de Haan is dead.'

'*You're* Kris de Haan,' the woman insisted. She slapped her hand down again as he tried to retrieve the flattened cigarette. 'Will you stop that! Give it to me—' She grabbed at the sad little mess of paper and tobacco. Wolf let her take it; she seemed to have some personal vendetta against the inoffensive roll-up. She shredded it without looking at what her hands were doing, glaring at him all the while a confetti of paper and tobacco rained down on her boots. Her eyes got very big and pretty when she was angry—which, Wolf had to admit, seemed to be a hell of a lot of the time. *At least*, he thought, *when she's angry, she looks **at** me, instead of past me.*

'I wish you hadn't done that,' Wolf said. The woman didn't seem to hear.

'This is important, you should know that! Don't you get it?' She almost stamped her foot at him in frustration.

'No,' Wolf said. 'Not really. You pulled me out of the canal last night, and I'm grateful. You saved my life. You can stay here for a few days if you don't have anywhere else to go.'

His little speech had the unexpected effect of rendering Robin momentarily speechless. Wolf took advantage of this phenomenon to reach past her elbow and retrieve his tobacco pouch. She did not seem to notice. He stuck it into his shirt pocket.

'You . . . ' Robin shook her head, and threw up her hands. Her expression softened. 'What am I saying? You've been in hiding, of course you don't know what's happened.'

'Oh?' Wolf managed. Robin yawned, and rubbed both hands over her face. She looked exhausted.

'Ufff. Sorry. Uh, where should I start?' This last was a mutter as she walked away scratching under her hair. Wolf kept quiet. She seemed to have him confused with somebody else. The ticklish bit was that the somebody else was him.

Wolf took a steadying breath. If he just encouraged her to keep talking, maybe something would click. He picked up his coffee cup, then remembered the soggy cigarette butt still floating in there and put it down again.

'All right.' Robin had propped her hip against the sink. She began, unwillingly, 'I guess the first thing you should know is that Carrie Bowman's in hospital.'

For a second Wolf just stared at her. Who the hell was Carrie Bowman, and how well had he known her? Was she a girlfriend? Was her illness good or bad? Robin's grey matter-of-factness gave him no clue. He realised he was leaving it too long. 'What happened?'

'They caught him,' Robin said, as if the words hurt her mouth.

Oh, realised Wolf—*Cary, not Carrie. And she's close to him, or I'm an Englishman.*

Robin folded her arms across her chest in an unconsciously protective gesture. 'It was after you sent that SOS a few days ago, from the cybercafé? He came to me for help, he was convinced someone was on to him, but I didn't listen. We . . . argued. I left him on his own, and they took him.' A scalding current of self-abnegation ran under the level words. 'They, uh . . . they beat him up,' Robin continued in a muffled voice. She did not look at Wolf. 'Then they dosed him with Nemesis and dumped him where he'd be found. I saw him in the hospital . . . ' Her voice faded away, then she jerked her chin up and sniffed, blinking. 'He, um, gave me a message for you.'

'*Me?*' Wolf felt blank with astonishment.

'He said to tell you that you were right about Nemesis,' Robin said. 'About it being for the military, I guess. He, uh, he said he couldn't imagine anyone wanting to feel like that for fun.'

'Right.' Nemesis. The word gave Wolf a funny feeling in the pit of his stomach. He rubbed his thumb over the pink welt where the hypo-gun had stung him. *Nemesis*. A military-designed drug? His pulse ticked dizzily in his temples. Kaleidoscope-fragments of memory twisted and tumbled. 'I remember,' he murmured, though he didn't exactly. 'I remember.'

Cary Bowman . . . a vivid image of the fair-haired man from the Hole sprang into Wolf's mind. Beaten up and forcibly inducted. Wolf closed his eyes: another friend he'd been trying to help, and he hadn't even recognised him. Was that his *geas* in this new life, always to be one step behind, one second too late? He forced himself to speak. 'How is he?'

'They won't let me see him,' the woman murmured. 'He's in a coma, they had to put him on a ventilator last night.' A brave effort to keep her voice normal. A shrug, a sniff. 'Lucky I found you when I did, huh. I just hope we're in time.'

'In time?' Wolf could not help it. A horrible sneaking suspicion crept through him like ice water. 'In time for what?'

'To get the antidote to Cary, of course.' The eyes were getting big again. 'I'm not *stupid*, De Haan, I can put two and two together as well as the next person. You were posing as a vagrant to get information on Nemesis, right?'

'Right,' Wolf said automatically. He rubbed at his forehead. Posing as a vagrant?

Robin did not give him time to think about it. She gestured. 'Out there last night— sure, you were hypothermic, but that wasn't all, not by a long chalk. You pulled yourself out of freezing water on to *ice*, for Pete's sake. You were photosensitive, confused—but you moved faster than anyone I've ever seen. Then just when you should have been getting better, you got sicker instead. It was Nemesis withdrawal. The symptoms were . . . similar to Cary's. Enough so I could take a guess what the stuff in that hypodermic-thing was. Antidote, or—or vaccine or whatever. The good old silver bullet.' She looked irritated, and a little sad, as if she thought he was taunting her. She uttered a short sigh. 'Look, I know this is a lot for you to—'

'It was Nemesis,' Wolf cut in. She stared at him, puzzled. He moistened his lips. The suspicion was crystallising into a really ugly certainty. 'What you gave me last night was Nemesis.'

'No. No, you're wrong.' Funny husk of a voice. 'It—it can't have been.' Her eyes were huge and dark.

Wolf had to turn away. 'I'm sorry.' He forced the words out through lips that tingled. 'They have a place—hidden place . . . they call it the Hole, it's like a lab. My friend was there. They gave us Nemesis, did tests. There was a doctor. She, uh, she didn't mention an antidote. I—I'm sorry . . . ' he repeated, helpless. 'Please, what's wrong, don't cry . . . '

Robin turned her back a little too fast. 'I'm not crying.' Savage, a little muffled. 'I thought . . . ' A complicated shrug.

'What?' Wolf prompted. The tension in her shoulders was weapons-grade. He did not dare touch her.

'I thought you had the antidote,' Robin said. 'Cary said you had something, something he needed. I thought he meant . . . When I gave you that shot last night I thought I was saving both your lives . . . and now you're telling me it was just more of the same goddamn *poison*—' She pressed a hand to her mouth as if she thought she was going to be sick.

'But it did save my life,' Wolf interrupted. 'If you hadn't given me the shot I would have died.'

'I know that,' Robin snapped. 'But what good does that do Cary? He's dying, he needs the antidote *now*.'

'Maybe he won't die,' Wolf said. 'Maybe there's something we can do.' Anything to take that look off her face.

'I promised Cary I'd find you and make sure you were OK,' Robin said, as if he hadn't spoken, 'and I promised him . . . ' Her voice got croaky with tears, and she cleared her throat. 'Uhm. Uh. I promised Cary I'd—you know, get the guys who did this to him. She looked round at Wolf after a long moment of silence. There was a world of misery in her eyes, but a flinty resolve as well, sharp enough to shave with. 'A promise is a promise. I want in on what you and Tekno-G do today.'

16

'ARE YOU SURE this is the right place?' De Haan was looking worried as I paid off the cab. I glanced up at the building Zia's instructions had brought us to. It was no uglier than most of the warehouse conversions this side of town. At least there wasn't too much jaunty painted pipework. This part of the Oosterdok ran more to etched glass and brushed aluminium. I shrugged.

'High-rent business units. Probably full of internet startups and design partnerships.' De Haan still jutted his lip and looked doubtful, so I tugged his sleeve and gave him what I hoped was an encouraging smile. 'Come on. We'd better go in.'

'I guess.' De Haan looked glum, but he waited while I punched in the door code, then followed me into the lobby. Our shuffling feet echoed in the pristine space. Wall-washers cast a discreet, nondescript glow. We dripped slush on the polished granite flooring in front of the lift doors while I tried to remember which floor we were supposed to go to. Everything smelled ozoney with newness.

'Hate this,' De Haan muttered.

'It's OK,' I soothed, and summoned another big, reassuring smile. 'These are the guys Cary was working for, remember? They're OK.'

'No,' De Haan said, looking as if he wished he hadn't spoken. 'I mean *this*—' and kicked at the burnished aluminium kickplate that ran up the stairwell. Echoes twing-twanged off plastic ceiling panels. 'This . . . sanitised corporate crap. It doesn't *fit*.' He sneezed, as if for punctuation, then blew his nose, glaring at nothing in particular. 'You needn't look so surprised,' he added, shooting a look at me. 'A fixed address isn't a legal requirement for a sense of aesthetics.'

'I never said that,' I protested, but I felt my treacherous face turn red.

'You didn't need to say anything,' De Haan muttered. His gaze was very sharp. 'Why is it so important to you that I'm just posing as a tramp? Would it be so terrible if I really *was* one?' I couldn't think of a single word to say. He shrugged and looked away. 'Never mind.'

So I'm an idiot. That doesn't mean I don't aspire to the qualities of a fool sometimes.

In the lift, De Haan stuck his hands in his coat pockets and gazed at the illuminated numbers in morose silence as we accelerated towards the top floor. I wished I could figure him out. He and Cary and Zia seemed to be playing out some kind of a game here, and De Haan was as close-mouthed about it as Cary had been. In the circumstances,

I couldn't blame him for not trusting me. Whatever the game, it was all too obvious that I wasn't being asked to play.

Gabriel met us at the lift doors. 'Hi, good to see youse.' His eyes lit on De Haan, and he grinned. 'Kris! Great to see you again, mate, how's it going?' He lunged forward to shake hands.

De Haan stared at the hyperactive Irishman, and retrieved his hand. 'Hi.' The nervous tic flickered in his left eye.

Gabriel led us off at a fast clip down a shadowy wood-panelled corridor towards an open door. He kept one hand on De Haan's shoulder. 'This is amazing, man, you've got no idea. Thought all that was out the window, you know? And then with Cary gettin' whacked like that . . . sorry, Robin,' he added, with a guilty glance over his shoulder at me. He returned his attention to De Haan. 'So, where've you been all this time?'

'Hiding,' De Haan said. He gazed around as Gabriel ushered us across the threshold into sunlight. The whites of his eyes showed.

Gabriel gestured expansively at nothing much. 'Take a seat.'

I had been right: you could imagine desks and computers and cubicles in here. Instead, there was a huge expanse of polished wood flooring, and a lot of glass with views over the harbour. Apart from some seating near the windows, and a mess of cardboard boxes, that was about it.

I marched over to the window and perched at one end of a fat leather sofa. De Haan settled himself at the opposite end. Gabriel regarded us quizzically. 'You two a comedy team or something?' He dragged up a swivel chair from nearby and stationed it midway between us, reversed so that he could rest his arms on the back. He tossed back his foxy hair and peered over the tops of his shades. 'So, what's the story?'

'A long one,' I said. 'Look, Gabe, things are a little more complicated than I thought. Kris got the information Cary wanted—'

'That's great!' enthused Gabriel. His grin slipped a notch. 'So what's the problem?'

'I was getting to that,' I said. I glanced over at De Haan but he didn't look as if he wanted to take up the story-telling. I took a deep breath and launched in. 'He got the information by getting into their lab test programme, Gabe. He got dosed with Nemesis, he's sick already.'

'*What?*' Gabriel took off the dark glasses to stare at De Haan. 'Holy crap, why'd you go and take a stupid risk like that? What the hell did you think you were playing at?' As always, the big anxious eyes undermined the sting of his words. De Haan shrugged.

'I, I don't know—look, my friends were in trouble, I went after them. It's no big deal.' His face took on a closed look that reminded me of Bowman: bad memories.

'Friends? What friends? Anyone we know?' Gabriel didn't know when to leave well enough alone. De Haan flinched, and rubbed at his left eye.

'No.'

I wanted to shoot Gabriel just to shut him up. He was still worrying at it. 'Where are they now, did they get dosed with Nemesis too?'

'They didn't make it.' De Haan stared off at nothing. Gabriel fell over his words, belatedly aware of his gaffe.

'Oh my—sorry, mate, I—I didn't—'

'Forget it.' An ironic twist to De Haan's mouth.

'Gabe.' I got his attention. 'I already told Kris, I want into this. So what's the plan?'

'Zia set up a video conference for this afternoon,' Gabriel admitted, and added with an attempt at noncholance, '—with Michel Rancoul.'

'*What?*' I leapt to my feet and yelled, 'Are you *nuts?*'

'There's no time to pussyfoot around!' Gabriel gestured angrily. 'DCI are on the point of closing deals with several major military powers—now they have the antidote, there's nothing to stop them any more. I'm sorry if it encroaches on your personal feelings, Robin, but this was always what we planned to do. I thought Kris would've told you. We can hit 'em where it hurts—with *him*,' he added, with a tight grin and a jerk of his chin towards De Haan. 'It's all set up. If they don't close it down and withdraw from the deals, we send it out broadband, multimedia. The whole world gets to know about Nemesis.'

'Wait, just wait one damn minute!' Now De Haan was on his feet. 'What do you mean, hit them with me? I'm not going back there.' He had gone white. I took a step towards him and he backed off, circling towards the door. 'No. I won't be handed back to *them*.' He spat the word. He was trembling.

'Calm down,' I said. 'Nobody's going anywhere. Right, Gabriel?' I turned to glare at Gabriel.

'Absolutely not,' he agreed, looking as startled by De Haan's reaction as I was. 'No question of anything like that. They don't even know where we are, I told ya, it's a video conference, just like we talked about before.'

'Before,' De Haan mumbled, half to himself. 'Everything's *before*.' He walked off to stare out of the window with his hands stuffed in his coat pockets. I felt suddenly sorry for him.

Gabriel walked off too, and vanished through a doorway. I heard the murmur of voices. I came up beside De Haan, a little hesitant.

'I'm sorry about your friends.'

De Haan shook his head. 'It's OK. You weren't to know.' He ran his hands through his hair in a distracted gesture I was beginning to recognise, and shuddered. 'Brought it all back, is all. I could feel her—' He glanced at me, then away. 'Maartje. Her name was Maartje Rijk, she was . . . kind to me.' His voice trailed off, and I was on the point of saying something when he began to speak again in a low voice, squinting as he stared out at the sunlit docks. 'We almost made it. They shot her, I—I couldn't do anything. Nothing.'

'You're not the one that killed her,' I said. 'You can't blame yourself.'

De Haan glanced at me again, and the pain in his eyes made me suck my breath in. He blinked and looked away. 'I don't . . . maybe I do, I don't know . . . we could sense each other, hear each other, did I tell you that? It's what Nemesis does, it—' He shivered. '—it stitches you together, inside. I felt it when her heart stopped beating.' He touched his own chest tenderly, as if it hurt. 'Felt it here.' He closed his eyes, and touched his forehead. 'And here. Like a door shut. She wasn't there any more.'

'It wasn't your fault.' I couldn't think of anything else to say. What he had just told me was impossible. I felt a tingle of fear. What was that thing Sherlock Holmes was always droning on at Dr Watson? *When you have eliminated the impossible, Watson, whatever remains, however improbable, must be the truth.*

Telepathy didn't exist. So where did that leave me?

'You think I'm crazy, don't you?' He wasn't looking at me, but that ironic look was on his face again. I swallowed the denial that leapt to my lips, and thought it over a moment before I answered him.

'I don't know what to think any more. And that's the truth. Maybe you're crazy, maybe you're not. But I promised Cary I'd look out for you.'

De Haan squinted at me, looking torn between amusement and irritation.

'A promise is a promise.' I held out my hand. 'I won't leave you.'

De Haan looked dismayed for a second. 'But . . . ' He caught himself, and shrugged, resigned. 'Ah, what the hell.' We shook hands like two horse-traders striking a bargain, and gazed out at the harbour for a few moments in silence.

Gabriel was waiting when we turned away from the window. He looked edgy but confident. 'Youse guys ready to go after big game now?'

'I don't get this,' I said. 'Where's Zia?'

'She's here,' Gabriel said. 'She's just not . . . *here*, exactly.'

'Sorry?'

'She's plugged,' Gabriel said. 'I told you, she's been setting up this video conference with Rancoul. It's going to need security, for sure. They'll try to track us, so she has to set up a whole rack of dummy accounts and stuff to throw them off the trail a bit. She finished that before you arrived, then she went inworld to sort out the settings— avatars and all that. We couldn't get all the *geister* inworld on such short notice, but most of 'em'll be there.'

'Avatars? We're going into some kind of VR environment?' De Haan walked off again, rubbing his hands through his hair. I thought he looked dazed. Odd—he had obviously been something of a hacker himself. Why should something as simple as a virtual reality program upset him?

Gabriel checked his watch, then gestured towards a door. 'Come and see. It's about time we went in anyway.'

'Come on,' I said to De Haan. 'You've used VR rigs before, haven't you?'

'I guess,' De Haan said, wretchedly. Again, he seemed to be on the point of saying more, but just added, 'It's Nemesis, it's—causing me a few problems, that's all.' He rubbed his fingers into his eyes as if he was tired, and shook himself, tried to smile. 'I'll be OK.'

He allowed me to shepherd him into the room that Gabriel had entered. As we crossed the threshold he ran his shoulder into the doorframe. I grabbed his arm.

'Kris?'

'Fine. I'm fine.' De Haan was mouth-breathing, a fine sheen of sweat on his face. I thought he looked far from fine, but now wasn't the time to be coming over all maternal.

This room must have been designed as an executive hospitality suite. I knew without asking that De Haan hated it as much as I did. It was carpeted and painted in deathlessly tasteful pastels. The windows were covered with blinds. There was a mirror-backed bar in the corner, and I glimpsed a wash-basin and toilet through an open door. The bar had a big basket of assorted fruit on the counter, standing next to an electric blender. I recognised Gabriel's touch.

Five bentwood recliner chairs upholstered in cream nubuck leather stood in a line against one wall. In the furthest chair, wearing what looked like a motorcycle helmet with the visor down, lay Zia. A thick cable trailed from the side of the helmet, across the floor to a bank of computer equipment on a bench against the wall.

She wore what looked at first sight like fanciful alien jewellery on her hands—sleek metal thimbles capped each finger and stretched a web of slender tendrils across the palms and backs of her hands. In a most un-alien fashion, they fastened at the wrist with velcro. She was making slow, intricate movements with her hands, like sloweddown sign language.

'What is all that stuff?' I demanded. Gabriel checked his watch again and shut the door.

'The helmet's basically our take on VR gogs. Bit clunky at the moment but we're still in prototypes right now. The cool stuff on her hands, that's what we call a finger rig. All our own work. Here,' he thrust a plastic storage crate into my arms. It was a tangle of wires and jack-plugs and ribbon cables. Several of the shiny thimbles peeped from among the spaghetti. 'Each rig transmits all its data to a black box over there, so there's no need for wires all over the damn place. We're hoping to do the same with the headset eventually.'

'Do we have to, ah . . . go inworld to do this?' De Haan licked his lips. He looked more spooked than ever. Perhaps he was the claustrophobic type.

'It's not 'The Matrix', you know,' Gabriel said. 'There isn't some big needle going to come up and stab you in the back of the neck or something. Don't sweat the chairs. It's just more comfortable to lie down if you're going to be plugged for a while.'

I sat down on the recliner next to Zia's, and put my feet up. 'Comfy. What next?'

'Next we all have a little smoothie.' Gabriel went over to the bar and started peeling bananas. He slotted them into the blender with half a lemon and switched on.

De Haan raised his voice over the whine of the machine. 'What's the drink for?'

Gabriel tipped orange juice and sugar in, sprinkled over a pinch of brown powder, and added a few drops of something from a small bottle. 'You mean apart from the social bonding?' He switched the blender to a lower setting and dropped in a glutinous chunk of vanilla ice cream. 'It contains a mild narcotic that acts on the sight and balance centres of the brain. That calms down any nausea you might feel and helps integrate the graphical experience. The bananas and the citric acid help with some of the biochemical stuff, potassium absorption and all that. Cushions the system. And it tastes great.' He poured three tumblers of violent-yellow sludge, and brought them over. De Haan raised his hands in a fending-off gesture.

'I'll pass.'

'Suit yourself, but you might regret it.' Gabriel passed a glass to me, and drank the third himself in a couple of fluid gulps. I sipped mine more slowly, trying unsuccessfully to identify the taint of the drug.

I licked the milk-moustache off my upper lip with the tip of my tongue, and caught De Haan watching me. He looked away. I handed the glass back to Gabriel and said to De Haan, 'are you sure you'll be all right?'

'No,' said De Haan after a pause. He lay down on the couch and folded his arms on his chest. 'But I'll do it,' he added. 'Just let's make it quick before I change my mind.'

'All right, here we go.' Gabriel fetched a headset over from the bench and fitted it on De Haan's head. 'It's a motorcycle helmet basically,' Gabriel said as he adjusted the chin-strap. The unconscious echo of my own thought made me want to laugh.

I bit my lips together and wondered if the desire to giggle might not have something to do with the narcotic, whatever it was. I felt warm and delightfully light-headed.

Gabriel was still talking. '. . . and we wanted something we could retro-fit easily. That feel all right?'

De Haan made a thumbs-up gesture. Gabriel shook one of the finger-rigs free of the cables in the box, and started fitting the metal caps on to De Haan's finger-ends. The first one fell off, then the next. Gabriel tried again, then bundled the contraption up with an exasperated sound. 'I don't believe this, your fingers are too big, the sleeves keep coming off. You'll just have to plug in without the rig.' He fitted a thick black cable to the helmet jack, and plugged the other end into the rack of holes beside Zia's.

I frowned. 'Doesn't he need the, uh, finger thing?'

'Not as such,' Gabriel said. 'It just means his avatar's going to be a bit stiff. No hand gestures or anything. And I'll have to navigate him around, 'cos he won't be able to point or press. It's not really a *problem*, it's just a pain in the arse.' He sat down beside me with another helmet. 'Here. Pop it on, that's it.' The helmet muffled his voice but I could still hear him. 'Is that chin-strap too tight?'

'It's fine,' I said. My voice echoed in a funny way. I added, 'Can you hear me? It sounds really funny in here.'

'Like talking in a dustbin,' Gabriel said. 'That's just because you're not in the system yet. There's a mike in that hollow bit in front of your face. When you're plugged, it feeds back your speech in real-time, sounds fine. Give your head a bit of a shake, see if it waggles.'

'No, it's fine.'

Gabriel took my hand and slotted the cold metal thimbles on to my fingers. The round battery-pack lay against my palm like a lucky coin. Gabriel tapped the top of the helmet. 'OK?'

'Sure.' *I think.*

'Then let's rock and roll,' Gabriel chortled, and slapped my leg. He seemed to be in a terrific mood, and I wondered if the smoothie was acting on him, too. 'Lie back, relax, you're going to like this.' I heard him walk over to his own couch next to the computer. 'Plugging in,' he said.

There was an instant of white-noise, white-light. I found that I was staring into a pixelated grey mist. I exclaimed out loud: you could even see little random cloud-shapes drift past. I had expected this to be like walking into a cartoon—just a 3-D V-Zone—but it was much more life-like. The effect was odd, trippy.

I twisted my head to the left. The world lurched and zoomed. I screwed my eyes shut and kept still. My heart pounded. My voice was a squeak. '*Help.*'

'Sorry, should have told you before.' Gabriel's voice in my left ear. 'This isn't like yer usual VR kit. The helmet reads eye movement primarily, not head movement. If you want to look round to the left, just move your eyes that way. Want to move, press the stud at the base of your right thumb, then point in the direction you want to go. Stud for directions, remember. Otherwise, the rig'll just read it as hand and arm movement. You'll get the hang of it pretty quick.'

'OK,' I said, and opened my eyes again. I swivelled my eyes to the left. A broad-shouldered male figure stood there, dressed in a green combat jumpsuit. It had a mane of fiery red hair and a goatee beard, and wore sharp shades. I laughed. 'Gabriel,' I said out loud. He had been right, my voice sounded more or less normal.

The figure nodded at me. The mouth moved. 'Lookin' good, Robin. Nice outfit.'

'Nice—?' I moved my eyes cautiously downwards. My avatar was dressed Lara-Croft-style in shorts and a vest tee. Kick-ass boots and hiking socks peeped out from beneath a considerable overhang. 'Whoa,' I murmured, stunned. 'Boobs at last.'

'You'll have to take that up with Zia,' Gabriel said. 'She picked it out for you.'

'It's not a problem,' I assured him. I looked down again, and smothered another fit of giggles. 'How realistic is this? I mean, do they bounce and everything?' The impulse to experiment was strong.

'Robin?' De Haan's voice. It came from my right, so I looked that way. Another avatar stood next to me—a slender oriental man in a dark suit. I blinked at him.

'Kris? Is that you?'

'I guess,' De Haan said. The avatar blinked, then grinned. 'You look great.'

'Yeah, thanks,' I said quellingly. 'Gabriel likes them too.'

'Let's go, guys,' Gabriel said. 'Zia's just dialled us into the loft.' His avatar made a complicated series of hand gestures, like the ones I'd seen Zia make. The grey mist thickened and boiled up into a swirl of muddy colours, so that I could not see my companions. It was rather like being shut inside the endpapers of an old book, except that the feathery patterns of colour *moved*. To my right, I heard De Haan draw in a sharp breath. I flickered glances left and right.

'Uh, Gabe? What's happening?'

'It's just a fill pattern,' Gabriel said. I was reassured to find that he sounded close by. 'We were in the system basic environment, sort of a lobby if you like. Now we're going elsewhere. Here you go,' he added.

The wavering mist vanished. I found myself standing in the doorway of a high, many-windowed room. Gabriel walked past me to the left, and waved a hand. 'Come in.'

'OK.' I pressed the stud at the base of my right thumb, and pointed forwards, feeling silly. To my relief, I moved forwards into the room. 'Wow,' I muttered under my breath. 'This is awesome.'

The room we had entered was rendered in the same lifelike way as the avatars. Sunlight streamed through multiple panes of glass and threw skewed oblongs of light on the wooden plank floor. As Gabriel walked into the light, the sun shone in his hair and his face was thrown into shadow. I gaped. I lifted one of my hands in front of my face and the sunlight winked at me through my fingers. 'This makes V-Zones look like email,' I muttered. 'Gabe, this is just . . . *incredible*.'

'Why, thank you,' Zia's voice drawled. A tall dark-haired woman in a floor-length silver fur cape walked towards us. Slender white arms beckoned us closer. I moved forward.

'Chili?' The woman's Asian-dark eyes had silver pupils, like two dots of mercury.

She smiled, and dimples appeared in her perfect cheeks.

'Sure is, honey. Do you like our little hacker clubhouse? We call it the Loft.'

'Some loft,' I said. 'Zia, this must use gazillions of megs to run. How do you do it?'

'Trade secret,' said a sharp voice. I looked: a computer sat on a low table near one of the windows. Its screen had lit up to show a man's sweating face. I looked from the fuzzy image on the screen to Zia's pixel-perfect avatar.

'Is that a video feed?'

'Clever girl,' the man on the screen said. 'We don't all have the hardware necessary to participate fully in Artemis' little fantasies. So she kindly splices us in this way.'

'Red, Kris—meet Rue,' Zia said. Her avatar's face somehow managed to convey humorous long-suffering. 'One of the top Dutch hackers of the eighties, still not too bad on a good day. Rue, this is Robin Carlson. And this is Kris de Haan, I believe you two know each other?'

'We met,' Rue said. The computer screen swivelled towards De Haan's immobile avatar. 'I hear you've been getting yourself in trouble on our behalf.'

'Something like that,' De Haan said. He sounded breathless, as if we'd just run up here. I interrupted.

'Look, uh, this is all very nice, but shouldn't we be getting on?'

'Yes,' Rue said. He grinned. 'Artemis was right about you. You don't fart around.'

'Thanks for the character reference, Chili,' I muttered. I looked down at my avatar again, and added, 'Thanks for the uh, equipment, by the way. Very thoughtful of you.'

'Glad you like it,' Zia said. 'I really wanted you to see what we have here, we've been working on this for quite a while now and it's almost finished. This sort of cross-media interaction's going to be the next big thing, but right now it's kind of avant garde. The smoothies were Gabriel's idea.'

'Surprise,' I murmured. 'So what now, Chili?'

'We just wait for Bear and Ozzy to turn up, then we can get on. You already met Rue. Maya, Geode, come and be introduced.'

'Don't these people *do* normal names?' De Haan muttered peevishly under his breath. I was about to make some witty remark about 'Wolf' not being exactly normal either, when I heard him utter a muffled noise, quickly bitten off. I turned towards him.

'Are you all right?'

'Not exactly,' De Haan panted. 'Ahh—damn. This . . . environment . . . doesn't agree with me. Too much input—'

'Input?' I whispered. 'What do you mean?'

'I'll be all right,' De Haan muttered. 'Don't fuss.'

I had to swallow my retort. Maya and Geode were identical twins. Their avatars were willowy elvish types, with cloaks and pointed ears. Their voices were filtered in some way to sound echoey and alien.

'Is this the dude with the lab data?' Two pairs of slanted green eyes turned to gaze at De Haan's unimposing avatar.

Maya—or maybe Geode—turned to Zia. 'You sure Rancoul's gonna buy this?' The curt idiom jarred with the elvish appearance of the two women. If they went to all the trouble of creating avatars and having their speech processed like that, you'd think they might go the whole hog and talk more like the elves in books talked.

'As sure as I can be,' Zia was saying in a level tone. 'There's always a chance that he won't bite—'

'You know what I think about this,' Rue cut in from his screen. 'Maybe he'll turn round and bite us in the ass, eh? What then?'

'It's a risk we have to take,' Zia said. 'I've set it up so there's minimum risk of a trace succeeding—'

'Here come the guys,' Gabriel said. I noticed that a yellow arrow above the doors had lit up. When the doors slid open, two more figures stood in front of us.

The first was a hulking cartoon bear, walking on its hind legs. I wanted to run my fingers through its luxuriantly-rendered fur. Its greeting was heavily Russian-accented. Its name, unsurprisingly, was 'Bear'.

The last arrival in the Loft was an Egyptian king, complete with golden mask and pleated linen skirt. He had a bodybuilder's torso under the sparkling broad-collar, and painted toenails. He looked even more out of place than the elves, especially with his waddling ursine escort. I quelled a rebellious urge to smirk.

'Hi Ozzy,' Zia said. My smile got away again. An Egyptian monarch named *Ozzy*? The gold-and-blue clad splendour inclined its head. Its voice boomed like the closing of crypt doors.

'Artemis. Gabriel. Are we all foregathered?'

'You were the last,' Zia said pointedly. 'Oz, this is Robin Carlson, that I told you about. And this is Kris de Haan. Robin, Kris, this is Ozymandias, King of Kings. But you can call him Oz, it's good for his ego.'

'Hi,' I managed. De Haan nodded again.

'I am pleased to make your acquaintance,' Ozymandias intoned, then added in a far more normal tone, '—play nicely, now, Artemis. You're just jealous because I'm more gorgeous and talented than you are.' A nasal, slightly camp inflection that made me suspect there might be more queen than king behind the golden mask.

'Are you two finished?' Gabriel asked.

'You're right, we should get on,' Zia said. 'You're all up with the latest?' A general chorus of assent. 'OK, let's just go through this: we'll be in a closed video conference. Just me, Gabe, Robin and Kris. We don't want to be in there longer than ten minutes, so watch the clock, people. Rue, you're going to be handling the security with Ozzy. Don't let 'em get closer than you have to. Bear, I want you to keep your eye on any techie problems, practical stuff. Report to Gabe. Maya, Geode, make yourselves available to whoever needs backup, all right?'

'What about me,' I asked. 'What do I do?'

'Keep quiet, mostly,' Zia said. 'You're kind of a bonus card, Red. Barnabas and his goons lost you—you're an embarrassment and a potential danger to them and it's going to be driving them crazy wondering exactly how much you know. Just the fact that we have you should be enough to send Michel into a flat spin. Exposure is a risk they can't afford to take. OK?'

'Sure,' I said. *Maybe. Help?*

'Yes,' De Haan said. His voice sounded gruff and breathless. I was just about to ask him if he was all right, when the wavering fill-pattern blotted out the room in front of me.

'Hey,' I protested. 'What's up?'

'It's time,' Zia said soberly. 'We're going to the conference room now. You'll see a set of screens like the one we use for Rue. All Michel will see will be a set of digital masks, no real faces. My voice and Gabe's will be altered, yours and Kris's won't—the whole point is he has to be able to identify you.'

'But we're not—' *ready*, I had been going to add.

A set of four screens blinked into being in front of me, and I swallowed the word. Three of the screens showed smooth, androgynous mask faces. I supposed they must be Zia, Gabriel and De Haan. The fourth was a video feed of Michel Rancoul.

I bit my lip. Michel looked irritable and twitchy. His normally-immaculate clothing was ever so slightly crumpled, the knot of his tie a touch off-centre. For Michel Rancoul, this was the equivalent of screaming and tearing at his hair. It was a rewarding moment, seeing him like that.

Evidently, he could see us as well, because he leaned forward towards the camera and snapped, 'Well?'

'Thank you for agreeing to this meeting on such short notice,' somebody said—a woman, I thought. One of the masks animated as she spoke. It must be Zia, but the raspy, flat vowels sounded nothing like her smooth Southern-States drawl.

'Get on with it,' Michel said. 'We're not doing lunch here, Artemis.'

'We have a proposition to put to you regarding the Nemesis Project,' Zia said.

All credit to his acting skills, Michel barely even flinched. 'Sorry, the what?'

'It's a long story,' said the Artemis-voice. 'Let's just say we've been following the progress of your research in battlefield pharmaceuticals for about two years now. From Glasgow to London to Amsterdam. We disapprove of what you're doing, Mister Rancoul. The world is a dangerous enough place without introducing drugs like Nemesis into the equation. The fact that you've been using your sister's charitable organisation as a cover for the whole thing is grotesque.'

'Spare me the sermon.' Michel leaned back in his chair, miming boredom. 'What is it you want?'

'We want you to stop making it,' another voice butted in—male this time, so it must be Gabriel, I thought. The masks and the odd voices were a surreal mixture. I concentrated on watching Michel instead. He was actually smiling—that lazy, indulgent smile I knew so well. I found myself aching to wipe it off his face.

'You don't want much, do you?' Michel said, mock-serious. 'Whatever makes you think you can make such a request of me?'

'It's not a request,' Gabriel shot back. 'It's an order, you smug little turd.'

'Artemis, do I have to put up with your dog's barking?' Michel was trying to sound bored. Only a trace of wariness in his eyes betrayed anything different.

'Yes,' Zia said, 'you do.'

'Could we get on?' Straightening the tie, leaning forwards at the camera. 'Why should I give in to the demands of—forgive me—a bunch of petty criminals?'

'Because if you don't, we'll expose the whole sordid little scam. We have all the proof we need.' The flattening effect on Zia's voice made it sound very sinister. Michel leaned back again, brows raised.

'If you don't mind my saying so, if you had concrete proof of a crime, you would surely have gone to the authorities with it already.'

Gabriel butted in again. 'No thanks! Not with your toy soldiers hanging around to clean up anything inconvenient.'

'Major Barnabas is getting careless,' Zia added. My heart jumped to attention. I moistened my lips, then did it again because my mouth was so dry. Michel had not-quite suppressed a glance to the side, and I stared at the periphery of the screen: was Barnabas in the room with Michel? The thought of actually witnessing Tom's duplicity filled me with dread.

'Major who?' Michel said. The tiny frown of incomprehension was perfect, if you hadn't seen that twitch.

'Major Thomas Barnabas of the United States Army,' Zia elaborated. 'Special Forces, currently listed as retired, actually on active service, black ops? Matter of fact, he's a Captain, not a Major, but what the hell, I guess you get promotion for the sort of stuff he does. Come on, Mister Rancoul, he's been working for you for almost two years now, surely you remember him?'

Michel didn't miss a beat. 'Oh,' he said, '*that* Barnabas. Well, naturally I know Tom, though I have to say your information is faulty if you think he is still working for the United States government. I assure you, his duties as head of security here keep him far too busy.' A prim, sanitised smile.

Rage rode over angels with guns blazing. I said, hotly, 'That is *such* a crock, Michel Rancoul!'

His blank double-take would have been funny in any other circumstances. '*Robin?*'

'I'm so glad you remember my name,' I shot back. 'What—didn't Tom tell you he lost me? Maybe he was embarrassed at being outwitted by a mere civilian. Or maybe he was hoping he could get me back under lock and key before anyone else noticed I was missing. Was that it, *Major*? I know you can hear this, Tom,' My voice got ragged just when I wanted it to be strong, and I gritted my teeth. 'I trusted you! How could you do this to me? And to Cary? How *could* you?' My heart boomed in the confines of the helmet. 'You—'

'That's right, Major,' Zia cut in. '*Big* mistake killing a British national on Dutch soil. You know, you've trodden on so many toes recently, people are going to have to get in line. Now,' she continued in a crisp tone, 'listen up, guys, and listen up carefully. We not only have Robin—who, as I'm sure you can understand, is willing to testify against you both in any court in the world—we have Kris de Haan.'

'Kris de Haan?' Michel sounded genuinely puzzled. 'Who—?'

'Just another of Major Barnabas' little mistakes,' Zia elucidated sweetly. 'You might have forgotten him, but we sure didn't. Kris de Haan is a PI, Mister Rancoul, a specialist in industrial espionage. He was investigating you on behalf of Cary Bowman, back in the spring. He had to go into hiding, but he still managed to infiltrate your repulsive little test programme. I understand he caused something of a stir when he left. Now here's the sting, guys: Menheer de Haan has a photographic memory. He's a walking bank of evidence, and we have him right here.'

'I have no idea what you are talking about,' Michel protested, but you could see his composure was rattled. He straightened in his seat, and smoothed at his tie again. 'I don't know what kind of vindictive lies this so-called specialist of yours has fed you, Artemis, but you are harassing a legitimate business—'

'Oh, don't you worry about that,' Zia cut across him. 'We anticipated that you'd need proof, so I had Menheer de Haan sit in on this meeting. He'll give you enough data to verify what we say. I hope your recording equipment is working? Kris, go for it.' I heard the satisfaction in her voice even through the distortion. She'd set up the trap and Rancoul was just about to be hauled wriggling out of the water.

There was a pause.

De Haan said, 'Now? Oh. Uh, OK . . . ' He paused, and cleared his throat, then started slowly, 'Nemesis is . . . a battlefield stimulant . . . um, based on manufactured, ah, substances . . . ' He trailed off. Michel uttered a short sigh.

'If that's the limit of your data, Artemis, I'm truly disappointed.'

'No.' Zia sounded startled even through the vocal distortion. 'He's just mapping it out. He has the hard data. He's going to give it to you now.' A pause. Nobody said anything. Zia prompted, 'Kris. Go ahead, we're waiting.'

De Haan's mask-face gave no clue to what was happening except that the mouth animated a couple of times without making a sound. Then De Haan uttered that same muffled pain-sound I'd heard before. Just once, nothing dramatic, then said, in an odd voice, 'I—can't.' He sounded as if his teeth were clenched. 'I can't—I don't—' He broke off.

Michel laughed loud and long, leaning back in his chair. Then he leaned forward, mock-serious. 'Artemis, I can't thank you enough. For the comedy show—' another amused snort, '—and for the advance warning of your intentions. You've just made somebody's job *so* much easier.' He winked, blew a kiss, and vanished from the screen.

17

A PANDEMONIUM of yelling broke out, Zia demanding to know what was going on, Gabriel bawling all sorts of commands in a mush of techie-speak, random voices interrupting.

None of it meant anything to me. All I wanted was to know what was wrong with De Haan. I ripped the tangle of wires from my hands, cursing, wrestled the chin-strap open. I shoved the helmet off my head. It bing-banged along the floor on its cable tether. The yammering voices cut off.

The room was preternaturally still. I could hear my own heart bumping as I swung my legs over the side of the couch and stood up. Zia's and Gabriel's voices were a muted, intermittent buzz from inside their helmets.

De Haan was sitting up on the side of his couch. He had removed his helmet. The blond hair was rumpled as if from sleep.

'Kris?' No reaction. I stumbled over the web of cables to his side. He was clutching the helmet to him with both hands. 'Hey,' I said, and tried to take it. His grip tightened reflexively. I pried his fingers patiently off the helmet, placed it behind him on the couch and perched beside him. He was trembling, a sheen of sweat on his face. 'Kris, what happened? Are you OK? Kris?'

'Don't call me that,' De Haan whispered. He turned his head towards me, as if by great effort. 'Please.'

'All right,' I said. 'Tell me what happened in there?'

'Nothing,' he said, and shut his eyes. 'Nothing happened.'

'*Nothing* is about right!' Zia was incandescent with rage. She stalked up from behind and surveyed the two of us slumped side-by-side on the edge of the couch. Then she folded her arms. 'We just got ourselves shafted. *Why?*'

The question seemed to be aimed at both of us, and De Haan—Wolf—still had his eyes shut. I sounded tired even to myself.

'Chili, just lay off. He's been through a hell of a lot. Gabe told you about the test programme, didn't he? This guy's lucky to be alive, let alone lucid. And he could still die. He *will* die if he doesn't get that antidote. So give him a break already.'

Zia's eyes bulged. 'Can you hear yourself? This guy just managed to screw up our one and only shot at Rancoul!'

'It wasn't his fault,' I said.

'You better be sure about that,' Zia spat, trenchant. 'You better be *damn* sure about that, Red, 'cos you just lost your only chance to get ahold of that antidote for Cary. You hear me? Your *only* chance. So you better know what you're talking about, girl.'

'I do,' I muttered, 'I do,' but I couldn't hold her gaze. Wolf shifted beside me on the couch. I looked at his knotted, trembling hands, then up at his face. To him, I added, '—don't I?'

Wolf met my eyes for a second. It was an incongruous moment to notice such a thing, but I guess I hadn't really looked him in the eyes till then; they were deep stormy blue, very beautiful. They were also filled with regret.

Then he blinked, that by-now familiar wince, and looked down at his hands. 'I was going to tell you.' Six words. They kicked the world out from under me.

There was a lot afterwards—shouting, and blame, and stumbling explanations—but it all came too late. Too damned late.

❖

They think I'm asleep.

Wolf opened his eyes, then hooded them again: his eyeballs felt like a pair of lightly-poached golf-balls. His head hurt, though not as much as it had. He lay still on the couch and listened to the hushed, querulous voices behind him.

The black woman who Robin called 'Chili' and Gabriel called 'Artemis' looked just like that supermodel off the TV. Except for the frown, Wolf thought, and winced. The frown sat between her perfect brows like the sight-notch on a high-powered rifle.

Her shadow slid back and forth on the floor beside the couch as she paced in front of the window. The spindly shadow-hands chopped and flickered as she spoke.

'. . . how can he not know who he *is*?'

'How in the hell should I know?' That was Robin. He could see her shadow too, hunched in a chair. She sounded angry and tired. 'I'm not a doctor. He said his memory's started to come back, like every time he gets a dose of the drug it's freeing up more stuff in his head—that's how he found his way back to the boat. But he still can't remember much. He was shot, for Pete's sake! So you've got Tom Barnabas to thank—again.'

'That doesn't change the fact that he lied to you, Red. *Think* about it!'

The black woman was American too. She fired words like bullets. *It must be something in the gene-pool*, Wolf thought in wonder. *Davy Crockett, Buffalo Bill, Annie Get Your Gun.* It would have been funny if he wasn't the one in the firing-line.

'It wasn't like that,' Robin insisted, obdurate. 'He's scared, Chili. He doesn't know who to trust and I don't blame him if he kept quiet.'

'Well I do,' the other woman snapped. The shadow halted, and the arms gestured wide. 'Robin, we planned this out months ago, me and Cary. Gabe and I have been working on it ever since Cary got that damned email—weblinks to every major newspaper and TV station in the world, every head of state, every political party, the UN—hell, even the Human Rights guys in Strasburg. I won't even begin to go into how much it all cost. Everything was ready. All he had to do was recall the data. Damn it,' and the pacing resumed, with a shake of the head. 'Cary called me from your place, did you know that?'

'No.' Wolf winced on Robin's behalf. Her voice had sunk to a listless whisper. 'He didn't tell me.'

'He told me about this miracle that was going to come save the day, this guy with a photographic memory who had all the data right here—' Shadow-finger jabbed at shadow-forehead. 'When Gabe told me you'd found him, last night, I could hardly believe my luck. I still can't,' she added with a bitter laugh. The shadow stopped, fists on hips. 'What is it with you, Red? Why are you defending him?'

'Someone's got to,' Robin snapped. 'If you'd just told us why you needed him, we wouldn't have gotten into this mess in the first place!'

'We thought he knew!' The accusatory shadow threw up its hands and started pacing again. 'Dammit, he knew there was something wrong, all he had to do was tell us! But he didn't, he let us get shot right out of the water. Still want to make excuses for him?'

'She's not making excuses.' Wolf's voice was a gravelly croak. He swung his feet to the floor and stood up. Bad idea: the world lurched sideways. He squinched his eyes almost shut, and stood swaying while the room slowed down to an acceptable rate of spin.

Artemis was glaring at the interruption, hands on hips again. She was dressed in combat pants and a crop camouflage vest, with nubuck Docs that looked brand-new. *God help us,* Wolf thought. *It's a designer-label hacker-terrorist chick.*

Robin glanced up at him and sketched a strained smile. Wolf's bad eyelid fluttered, and he knuckled at it. *Great, now she's going to think I'm winking at her.* He settled for looking at Artemis. Things were more straightforward there: her antagonism was as direct as a slap in the face. 'She's not making excuses for me,' he repeated.

Artemis' eyes were dark brown, and bloodshot. Confusing; he remembered them being yellow. She stared at him and curled her lip. 'What, big guy, you've come to make your own excuses now?'

'No,' Wolf said. 'But you're writing this off too quickly. Yes, I screwed up your little video conference, and I'm sorry—'

'Ohh, he's *sor-ry*,' Artemis mocked with a sneer. Wolf's temper rose.

'You're the one who ought to be sorry! If you'd stopped to *ask* me instead of just shoving me into your ready-made little scenario, maybe there wouldn't have been a problem in the first place. But you didn't even stop to think about it, did you?'

'*I* should be sorry?' Artemis looked savage enough to bite. Wolf stuck his face in hers and bared his teeth right back at her.

'That's right, darling, just think about yourself, that's what you do best! Didn't your bitch of a mother ever teach you to say 'please'?'

'You just leave my mother out of this, you—'

'*THAT'S ENOUGH!*' Robin had jumped to her feet. She was pale with anger. Wolf shut his mouth with a snap. He might be crazy, but he wasn't stupid. Artemis drew breath to argue, and Robin stuck one rigid finger under the taller woman's nose. 'Not one more *word* out of you, Constanzia Roccaro! Not. One.'

Artemis blinked, shot Wolf a dirty look, and strode off. A door slammed. Wolf looked at Robin, and caught the full force of her glare. After a second she looked down. Her voice was very low. 'I wish you'd trusted me. I just—'

The chirrup of a cellphone interrupted. Robin made an apologetic shrug to Wolf, and went over to the sofa to yank her bag open. She turned away to look out of the window as she answered the call, flipping her hair back. 'Hello? Hi Sunny, what's up? Did you—' She had been twiddling the ends of her hair; her hand stopped moving suddenly. Wolf heard her snatch a quick breath in, then she muttered in a tight voice, 'OK. No. No . . . look, I'll call you back in a minute. Bye.' She lowered the cellphone from her ear and fumbled to switch it off, still gazing straight ahead. Wolf walked over, cautious.

'What's wrong?'

Robin's skin in the sunlight was paper-white. Her freckles stood out like a rash. She spoke in a rough whisper. 'Cary's dead.' She dragged in a breath, and blinked, as if waking from a bad dream. 'Excuse me.' She brushed past Wolf as if he wasn't there. The bathroom door banged shut, and he heard the rapid babble of her cellphone speed-dialling.

Wolf took himself over to stare out the window. A big container ship was moving slowly out from the docks. Its rusty white superstructure glided just beyond the rooftops, noiseless, as if by magic. Its multi-coloured patchwork cargo of steel boxes scrolled past, taller than a house. Wolf made a desultory attempt to estimate how many containers it was carrying, then gave it up as a bad job.

Another face from the past wiped out. Cary Bowman. Wolf dredged up the memory of the last time he'd seen him in the Hole, drugged and bloodied. Dead now. It refused to feel real.

His thoughts were interrupted by the bang of the bathroom door. Robin came out, wearing her coat.

'I'm going out, I'll see you later.' She scooped up her bag from the sofa, slung it over her shoulder and headed for the door, pulling on her gloves. Wolf moved to intercept her.

'You can't go out!'

'Don't tell me what I can and can't do.' She accompanied this flat ultimatum with a straight-armed shove. Wolf gave ground, but kept between her and the door, arms outspread. He shot an appealing look at Artemis and Gabriel, who had appeared from the computer room at his raised voice.

'She's leaving.'

'Red, honey!' Artemis loped gracefully over and stationed herself beside Wolf. Robin heaved a short sigh, and folded her arms. Her face was still very white. Artemis laid a hand on her sleeve. 'He's right, sweetie, it's too dangerous. Barnabas and his goons are desperate, they'll be looking all over for you.'

Robin rolled her eyes. 'Look. I'll wear a hat or something. Dark glasses,' she added, looking at Gabriel. 'Whatever. But I *am* going out. It's not a topic for discussion,' she snapped as Artemis opened her mouth. 'Sunny's meeting me with a bag of stuff. I pick it up, then I come back here, OK? I need to get out for a while,' she added in a small, obstinate voice. A thread of desperation in there, Wolf thought. From what he knew of Robin, she'd sooner shoot herself than admit it. Hence the steel-gauntlet act. She stuck her chin out, in a gesture Wolf remembered. 'I'm suffocating in here.'

'Here,' Wolf said, surprising himself. He shucked off his jacket and offered it, valet-fashion. 'Take this.'

Robin stared at him for a long moment, then at the coat. Then a reluctant grin broke surface. 'Thanks.' She shrugged out of her own coat with its tooled-silver bosses and suede tassels, handed it to Artemis, and pushed her arms into the sleeves of the coat. 'I won't be long,' she added, fumbling with the buttons and not looking at him. Wolf tugged the collar up round her ears.

'Just be careful, OK? I want my coat back.' He met her startled look with one of his own. She hesitated, then nodded.

'Sure.'

Artemis had hurried off. Now she came back carrying a voluminous, bright purple pashmina. 'Here, put this on. We have to hide that damn carroty wig of yours or you've had it.'

Wolf touched the shiny copper hair that curled over the collar of his coat. Less than no point in trying to stop her going. It would just piss her off and she'd go anyway. At least this way, there was a better chance she'd slip through whatever net Barnabas had waiting. He spoke very softly. 'A promise is a promise, right?'

'Yes,' Robin said.

Wolf nodded, and stepped back. He watched as Artemis wound the ridiculous purple shawl round Robin's neck and over her hair. Robin suffered the other woman's sharp-tongued worry patiently enough, but Wolf could see she wanted to be gone.

He shut himself in the bathroom, ran the handbasin full of cold water and immersed his face. The chill pressed into his flesh like a concrete mask. Wolf stood it as long as he could, then breached, hyperventilating, and stared at the dripping madman in the mirror.

He wouldn't go out until she'd gone. Holding the words in hurt too much, and he felt sure that Robin would despise him for saying them, almost as much as he would despise himself.

Wolf blinked water out of his eyes, and straightened in front of the mirror. 'I have a really, really bad feeling about this,' he informed his reflection in a hoarse whisper, 'and I don't want you to go.'

He was right, it would be insulting even to say it. Pleading would make things exponentially worse. The trouble was, knowing this did not diminish the bad feeling even a tiny bit. Something awful was going to happen.

It is the weirdest feeling in the world to walk through your everyday surroundings and know that there are people out there hunting you with guns. Did I say weirdest? Excuse me, I think I mean *scariest*.

The taxi dropped me at the supermarket on the far end of Museumplein. It was only four o'clock, but it was already getting dark. I leaned in to pass over a handful of Zia's cash. The welter of traffic noise almost drowned my voice. 'Can you meet me back here in ten minutes? Ten,' I mouthed, and flashed my fingers at the driver twice, *five-five*.

The driver flashed a thumbs-up and slammed the door. I stumbled over strange ice cream shapes of frozen black slush to the kerb. Behind me, the driver revved his engine and launched the taxi neatly into the path of an oncoming truck.

Museumplein was crowded, and I relaxed a bit as I walked between the spindly sapling trees. A trio of snowboarders were destruct-testing their limbs on the half-pipes provided for summer skateboarding, and more kids and their parents milled around, dragging sleds and throwing snowballs. The more people, the happier I'd be: less chance of being spotted, less chance of anybody grabbing me or shooting me if there were plenty of witnesses around.

People were out skating on the smooth oval rink that was a paddling-pool in the summer, and the cafés looked as if they were doing a good trade. The sushi bar where Sunny worked looked quiet. Not much demand for cold raw fish at this time of year, I guess. At least she'd be able to slip out pretty easily. I made myself small and kept my head down as I wove in and out of the crowds.

I felt ridiculous, as if I was the mark in some mad omnibus edition of *Candid Camera*. At the same time, I felt dizzy and hot because I was so scared.

The heat and dizziness might have been impending asphyxiation, of course. Everyone had pitched in for the disguise, so I was wearing Wolf's big black jacket (more of a topcoat on me), Gabriel's knitted beanie-hat with a yellow smiley face on the front, and Zia's old pashmina. The tassels on the pashmina tickled but it masked the lower half of my face. The hat met it in the middle, and the coat collar came up right over my ears. I was being steamed alive, but I figured I was pretty safe unless Tom had told his guys to look out for a medium-rare steak dressed by Oxfam.

The ass-end of the Rijksmuseum is as pretty as the façade, and it *towers*. With icicles hanging from the leaky gutters, and snow capping its peaked rooflines, it looked even more like a fairytale castle than usual. A lone busker had braved the cold wind that whisked through the great arched tunnel—classical guitar—notes ringing clear as fairy bells in the hard acoustics.

I turned in through the iron archway that led to the gardens. A brown tangle of winter-dead creepers made a kind of triumphal arch over the bark path. I walked to the far end, and down the snow-crusted steps to the little formal garden. The fountains had been turned off months ago, and snow filled the bowl.

My breath trailed me like a nervous ghost. I walked round the fountain, running my gloved fingers along the stone rim. It was quiet. Up above on the road, streetlights were flicking on. My footsteps were little crunching noises as I completed the circle.

'Robin!' Sunny was coming down the steps from the path, her afghan coat slung on over her waitress' uniform. She carried a bulging sports bag that I thought I recognised as one of Marik's.

We hugged for a long moment. Sunny is awfully strong for such a tiny person, and she had my ribs in a death-grip. Eventually, she let me go, and stood back.

'Wha' the frock's going on?'

'No time to explain,' I hedged, and tried to take the bag. She held on to the strap.

'You not in trouble with the police, are you?'

'Nooo,' I said hastily, and got the bag on the second try. Sunny gave me an unimpressed look.

'I'd better get a longer explanation than tha' one,' she said ominously. I grinned, and hugged her again.

'Course you will. Look, I have to go, there's a taxi waiting for me.'

'Actually,' a familiar voice said behind my shoulder, 'there isn't.'

Tom Barnabas.

'Wha' the—' Sunny's shocked expression must have mirrored my own. Then I whirled round and aimed a side-kick at his head.

Something kicked back. Next thing, I was lying on the ground with my face pressed into the snow. I could see and hear, but I couldn't move a muscle or make a sound. I thought he'd shot me. I was so scared I wanted to cry, but I couldn't even do that.

Sunny was screaming, hands pressed to her face. Barnabas slapped her, hard. She gulped and shut up. A guy with neat, blow-dried hair and a beard took her by the arm and led her away. It seemed that I should know him—had we met before?—but I couldn't think straight. Where was he taking Sunny?

Hard hands gripped my arms, and I was suddenly dragged upright. I managed to roll my eyes to the left. Tom. Tom and someone else. They lifted me up between them like a drunk.

Didn't anyone care that I was getting kidnapped here? I got a glimpse of a couple holding hands at the top of the steps, staring. Another black coat walked towards them, holding up a badge-wallet as if he was a cop.

My feet dragged as they marched me along the bark path and through the windy archway of the Rijksmuseum to the Stadhouderskade. Light high above, peaceful globes of white light. People passing by whispered and stared, but they didn't help me; why should they? I must have looked like a drug-addict or a drunk being taken away by plain-clothes police.

Somewhere in a parallel universe, Barnabas was talking. I made a massive effort at concentration. '. . . is everything prepped? Yeah, 'bout ten minutes. Send the lift up in five.'

There was a black car waiting. They posted me into the back seat like a letter into a pigeon-hole: file under *dumbass*. The car rocked, doors slammed. We were moving. Street-lights flicked past faster and faster until I thought I might throw up.

After an unmeasurable time, I managed to blink. I could feel my face again, and smell the leather of the car seat. I swallowed again and again: my tongue felt thick, too big for my mouth. Sensation returned and bestowed a pounding headache on me. I groaned and wished for oblivion. *No heroine should have to do her stuff with a headache. I bet Lara Croft never gets headaches.*

Lara Croft, admittedly, had the inestimable advantage of being fictional.

'Sorry about that, Birdy.' Barnabas was leaning into the back seat. 'Taser. I had a hunch you wouldn't be pleased to see me, and I know what a little devil you are with the old Kung Fu. So take it easy, kid. The numbness'll wear off pretty quick now.'

'What did you do with Sunny?' At least, that was what I meant to say. What actually came out was more like 'Wha' yoo doow' Thunnergh?'

'Aw, nothin' much,' Barnabas said, unfazed by my sudden speech impediment. 'Had one of the boys explain things. I don't think we'll have any more trouble off've her.'

'How did you know?' *Owd' yoo doe?* Getting better. I pulled dentist-faces in the dark, and bit my tongue by mistake.

'Where to find ya? Easy.' Barnabas' smugness infuriated me, then scared me. 'I figured you'd try to get in touch with your good buddies at the Club sooner or later, so I had their phones tapped. You told me yourself. Oh—' A big, malicious grin. He held something up. '—and thanks for the info, Birdy. I'll get someone over to Oude Schans right away.'

He held my green fur notebook. Complete with a photo of Kris de Haan, and every scrap of information I had on him. Including the rent demand for *Questor*.

Like I said, I do aspire to the qualities of a fool sometimes. I bit my tongue again, for sheer chagrin. It hurt more than the first time, which I suppose was a good sign.

I tried to sit up and flopped on to my side with my face buried in a cushion. My limbs were a mass of pins and needles. 'Ow.'

'You always did have to do things the hard way,' Barnabas said soberly. The driver said something to him, and he peered over his shoulder. 'Nearly there.' He banged shut a tinted partition that I hadn't seen till that moment.

I cursed and wriggled and grunted until I was more or less in a sitting position. My head kept wobbling over to one side.

The windows were tinted as well. I could see out, a little, but nobody would be able to see in. There were no doorhandles. Tears sprang to my eyes: I'd gotten myself into this, which was bad enough—but knowing I'd gotten Wolf and Zia and Gabriel into it too made it worse to a power of ten. If they went back to *Questor* . . .

The car slowed, and bumped over rough ground. I plastered my nose to the window and made out chain-link fences and squat ugly buildings. No people around that I could see. *Welcome to the armpit of Amsterdam.* My breath bloomed in sudden white shapes on the glass.

The car lurched in a right-angle turn through some rusty gate-posts, and I banged my forehead. I fended off the window with one shaky arm. My muscles weren't up to snuff yet, evidently. They'd just have to do.

I had a plan, for what it was worth: when Tom opened the door I was going to pretend to be weaker than I really was, and when he came to see what was wrong, I was going to kick his face through the back of his head, hack my way past the probably-armed driver with my bare hands, and make my escape. Not a terrific plan, but it was the best I could do in the time available. The car pulled up alongside a derelict-looking concrete building. Now or never.

Never, as it turned out. It wasn't Tom who opened the car door, but a dark-haired guy with sad brown eyes who looked at me and said, 'Out.' He had a gun in his hand. I fumbled my way out of the backseat, trembling—and only half of it, I swear, was because of the taser. Being threatened with a gun by a complete stranger is one of the nastiest feelings I know.

Also, I had a hunch I knew where I was. Wolf had told me about it only a few hours ago: the Hole. The secret lab. The odds against my walking out of here in robust health seemed pretty minuscule at that moment. My backbone suddenly had no marrow.

If you think that's a pathetic excuse, you're right, but you try it. Being Lara Croft in real life is nothing—and I mean *nothing*—like playing Tomb Raider. Trust me on this.

'Smart kid,' Barnabas said, as I clung to the open door and tried to persuade my knees to hold me up. 'Mulder, cuff her. And make it nice and snug, we don't want our guest checking out of the hotel before happy hour, do we?'

Mulder was good at his job. He was also a creep. He yanked my hands behind me and cuffed wrist to elbow so damn tight I couldn't feel my hand, then hustled me stumbling across the snowy yard and through a door.

We stood in a dimly-lit breeze-block corridor. Outside, I heard Barnabas' voice, and the crunching of car tyres on snow. There must be more men coming.

I was in more immediate trouble. Mulder shoved me face-first into the wall. Hoarse hot breath right in my ear. He was bigger than me, and a lot stronger, and I was fairly sure that wasn't a gun in his pocket.

I tried to kick his shins and he jabbed me in the kidneys. It hurt so much I nearly passed out—would have fallen to the floor if he hadn't been pinning me. His hands were everywhere. I couldn't make a sound. I struggled feebly, more out of pride than any conviction that I could make him stop.

'Mulder, get your dirty paws off.' Tom's voice. Mulder left off instantly, like a well-trained attack dog.

Barnabas took my arm and propelled me down the corridor in front of him at a smart pace. Humiliation on humiliation: I felt like sobbing my thanks, had to bite my lips together to keep from doing exactly that. My chin trembled.

Mulder stared at me all the mercifully-short ride in the lift. Not at my body, as I might have expected, but at *me*, like a fighter trying to psych-out his opponent. His eyes weren't sad, not up close. They were dirty windows into a dark interior. He didn't blink once.

The lift doors opened on a sterile white corridor. Barnabas hustled me out and straight ahead into a bare little office room. Mulder went off somewhere else. It's amazing, the things you feel thankful for after a bit.

A zed-bed had been made up in the far corner. Barnabas made me sit on the bed, then cuffed my wrists separately to the steel frame. I wanted desperately to reason with him, but I had a feeling that he'd heard it all before, so I kept quiet. I wasn't sure that I could speak without bursting into tears anyway. His brisk matter-of-factness was, I suppose, better than the false front he'd put on for me, but it was pretty horrible nevertheless.

I stared into his face as he went about securing my feet to the bed frame with orange plastic cable. I think I was trying to discern some difference in him, some fatal flaw that would make hating him easier.

It was impossible: this was Tom Barnabas, the same man who had taught me to shoot and spit, who'd taken my part in the endless rows with Dad after Mom died. This wasn't *Invasion of the Bodysnatchers*, there was no alien entity lurking in there. Just Tom, with his own drives and needs and his own reasons for doing what he was doing. Somehow, knowing that made it more sad and scary than ever.

A brisk rattle of noise in the corridor. The door opened to admit a steel trolley—source of the rattling—pushed by a slim woman with a white doctor's coat slung casually on over a stunning Dior suit. She flicked her glorious blonde hair back, smiled, and said, 'Hello Robin.'

The final piece of the puzzle fell into place with a doom-laden clang: Dominique Rancoul. I stared at her, remembering Zia's voice in my ear as I sat in Tom Barnabas' kitchen. *We're pretty sure she's involved too.* And how.

Domi always had been the clever one, and left the charm to Michel. Now she looked at me with a calculating eye and said, ridiculously, 'How much do you weigh?'

The question startled me back into speech. 'Pounds or kilos?'

Dominique made an impatient gesture. 'Kilos, naturally. Fifty?'

Bitch. 'Forty-three last time I looked,' I snapped. Honestly. Some people just can't resist the chance to stick the knife in. Domi seemed to be taking the opportunity a little too literally: she'd picked up a syringe from the trolley and was filling it with pale blue liquid from a plastic bottle. She flicked the barrel of the thing with an immaculate fingernail, and glanced at me again.

'OK. Do you suffer from hypertension, heart condition or diabetes?'

From somewhere, I found a spark of outrage that pierced through the bad-dream numbness. 'How could you do that to Cary? You slept with him—'

'For one week only,' Dominique objected fastidiously. 'Anyway, he was only screwing me to get his precious information. Believe me, it was a great pleasure to stick it to him for a change.' She waggled the syringe, and smiled. Or it looked like a smile; I wasn't sure there was any humour behind it that a normal human being would recognise. The resemblance to her brother was strong.

'He's dead,' I said in a small voice, 'and you killed him, out of spite.'

'Don't be so melodramatic,' Domi said. 'He knew the risks he was taking. And I imagine he got all the data he wanted at the end.'

'You bitch!' A dizzy surge of anger deprived my brain of oxygen just when I needed it to give her a good cussing-out. All I could do was repeat, weakly, 'You *bitch*.'

Barnabas had been standing in the doorway with his arms folded. Now he interrupted. 'Can we get on with it? The sooner we get De Haan back here under lock and key, the happier I'll be.'

'What—what do you mean?' I realised I was struggling against my bonds in a ridiculous heroine-in-a-fix kind of way, and stopped with an effort. I stuck my chin out at Dominique as she bent over me with that damned syringe in her hand. 'Am I a hostage?'

'Not quite,' Dominique said, and stuck the needle in my leg right through my jeans.

It hurt. She smiled into my eyes from far too close, and patted my cheek. '*Now* you're a hostage.'

❖

'Is she always this . . . intense?' Wolf peered through the half-open door of the hospitality room at Zia's pacing figure.

Gabriel shot Wolf an amused look over his shoulder from the sink. 'Who, the Überchick? You better believe it. High-octane A-type personality, driven as hell. Plus she's a Yank,' he added, and passed Wolf another dripping cup. 'Here you go. Serious bunch, the Yanks.'

'Tell me about it.' Wolf wiped the cup and placed it with the others on the mini-bar. 'If you don't mind my asking, what's your interest in Nemesis? Artemis—well, she didn't exactly stop to fill me in.'

'I heard her,' Gabriel said, and passed Wolf another cup. 'There you go, that's the last.' He wiped his hands on the tail of Wolf's drying-cloth, and got out a packet of cigarettes. 'Want one? No? OK then,' lighting up with immense enjoyment and hopping his rear up on to the bar. He squinted at Wolf through the smoke. 'We had a close friend that died in the first round of tests in London a couple of years ago. It's the same story as you and Robin—someone you cared about got offed for no better reason than some arrogant arsehole thought they wouldn't be missed. Only difference—' Gabriel shrugged and grinned, 'Artemis has money. A *lot* of money.'

Wolf was about to reply when a dart of pain shot through his head. He dropped the cup. It somersaulted to the floor in slow-mo. The impact was a white smack of noise. Pieces of china wobbled about like broken eggshells.

His balance went. He dropped to hands and knees and the square of vinyl flooring, chequered steel and black, stabbed cold up his arm-bones. The room rippled around him like a mirage. He could see lights, lights that shouldn't be there. He screwed his eyes shut but the lights didn't go away.

His senses were peaking and dropping out as if someone was fiddling with the volume knobs: a knot in the wooden kick-board below the sink resembled a crevasse, a glistening bubble of amber sap set hard as epoxy on the edge; dust and floor-polish and sour food odours from the garbage.

'Jan? You all right?' Gabriel's voice, too loud. Wolf whimpered and wrapped his arms round his head. Loud footsteps. Gabriel again, not so close. 'Just happened. One minute he's right as rain, next thing I know he's on the feckin' floor.'

'Let him be for a minute.' Artemis. Sensible woman, Wolf thought. Let me be.

The nausea eased, but not the confusion. He could feel his own body, sturdy dependable thing, curled on the floor in the polite-beige hospitality room.

At the same time—as if the two things occupied the same space in his mind—he was flat on his back on a bed, handcuffs hurting his wrists, with the doctor—she was called Dominique—bent over him. And he wasn't a him at all. He was Robin, and she was very frightened.

Wolf pushed the sensations away with an almost physical effort. He was panting as if he'd run a mile. He rolled up to a sitting position, clutching his head.

'Man, you had us worried for a minute!' Gabriel, squatting on his heels and peering at Wolf with big liquid eyes. 'You OK there?'

'Be fine,' Wolf said, and gulped air. 'O God. O God. Robin.'

'What about Robin?' Artemis stood in the doorway tapping one foot, arms folded tight. Wolf hung his head while he got his breath back, then looked up.

'They caught her. They're holding her at the Hole.'

'What do you mean? How do you know?'

Wolf rubbed a hand across his mouth to quell a shudder. 'They gave her the drug.'

'Nemesis?' Gabriel said. Wolf nodded.

''S'right. Nemesis. It makes you . . . feel things. People,' Wolf persisted doggedly, screwing his eyes shut. 'Other people who've taken it. That's what it does. It was like I was there, seeing things through her eyes.' His voice shook. 'She's really scared.'

'I don't understand,' Artemis said into the silence that followed. 'Why would it have that effect?'

'It's the psychoactive,' Gabriel said suddenly. 'You remember that design element Cary got the name of, whassit, PSA? Psycho-something, he reckoned. That must be it. Bloody hellfire.' Reluctant admiration in his voice.

Out in the main room, a phone rang. Gabriel jumped as if someone had stuck a pin in him. 'That's my phone.' He disappeared, and Wolf heard his voice. 'Hello? Yes. Yes. Is she OK? Well, can I talk to her? OK. OK. All right, I'll tell him.'

Wolf had a foolish impulse to rise to hear the bad news, as if it would be a mark of respect or good manners or something equally fatuous. He was bone-tired, and he already knew what they were going to say, so he remained where he was on the floor when Gabriel came running.

'He was right.' The Irishman's voice was a panicked falsetto. 'They got her. What're we going to do?'

'I don't know.' Artemis sounded grim. 'What do they want?'

'Me.' Wolf buried his head in his hands so he didn't have to look at the pity on their faces. He spoke to the floor. 'They want me.'

18

THERE ARE DREAMS that come and go too quickly, all melted and running together so that nothing makes any sense. I am at the club, power-walking on the treadmill, Gabriel shouting instructions at me, sweat running down my sides; or I see Wolf's face, close as if he's bent over me. He is yelling something—something important—but his voice is less than a whisper, as if he's simultaneously by my side and miles away. He takes my shoulders in his big hands and shakes me, gently at first then harder. I shout for him to stop but he keeps shaking and shaking me. Somewhere in the dizziness, his face goes shadowy and strange, and suddenly Dominique Rancoul is there in his place, and it's her hands that grip my shoulders, fingernails digging into my flesh; or else it's the night of the crash and I limp along the roadside with the grass wet under my bare feet—bare because my tennis shoes have been squashed into the passenger footwell of the Land Cruiser and when I dragged my feet clear, the shoes wouldn't come. So, wet earth and a smell of torn grass and spilt gasoline. Cars pull up, people shout and run, and I just keep on walking—little hurt steps because if I put any weight on my left ankle it feels as if someone is sticking hot needles into it. My left arm is warm, and wet too: warmth tickles the back of my hand and drips from my finger-ends. If I keep walking, I'll find someone to help Mommy, help her wake up. Even at eight years old, I know it is bad when someone won't wake up. It's up to me. Nothing can happen to Mommy so long as I keep going.

Afterwards, I knew it was my fault. They tucked me up tight in the high hospital bed, and wrapped heavy wet bandages around my foot, and when I woke it had gone hard like a big Mickey Mouse shoe, and even if I could have untucked the hard white sheets I couldn't have walked away. That was when I knew something bad had happened.

Responsibility is a familiar pain in the ass, and I bring it back with me.

The first thing I see is Dominique Rancoul, so that wasn't a nightmare after all. Pity.

She bends over me, watching my face with the hungry concentration of a cat at a mouse-hole. I let my gaze slide past her. Everything has changed.

Only one of the lights is on, but everywhere seems light anyway, flat grey light even where there should be shadows—not daylight but something else—more efficient, less wholesome.

The greyish light would look drab if it wasn't for the colours that crawl and slide on every surface.

Everywhere I look it is the same: rich brocade textures, all flaring and sizzling with scribbled outlines of colour. Multiply that level of sensory detail by five, and it is almost drunkenly hypnotic. I get a sudden insight into what Wolf meant by 'too much input'. I want it to stop.

Maybe I'm still dreaming, maybe I fainted or something and Wolf is trying to wake me up. I squeeze my eyes tight shut and try to visualise Wolf's face as he appeared in the dream. OK, hold on to that. I open my eyes again.

Finding Domi still there is a nasty jolt. She ignores my dirty look and busies herself taking my pulse.

'How do you feel?'

'What the hell do you care how I feel?'

'If you're dead, we can't trade you for De Haan,' Domi says calmly, as if discussing the price of bacon, and drops my wrist. 'Well, you seem to have assimilated the shock quite well, all things considered. Clean yourself up, you stink.' She drops a box of tissues and a drum of wet-wipes on the floor by my side, and walks out of the room. Her stilettos tip-tap away down the corridor.

I lie still, staring at the tissues. Domi has always been charmless, but meeting this side of her head-on is a bit of a shock. At the same time, I am aware that she is right: the office smells like a sick-room, foetid and musty. I check discreetly. Yup, it's me.

I sit up, feeling shaky, but glad to find my hands free, and wash as thoroughly as possible. The wipes are cheap, scented with a cloying perfume that is only marginally better than what it replaces. I hold my breath and get on with the job.

The office isn't exactly private. The windows either side of the door are covered with venetian blinds, but they are open. There is no way to retire to a discreet corner for my cat-bath; my feet are still secured to the bed-frame with that stupid jelly cable, and I can't even stand up, let alone turn round.

A guy in a black coat stands outside the door with his back to me. My guard, I suppose.

By the time Domi comes back with Tom I smell better, but that's about it. I can see my bag, which someone has dropped casually over in the corner by the door. I sit and fret. What I couldn't do if I got my hands on that bag! I could shoot 'em, zap 'em, gas 'em . . . which is probably why it's safely out of my reach.

And anyway, I berate myself, what will I do after I've shot Domi, zapped Tom and gassed the guard? Lie back and think noble thoughts while Mulder does his funky S&M thing? As matters stand right now, I'm valuable, kind of. Tom will keep Mulder off of me for that reason at least. I hope he'd do it for old times' sake as well, but I'm not exactly confident about that any more.

'How you feelin', Birdy?' Tom has a grim, concentrated look that I recognise. It is a soldier's look. Any tentative hopes that he might let me go while Domi's back is turned wither. I clamp my jaw tight.

'I feel like a prisoner.' I knot my fists in the blankets and glare at nothing. Barnabas squats down in my line of view.

'Just checkin' you were OK, kid. We'll let you go as soon as we have De Haan, I swear.'

'And you expect me to thank you for that?' I meet his gaze for a second. He looks right back at me.

'No. No, I don't expect that. I'm not a barbarian, Robin.'

'Yeh right,' I mutter. 'That's why you're working for *her*.'

'I'm not working for her,' Barnabas says. 'I'm working for Uncle Sam, just like I always have. This is a matter of national security. I don't always like my job, kid, but I always do it to the best of my ability.'

'I need the bathroom,' I say, 'and I want my bag back.'

'I don't think—' Domi begins, peevish, but Barnabas has already scooped it up. He roots through the contents.

'Let's see now . . . ' He comes up with the Glock-17 between finger and thumb, and lays it on the table at his side. 'Think I'll keep an eye on that for you, if you don't mind. Oh. This too.' The little taser joins the gun, then my cellphone. Barnabas drops the bag in my lap with a wry grin for my transparent hopes. 'Have fun.' He jerks his head at the door guard, a fair-haired guy with blandly forgettable good looks. 'Louis here'll take you along to the bathroom. You try to escape, he's got orders to incapacitate you. He's also better at the martial arts crap than you are, so forget any smart ideas, OK?'

Louis is almost civilised next to Mulder, but I am never in any doubt that Tom is telling me the truth about him. He accompanies me into the bathroom and waits outside the cubicle while I pee.

Under cover of rushing water, I check quickly through what Tom has left me. Lip-salve, tissues, the little computer in its soft case. Biscuit crumbs, and an empty chocolate wrapper.

My fingers shake as I fish out the tiny can of Mace. It looks like a lipstick in its chic little gold canister.

I've used it only once, to knock out a huge guy who'd tried to take on Taz in the Gents at EyeKon. I don't think he appreciated the fact that I saved him from broken bones. How much have I used? I don't know how many squirts you get from this thing. Maybe only one more, maybe four or five, there's no way to tell. I'm not sure how much use it'll be if it comes to a fight, but just knowing I have a weapon they don't know about makes me feel better. I stuff it back under the rest of the rubbish, and allow Louis to escort me back to my malodorous little cell.

Domi is waiting in the office. She has closed the venetian blinds. I look at the wall while Louis locks the cable tight on my ankles, then lie down and shut my eyes. I hear Louis go out, and the brush of his coat against the door glass as he takes up his position in the corridor. Domi is a whisper of sound and scent that makes the skin on my back crawl.

'What's it like?'

I open my eyes. Dominique has an odd look on her face, compounded of distaste and a sort of hungry prurience. She leans against the bare table near the door with arms folded, the picture of chic detachment, if you don't know what to look for. I learned a lot from Michel. She is tense as hell.

'Why don't you try it yourself,' I say. 'Oh, I forgot, you don't have the guts. You just get other people to take risks for you.'

I should have saved my breath. My scathing words bounce off her iron-clad self-regard like ping-pong balls. She shrugs elegantly. 'You know, to make an omelette—'

'What?' I cut in, 'you have to make a mess? To make an omelette, you have to tell lies? No, let me guess, to make an omelette, you have to *use* people. Am I getting warm yet?'

'I don't have to listen to this.' Domi walks to the door, but she's a Rancoul, she can't resist a parting shot. She pauses with her hand on the doorknob. 'As soon as we have your Dutch friend safely, ah, debriefed,' pause for a smirk, 'I will be leaving. Our customers are paying a lot of money for Nemesis. They are most anxious to take delivery as soon as possible, so if you'll excuse me, I'm busy.' Smile. Flick hair. Exit, stage centre. The key turns in the lock.

'You crazy bitch! What do you think this is, a Bond movie?' For want of a more fearsome weapon, I throw the drum of wet-wipes. It bounces off the door-frame and rolls into a corner.

I drag the pillow half way down the bed so that I can curl up, and pull the single thin blanket over my head. It feels scratchy, and smells of God-knows-what. My head is spinning as if I am drunk, and I have that horrible fluey feeling as if some practical joker peeled me while I was asleep and put my skin back on nerve-side-out.

I should have listened to Wolf. He tried to tell me what Nemesis did to him, and I just assumed he was a flake. I wish he was here, then bite my lips together at a sudden realisation: he soon *will* be here, and it's all my fault.

❖

The only sound in the Alfasud was the whirr of the heater. Wolf sat hunched over in the passenger seat, staring through the curved vignette created in the snow by the windscreen wipers.

In the shadows beyond the iron railings, *Questor*'s main hatch squeaked back and forth in the wind.

Artemis worried at one perfect fingernail. 'You're *sure* you locked it?'

'Of course I'm sure,' Wolf said for the third time. He shook his head, unbuckled his seatbelt. 'I'm going over there.'

'You can't,' Artemis said. 'What if they're still there?'

'They'll wish they weren't,' Wolf said—acutely irritated to find that he sounded like an action hero—and fumbled for the door handle. Artemis grabbed his sleeve.

'Wait a second! Those guys blew Robin's apartment sky-high just yesterday. There might be a bomb in there.'

Her voice cracked on the word 'bomb'. Wolf looked into her face, very close to his. Her eyes were enormous, wide with fright. He could hear her heart.

'Stay here,' he said, and put her hand away from his arm. 'Keep an eye on the street. If there's anything or anybody down there, I stand the best chance.'

'No,' Artemis said. 'What if you get yourself blown away?'

'I have no intention of dying,' Wolf said.

'Yeah, well, we all know about good intentions,' Artemis hissed.

'Let the guy do his stuff,' Gabriel said from the shadowy back seat. 'C'mon, Zia. He's right.'

Wolf was surprised when Artemis—after only a second's hesitation—gave a quick nod and sat back in her seat. 'Just be careful.'

Wolf did not reply, just opened the car door and clambered out. Colour was leaching into the monochromes of night, and he stood for a second stretching the kinks out of his back. The smell of beer and tobacco smoke from the jazz club a few doors away across the road made his stomach churn. Now or never. He walked briskly across to the iron railings, and vaulted down on to *Questor*'s deck.

There were no lights on in the saloon. Wolf moved quietly to the top of the companionway, poised for fight or flight—they seemed equally appealing—but nobody came. He leaned in, and peered suspiciously at the light-switch. It didn't look as if it had been tampered with. He left it alone all the same. Darkness gave him an edge that he was unwilling to relinquish just yet. He slid noiselessly down the ladder, and turned to scan the room.

Wolf felt as if someone had scooped the contents of his chest out with a sharp spoon. The saloon was a mess. Books and pictures had been swept off the shelves on to the floor. His old armchair had been slashed open. Tufts of horsehair stuck up from the disembowelled seat with an odd, jaunty air. The kitchen drawers had been yanked out of their frames and the contents spilt carelessly in a heap on top of the splintered remains.

Wolf smelt traces of himself and Robin, both overlaid by the bodily odours of two or more men. The hairs at the back of his neck prickled, but the scent wasn't fresh. He strained his ears, holding his breath, but apart from the over-excited pounding of his own heart, there was no sound.

He bent to pick up a broken cup. Ridiculously, he felt close to tears. *Questor* had been his secret, his hidey-hole. The calculated destruction hurt more than Wolf would have thought it possible to be hurt by the breaking of mere things. *Foolishness*, he told himself. *Yesterday you didn't even know you had a home.*

'All clear down there?' Gabriel's stage whisper racketed off the panelled walls. Wolf winced and brushed his fingers across his eyes before he answered.

'Come on down. There's no one here now.'

'You mean there were people here? How can you tell?' Gabriel's steps fumbled down the companionway, then the lights flickered on. The Irishman's face looked pale as he gaped round. 'Holy crap.'

Artemis vaulted neatly down from the deck, landing like a cat. Her yellow eyes widened as she took in the mess. 'Nobody about up there. What were they looking for?' Straight to the point, as always. Wolf blinked, and shrugged.

'Papers, I suppose. Disks. Hard data.'

'And did they get it?'

'I . . . uh, I'm not sure.' Wolf pushed at his forehead. 'I don't think so. I don't think I kept things like that.'

'Oh, great.' Artemis collapsed gracefully on to the torn armchair. Her long fingers picked and twisted at the protruding lumps of stuffing as she stared at Wolf. Silver rings on her fingers winked in the light and reminded him suddenly of Maartje. He rubbed one hand numbly over his face. So many people tangled in this now. It wasn't just him any longer—if it ever had been.

He gazed at Gabriel rootling curiously through the litter of ruined books, and closed his eyes. *Questor* had never been the solution to his troubles. He'd been foolish even to allow himself to hope that he could just go to ground here.

'So why're we here?' Artemis was still gazing at him with those disconcerting eyes. Wolf recalled himself from his recriminations with an effort.

'To find something.'

'You said there wasn't anything here to find,' Artemis pointed out.

'I said *they* didn't find anything,' Wolf corrected her. He picked his way among the debris of his possessions to the kitchen nook. He braced his fists on the sink, suddenly at a loss. It was here—right here—but where? The sudden blankness was infuriating. It was on the tip of his mind . . .

'So, if we're not looking for hard-copies of data, what are we looking for?' Gabriel's soft voice at his elbow made Wolf jump. He turned to answer, and got his head tangled in the stupid plastic mobile, wobbling around on its string.

'Damn!' Wolf pawed at his head, feeling acutely foolish, and ducked free of the lopsided mess of rods and balls, clutching them in his fist so that they couldn't ambush him again. He remembered the last time he'd touched them. *I must have put this here.* Suddenly, he knew why.

A warm liquid twist of relief. Wolf smiled, and reached up to snap the thread that fastened it to the ceiling. 'I'll show you.'

He cleared a space on the refectory table by shovelling an armful of books off the end. Gabriel and Artemis crowded close as he began to dismantle the hollow plastic rods and balls. Empty pieces rolled and fell to the floor as he worked. Then the welcome, unexpected weight of a blue rod. He upended it into his palm with infinite care: a slim plastic ampoule slid out into his hand. The liquid inside was the pale blue of an early-morning sky. Wolf held it up between finger and thumb, and had to sit down. 'Nemesis. I stole a sample.'

'I don't understand,' Artemis said after a second, and sank down on the bench opposite. 'Just a sample of the finished product doesn't do us any good. We have to have evidence of who made it.'

'If we can find some way to get the data out of my head *now*,' Wolf said slowly, 'could you still put it on the web? I—I mean, are all the links and things still in place?'

'Of course. But how?'

'I don't know if it'll work.' Wolf glanced around at the devastated saloon. 'Robin told you it affected my memory block before. It has a psychotropic base, right?' A nod from Gabriel. Wolf went on doggedly, 'I had a dose only yesterday. Maybe if I take this as well, it'll be enough to kind of jog my memory.'

'Yeah, and maybe it'll be enough to kill you,' Gabriel put in acidly. 'This is the dumbest thing I've ever heard.'

'It sounds like an awful lot of ifs and maybes to me,' Artemis said. 'I don't think you should do it. You don't *have* to do any of this.'

'Yes I do,' Wolf said. He rubbed his fingertips into his eyes, hard. 'Either we get that data out of my head, or I have to go back. I can't leave Robin there. But thanks for the sentiment.' He drew a deep breath, wishing he was really as calm as he sounded, and glanced around the room. 'There's a hypo-gun somewhere.'

'I'll find it,' Gabriel volunteered.

'Try down in the engine compartment,' Wolf said. 'First door on the right, it might be on the floor under the steps. If they didn't take it,' he added, more to himself than anybody. Artemis reached out one silver-tipped fingernail to touch his wrist. 'Scared?'

Wolf stared into the glowing yellow eyes for a long moment. 'Of course I am.' The words came out with some difficulty, and his bad eye threatened to spasm, but he held her gaze. She nodded, and a luminous grin broke over her face, like moonrise.

'You're all right, Jan Wolf.'

'You're not so bad yourself,' Wolf said, and left it just long enough before he added, '—for a spoilt-brat rich bitch.'

Artemis burst out laughing, and Wolf grinned. Gabriel, just closing the door to the engine-room, looked at the pair of them as if they were certifiable. He set something down on the table with a thump.

'This the right thing, Jan?'

'Yeah, that's it. Thanks.' Wolf picked it up and turned it over a couple of times, unsure of what to do next. Artemis surprised him again by taking it and working the action with a capable touch.

'When you're patron of a medical charity, you get to play with all the best toys,' she said. 'These things have a compressed-gas cylinder in the grip. Here, give me that.'

Wolf handed over the ampoule. Artemis snapped off the end and poured the blue liquid carefully, then twisted the opening shut. 'You make sure the seal's good, then it's ready to go. I guess the reservoir should be sterilised or something in between uses, but . . .' She shrugged, and held the gun out to Wolf on her open palm. 'It's all yours. What do you want us to do?'

'Keep an eye out upstairs,' Wolf said. 'This won't take long.' I hope.

He picked the hypo-gun up and waited until Zia and Gabriel were climbing up on to the street. He placed the muzzle of the hypo-gun against his throat and pulled the trigger.

A shot of cold to the head, just as before. Wolf dropped the gun on the table and leant back against the wall, shutting his eyes. Dizziness plucked at him. He gripped the edge of his seat and tried to breathe deeply. Panic. Gabriel was right, this was stupid. How often were you supposed to take this stuff?

He tried to sit up, and fell in a clumsy sprawl of limbs. On to the floor, books sliding under his shoulders, broken pottery digging into his left hip. Wolf scrabbled vainly for a handhold. He was sinking. A shifting sea of dreams. The grey walls of the maze crumbled under the sly lick of its surf.

He thought of Lisette suddenly, as if she had just slipped his mind for a moment. Lisette, with her long brown hair and brown eyes and soft full lips that tasted of the best Belgian chocolate. Wolf closed his eyes for a second at the reality of that memory, heart pounding a little. Her mouth was always cool, even in summer. They'd been married for three disastrous years. He didn't contest the divorce, but he'd kept the ring all this time out of a kind of guilty sentimentality. She'd married a civil engineer from Innsbruck called Rufus or Brutus or something. They had a whole brood of kids—five or six—he forgot exactly how many.

Too much. Wolf moaned and covered his eyes with his fingers, as if that could help. Images leapt at him like speeded-up VR graphics for some Grand Prix race game: Pete, Maartje, Klaas, Mademoiselle la Docteur, all there for an instant then smashed aside in the rush. He groaned out loud and struggled to sit, but his balance was gone. He could not even lift his head.

He was hyperventilating. Boots and fists rucked up the rug as if his body wanted to crawl away and hide. The maze rushed towards him, clear as glass.

He watched his Oma shaking a colander full of damsons, knobbly-jointed fingers picking out stalks and bits of leaf. He was eight years old and hopping with impatience because he wanted to slot the shiny hard damsons one by one into the jars of *jenever*—his particular job, his privilege—and Oma was taking an unconscionably long time over washing them. Heady sour juniper-smell from the open jars, and Oma's perfume composed of lavender-water and cigarette smoke and wintergreen ointment. The stifling scent always made him cough when he walked into the blue-painted house, no matter how long he lived there.

He fell away from it through the glass walls.

Fragments from his two years aboard the HNLMS *Wolf*: Lieutenant Van Reep and his bristly ginger beard and endless safety lectures. *Rijstaffel* on Wednesdays and pea-soup with black rye bread on Fridays, world without end.

The time he went overboard near Macao and almost got eaten by a great white (he even remembered the sandpaper rasp of the shark's flank against his arm, and the flat boot-button eyes the size of his palm)—he'd been clowning around for a bet, and got himself thrown in the brig for three days—the shark got off scot free.

Seeing the phosphorescent spume of breaching whales when he was up on the deck on night watches, and the spit and splash of eerie green-white fire where the dolphins rode the bow-wave. Falling in terrified love with the ocean.

Sweat drew wavy lines on his scalp. Wolf struggled to open his eyes. Snowflakes drifted in the open hatchway like infinitesimal galaxies and prompted a gentler memory.

An attic. Music, and the smell of wet earth. Hot coffee cup in his hand, and grit under his fingernails. If he turned his head coming up the last few steep box steps from the landing, the tall rectangle of the window looked like a sunny doorway into the sky. Dust moved in lazy patterns in the light. The panes were old, and the glass had sagged at the bottom, twisting the view of trees and the canal bridge like liquorice.

It was a peaceful image. Wolf turned it dreamily in his head, tested the sensations of memory as a craftsman might turn a carving in his hands, running critical fingers over the grain for flaws.

He let the memory slide away. His head ached. He felt insubstantial—almost transparent—as if the images had passed through him like a prism and left him unchanged. All that was left was the monotonous murmur of traffic, and the blat of boat sirens from the docks. He heard Zia and Gabriel murmur together, their boots shifting on the deck above him.

Wolf lay spreadeagled among the debris on the floor and watched the warm glimmer of his own breath dissipate into the chilly shadows that surrounded him. Shadows full of someone else's past.

Stars were out in the scrap of sky visible through the hatch. Aeroplane lights drew coloured lines between the stars.

His head felt fragile, transparent as glass. His thoughts were a dense, spinning swarm of lights, infintesimal planets whirling in their elliptical orbits. And music—he could hear the music of his own body, his bones singing in harmony with his flesh, all overridden by the dizzy symphony of his brain. He was a creature made of crystal, all sharp edges and gleaming facets, thrumming with power. The music was winding up to an impossible pitch, higher and higher until he felt as if it would shatter his bones. Wolf felt tears slide down his face, searing hot. He could only lie there paralysed and wait for it to happen.

'Jan?' Sound crashed in on him. Wolf clapped clumsy hands to his ears and for a moment entertained the novel notion that he'd smashed his own skull into pieces. His thoughts scattered like a puff of pollen on the wind.

A hand grasped his wrist and pulled his hand firmly away from his ear. 'Jan?' A whisper this time, but it shook him like thunder.

'Too much . . . ' Wolf tried to focus on Artemis' face as she crouched down in front of him, but there was no image to hold on to. Crystal and light. He fended her off with trembling hands. Her voice crashed around in his head like percussion.

'Jan? Did it work?'

'No. No.' Wolf buried his face in his hands. 'No.'

A long pause. 'It's almost time.'

'Wait.' Wolf gathered himself. 'Gabriel said you have . . . lot of money, right? Could you find someone for me, if I told you where to look?'

'I have a few cents,' said Artemis. 'What's on your mind?'

I wasn't crazy before I went to sleep. But how can you tell? For all I know, convincing yourself that you're perfectly rational is an early sign that you're a complete fruitcake. Denial or something. Maybe, maybe it's a sign of a healthy mind to wonder if you're going crazy, in which case I'm fine.

Or not.

I sit hugging my knees and stare at the zigzags of harsh white light that mark the edges of the venetian blinds. The air-conditioning shut off a while ago, and the room is silent. Footsteps shuffle and tap in the corridor, trolley-wheels squeak and voices mutter, but I'm trapped in an eerie bubble of quiet. Not peace, just quiet.

I slide one hand under the hem of my t-shirt. I inch my fingertips across the flesh of my belly to my ribs. It tickles. I think I know I'll find nothing there, but the dream was horribly vivid.

I tug my shirt down and flop back on the bed, feeling foolish and relieved. It had felt so real.

Maybe it's the drug. Maybe it . . . I don't know, amplifies dreams or something, makes them realer just like it makes everything else realer.

Sure, that must be what happened. I fell asleep worrying about Wolf, and I dreamt about him getting shot, that's all. I saw the scars when I fished him out of the canal the other night, I knew it was the Black Coats who did it—my mind just supplied the missing details and cooked up a real good nightmare out of it.

I fold my other arm across my eyes. It's a good theory, it might even be the right theory. I frown against my arm. Since when does a good all-American girl dream in Dutch?

I groan and roll on to my side, clutching my aching head. Thinking of Wolf calms me for some reason and I linger on the image I have of him. He looks better without the beard. Good bones, Mom would have said.

He has a funny smile—kind of lopsided and wry, as if he knows something you don't. It would be rather a mocking smile if it wasn't for his eyes. Not anything premeditated, but a kind of nakedness, as if eye contact is a vulnerability to be guarded with great care. It touches a nerve somehow, gets under your guard.

It was that way last time we spoke: he touched my hair, and looked at me very seriously and said 'a promise is a promise'. Sexy as hell, in any other circumstances. I can see his lips shape the words, can almost hear his voice . . .

The picture darkens, slips sideways, then snaps back into focus. The image rushes towards me. My arm trembles. Sweat tickles my forehead.

My heart slams against my breastbone. I can't move. Part of me is very calm. *I'm hallucinating.*

'*No!*' I shoot upright in the camp-bed, gasping. Drenched with sweat.

The door clicks open, and Louis pokes his head in. 'Is everything all right?'

I manage to nod and smile somehow as he crosses over to check my bonds. My voice has no power. 'Just a bad dream.'

'Sleep well,' Louis says, and closes the door behind him. His broad silhouette takes up its usual position. I slump against the wall.

He touches my face. I bolt upright and stare wildly around the room. Nothing, nobody. Except even with my eyes open, Wolf is there, an earnest ghost. (*Robin? Robin, don't be scared.*)

I'm not scared. Not of him. Scared of going crazy, yes—scared to death I'm going to lose my mind. Confusion and hallucinations, that's how it started with Cary, that's how it started with Wolf. I press my hands to my face and even that scares me because I know what lies beneath and my bones are indelibly etched with the strangeness of what's passed over us.

I hug myself instead and rock, back and forth, back and forth. 'Wolf, if you can hear me, don't come here, they're going to kill you. Oh God, go away, please go away, please Wolf, *please* . . . '

19

WOLF STOOD with his back pressed to the iron railings of the zoo, half-hidden by the overhanging branches of a fir tree. The noise of traffic battered his senses. The air was heavy with exhaust fumes.

All the same, he supped the cold air slowly, savoured it. His knees quivered. In ten minutes' time, he would be breathing the ammonia-tainted, lukewarm air of the Hole. The mere thought had claustrophobia paddling damp fingers along his spine. His own terror made him ashamed, but it seemed there was nothing to be done about it. Only a saint or a madman isn't frightened when he sees death coming for him.

Think of it as unfinished business, Wolf prodded himself. You were never meant to survive that shooting. Everything since then has been borrowed time. Does it really matter whether the end comes above ground or below, in warm air or cold? Dead is dead, whether it comes with a butterfly-kiss or a bullet. There's no good way to do it.

All the same, he thought—all the same, I'd rather go for the kiss.

He stood very still. Two police cars had already rolled past; he did not wish to attract their attention. What appalled him most was not the thought of what the police might do if they stopped him, so much as what he, Wolf, might then do to them—intentionally or otherwise. Every time he allowed his thoughts to stray along those lines, he saw vividly-animated clips of the moment when he had hit the man in the alley—so vivid that he seemed to feel the actual brute sensation of the two blows compress the bone and muscle of his forearms. His hands ached, and he kept them stuffed in his coat pockets. Hallucinatory thought: could he be prosecuted for carrying concealed? What kind of license would you need to be whatever it was he had become?

Wolf clenched his fists inside his pockets and watched the cars fly past, all filled with people. People talked, or kissed, or argued or sat lost in thought until the lights changed at the junction, then the cars sped away and were replaced by others. Wolf gazed and gazed, and envied them their neat, oblivious lives.

He did not belong in the same world any more. Funny, he'd thought he was a nobody when he lived on the streets, but this—this was like being dead. The unreal nature of what he knew had broken over him in a silent wave and carried him with it into intangibility.

All around him, the city growled and lumbered and stank, like the composite beast it was—solid and touchable. Wolf felt quixotically certain that the currents of cold air that whisked through the branches and raised gooseflesh on his arms would pass through him, bone and flesh, without a ripple. Mister Nobody. Robin had called him that.

Wolf did not want to think about Robin. When he thought about her, a big empty place opened up inside him, no matter how hard he tried to stop it happening, and she came in. Not deliberately—she didn't seem even to be aware of his frantic efforts to fend her off—but like water flowing through a breach in a dike.

It was happening now. He was with her, huddled on the narrow camp-bed under a scratchy blanket, hugging herself. A jumble of guilt and panic. She'd been crying again.

Wolf was torn between wanting to get away and wanting to cradle her. He could do neither. He was faintly aware of his own body, much more aware of hers, as if the drug had somehow shoehorned them both inside her skin and bones. The sensation went several light-years beyond voyeurism into an acute consciousness of supple muscle and soft flesh. She had a dinger of a bruise on her upper arm.

A car slowed and stopped, directly opposite Wolf's hiding place. A long black car with tinted windows.

The blinding sizzle of battle-colours snatched Wolf back to himself. The car's rear passenger door swung open. The interior was unlit, but Wolf made out the rippling outline of a human body. A body with a scent that nagged at his memory.

Decision time.

Wolf closed his eyes for a brief moment. He smelt pine sap, and snow thawing, rainwater and ozone mixed. The pine-scent made spiky green shapes in his head. He breathed deeply. There was still time to run. They wouldn't be able to catch him.

(Sorry, Robin. A promise is a promise.)

Wolf walked over and bent down to peer into the back of the car.

'Happy Sinterklaas,' said the American, and winked at Wolf. He had a sprig of holly in the lapel of his black topcoat. 'Hop in, Mister De Haan. We've got a lot to talk about.'

Wolf got in and slammed the door. The car swung out into traffic. Wolf didn't bother trying to see where they were going: he knew, and in any case, something else was taking all his attention.

His murderer. Wolf stared, hypnotised: buzz-cut hair somewhere between blond and white; big fleshy hawk face, grim mouth, watchful smiling blue eyes. Muscles moved along the man's jaw, as if he was in the habit of grinding his teeth. Expensive grey suit under the black overcoat, and that jaunty sprig of green in the buttonhole, red berries shiny as fresh blood. Expensive blued-steel gun in the manicured hand.

The recognition was so profound that Wolf almost distrusted it. Almost, but not quite. Emotion, it seemed, was a hardwired connection to the past. He had not realised that he was capable of such hate. His own voice sounded terrifically, admirably calm.

'Major Barnabas.'

'Ahh, I'm touched.' A hard grin. The sapphire eyes twinkled. 'You remember me.'

'I remember what you did to me.' Wolf met Barnabas' gaze for a second, then looked at the gun. The hole in the end of it looked like the IJ Tunnel from here. Sweat sprang under his arms. A strange singing in his skull, stars in the black sky. From somewhere, he summoned a shaky sneer. 'Going to finish the job yourself?'

Barnabas uttered a humourless bark of laughter. 'You in a hurry?'

Wolf did not reply. He was having to breathe very slowly and carefully because every cell in his body was screaming at him to crush these idiots—hit them hard before they realised what he was capable of. The strain of sitting still made him light-headed. Salty blood-taste in his mouth. It would be so easy.

Unfortunately, freeing himself with a single bound wasn't part of the game-plan. Wolf shivered, and worried at his thumbnail.

'I'm trying to figure you out,' Barnabas said. 'You know, I think a lot of Robin.'

Several responses sprang to mind, but none that would be safe to speak out loud. Wolf settled for raising his brows a fraction. Barnabas had the grace to look embarrassed.

'Her Daddy and me go way back. She's a good kid, shouldn't have gotten mixed up in all this.'

'Right,' Wolf agreed cautiously. Barnabas scowled at him.

'It's like everything else in this sorry mess. Everything comes back to you. You start snooping around, get too clever, get too close, and we had to whack you, but you wouldn't just lie down and die, oh no.' A shake of the head. 'Then what do you do? You infiltrate the test programme.'

Wolf opened his mouth to say that was mostly by accident, then shut it again. Barnabas was on a roll, leaning forward with the gun dangling from his fingers.

'Now that should have killed you. Y'know? That's what's supposed to happen. But you do it again. You get away, and I can't find you. You're a walking goddamn nightmare. And then Robin comes along. Her Daddy's the stubbornest sonofabitch I ever met, and she's just like him, and she's looking for you. I tell ya—' Barnabas placed one hand on his stomach. 'That was when I started getting ulcers.'

There was one black car parked on the crumbling concrete apron in front of Goudberg's. Barnabas hustled Wolf past it and into the dusty office at a fast walk.

Wolf stumbled over the threshold of the lift, and the doors hissed shut. There was a slight jolt as the cage began to move, and Wolf's knees wobbled. He leant against the wall.

'Want to see her?' Barnabas' question flipped Wolf's eyes open in surprise. He stammered.

'Wh-what?'

'Do you want to see Robin?' Barnabas had the embarrassed look on his face again, as if he was breaking the Tough-Guy Code and would have to do penance, twenty Hail Marys, or whatever the mercenary equivalent was. Die Suckers, maybe.

Wolf nodded. 'Yes.' The offer had a distinct flavour of *the-condemned-man-had-a-hearty-breakfast* about it, but right now he'd overlook a lot for the sight of a friendly face. Especially Robin's.

Thinking of her had the same effect as before. Wolf stared past Barnabas' right ear at a blob of rust on the back of the mirror-glass. At the same time, he sat up suddenly on the creaky camp-bed. Wolf looked at his reflection in the mirror behind Barnabas, and felt her shock.

Of course, it might have something to do with how he looked. Gabriel had found an army-surplus flak jacket from somewhere, patterned in desert camouflage. Combined with his hair all stuck on end, the white face and the crazy, unblinking stare, it was enough to give anyone a shock—including yourself if you weren't careful. Wolf shut his eyes quick.

'What'n'the hell are you doing?' Barnabas grasped a handful of Wolf's jacket as the lift jolted to a standstill, and turned him towards the doors. 'Never mind. Let's go.'

A Black Coat was standing outside the door of the little office. As they emerged from the lift, Barnabas nodded to him. 'Open up, Louis.'

The man obeyed instantly, and Wolf found himself pushed roughly inside. 'Five minutes,' Barnabas said in his ear. The door slammed shut, and the key turned in the lock.

Robin was sitting stiffly upright on a camp bed in the far corner of the room. She stared at Wolf as if he had just risen through the floor. Her voice was husky from crying. 'You stupid sonofabitch.' She crossed her arms protectively over her breasts, kneading at her own shoulder muscles. 'I told you not to come.'

'I had to.' Wolf sank to a crouch in front of her. (You know I had to.) Their eyes met, and she looked away quickly.

'I'm sorry.'

'For what?' He knew.

(Getting you caught again.) Robin covered her mouth with her hands. She met Wolf's gaze with a kind of wince of recognition. (What did they *do* to us?) Awe, mixed with revulsion. Wolf recognised the emotion. Robin shuddered and leaned forward to grasp Wolf's hands tightly in hers. (What's happening?)

(It's called psycho-spatial awareness. It was part of the drug design.) Wolf shrugged and looked down. (It's . . . more than they intended. A lot more. The drug's reacting with our body chemistry . . . kind of a synergy effect.)

(How do you know all that stuff?) Robin frowned at him; her curiosity/apprehension tugged inside his head like a fish-hook.

(I took another dose.) Wolf pulled his hands free and stood up. His own voice sounded rough. 'I thought it might break through the memory block. It worked . . .' He dragged his hands through his hair, and shrugged again, helpless. 'Not quick enough. Now I got all this data swimming round in my head and no place to shove it except up my own ass.' His chagrin was hot enough to make Robin flinch slightly as he sat down on the bed beside her.

'What's going to happen now?' She leant hesitantly against Wolf's side. He put his arm round her and she snuggled closer, trembling. He could feel her heartbeat, smell her hair.

It was strange to draw comfort from her feeling of being sheltered by *him*. Odd, seeing yourself through another's eyes, and feeling their surprise when they saw how they looked to you . . . mirrors inside mirrors. Wolf closed his eyes and held her tight. No matter how it was done, there was really nothing left to say. Five minutes was over all too quickly.

❖

They put him in the same cell he'd occupied before. No furniture this time. Barnabas stood back in the open doorway, hands folded, as Mulder went over Wolf for weapons. Wolf stared the man in the eyes and thought, *the only weapons that matter are the ones you can't take away from me, asshole.*

'Clean.' Mulder stepped back, looking at his boss. Barnabas drew something out of his coat pocket and handed it over without taking his eyes off Wolf. A hypo-gun. Mulder gestured at Wolf. 'Chin up.'

Wolf stood still and allowed Mulder to jam the muzzle into his neck and pull the trigger. He didn't get it in quite the right place, and the gun kicked against tendon. It hurt, and Wolf could not muffle a grunt of pain.

'Just a precaution,' Barnabas said, holding his hand out for the gadget. 'It's the antidote to Nemesis. Acts pretty quick, or so I'm told. We'll be back shortly with a few questions for you.' Anticipation in Mulder's wrinkled eyes.

'Oh?' Wolf had to suppress the urge to rub his neck where the gun had stung him. The shot had missed—not completely, but enough for it to take longer to do its job. Combined with the fact that they didn't know how much Nemesis he'd taken . . . well, it might not make enough difference, but hell, at this point he'd play whatever cards he was dealt.

Barnabas smiled. 'You've been a real pain in my ass, De Haan. That ends today.' He nodded to Mulder. 'Karel.'

Mulder gave Wolf a look so lingering it was almost lascivious, and walked out behind Barnabas. The door clanged shut, and Wolf heard the bolt drop.

He sank to his haunches, and blew out a shaky breath. Robin's curious presence nudged at him.

(Why'd they bother giving you the antidote?)

(Cut me down to size.)

He felt her consider it. (Mulder's scared of you.)

Wolf snorted. (Your friend Barnabas isn't.)

(He's not my *friend*.) A violent revulsion. Wolf soothed at her without words, and felt her rage subside, replaced by dejection.

(I wish this wasn't happening. I wish we were back on the boat.)

(Wish away.)

(Wolf, I hate this place. I'm so scared.)

(I'm scared too, but it's OK—)

(Sez who?)

(Insofar as anything **can** be OK, it's OK. OK?)

(All right. Wolf?) A ghost of a whisper. (I'm glad you're here.) A feeling as if she tried to smile. (It's like having an imaginary friend, only better.)

(Mister Nobody?) Helplessness, isolation. He couldn't hide it.

(Don't, Wolf.) Distress. (You're not nobody.)

Wolf scooted his butt along the floor and leaned back against the cool metal. He was feeling neauseous, a little feverish. (Don't know how long this is going to last now they've given me the antidote. Don't want to be on my own down here, Robin . . .)

(Hey, I'm here. Doesn't matter if we can talk or not, I'm still here for you, Wolf. They can't take that away, right?)

That was when Wolf got the idea. He actually yelped out loud, 'That's it!'

He clamped his mouth shut, but he couldn't keep himself from scrambling up and pacing. (Robin, listen, do you still have that toy computer in your bag?)

(Yeah, they let me keep it. Not much of a weapon, I guess.)

(No no—it's the best weapon we've got.) Wolf peered cautiously out through the glass porthole into the corridor. He could see the right foot and elbow of the Black Coat outside the office door. Other than that, nobody in sight. He slid down to his haunches, leaning in the corner beside the door. A flutter of excitement in his belly. (Robin, look round the room and see if there's a phone socket.)

(Phone socket?) Puzzled. (Yeah, there's one right here, why?)

(Plug the computer in without anyone seeing you, get online and go to Zia's website. Can you do that?)

(Oh!) Comprehension, and painful hope. It had cost her a lot to be stoic, Wolf realised. (OK, OK, the blinds are shut, it'll be easy. The guard's got his back to me. If I can plug in and just kind of slip under the blanket . . . All right, here we go . . . I'm in. What's the site called?)

(Nemesis.com.)

(Right . . . OK. There's a text box, what now?)

(Now I give you the data and you type it in as fast as you can.) Wolf closed his eyes and pinched thumb and forefinger over the bridge of his nose. Get it right first time, it all had to be in some sort of order . . . 'OK,' he said out loud. 'I'll just talk it to you, piece by piece. From the start. Ready?'

(Ready.) That wicked lick of excitement again, like the flare of a match flame. Her fingers trembled a little on the tiny keyboard.

Wolf clasped his hands on top of his knees. He'd given Nemesis a doorway, he remembered now: that silly plastic mobile on the boat where he'd hidden the drug sample. He pictured it carefully in his mind's eye, and followed where the image took him. 'Report on the Nemesis Project,' he began. The information lined up and marched out at his will. Wolf gripped his hands tight and kept his voice to a murmur.

He spoke quickly. They'd be coming back. He had to be done before then. If he wasn't . . . Wolf grimaced, and glared at his knuckles. No time to think about *if*.

He was reciting the last-but-one page of his report when the door-bolt rattled. Wolf got to his feet, heart bumping.

'Mister De Haan.' Barnabas walked into the cell, followed by Mulder, who carried a solid-looking metal chair. He set it down with a clang in the middle of the floor. Barnabas gestured politely. 'Take a seat.'

'Thanks. I'll stand.' Wolf backed off until he ran out of room. Sweat tickled the back of his neck. No way of telling how much the antidote had affected him yet. His heart pumped painfully, but the flaring battle colours were slow to come. It was only when Mulder pointed a gun at him that they stuttered into being—even then, they were a sickly parody of their usual energy-burst. Wolf walked to the chair and sat, a bubble of panic swelling in his guts.

'Now.' Barnabas took up his usual relaxed stance in front of the door. Wolf was uneasily aware of Mulder moving to stand just behind him. Barnabas held up one finger. 'I'm going to ask my questions just once, Mister De Haan. I know you wouldn't want anything to happen to Robin, and because of this, I know that you'll answer the questions. Am I right?'

Wolf nodded stiffly. He could feel Robin's fear/outrage like an ache in the back of his head.

Wolf moistened his lips. (Stay sharp, things are going to get a bit rough down here.) He cocked his head to one side as if easing the tendons in his neck. Mulder was right behind him, slightly to the left of centre. He was right-handed, so his left hand and shoulder would be forward if he was preparing for a blow . . .

'Now,' Barnabas said. 'Who have you told about Project Nemesis?'

'Nobody.' Wolf sensed Mulder's movement behind him. A final breathtaking stab of colour. He twisted with a snarl, grabbed Mulder's fist as it drove forward. He yanked the man off the floor and cracked his spine in mid-air like a whip. Mulder crash-landed at Wolf's feet in a sprawl of limbs. The angle of his neck made it clear that he wouldn't be getting up again, ever.

Stunned silence. Wolf shoved the body away and stood up, teeth bared. 'That was for my friends.'

'Sonofabitch!' Barnabas backed out of the door so fast he almost tripped. The door slammed, and Wolf made it to the porthole window in time to make Barnabas jump as he was fumbling with the bolt.

Dominique Rancoul appeared through the swing doors from the lab. Her voice was sharp and Wolf had no trouble hearing what she said. 'Why isn't he dead yet?'

Barnabas looked flustered. 'He just killed Mulder.'

'Mulder was an incompetent idiot,' snapped the doctor.

You're all heart, sweetie, thought Wolf.

'We were questioning him. We have to be sure exactly how much information he passed on—'

'And?'

'Nothing,' Barnabas growled. 'We only just got started.'

'If he had passed information to anyone, he wouldn't be inside that cell, we would. He's no risk to us now.'

Wolf stared at the doctor with his best poker face. *Guess again, superbitch.*

Dominique glared thoughtfully at Wolf through the little circle of reinforced glass. Her grey eyes flicked over his face and dismissed him. 'I'm going to check on Carlson. See to him yourself.'

❖

(Robin, she's coming!)

Wolf's yell in my head nearly stuns me. My fingers spasm on the keyboard. I do a whole line that goes ';dsfjhKJhjbc#' before I recollect myself. By then, Domi is snarling in French at Louis outside the door.

I duck deeper beneath the blanket. My hands tremble as I place the little computer carefully beneath the bed. The dark under there is suddenly full of bright colours.

The key rattles in the lock. Another burst of brilliant magenta that pulses in time with my blood. I blink, nerves at full stretch, and try to lie still. I'll have only the one chance.

Clattering steps. I twitch, can't help it. I want to fight. I want to run away. Blood-red fireworks splash against the dark inside my eyelids. Three. Two. One.

Domi snatches the blanket off me and grabs at my shoulder. 'Sit up!'

Stupid, but then I was counting on that. I open my eyes a slit, and draw a discreet breath. Domi is bent over me with that pretty mouth of hers pursed. Louis is right behind her, peering over her shoulder.

I squeeze my eyes shut, and let them have the pepper spray at point-blank range. There isn't much left in the can, but it's more than enough, in the circumstances. The two of them go down screaming and clawing at their faces. Domi crawls away to puke in the corner.

Louis is trained, and tries to get at me, but he isn't functioning at his best. His attack scares me though, enough so I forget myself and breathe in to scream.

The air's still full of red hot chilli peppers. I choke. Louis is still grabbing at my clothing. I club him on the back of the neck as hard as I can and he flops over for a quick sleep.

I scrabble through his pockets and find the key to my hobble, then spend too long fumbling—eyes still tight shut—to get the key in the tiny lock. I shove Louis off my legs and stagger to the door. Dominique is crawling that way. She has lost one elegant shoe, and there are loops of drool swinging from her mouth. I put my boot on the point of her bony ass and give her a hard push. She squeals and lands on her nose in the corridor. Shame.

I drag in lungfuls of air, wheezing. The corridor is deserted. This happy situation won't last long if the noises Domi is making are anything to go by. I grab the key from the outside of the lock, slip back inside and lock myself in.

Louis is starting to revive. I take his gun away from him and use the hobble to tether his hands and feet together behind his back. Then I roll him against the door like a draught-excluder, and arrange my shelter.

The two tables are veneered chipboard, which is pretty damn heavy. I drag one over to the camp-bed, then drop the other on its side and drag that across as well. Now I have a little den. Not perfect by a long chalk, probably as bullet-proof as a waxed paper bag when you come right down to it, but it makes me feel better.

I crawl inside and retrieve the palmtop from under the bed. It's still connected. Wolf's anxiety flutters in my throat, and I reach for him.

(I'm OK.) I show him what happened. I think he laughs, but it's sort of difficult to tell. His heart's going mad and his fists hurt. I can feel that there's been some kind of violence, but he's trying to block it out—or stop me from seeing it. He's tired, and the brutality of what he's just done revolts him. Barnabas is unlocking his cell door.

(No time left. Sorry, Robin.) Wolf closes his eyes and suddenly I'm right inside his head, he's laid himself wide open to me. The violation tears at him, but he holds the moment, teeth clenched. (Quickly. Get the report—) I'm disoriented, bewildered by perceptions so different from my own. His memories crowd my head. I grab clumsily for what he shoves at me.

(Wolf, I got it, let me go!) There's a panicked second when neither one of us knows how to disentangle what we've done. We struggle in silence, fighting for identity in a red/black sprawl of emotion and memory. Losing it.

Abruptly, I'm alone, crouched trembling on the creaky camp bed. I can't feel Wolf at all. There is so much in my head that I feel if I move too quickly I might explode. On the computer screen, the cursor winks at me, waiting.

I settle down on the bed with Louis' gun in my lap, and start to type.

❖

Barnabas let the door thunk to behind him. Wolf stared at him for a second in silence, then Barnabas' gaze flicked away to the body still huddled on the floor by the chair. 'He dead?'

'Yes,' Wolf said. He wondered why he felt so calm. Maybe because he'd burnt all his bridges now. He wished he could reach out for Robin, but his head still hurt from the way he had torn himself loose from her. It shouldn't be possible to do such things. He shuddered involuntarily.

Barnabas breathed in deeply through his nose, a reasonable man sorely tested. 'Now that's really gone and made me mad. Do you know how hard it is to get decent help these days?'

'I'm heartbroken,' muttered Wolf. He brought his hand out from behind his back. Mulder's gun was a Walther TPH .22, pretty pathetic as far as firepower goes but enough to give even a macho jock like Barnabas pause for thought. There was indeed a short, thoughtful pause.

'You should put that down before someone gets hurt,' Barnabas said, and drew his own gun. The difference in size was considerable. Wolf shook his head.

'Put it away.'

There was another pause. Neither gun wavered. Then Barnabas heaved an elaborate sigh, and shrugged. 'All right, have it your way, Kris. If it makes you happy . . . ' He held up his gun between finger and thumb, and pulled his coat aside with his left hand while he returned the automatic to its holster under his left arm.

The American's left hand flicked out, horribly fast. Wolf flinched aside, and the knife which had been intended for his throat bounced off the rear wall with a clang. Barnabas roared, and sprang.

Wolf was stunned. Nothing was happening—no slow-mo, no coloured lights. Most importantly, no speed, no strength. He felt like a snail in the path of a juggernaut.

Barnabas' leap knocked Wolf to the floor. He grabbed Barnabas' arm and tried to roll out from under. The American grinned and pinned Wolf's arms with his knees while he retrieved his knife. He was breathing heavily, but there was a professional relish in his eyes. 'Not a bad try, Kris. But you gotta understand, it was always going to end like this. You're a lucky sumbitch, but you're no kind of match for me. See this?' He was rolling up his shirt sleeve to display a tattoo that Wolf recognised.

'Special Services?' he croaked. Barnabas grinned.

'You bet. Black Ops. Been to Bosnia, Kosovo, Albania, South America, Angola . . .' Not for his holidays, Wolf assumed. He panted, at a loss for words. Barnabas gripped him by the hair, leaned forward and placed the knife-tip at the right side of Wolf's neck. He winked. 'Nice and quick. Say goodb—'

Wolf kicked upwards with all his strength. His knee connected with something soft, and Barnabas screamed. Wolf knocked the knife away from his throat and scrabbled out from under the writhing American.

He was half way into the corridor on hands and knees when a hand clamped on to his boot. Wolf yelled in fright and kicked, twisted free and staggered to his feet. The double doors to the laboratory. He limped towards them as fast as he could.

Barnabas cannoned into him from behind, and the two of them fell through the doors in a heap, grappling. Wolf grunted with the effort of keeping a grip on the American's wrists. Gun or knife? Some choice. Barnabas gave suddenly with his arms and tried to headbutt Wolf. He jerked his head aside, then shoved the American back to arm's length.

Barnabas growled and pressed down, concentrating on his knife hand. Sweat made Wolf's fingers slippery. Barnabas grinned in triumph and bore down with all his strength. His sweat dripped into Wolf's eyes. The point of the knife touched Wolf's cheek. He groaned and twisted desperately, but he was trapped. The knife sliced downwards, and Wolf gave a jagged cry of pain. Hot blood ran down past his ear. Barnabas laughed.

Wolf let his hands drop, and the American lurched forward, off-balance for a second. Wolf headbutted him, or tried to: his forehead connected with Barnabas' chin. Stars exploded behind his eyes.

Wolf dragged himself free and lurched to his feet. His heart laboured in his chest. He was losing this fight. He might be able to pull one or two more tricks out of the bag, but Barnabas was right—Wolf was no match for someone trained in hand-to-hand combat. He was running out of time.

'OK.' Barnabas had recovered his wits, or enough of them to be up on his hind legs again. He pointed the big gun at Wolf and cocked the action. 'I think I've had enough of you now.'

The lights went out.

Wolf dropped and threw himself forward, shoulder-first into Barnabas' legs. The gun went off with an almighty bang. The two men went down together in a mad tangle. Wolf hit his head on the floor. Something metallic skittered across the lino. *Gun or knife?*

Wolf rolled to his feet. Nemesis still gave him a dim twilight illumination. All the voice he could command was a strangled whisper. 'Come on. Come on! You son of a bitch, how many tries does it take before you manage to kill me properly?'

'You in a hurry?' Barnabas panted, getting up on to one knee. The bloody knife was still in his hand, so it must be the gun that Wolf had heard fall. 'Just coverin' all the bases, pal.' He seemed to be addressing his words to Wolf's left shoulder, and Wolf realised abruptly that the man couldn't see. It must be pitch black down here. Well, thank God for small mercies. The gash on his cheek hurt in a dull way that suggested it was probably just waiting till it had his full attention.

Wolf backed off soundlessly. Barnabas was just getting to his feet, and the harsh noise of his own breathing probably eclipsed any sound that Wolf made as he circled round the bench to come up behind the soldier. He hesitated: now what? He gawped round desperately. The only thing that looked remotely useful was a shiny steel electric kettle left on the nearest bench with a couple of folorn-looking mugs. Wolf lifted the kettle stealthily, and inched up behind Barnabas, who was grumbling and making threatening sweeps with the knife. Wolf lifted the kettle for a quick blow to the back of Barnabas' head.

The kettle lid fell off with a clang, and Barnabas whirled. Wolf bashed at his head with the kettle, and caught the American a sharp blow on the left temple. Barnabas thudded to the floor.

It was so sudden Wolf almost didn't believe it. He skipped back, then kicked Barnabas hard in the side of the knee. Barnabas didn't move, which meant either he was Laurence Olivier reincarnate, or he was unconscious. When he woke up, he was going to limp for days.

Wolf rifled through the American's coat pockets and found the hypo-gun. He held it up, squinting: the reservoir was still half-full of antidote. He had to get it to Robin.

20

EMERGENCY LIGHTING made odd dull-blue puddles of light at ground level in the corridor. Wolf scooted along cautiously, as fast as he dared. The lift doors were open, and a plastic crate stood in the corridor. As Wolf crept up, hugging the wall, Dominique Rancoul walked out of the lift, grabbed the crate and froze as she spotted him. Her glossy perfection was spoilt: her eyes were red and teary, her lips were puffy and her mascara had run. She was barefoot.

The sight was so unexpected that Wolf gaped. Dominique recovered from the shock first. She uttered a shriek, dropped the crate with a crash and darted backwards into the lift. The doors closed, and Wolf heard the cage start up the shaft.

He ran to the doors and tried to pry them apart, but the seal was tight. He pressed every button on the panel. Nothing. He hammered on the doors with his fists, and yelled, 'Bitch!' The panel lights winked smugly at him.

Red rage. Wolf smashed his fist into the panel. Miniature lightning arced over the broken casing, and there was a whiff of acrid smoke. Wolf snatched his hand back hurriedly, sucking at his knuckles. In the lift shaft, grinding noises, and a squeak of brakes. A faint, echoing shriek of outrage.

'Wolf?' The faint voice snatched him back to the here and now.

'Robin?' The blinds were all shut in the office. He tried the door. It was locked. 'Robin, let me in!'

'I can't.' Her fatigue was palpable.

Wolf took a step backwards and tried to kick the door in. The lock splintered, but the door didn't open. Wolf put his shoulder to it and pushed. There was something preventing it from opening. He heaved at the door, and felt the something slide. He peered in through the gap he'd made: the something was a body. The guard, by the look of it. He experienced a second of shock at the thought of Robin killing someone in cold blood. Then the corpse wriggled and vented some furious grunting noises. Wolf grinned in relief, and shoved the trussed-up man out of the way.

There was a kind of barricade of tables where the camp-bed had been. Wolf peered over the top. 'Robin? It's me,' he added hastily as her hand swung up clasping a gun. Her hair was dark with sweat, and her breathing had an effortful sound Wolf didn't like. She stared at him bleary-eyed.

'Wolf . . . ?' The gun wavered.

Wolf heaved the table away and knelt in front of her. 'You're going to be OK, look.' He held up the hypo-gun.

A bare nod. She slid down on to the bed with a sigh. Wolf primed the hypo-gun, pressed the muzzle against her bare arm and pulled the trigger. It made the usual noise, between a thud and a click. Wolf rubbed his hand over the spot. Difficult to tell, between the murky blue glow of the emergency lights and his own failing grey illumination, if she was pale or not. Her eyes opened, then slowly closed again. 'That hurt,' she murmured.

Wolf took her hand. Her skin was hot and damp, but her fingers moved inside his.

(Tired . . .) She was a bare flicker of sensation, a wisp of smoke. Wolf compressed his lips. Was that good or bad? Maybe it meant the antidote was doing its job, cleaning Nemesis out of his system. He grappled with rusty retrieval mechanisms for a moment. *Vaccines are made from neutralised viral or bacterial matter, right? And they produce an immune reaction in the parts of the body most affected by the live bug. Only trouble is, Nemesis is no bug, and the antidote isn't exactly a vaccine, so who's to know exactly how it's supposed to work?*

'I'm going to find us a way out of here,' he said out loud.

No response at all, outward or inward. Wolf pulled the thin blanket gently up around her shoulders, and slipped out into the corridor again. Something had been bothering him for several seconds, and he had to cast around for a while before he realised what it was: a smell, faint but familiar.

Wolf wrinkled his nostrils and grinned. *I never thought I'd be grateful to get that stink up my nose.*

He sniffed cautiously, weaving his head side to side. That way. Towards the lab. He set off down the corridor at a run. *Just so long as the crazy son of a bitch doesn't shoot me by mistake.*

He was still a few metres from the swing doors when they banged wide and a bedraggled figure leapt into the corridor.

The Fireman looked—if possible—even more bizarre than the last time Wolf had encountered him. The Peruvian woolly hat was still in place, but now he wore a pair of night-sight goggles as well, which gave him an alien, insectoid look. Whether aliens wore multi-coloured woolly mittens was something Wolf didn't feel equipped to go into at that moment. The nasty looking submachine gun clutched in the mittens was of more immediate concern. The Fireman was pointing it at Wolf. The goggles did not seem to be very well adjusted. They waggled as the Fireman cocked his head on one side. Wolf stopped and held his hands well away from his sides. 'Hey, *mon ami*! It's me, Jan Wolf—remember? Jan Wolf,' he repeated loudly, nodding and smiling like a maniac.

Inwardly, he rolled his eyes. Who else but a maniac would be having this conversation?

'Wolf,' the Fireman said. The muzzle of the submachine gun dropped, and the dazzling white grin flashed. 'Wolf! That guy said you were in trouble down here, needed help. You need help?' he repeated in a hopeful tone, like a labrador waiting for the stick to be thrown.

Wolf had to be sure. 'A guy?'

'Sure.' The Fireman scratched behind his ear. 'Red hair, dark glasses . . . '

Gabriel. Wolf sent a silent blessing up for the Teknogeister. Money did have its uses. 'Did he tell you what kind of trouble?'

The Fireman moved up close, and held his coat wide, like a black marketeer flogging fake Rolexes. '*Any* kinda trouble, *mon ami*, no problem.' He wasn't joking. The lining of his greatcoat sagged under the weight of enough firepower to depopulate downtown Amsterdam. Besides spare clips and two dangling bandoliers, Wolf counted three different types of grenade, four guns, rolls of cable, pliers, two knives, and a can of deodorant.

'Great,' he croaked.

'Listen, guy gives me that much money and tells me my friend's in trouble, I bring the best I got, eh?' Happy, selecting items from beneath the voluminous coat. He handed something to Wolf. 'Machine-pistol, OK? Don't squeeze too hard or you be out of ammo in ten seconds flat. Spare clip.' Wolf thrust that into his pocket, and stared at the brutal-looking contraption he held in his hands. The Fireman grinned. 'Ready now.'

Wolf managed a nod and some kind of teeth-bared grimace in return. 'You take the corridor,' he whispered. 'There's a doorway back in the lab, I think it must meet up, we can sweep the place from both ends. Just don't shoot the girl.'

'Don't shoot the girl. Sure thing.' The Fireman lifted his own gun, a bigger, badder-looking version of the machine-pistol he'd gifted Wolf with, and scurried off down the corridor. Wolf ducked through the lab doors.

A muffled, muzzein-like wail echoed down the corridor, calling anyone unfortunate enough to meet the Fireman to an early demise.

Wolf made for the far door, skirting benches. He should see to Barnabas, lock him in a cupboard or something. As he turned the corner of the far bench, he renewed his grip on the gun.

Barnabas was gone. Wolf stood on the spot where he had left the American, and knew a moment of sheer panic.

The muffled stutter of a submachine-gun, not far away. Wolf came to a decision. He had to get back to Robin, protect her from Barnabas. Let the Fireman deal with the rest.

There was a door that looked as if it might link up with the main corridor at the far end. That would be the best way to go. Wolf hefted the gun and found that he'd left the safety-catch on. He pushed it aside.

He was almost at the door when it started to open.

Coloured fire leapt up like a *suttee* pyre. Wolf jumped forward and slammed the door back into the face and shoulder of the man who was opening it. There was a *crunch*, and a yodel of surprised agony.

Wolf did not wait to find out what the man might do next. He yanked the door open and pulled the trigger.

It was like a photograph, frozen in the spitting yellow light of the bullets: a bearded man in a black suit and overcoat, his automatic dropping with surreal slowness from his outstretched hand, knees slightly bent, one hand to his bloodied mouth. It was Orthodontic Man, and he was never going to forgive Wolf for ruining his expensive smile. He crumpled backwards softly, a discarded coat.

There was a short corridor, and another door. Wolf skirted the dead man and walked forward slowly, holding the gun in numb hands. The door was ajar, and he nudged it open with the muzzle of the gun.

A dingy crew room, the walls lined with chairs. Wolf lowered the gun. Someone had been here before him. Water still spurted from several holes in the cooler, and a paper cup twirled on the spreading pool. It was the only thing moving. The water was tinged pink in places. Bodies sprawled everywhere.

Footsteps approached at a run. Wolf swung the gun up again with a clutch of dread.

The Fireman barreled into the room, clutching at him. 'Shut the door! Shut it!'

Wolf kicked it shut, dragged the Fireman roughly to one side and dumped him in a chair. The little man gave a grunt of pain. He had lost his night-vision goggles and his woolly hat. His greasy hair stuck up in wild goaty curls. His eyes stared, and his breathing sounded wrong. The front of his coat was stained deep blackish-red.

Wolf had no time to assess things further than this, because an explosion blew the door he had just closed out of its frame. The blast flung him against the far wall, spatchcocked like an oven-ready chicken. The door struck his left arm a jarring blow, and cartwheeled on into the passageway, broken-backed.

Wolf couldn't attend to his arm immediately, because the impact with the wall had knocked all the breath out of him. He flopped about on the floor, mouth gaping vainly for air that wouldn't come.

When he could breathe again, he attempted to get up on hands and knees, and discovered in this empirical fashion that his left arm was broken just above the wrist. It must be, he thought fuzzily from the floor. Nothing that wasn't broken had any right to hurt so badly.

He levered himself up with his good arm, and cradled the broken one against his chest like a hurt kitten. He tried not to look at it too much.

Flames roared and gushed around the empty doorway. Smoke rolled fat python coils around him.

The Fireman. Wolf started in that direction, coughing. Tripped over an arm or a leg in the jigsaw of Black Coats and went down on one knee with a cry of pain.

'Got you, *mon ami*.' The Fireman sounded worse than he did. He got an arm round Wolf's body and heaved him to his feet; he was surprisingly strong. Clinging together like a pair of old ladies, they staggered towards the fresher air of the laboratory.

The Fireman slammed the door shut behind them and leaned on it, panting and coughing. His little black eyes glittered hectically. 'They told me that one had a good blast radius, I jus' didn't believe them. Hoooh.'

'Listen!' Wolf grabbed the smaller man by the shoulder. 'It's important. Did you shoot a big guy, white hair, carried a knife?'

The Fireman frowned, then shook his head. 'Sorry, *mon ami*. Just those sons of bitches in there.'

'Then he's still down here somewhere,' Wolf said. 'Watch yourself, he's fast and he doesn't play fair. We'd better find the girl and get out of here before that fire really takes hold. How did you get in? The lift?'

'I show you.' The Fireman jerked his head. 'Come on.'

Through the swing doors and into the corridor. Smoke hung low from the ceiling. Wolf and the Fireman limped up the corridor, bent double to keep clear of the smoke. Sweat stung Wolf's eyes. He wiped his face with his sleeve, gasping.

The office was empty. Robin's makeshift shelter had been hurled aside. The little computer lay smashed on the floor. The guard lay still tied up in a corner. He had been shot between the eyes.

'She's gone!' Wolf's heart picked up the pace. 'Barnabas must've done this.'

The Fireman looked nervous. 'We better go, man, those grenades, they're on a timer switch.'

'Timer switch?' Wolf swivelled to stare at the man. 'Grenades?' He took a gentle grip on the Fireman's collar. 'How—many—grenades?'

His calm monotone unnerved the smaller man. 'N-nine,' he stuttered. 'Napalm grenades, best I got . . . ' His smile faded at Wolf's stricken expression. 'Hey, it's no problem, we got another . . . ' he checked his wristwatch, and went a grey kind of colour under the dirt. 'Uh, we got another three minutes before they go off.'

'You weren't supposed to blow the place up!' Wolf redoubled his grip on the Fireman's collar, then let go with a growl of frustration. 'Come on, we have to find the girl and get out.'

At the bend of the corridor, there was a door. Wolf peered inside: a long narrow room that had obviously served as a dormitory for the orderlies and Black Coats. Lots of beds, not much else. The Fireman jostled his shoulder, and pointed.

'In here, see? I come down the shaft.' Wolf followed his pointing finger. A hatch was just visible through the smoke. Staples in the wall led up into the dark opening.

'Where does it come out?'

'In the yard at the side of the building,' the Fireman said. 'Emergency access.'

'Great,' Wolf said. 'Stay here, I'll go find the girl. Maybe she's jammed herself in a store cupboard or something.'

'Wrong,' a familiar voice croaked from someplace near his feet. A slender hand waved from beneath the nearest bed. 'Help me out, will you?'

Wolf grabbed the hand and pulled. Robin slid out covered in dust, coughing. 'I thought you were never coming back, I had to find someplace to hide, Tom's still down here.' She looked at Wolf in the blue glow of emergency lights, and her eyes widened. 'Omigod, what happened to your arm?'

'Caught it in a door,' Wolf said, and grasped her wrist to yank her to her feet. 'We have to go, Einstein here wired the whole place to explode.'

'In one minute, forty seconds,' the Fireman supplied with a professional flourish of the wrist.

'Let's go.' Wolf jerked his chin at the hatchway. 'You go first, Fireman. Then Robin.'

'Sure thing.' The Fireman hobbled across and started up the staples. Robin hesitated, gazing up into the black hole.

'I don't know if I can do this, Wolf.'

'We can discuss it on the way up,' Wolf said with a clutch of misgiving. He placed her hand on a staple. 'Come on, you can do it. Look, I'll be right with you, see? Just hold on to one rung, then step up on to this one. That's it . . . now I step up behind you. You can't fall. Just keep moving up, c'mon . . . that's it . . . '

Quietly, with murmurs of encouragement, he coaxed Robin up from rung to rung. It was slow going. Robin's breathing was effortful even to begin with. Soon she was wheezing for air, and Wolf had to steady her against the ladder for long moments in between steps up. In point of fact, he was grateful for the rests himself: his good arm was becoming less good all the time. The first stretch, when a little light still leaked up the shaft from below, was very hard.

Then there was just the Fireman's cracked army boots clambering up into blackness. Wolf stared into the dark with something approaching awe. He hadn't been without light for such a long time. The absence lapped over his sore nerve-endings like cool water. He shuddered.

'What's wrong?' Robin twisted her head vainly in the dark. Her hair tickled his arm. 'Wolf, what is it?'

'Nothing,' Wolf said. 'I'll tell you later.' He leaned in and hopped his good hand up another rung. 'Come on, we'd better keep moving. It's getting pretty warm in here.'

Robin sighed, and leant her forehead on his hand for a second. 'OK.'

She was just wriggling up between Wolf and the ladder when a wave of heat billowed up from below, accompanied by a reverberating roar. The grenades. A dull orange glow picked out detail in the shaft wall in front of Wolf. He hung on grimly as the burning-hot shockwave buffetted them.

It passed. Robin's hand found Wolf's, and gripped tight.

Then a voice echoed up the shaft.

'*De Haan!*' Barnabas' voice, thick with rage. Wolf risked a look down. Barnabas was a dark shape on the ladder, backlit by fire. Yellow-white flames streamed through the opening far below with a ragged, tearing sound. The heat was intense, and a sharp chemical smell filled the air.

Barnabas was climbing fast. A knife glinted.

Wolf froze for a second, looking down. They were trapped. He couldn't leave Robin to climb on by herself, and he could hardly engage in hand-to-hand fighting on a ladder when he only had one good arm. His brain was freewheeling in neutral, blank with fatigue and pain. They weren't going to make it.

'Wolf, move!' A whisper right by his ear, rough with fright. Wolf turned his head. Robin's face next to his was a taut, desperate mask painted in shades of orange and black. Her breath on his cheek was rapid. 'Quick,' she commanded, and hauled at his shirt. Wolf obediently moved up, then paused to allow her to join him; moved up again, aware with a kind of dizzy wonder that his right hand and arm were getting tired. Great timing.

'De Haan!' Barnabas' voice made Wolf start violently: he was much closer now. Wolf could hear the man's harsh breathing as he climbed.

In the crook of his arm, Robin twisted frantically. 'Tom! Let him go, why can't you just let him go? Let *us* go?' Her voice cracked. Her legs and arms trembled, and Wolf realised with that dreamy focus that she was on the point of collapse. Only her stubborn will had kept her moving this long. He braced his leg across the ladder, pinning her so that she could not fall. Below, Barnabas had stopped. Wolf wondered if he imagined the tinge of regret in the gravelly voice.

'Sorry, Birdy, can't do that. National security.' The bright eyes shifted to Wolf's face. Wolf gazed back with a sort of frozen fascination: here was death coming for him with a big shiny knife, and there was nothing he could do. Nothing at all. Barnabas' voice had dropped to a whisper. 'I'm sorry, Mister De Haan. Orders are orders, and the word is, you don't get out of this place alive.'

Barnabas had begun to climb again as he spoke—slow, stealthy, a big cat stalking its prey, confident of its ability to strike. Wolf twitched away from the bright, hypnotic gaze with a physical effort. He hauled Robin up another rung, and another. The palm of his hand was slippery with sweat, and he had to hook his elbow through the ladder to be sure of his grip. 'What about the girl?'

No response. Barnabas did not even hesitate. Wolf imagined something inside that buzz-cut skull, flashing red letters saying *targets acquired*. Wolf raised his voice, his only remaining weapon. 'I said, what about the girl? What about Robin?'

'I'm sorry,' Barnabas repeated flatly. His head was only a few rungs below Wolf's feet now. Wolf cursed and chivvied Robin into one more step up. Her boot slipped, and she whimpered. Hot tears fell on his arm.

'I can't . . . can't go any further. I'm going to fall—'

'Shhhh. Shh.' Wolf tucked her head under his chin, in lieu of holding her. Ridiculous moment to notice how nice the top of a woman's head smells. He breathed in deeply.

He seemed to have slipped beyond the paralysing terror of a few moments before, into a sort of cold practicality. He'd try to shield her with his body, but he wouldn't be much of an obstacle, and she was too weak to climb much further. The only thing that might give her a chance was hurling himself down the shaft on top of Barnabas. Wolf's heart turned over at the prospect. He kissed Robin's hair very gently, and closed his eyes. 'Hold on to the ladder.'

A gloved hand gripped him by the back of his neck. Wolf managed not to shriek as a body slithered down beside him. The shimmering air was enlivened for a moment by a very human stench: it was the Fireman. He had monkeyed down the ladder and now sat in mid-air, braced between ladder and wall with his pock-marked, grinning face inches from Wolf's. He inhaled deeply through his nose, as if the choking chemical stink was dewy spring air. 'Ah loooove the smell of napalm in the morning!' The dark stain on the front of his greatcoat was larger, with a wet sheen. His breathing was hectic, shallow, but the grin was of megawatt proportions. 'I owe you one, *mon ami*. Au'voir.'

A quick, calculating glance downwards. He let go.

Wolf could not even cry out. The Fireman hit Barnabas squarely, and snatched the mercenary off the ladder like the hand of Allah swatting a fly. Then they were a tangled shape tumbling down the shaft into a blowtorch flame. Their cries bellied up the steel chimney for a second. Then they were gone. Wolf hugged Robin against the ladder, shuddering.

It seemed a long blank time before he could move. The sound of the flames down below had taken on a whistling, pressure-cooker note, and the ladder was getting warm to the touch. Wolf looked down. Coils of smoke twisted up the shaft, reached for his feet with the lazy malice of unbottled genies. He coughed hastily, and shook Robin.

'Robin! Robin, we have to move.'

'Nooo . . . ' A drowsy groan. Wolf had to bully her awake. They inched up into the darkness with hot smoke twining against their legs like a friendly cat.

❖

Wolf didn't remember passing out. He wasn't even really sure that he *had* passed out. The world was a muddy blur, and his chest hurt with a nasty constricting pain when he breathed. But there was faint grey light above him. He was lying on his side in the open air with something spiky digging into his cheek. Robin lay curled against him. He felt her ribcage rise and fall.

Her hair had tumbled down over Wolf's right hand. He rubbed the cool, silky strands between finger and thumb, like an amulet.

❖

Somewhere, someone opened a door, and sweet rich air flooded into his lungs. Wolf gulped at it. His chest ached with the intense cold, but it revived him. He was sitting up, propped against something hard. How had that happened? There had been something . . . a scratch in his arm. A needle.

Wolf groaned and opened his eyes. Blue lights flashed; he moaned and shut them again. He pawed clumsily for the silky texture of hair in his right hand. Nothing. His heart gave a sick lurch.

'Robin?' Wolf jerked his eyes open. 'Robin? Robin!'

'Keep still, Menheer, don't try to move.' Calm voice. Strong hands pressed him back. Wolf slashed out in panic. An alarmed staccato of shouting over his head. More hands came to hold him, pinned him where he sat. His injured arm was a blood-red universe of agony. Wolf sagged. His throat was thick with tears. They didn't understand, she'd *gone*—

'He's hyperventilating, give him a bit of space. Here.' Someone pressed plastic to his face; the air suddenly tasted strange. Wolf gagged and pawed feebly at it before he realised it was an oxygen mask. He opened his eyes again, got a glimpse of the uniform jacket of a paramedic and past that, a jumble of vehicles. He craned up, and the paramedic eased him back again.

'There, friend, don't try to move, we'll have you out of here in no time. They're backing the ambulance round now. Just take some deep breaths for me, hey, nice and slow—'

'Where's the girl . . . ?' The mask muffled his voice. A second man was just withdrawing a needle from Wolf's arm; strange, he hadn't felt a thing. His face tingled as if he'd been to the dentist. 'The *girl*,' he insisted, suddenly frightened that he would pass out before they understood.

The man who'd just injected him so skilfully leaned closer. He had a strong German accent. 'She is all right. I'm a friend of hers, a doctor. You're safe.'

Wolf was just going to object when the man's face swam into focus: shaven head, and heavy blue moustaches. A leering mask of Maori tattoos.

'You're a doctor?' Wolf muttered. The man seemed familiar. Wolf wondered for a distracted second if this was what life was going to be like from now on: caught between strangers and friends and not knowing which was which.

The apparition grinned at him, and patted his shoulder. 'I'm a vet too, if that makes you feel any better. Take it easy, Miss Congeniality there has it all under control.' He uttered a snort of laughter, and jerked his head to one side.

Zia Roccaro stood nearby amid a jostle of microphones and cameras, completely at home in the glare of the TV floodlights. She was talking to a fat man in dull, smart clothes. The man looked acutely unhappy, but Zia was ticking off the points she was making on her long fingers, and she didn't look as if she was half finished. A nervous-looking cluster of high-ranking policemen awaited their turn on the spit. Wolf grinned behind the oxygen mask.

Wolf heard the tattooed man's gruff voice hail somebody. 'Got a second, mate?'

Wolf waited, watching woozily while the tail-lights of a fat white ambulance backed towards him through the jumble of television vans. The paramedic jumped up and banged on the panelling, and it squeaked to a halt.

The tingling sensation was all over Wolf now, not exactly pleasant but better than the alternative. The oxygen was making his throat dry and he tried to take off the mask but his arm wouldn't work. It felt as if he'd been served with a quickie divorce from his body. It wasn't answering his calls any more. He groaned out loud.

'All right, Kris?' The tattooed doctor again, squatting down at his side. Dancing grey eyes assessed him, and deft hands removed the mask.

Wolf licked his lips—or tried to—and gasped, 'Thanks. Dry.'

'Can't have a drink, I'm afraid,' the doctor said relentlessly. Wolf rolled his eyes.

'Every damn doctor I meet tells me that. What are you, all sadists or something?' He sucked at the clean night air. The doctor didn't answer. He had gone away again. Wolf grumbled under his breath. 'Great. Just great . . . '

'Wolf?' Robin's voice. Wolf's head jerked round so fast it was a wonder he didn't give himself whiplash. She was leaning on the doctor, filthy, haggard and bleeding from a cut on her forehead, but alive. Wolf couldn't speak for a second. It was like being visited by a rather grubby angel.

Robin eased down beside him. Wolf wanted very badly to hold her so tight she'd never disappear again, but the tingling and the weakness prevented him from doing much beyond a twitch of the eyebrows. 'Hi.'

'Hi yourself.' Robin looked at him, and Wolf found himself reaching automatically for the touch of her mind. He saw from her face that she did the same. She gave a grim, lopsided smile. 'It's gone, isn't it?'

'Doesn't matter,' Wolf murmured. 'Better this way.'

'I guess.' Robin leaned against him, as one might lean against a handy rock. 'Could get kind of inconvenient.'

'Embarrassing,' Wolf rasped, and managed a laugh that turned into a coughing fit. Robin's doctor friend—Kurt, wasn't that his name?—held the oxygen mask over Wolf's face until he stopped wheezing.

'We have to get you to the hospital now,' the doctor stated. He helped Robin to her feet and signalled over his shoulder to the waiting paramedics. 'Let's go!'

'Wait a second.' Robin bent over Wolf and took his good hand in hers. He gazed into her eyes from a distance of six inches and wished he had the power of movement because a red-blooded male oughtn't to pass up such a golden opportunity for a kiss. Doctors really are sadists, he thought peevishly.

Robin bent quickly and kissed him. Wolf's eyes came all the way open in a hurry. It wasn't a peck, or a polite brush of the lips. This was a warm, searching caress, eyes locked, breath mingling; maybe she could read his mind after all.

Robin squeezed Wolf's hand, and straightened. The tattooed doctor took her arm, grinning, but she had her eyes fixed on Wolf's. 'Still want your coat back?'

Wolf's world was getting dim and fuzzy, but he struggled to keep her face in focus as the doctor helped her up into the ambulance. He nodded. Robin's face was a flash of white surrounded by a halo of flames. Her voice suddenly had an edge of tears. 'Where will I find you?'

They'd be taking her away, Wolf realised as his focus went. America, probably. 'Questor,' he said; then, worried that she wouldn't hear, 'The boat. Come to the boat.'

'The boat,' he heard her say, then the white doors closed.

The medics eased Wolf down on to a stretcher and wheeled him away with a plastic bag jouncing on its stand by his head. There was a lot of fuss and flashing cameras when the famous supermodel gave him a very public kiss before they loaded him into the ambulance, and let one topaz eye close in a saucy wink.

Kissed twice in one day. But only one kiss mattered. A kiss, and the gold signet ring that she'd left folded in his fist. Wolf clutched the warm smooth metal tightly, afraid his numb fingers would let it slip. A magical ring, a token of numinous possibilities: somebody knew who he was. Knew, and cared.

Wolf considered it as the ambulance bumped over the rough ground, in the same sort of way that a tongue explores the cavity left by an extracted tooth, and smiled a little.

It wasn't much—not really very much—but it was more than Jan Wolf had had for a very long time. And for now, it was more than enough.

❖

I wish I'd been there when they finally hauled Dominique wriggling and screaming out of that lift shaft. Zia told me later that she was done medium-rare, shiny red as a boiled lobster from the heat, with mad frizzy hair. (An unworthy part of me is jumping up and down shouting 'Yes! Yessss!') I guess I'll have to be content with the tabloid pics that Gabriel scanned and emailed to me. I saved them. The rehab clinic Dad booked me into is so soothing it's tempting to slip into a coma; I could use a good belly-laugh now and then.

Anyway, the cases of Nemesis that they brought out of the lift cage with her should be enough to keep Domi busy breaking rocks or making car license plates for quite a long time. Even the European Court of Human Rights got a few whacks in before close season.

Only one regret: Michel insulated himself from the whole business with depressing efficiency. The duplicitous little asshole. With Tom Barnabas gone, there's no material witness against him, and Domi refused to implicate him. She always did let Mich get away with murder. One day, it'll be different.

❖

It's a funny thing. I imagine Wolf, and I can see him. Not like with Nemesis. More like a pleasant echo of what it did to us: he's sitting by an open window watching rain fall on tiny crimson flowers that bob and pirouette like dancers. I don't think he's slept. His eyes are ringed with grey. But he's lost that wary look, the frightened flinch that was always there just under the surface. I wonder if he can see me too.

He's not Kris de Haan any more. But he's not the Jan Wolf I first met either. He's someone different from both of them. I catch myself wondering if giving him Cary's ring was a mistake. Something got mixed up between the two of us in that crazy place: memories, feelings, things that blur with my own life and make me scared to go back there. Maybe what's different about Wolf is something to do with me. I don't know whether I could bear to find out. I can't go back, not yet. Maybe not ever.

One last, long look, to fix him in my mind's eye. He has his face turned up slightly to the daylight, and I can see the micropore tape along the livid-looking scar that runs down his cheek. His hair needs cutting. There's a scary-looking plastic and steel brace on his broken arm. It encases everything except his fingers.

He's rubbing the thumb of his right hand back and forth over the signet ring on his left middle finger. And he blinks, lazy as a cat, and smiles as he watches the flowers dance in the rain.

THE END